DON'T TEASE ME....

"The monster in me is still there, just below the surface," Eli continued, and his lips barely grazed the skin on the side of my neck. I shuddered, and I know he felt it. "Never forget that. Even with your Gullah magic inside you, I can smell your unique blood," he said, his mouth next to my ear. He inhaled a long, deep breath. "You have no idea how much of a temptation you are to me, Riley Poe," he said, the slight French accent making his voice erotic. "No . . . idea how much control I truly have not to simply taste what rushes through your veins, with barely more than a paper-thin layer of skin to stop me." I shivered as his breath rushed over my neck.

With what strength I had, I pushed hard against him to escape; he easily turned me around, and now we were face-to-face, body to body, and panic etched into my brain. Exerting the slightest pressure, he bent me backward until I felt the cool iron handrail press against my back. I felt every hard ridge and muscle Eli possessed pressing into me. And I mean *every one*. His eyes searched mine, then dropped to my mouth, where they lingered. "Vampiric cravings aren't the only ones I possess, but they're the only ones I can halfway control, heightened times a hundred by *what* I am." He dropped his head close, his lips a breath away. "Don't tease me again, Riley, unless you mean it. I can't promise that kind of control." He lifted his head and stared, his eyes dark as he searched mine. "I don't think you could handle me."

Afterlight

THE DARK INK CHRONICLES

ELLE JASPER

A SIGNET ECLIPSE BOOK

SIGNET ECLIPSE
Published by New American Library, a division of
Penguin Group (USA) Inc., 375 Hudson Street,
New York, New York 10014, USA
Penguin Group (Canada), 90 Eglinton Avenue East, Suite 700, Toronto,
Ontario M4P 2Y3, Canada (a division of Pearson Penguin Canada Inc.)
Penguin Books Ltd., 80 Strand, London WC2R 0RL, England
Penguin Ireland, 25 St. Stephen's Green, Dublin 2,
Ireland (a division of Penguin Books Ltd.)
Penguin Group (Australia), 250 Camberwell Road, Camberwell, Victoria 3124,
Australia (a division of Pearson Australia Group Pty. Ltd.)
Penguin Books India Pvt. Ltd., 11 Community Centre, Panchsheel Park,
New Delhi - 110 017, India
Penguin Group (NZ), 67 Apollo Drive, Rosedale, North Shore 0632,
New Zealand (a division of Pearson New Zealand Ltd.)
Penguin Books (South Africa) (Pty.) Ltd., 24 Sturdee Avenue,
Rosebank, Johannesburg 2196, South Africa

Penguin Books Ltd., Registered Offices:
80 Strand, London WC2R 0RL, England

First published by Signet Eclipse, an imprint of New American Library,
a division of Penguin Group (USA) Inc.

First Printing, November 2010
10   9   8   7   6   5   4   3   2   1

To Ben Burnley and Breaking Benjamin, this is for you.
Your lyrics echoed Riley's thoughts, and your music
guided me throughout the writing of Afterlight.

ACKNOWLEDGMENTS

Scores of people contribute to the birth of a novel, and so I'd like to thank the following for their time, friendship, encouragement, and hard work for the birth of *Afterlight*.

To my husband, Brian, son, Kyle, and daughter, Tyler, for their love, encouragement, and enthusiasm. You are all my love and joy! And for Kyle's gorgeous Lyndsee, who always reads my books, and for Tyler's adorable Jonathan, who genuinely wants to know the progress of whatever current project I'm on. Thanks, guys!

To my mom, Dale, who is my biggest cheerleader and best friend, and Ray, my dad, who chats my books up with any and all who will listen. I love you both!

To my beautiful sisters, Sheri, Tracy, and Nikki, and sweet brothers-in-law, Jerry, Jordan, and Will, who believe in me and always support me. To my brothers, Vince and David, and the rest of my enormous family who always chats up my books!

To my sister writer and pal Kim Lenox, who has encouraged me via phone, e-mail, and text endlessly throughout the years. We're gonna kick BUTT!

To my crazy pals Betty, Chapper, and Grandmother, for traipsing around Savannah's historic district in the rain with me, and Bonaventure Cemetery for those perfect, inspiring photos, as well as to Bunt, Mol, Walowee, Bhingaling, Vic, Lay-ha, and Anna—thanks to all of you for your treasured friendship and constant encouragement. To Kelly, for phrases like "Oh, Father." I love you guys! You're all so nass!

To my sister writer and pal Leah Brown, for the fabulous Strigoi aspect of *Afterlight*, and for the high-octane enthusiasm, friendship, and cheering. Mu-ah!

To my sister writer and pal Virginia Farmer, for all the support and great ideas and encouragement. Hugs!

To my Denmark Sisterhood, who are always cheering me on!

To Victorian and Valerian (yes, they're brothers and they're REAL!), for the use of their awesomely cool names.

To my agent, Jenny Bent, and my editor, Laura Cifelli, and to Jesse Feldman, for all the support and leadership. Thank you, and to everyone else at NAL who worked on *Afterlight*! Your hard work is appreciated!

To Oceana Gottlieb, fabulous designer of *Afterlight*'s cover. Thank you so much! It is PERFECT!

To the band Breaking Benjamin, whose music totally rocks! I love you guys!

Finally, to Mike Cummings, owner of Inksomnia Tattoo in Alpharetta, Georgia, for allowing me to use his wicked-cool shop name for Riley's. Thanks!!

PREFACE

Savannah, Georgia
City Market
October

*A*fterlight. According to the Gullah, it meant two things. One: darkness or dusk. Two: death, the life after, or beyond. I'm familiar with both.

Death I've known for a long time. I've seen it first-hand, and it left a gruesome imprint in my mind that will haunt me forever. But like most crappy things that have happened in my life, I've just dealt with it, and maybe death has made me stronger. One thing I've learned is no matter how you face it, and no matter the situation, there's one constant present: *finality*. There's no getting around it.

My vision blurred as I watched the rain pelt the window of the corner booth where I sat at Molly McPherson's pub, and I blinked to see clearly through the evening shower outside. God, I wanted a smoke, but these days it made me want to puke, so I fished out a piece of nic gum from my bag and popped it into my mouth. October twenty-third, nine p.m., and it was rainy and warm—nearly seventy-five degrees. Nothing was the same anymore, and although the changes were subtle to most, to me they were in-my-face obvious. I knew things others didn't, and to be perfectly honest, I'm as glad as hell. I'd much rather be totally prepared to face my fears and enemies head-on than be sucker punched because of ignorance—no matter how innocent. And trust me—I was ready. Beneath my short gauzy skirt, the weight of a pure silver blade rested against my bare thigh as a constant reminder.

"Hey, Riley, you want another pint?" The shout crossed the small pub and caught my attention.

I lifted a hand at Martin, the bartender, and shook my head. "No, thanks. I'm good." He winked and grinned and went about his business. Molly's wasn't too packed tonight, but the constant mumble of patrons was a low drone inside my head. If I stayed much longer, my temples would start to throb.

With the palm of my hand I wiped the moisture from the window and scanned the busy, lamplit cobbled streets of Congress Street and City Market. I spotted him beneath the awning at Belford's. Jesus—how long had he been standing there? Even though I couldn't see his cerulean blue eyes at such a distance, I knew that Eli had absolutely no trouble at all seeing me, and that his gaze locked solidly onto mine. An unstoppable, relentless thrill shot through my veins, and I shuddered. He stood there for a moment, watching me, and when he stepped into the throng of people out on the wet Friday night, he moved easily through the crowd toward me, effortless and commanding—almost floating. His features were young, flawless, and ancient all at once. Dark brown hair swept tousled and sideways across his forehead, giving him an easygoing, sexy look. It stood stark against the palest, most beautiful skin.

As I watched him grow closer, his features became clearer, and I realized just how deceptive looks really could be. For instance, to most I probably looked like a total freak, with black hair and red-fuchsia highlights, tall leather boots, a fishnet tee, and pale skin with bloodred lips. And I'm pretty positive the dragon tattoos—visible beneath the fishnet—that crept from my lower back up my spine and down both arms made people do a double take, as did the ebony angel wing inked into the skin at the corner of my left eye. I didn't mind—although an angel I was not. I may not look it, but I'm probably the most responsible person I know. Now, anyway. I've a successful business, I pay my bills on time, and after I cleaned up my act I did a pretty good job raising my little brother. So while I was scrutinized, Eli blended right in, and it intrigued me to see him interact with people; they were clueless, oblivious to what was right beneath their noses despite the faultless, boyish, breathtaking good looks and charm. I wasn't. Not anymore.

The bad thing, and this I knew with complete clarity, was that I'd die for him. And if such a thing were possible, he'd die for me. Was that love? Obsession? Maybe it was both. But it was definitely something powerful, and I no longer had control over it. It was terrifying and exhilarating all at once. Talk about a high. It topped any drug I'd ever done.

I scooted from the booth and stood, dropped a five-dollar bill on the table, and waved good-bye to Martin as I headed out into the now-constant drizzle. As the distance between us grew shorter, I could finally see the lamplight shine off his disturbing eyes as they searched mine, and my heart slammed against my ribs. I knew that there were much greater horrors, and sorrows, than death. Unimaginable things that just a few short months ago I would have vehemently disputed ever existed. *Vampires*. They're real. They *exist*. And they're *so* not what you think they are.

And I was utterly, irrevocably in love with one.

"You know, looking back now I can nail the exact moment everything around me changed. What's funny is, I noticed it right away, but it never really registered. I just didn't get it. Not until later, after I realized vampires existed. Know what it was? Cicadas. The moment it happened, the cicadas silenced. I've not heard even one, much less the thousands that filled every single summer night since I was a kid. They were my white noise, and they've gone. Fled. And it's annoyingly quiet around here. How effed up is that?"

—Riley Poe

Part 1

+⚬+━⚬━+⚬+

DISTURBANCES

I am not afraid to die having thought of the issues of a dying hour.

—Anonymous epitaph, Bonaventure Cemetery

Savannah, Georgia
Bonaventure Cemetery
August, after midnight

"**P**oe, you wiener, get your ass over here!"

"Shut up! I ain't a wiener!"

Broken, adolescent male laughter echoed through the night air, and if I hadn't been so damn mad, I'd have laughed, too. Something about hearing a group of idiotic pubescent fifteen-year-old boys say *wiener* just cracked me up. But right then, I wanted to strangle all four of them—especially the wiener. My younger brother, Seth. That little butthead knew I'd check up on him—especially when his plan included sleeping over at Riggs

Parker's house. Yet there I was, after midnight on a Friday night, peering through the fence surrounding Bonaventure Cemetery. *After* I'd worked all day. With the moon a waning crescent, shining through the canopy of trees, I could vaguely see their skinny little Levi's weave and dart through the aged headstones and shadows.

Sleepover at Riggs' house, my ass. They probably all told their parents they were sleeping over at each other's houses. Didn't they realize you can't con a con? Guess not, because here I stood in the middle of the freaking night, just to make sure my little brother kept out of trouble. I watched them edge toward the back of the cemetery, and I followed down the fence line toward one particular live oak, stepping over several gnarled roots—not easy for those inexperienced in six-inch-heel boots. But I'd managed that fine art during my partying days on the cobbles of River Street. I was a total pro. Finally, they got within earshot once again, and they were so busy shoving and calling each other perverted names that none of them even knew I was around. *Good*. I'd sneak up on them, scare the crap out of them, then drag them all home before someone called the cops.

I gave my outfit a quick glance and then gauged the challenge before me. It just figured that the day I wore my leather miniskirt and spike-heel boots to the shop, I had to scale an eight-foot chain-link fence. If Riggs' mom had called a little earlier, I would have changed. But I'd locked up and hurried out, and when I'd caught sight of them on Victory, I never would have thought the goofballs would sneak into Bonaventure. It wasn't as easy to do as it'd been when I was a teen. So there I was, skirt, spiked boots, and all. Good thing no one but the dead would see my hiniesca (*high-nee-sca* is a juvenile, made-up word for *ass*, and I use it frequently) when I shimmied over the top. I drew a deep breath and gripped the bars with both hands. Even in hot, muggy August, the dew-covered steel felt cool beneath my palms. I found the old notches in the oak—the same ones my friends and I had used back in my wild days—dug the toe of one boot into the gash, and stretched my other leg out until it hooked the top of the fence. I used to hate being so tall, but once again my five-foot-nine-inch frame came in handy. Using my stomach and arms, I braced myself and eased my other leg up and over, then slowly slid to the ground. My skirt caught on the damp steel and inched completely up around my waist, and my heels sunk into the mossy dirt as I landed. I swore silently, pulled my heels free, yanked my skirt back down, and crouched, listening. Those little pecker-heads would pay for this.

A crash followed by a string of swears cut through the still air and drifted to my ears. What in the hell were they up to? Easing through the damp moss and fallen oak leaves, I made my way to the far back corner of the cemetery, close to the river; I followed their voices silently. I probably knew every single headstone at Bonaventure—my friends and I used to camp out here on a regular basis back in the day. Sick, I know, but true. Smoking joints while jumping headstones wasn't my proudest moment in life, but neither was having sex against one. For the record, I gave up joints and grave jumping a few years back. Sex I still had, just not against headstones. As I crept closer, I dodged and toed my way around pinecones and cockleburs, pushing aside the long

hanks of Spanish moss that dangled from the branches.
Finally, beneath the shadows and moonlight, the boys
came into view, and I stared, dumbstruck, as Seth and his
pals disappeared into an old crypt.

That explained the crash. Damn—even I'd never
done that, and I'd done a lot of crazy crap. But knowing what I knew from the Gullah? Hell and double no. I
couldn't believe Seth was going along with it. The name
on *that* particular crypt was ancient; the words were
nearly sanded flat with the stone, the rest covered by
sap, moss, and age. Couldn't read but maybe one or two
letters at best. Preacher—a well-respected Gullah elder,
herbalist, and conjurer, as well as a practiced hoodoo-
ist—had been a grandfather figure to me and Seth since
Mom's death. He'd called it *da hell stone* and told us a
long time ago to stay away from it. When a Gullah conjurer warned you about something, you'd better believe
it was nasty-bad. If you had even a scrap of gray matter in your crane-cap, you'd listen. They were descendants of the Africans brought to the eastern seaboard
during the slave trade, and they knew some wicked-bad
magic. *Dark stuff.* Some voodoo, some hoodoo, some
traditional root medicine and herbal cures, some conjur-
ing. All of it highly respected in the Gullah community.
Jesus, Seth must have lost his friggin' mind. I listened
for a few seconds; the deafening cacophony of cicadas
nearly drowned out the boys' low chatter inside the old
tomb. Damn, those bugs were loud.

With my backside pressed close to the aged stone, I
slid sideways toward the crypt's new, ragged opening.
Mosquitoes sank into my bare thighs, and I swatted at

them without making contact with my skin. They kept right on biting.

I pushed through a final fall of moss and peered downward, my breath catching in my throat. The mausoleum looked more like an old stone shanty—a slab about eight feet long and five feet wide, maybe four feet off the ground. From what Preacher said, though, the crypt itself was a helluva lot bigger belowground—even here in the low country. They had kicked in the old rusted iron gate at the entrance and had lowered themselves inside. I couldn't see them, but I saw a light flickering and their shadows moving about. Great. They were probably waving around their lighters. They'd catch the poor old dusty corpse on fire and themselves right along with it. *Dumbasses.* I wasn't a chicken or anything, but *no way* was I going down in there. This was *da hell stone*, and I wasn't taking any chances. I'd just scare the hell out of them and watch their bony rumps scramble out of the crypt. Then I'd yank Seth by the ears and drag them all home. Juvenile, I know. But it was the best I could do. *If only I had some classic firecrackers, like Black Cats or Whistling Moon Travelers . . .*

With a deep pull of air, I steadied myself and deepened my voice as much as I could. Not too hard, since it was naturally raspy and a little deep anyway. "Savannah PD! Get your asses out of there *now*!"

Waiting for the scrambling of bony behinds was almost fun. I stood there listening to their cursing, calling of vile names, and climbing up stone with one hand over my mouth, the other hand viciously swatting at the mosquitoes sucking the blood out of my hide. Then, many things happened all at once.

Another crash sounded, almost like glass or pottery being broken, and a gust of wind seemed to *whoosh* from the crypt, high-pitched, almost like a howl. I turned my head to avoid the brunt of it because it smelled gross, like decay. Then one of the boys swore, and they all yelled with squeaky voices and piled out of the grave, flinging themselves onto the ground and then scurrying to get up. The wind abruptly stopped. The deafening chirping cicadas had grown completely silent. Bonaventure was as still as the death that lay buried beneath it.

Seth stumbled by, and I grabbed him by the shirt, pulling him to an abrupt stop. He whipped around, his eyes glazed; they turned angry when he recognized me. I let him go and lifted a brow.

"God, Riley!" he hollered. "What are you doing?" He frowned. "Let me go!"

The other boys stopped their scrambling and turned. They all fell to the ground, laughing. One whistled. Riggs, whom I'd known since he was seven, said, "Poe's sister is freakin' hot!"

"Damn, Poe—where you been hidin' her?"

"She married?"

"Who cares, man?!" Riggs said. "Her ass is smokin'!"

They all laughed.

Seth's gaze left mine, and he lunged toward his friend. "Shut up, Riggs!"

I smiled. A small piece of me felt proud that my little brother—idiot that he was at the moment—would want to defend me against his pervy friends. Maybe I hadn't done too bad a job in raising him after all. Again I grabbed Seth's shirt and yanked him backward—not easy since the kid was already as tall as me with my boots on. "Let it go, Bro," I said, and began tugging him toward the back of the cemetery. There was a place near the very back left fence where the ground sloped upward—enough for us to climb out. I glanced at Seth's friends and inclined my head. "Let's get out of here before the cops show up for real. I'm pretty sure you guys don't want your parents to get a knock on their doors tonight. It's a federal offense to desecrate a grave, you know." That was all we'd need, especially since the cops already knew *exactly* who I was.

"Dude, what's desecrate?" one of the boys said.

"You want *us* to go with *you*?" Riggs said, a smirk on his adolescent face. "So you can rat us out to our parents? No, thanks, babe!" He turned to the others. "Come on!"

"Hey, wait!" I called, taking several steps and thinking that I'd let Riggs find out on his own that his mom already knew about his little scheme. "Come on, guys! I'll drive you home." I couldn't just leave them out in the middle of the night. No way. "Swear to God, I won't rat you out."

"No, thanks, sexy!" Riggs hollered, laughing, and he and the others took off into the shadows. He called back, "You're fine as hell, but I ain't letting you hand me over to my mommy!" More squeaky male laughter; then their voices grew faint as they slipped off into the night.

Somehow, that made me very uncomfortable, and yet as agile as I was, even in spike-heel boots, I knew I couldn't catch Riggs and his friends, corral them, and drag them all to my Jeep. I gave a sigh and shook my head. "Come on, Bro. Let's get out of here."

I looked at my brother. Even in the dimness of the oaks, I could make out Seth's venomous glare as he

stared after his friends. He was truly pissed at them.
"Whatever," he mumbled. He kicked the dirt and threw
a lanky arm over my shoulders. "Didn't wanna come
here anyway. Stupid idea."

I glanced at him. "Why did you?"

He shrugged. "Just a lame bet."

More adolescent male giggling cracked through the
night as Riggs and the others blew us off and ran in the
opposite direction. I had half a mind to call the cops.
Maybe that was exactly what they needed: a little heat.
But since Seth would be the one to catch hell, I let it go.
I'd circle Bonaventure to make sure they got out, and
then I'd follow their stupid little keisters home.

"Schmucks," I muttered at them; then I turned back
to Seth. I knew from experience not to pound him with
why's and *how come*'s—it'd been done to me plenty
of times when I was his age, and it didn't do anything
but royally piss me off. I'd talk to him later. Besides, I
could tell he regretted even hanging out with those
guys, even though he'd known Riggs since grade school.
"Hey, wanna grab some Krystal's? I haven't eaten yet."
I asked. Best fast-food burgers in the South, and they
were open twenty-four seven. Nice and greasy.

"Yeah, sure," said Seth. "Hey." He stopped at the
sloped ground and faced me. In the moonlight I could
see the patches of whiskers he'd tried shaving. His eyes,
though, were completely sincere. I loved that about my
brother. You could tell just about everything he was
thinking and feeling in the depths of his eyes. "Sorry
about tonight," he said. "I know you gotta work in the
morning."

I gave him a playful punch to the gut. "Yeah, well, not

until eleven, so it's no big deal." I elbowed his ribs. "You can come in and sweep the floor for me." I grinned and dug my boot toe into a gnarled bump in the tree. "You'd better turn your head unless you want an eyeful." No doubt my skirt was about to take a ride up my fanny again.

"Don't have to ask me twice," he said, and turned his back.

As I crawled over the fence, I could hear Riggs and the others whistling. The sound wasn't that far away, and I knew they watched from close-by shadows. Freaking little perverts. A growl escaped Seth's throat, and I imagined that if Riggs had been close enough, Seth would have laid into him. My brother was lanky but as strong as hell.

As I landed on the soft ground and my heels sunk into the dirt, I noticed how deathly silent Bonaventure was. Not a single night bird, bug, or frog—or Riggs and the guys—made a single sound. The fine hairs on the back of my neck and arms rose, and I quickly brushed the uncomfortable feeling off.

"What's the matter?" Seth said as he dropped to the ground beside me. "You look like you've seen a ghost or something."

My gaze swept the graves, the luminescent marble statues that peeked through the trees, and the longer I stood there, the stronger the bad feeling became. "You don't feel that?"

Seth was silent for a split second. "Yeah. What is it? It's creepin' me out." He scanned the cemetery. "Too quiet."

I glanced at him. "You know what crypt you were in, right?"

He pushed his floppy bangs off of his face and nodded, his glassy-eyed stare reflecting the night. "Not until after. I tried to talk Riggs into leaving it alone, but he's an idiot. He'd kicked the gate in before I could stop him."

I wholeheartedly agreed. Riggs was an idiot. "Well, let's get out of here, huh?" I pointed. "Jeep's over there."

"Can I drive?" he asked.

"No."

"Damn."

I grinned as we hurried across the sandy lot outside the cemetery and past the two pillars of the entrance. But the weird feeling stayed with me, grated at my insides, even after we pulled away. I eased down the one-lane street, waiting for a glimpse of Riggs and the guys as they stumbled from the cemetery, and the raw gut feelings that clawed at my insides disturbed me. I'd spent too many teenage years looking over my shoulder in the shadiest streets of Savannah. I had to watch my own back, and gut feelings were things I paid attention to.

I felt as though someone watched us. And I didn't think it was Riggs and his friends, either. Weirdest damn feeling I'd ever had. I *never* get spooked. When I was Seth's age, I was one badass punk kid. I didn't have a scared bone in my body, and I'd do anything anyone dared me to do. I'd even looked scary as a teenager, with my naturally pale skin and, back then, red hair streaked black, kohl-rimmed eyes, and black lips. I've walked Savannah's cobbles the whole of my life, been in the darkest alleys, and I've seen a lot of crap go down. I've been *in* a lot of crap as it was *going* down. I was one effed-up

kid back then, and if it weren't for Preacher, I still would
be. But I'd never had a feeling creep over me like this
one. I wanted to continuously look over my shoulder, or
worse—*overhead*. What the hell would I be doing that
for? What would be overhead?

The muggy brine from the marsh whipped at my face
as I shifted into third, and I glanced at Seth. He was
biting his nails and staring out what would have been
his window, had the Jeep's top been on. I knew why he
was acting funny. He'd been inside da hell stone. I'd be
freaked-out, too, were I him. Dammit, he knew better
than to go inside something like that. But I wouldn't torture him by asking a load of questions tonight. Tomorrow. I'd wait until tomorrow.

"There they are," Seth said, pointing off to the left of
the narrow street. Sure enough, there were those ding-
dongs, cutting across someone's yard. They disappeared
around the back of a small, white, concrete house.

"That's Todd's grandma's," Seth said. "They're staying there tonight."

I downshifted into first and slowly drove by the old
home. After I saw a light flicker on near the back of the
house, I felt relieved. At least the boys were off the streets.
We pulled away and headed into the now-thinned traffic
of Victory Drive.

After going through the drive-through at Krystal's,
we headed home. The smell of grease-soaked bread and
fried burgers wafted from the paper bags, making my
stomach growl. I was a proud JFJ (junk-food junkie),
and I'd bought a dozen. I'd probably polish off at least
five or six myself. If you've never had a Krystal burger,
they're glorious—or hell on the stomach. Lucky for me,

they worked perfectly fine for my digestive system, and I was starved. I turned onto Abercorn, hit all the squares, crossed Bay Street, and finally pulled onto the cobbles. The moment I turned onto the merchant's drive, the scent of urine from a busy Friday night stung my nostrils. That's something they don't put in the tourist mags of Savannah—weekend public urination in the historic district. Nasty. Just freaking nasty.

I parked the Jeep at the back entrance of Inksomnia, pulled the emergency brake, and shifted it into first. I grabbed the drinks. "Let's go, Bro, before I start gnawing on that paper bag. Hey, will you take Chaz out for a walk? He probably needs to pee." Chaz was our three-year-old Australian shepherd. Blue merle, one blue eye, one brown. Cool as hell, that dog, and we'd gotten him from a rescue organization two years before.

Seth's eyes still looked hazed as he climbed out. "Yeah, sure."

It was then that I truly noticed the silence in the streets. Not human silence, as I still heard music pouring from the Boar's Head, laughter, and the occasional blast of a horn or the wail of a cop car in the distance. I even heard old Capote playing his saxophone on the river walk. But the cicadas? Crickets? Night birds?

Dead silence.

I shoved the key in the lock and went inside, Seth on my heels, and immediately Chaz was there, barking and wagging his backside. "Hey, boy," I said, scrubbing the fur between his ears. "You miss us?" Seth grabbed the leash hanging from the wall, snapped it onto Chaz's collar, and headed out with a waste bag. I watched him for a minute, until they disappeared up the walk. Before I closed the door, I glanced over my shoulder, out into the afterlight (the Gullah pronounced it *afta-light*).

I saw nothing; I felt everything.

Seth and Chaz came jogging up the cobbles, so I waited until they were inside; then I locked the door and threw the second bolt. Soon, though, I'd find out that locks and bolts were for the ignorant. In reality, they were absolutely freaking worthless.

Part 2

THE BEGINNING

When the alarm went off at eight the next morning, I was surprised to find I'd actually had enough sleep despite the late-night escapade at Bonaventure. Although I didn't open shop until eleven, I loved the morning on the riverfront, and although I was completely unpredictable ninety-eight percent of the time, I was a total creature of habit for the last two percent: Gullah tea. I know—to look at me you'd never think for a second I enjoyed strong-steeped African tea with cream and sugar in the mornings. I looked more like a . . . Red Bull type of girl (I saved the Bull for midday). But Gullah tea was absolute heaven, and I drank it every single day. Slipping out of bed, I threw on a black tee and a pair of frayed jean shorts, pulled my hair into a ponytail, slipped into flip-flops, and eased downstairs. I took Chaz for a short walk, poured a heaping serving of dog food into his bowl, and eased out the back entrance of Inksomnia. I briefly glanced down as I left and made a mental note to paint my toenails later. The black-purple polish I'd put on just two days before was already chipping off. I hated chipped polish. Total trash.

The thick, humid August air smacked me in the face and clung to my skin as I made my way down Factor's Walk to the back side of Preacher's store, which sat directly next to mine. Da Plat Eye. Literally, it meant *the stink eye*, or *the evil eye*, in Gullah, and was a wicked-cool herbs, potions, and magic store. Preacher and his wife, Estelle, belonged to a small but tight-knit community of Gullah who grew their own loose tea and other herbs out on what they simply referred to as Da Island—one of the small barrier islands off the coast of Savannah. The tea was out of this freaking world. As I said, Preacher was an herbalist and conjurer, highly sought after for all sorts of cures for illnesses, hexes— you name it. Although Preacher was the quiet, stoic type and was as gentle as a kitten, it took only one look of disappointment from him to make you want to curl up and bawl with regret (I know—I've done it). So I'd decided to hold off on telling Preacher about Seth and da hell stone—at least until I'd gone over there during the daylight hours to check out how much damage had been done. Hopefully, nothing more than a gate and an old piece of pottery had been broken. As I pushed into Da Plat Eye's narrow double doors—painted haint blue to keep the evil spirits out—the ever-familiar bell tinkled above my head, and Estelle immediately emerged from behind the blue curtain that led into their living quarters upstairs. A big, warm, blindingly white smile stretched across her ebony face, and the brightly colored red, black, blue, and yellow scarf traditional to Gullah women that she wore wrapped around her head and knotted in the front matched the flowing skirt that reached her ankles. A haint blue Da Plat Eye T-shirt hung past her hips. She was probably all of five feet two inches high. My little Gullah granny.

"Ah! Dere's my Riley Poe," she said, and, as she did every morning, rushed over to hug me as if she hadn't seen me in forever. I admit that it felt good to have someone care so much. With a pair of strong, worn palms on either side of my face, she squished my cheeks, pulled my head down, and kissed me square on the nose. Dark, fathomless eyes stared up into mine, and she gave a mock frown. "Where's dat brodder of yours, huh?" she asked in that unique Gullah accent that I never tired of hearing, even the more relaxed version they spoke around Seth and me. The cadence and pitch of that Creole blend of Elizabethan English and mesmerizing African drew the listener back in time. I loved it. "Dat lazybones boy still abed?"

"Of course," I answered, and linked my arm through hers as we made our way to their kitchen. The aroma of fresh-brewed tea filled the two-hundred-year-old building, along with aged wood and fried bacon. My stomach growled so loud, Estelle turned and giggled.

"You poor tang; you don't eat enough," she said, shaking her head. "Now, git on in dere, girl. Your Preacher man is waitin' wit your tea. I'll bring da bacon and biscuits."

"Sweet," I said. I gave Estelle a quick smile and hurried past stainless-steel pots, crockery, clay pots, and handwoven sweetgrass baskets hanging from the ceiling, and the newsprint-covered walls (newspaper print covering the walls keeps evil spirits at bay since they have to stop and read each word before taking action—another cool Gullah belief) to the breakfast nook just off the kitchen. Preacher was in his usual straight-backed wooden chair, which was probably a hundred years old, near the corner window facing River Street. And no matter how warm the weather, he always—*always*—wore a plaid long-sleeved cotton shirt tucked into a pair of worn jeans. With a cap of short, pure white hair standing stark against his satiny black skin, he looked every bit the part of a Gullah root doctor. All-knowing brown eyes evaluated me as I walked toward him, and somehow, even after so many years, Preacher still had the ability to do something no one else could: make me squirm. I'd never let it show, of course, and he knew it. It was a game between us, and one that wily old Gullah totally dug.

I met those ancient brown eyes with a stare of complete confidence, scrutiny, and an air of arrogance, and we continued our stare-off in silence until Estelle bustled into the nook.

"Ah, you two fools, stop wit da starin' dis mornin'!" she said, laughing. "Don' you ever git tired of playin' dat game? Sit down, girl, before I take a switch to dat skinny backside. I already ate, so dig in."

A small twitch in Preacher's lip made me laugh, and the game was over. "Yes, ma'am," I said, and did as I was told. Estelle set a platter of thick fried bacon and biscuits on the table between me and Preacher, along with a bottle of cane syrup. A pot of tea sat steaming and ready.

Preacher grinned, a large white smile similar to his

wife's. He stared at me a bit longer, then nodded at my plate. "Eat up so I don' have to listen to your stomach cry," he said with a chuckle.

"Don't have to ask me twice," I said, and dug in. We ate in silence for a few minutes, and after two biscuits drenched in cane syrup, and three slices of bacon, I pushed my plate aside and, dumping in a couple of spoonfuls of brown sugar and a splash of cream, started on my first cup of tea. The whole while, Preacher seemed to watch me with more depth than usual. Maybe that was guilt speaking for not telling him immediately about da hell stone. I brushed it off the best I could and sipped my tea. The pungent mix of odd and mysterious Gullah herbs at first stung my throat, as always, and then an irresistible smoothness settled in and warmed my insides. I glanced at Preacher over the rim of my cup, and he sipped his own brew—straight black.

"You send dat brodder of yours over dis afternoon," he said, his voice deep and silky. "He can paper da walls upstairs for me, and I'll pay him. Can't give dem *wudus* idle eyes, and dat old paper up dere is fallin' down in places." He sighed and rubbed his neck. "I been meanin' to replace it, but I'm gettin' old, girl. Joints are achin'."

I leaned back in the chair with my tea and frowned. *Wudus* was Gullah for evil spirits, something Preacher believed in wholeheartedly. I can't say that I totally bought it, but I wasn't completely opposed to the idea. I scrutinized him for several seconds. "My ass you're getting old. You look exactly like you did the first time I met you." I wiggled my brows. "You're hot, Preacher man. Seriously."

Estelle's high-pitched cackle rattled the pots hanging from the rafters. "Ha! Oh, girl, for shame!"

"You are a crazy painted white girl," Preacher said, his eyes smiling. "I love ya like you was my own child, you know dat? Seth, too." He watched me closely, and I felt clear to my bones that he suspected something was up. Even if you didn't believe in Gullah ways, there was no getting around the power Preacher radiated. It was what saved me as a punk kid, dragged me from a total path of self-destruction.

That was what the Gullah called me, because of my inked skin: *painted*. I'd always loved it, and thought it fit me to a T. I drained my teacup, got up, and walked over to Preacher, who in fact did look a little tired today, and to be honest, that fact bothered the hell out of me. I wrapped my arms around his neck and hugged him tightly. "Yeah, I know, and we love you, too." I kissed his cheek, his unique, familiar scent of homemade soap and Old Spice wafting to my nostrils. "I don't know what we'd do without you and Estelle." I met his gaze. "You guys saved my life. Mine and Seth's." They knew it, too, and it wasn't the first time I'd told them. For some reason, the need to assure them that I still felt that way overtook me, and they allowed it.

Preacher sat silently, as was his way, and we stared at each other for what seemed like a long, long time. He and Estelle and their extended community were the only family Seth and I had. Our father? I remember only vague glimpses of him, and I'm as glad as hell. He left us right after I'd turned ten, and Seth was a baby. I remember Mom crying for hours on end, days on end, and I'd always hated him for that. Effing idiot. Last I heard, he was somewhere in the Louisiana prison system. I didn't care if I ever laid eyes on him again. Sometimes, though, Seth asked about him, and I figured he was at that age when his curiosity was getting at him. Every guy wants a dad—even if that dad was a total fuckup.

Estelle bustled back into the nook and swatted me on the rump, breaking my hateful thoughts. "You'd best git, girl," she said, gathering plates before I even had a chance to pick mine up. "Unless you plan on paintin' folks in dem high shorts, dere."

I laughed, gave her a quick peck on the cheek, and smiled at Preacher. "Peace out, Preacher man. I'll send Seth over in a little while."

Preacher gave a single nod, and I was already at the blue curtain before he said anything. "When you feel like sayin' what it is you don't wanna say right now, come on back," he said. "I got ears for you."

I looked at him over my shoulder and stared in wonder. I knew he could tell something was up. "How do you do that?" I asked. Seriously. I had one major poker face, and he *still* could tell I was keeping something from him. Damn.

Preacher merely lifted one plaid-covered shoulder. "You come back den. We'll talk right."

I met his gaze. "I will." I scooted through the curtain and left Da Plat Eye fast. There was hardly anything worse than Preacher knowing something was up, and that he had endless patience waiting for you to spill the beans. Trust me when I say he reveled in knowing he made you squirm—even if it didn't show on the outside. It made me feel guilty as hell for withholding info, but

I needed to see exactly what the boys had done at da hell stone. It was a big deal, and I knew it would be to Preacher.

I made my way back to Inksomnia, stepped inside, and glanced at the Kit-Cat Clock (eBay, Classic Black, seventy-fifth-anniversary edition, $49.99 with free batteries and shipping!) on the wall: eight forty-five. I had time to run over to Bonaventure, check out the damage, and get back in time to shower and get ready to open shop. My first appointment was at eleven thirty, so no sweat. Grabbing my keys, I listened for a minute, heard nothing, so figured Seth was still crashed upstairs. "Chaz, come on, boy," I hollered, and Chaz came trotting down the steps, anxious to go for a ride. We hurried out the door and in minutes were on Bay Street, heading toward Abercorn. Chaz sat in the passenger seat, the wind blowing his ears back, as happy as a puppy. He was smart and completely obedient. Great dog.

Being that this was the first Saturday of the month, the historic district was already crowded with tourists and local shoppers on foot. The first Saturday included outdoor music, sidewalk shopping (the stores pulled merchandise out onto the sidewalk to sell), and food vendors along the river walk (I reminded myself right then to get a funnel cake later), and to top it off school would be starting up soon, so people would be grabbing their last little bit of vacation time. By noon there wouldn't be a single cobble visible, which was okay by me. There were always tourists who got a burr in their Levi's to get a spontaneous tattoo, and if I had an available spot, I'd give them a one-of-a-kind piece of body art.

As I rounded LaFayette Square, I saw Capote knelt

down by a park bench, pulling his sax from its case. I
knocked the horn twice, Chaz let out a bark, and Capote
glanced up, waved, and flashed a broad, white smile. He
was Gullah, one of Preacher's cousins; he lived in a tiny
apartment on Gaston Street. What a sweetheart that old
guy was, and he could play the sax like a raving mofo. I'd
asked him once why he'd never gone professional, and
his simple answer was *I don't need all dat fancy stuff, girl.*
He was a permanent Savannah fixture, Capote.

The closer I got to Bonaventure, the heavier the marsh
scent became, and with the top off my Jeep, it surrounded
me; I inhaled a lungful. Some hated the smell of brine,
but I liked it. It reminded me of my childhood, the innocent part, after we'd gotten over my dad leaving, and before I'd turned into a head-banging wild child. God, how
I wished I could take all that crap back. I gave my mom
hell, and she so hadn't deserved any more hell. The pain
of that last moment with her, while she lay dead, lifeless
in my arms, still haunted me, even in my sleep. I missed
my mom so bad it hurt my chest to think about it, and
yeah, I thought about it every damn day, even if I didn't
want to. It just happened, invaded my gray matter and
made me remember things I didn't necessarily want to
remember. My penance, I suppose, since I was to blame
for my mom's death. Probably why I'd partied every last
drop of craziness out of myself back then. I might look
like I party hard now, but I'm as domesticated as they
come. An occasional drink at Molly McPherson's is all
I'm good for anymore. I left that wild life far behind, and
only scars and remnants of my past were still visible and
present. And all that by my ripe old age of twenty-five.

I pulled the Jeep into the left-hand-turn lane at the

Victory Drive traffic light and threw it into neutral as
I waited. The sun beamed down through the canopy of
live oaks and Spanish moss with ferocity, making me
squint through the tint of my shades—and it was only
nine a.m. I was neither a morning person nor a night
person—I dealt with both times of the day equally well.
But as my lily-white skin revealed, I wasn't particularly
fond of the sun. I burned fiercely. A thin sheen of part
sweat, part humidity covered my exposed skin, and the
slightest of breezes cooled me off. I watched patrons and
traffic as I listened to the sounds of early-morning Savannah mixed with horn blasts, lost in my thoughts until
a smooth voice from the car beside me interrupted.

"Hey, babe, nice dog. Really nice tats."

I stared straight ahead, uninterested. A low growl
sounded deep in Chaz's throat, and though the double
rejection probably pissed the guy off, he didn't show it.
I could feel his eyes on me, though, and I hadn't even
spared him a single glance yet. It was just a creepy feeling I'd come to pick off rather fast, and ignore even
faster.

"Hey, don't be shy, baby," he said, as if I had a shy
bone in my body. "You want to meet later? Show me
all your tats?" He laughed. "You can leave your dog
home."

My arrow turned green, and I threw the Jeep into first
gear. I held the clutch for a second as I glanced over at
the guy and peered at him over the rim of my shades. Figured. A smart-dressed older guy in a new Lexus, wanting to get it on with something he probably thought was
freaky—me. He probably had a wife and kids at home.
He was so not on my agenda—now or ever. For some

reason, guys seemed to think alternatively dressed and
inked skin equaled an easy lay. Funny thing was, I really
wasn't anything, as in, I wasn't Goth, or any other sort
of character. I just had a . . . quirky, artistic sense of style.
I smirked, then shook my head in amusement, because
to me he was a sick freaking idiot. "You wish, gramps," I
said. Chaz barked, and I made the turn. I heard him call
me a bitch, and for some reason it made me laugh. Even
Chaz looked like he was smiling, with his tongue hanging out of his open mouth, the wind picking it up and
flopping it all over. I'd been called way worse; you can
believe it. Sticks and stones, baby. It took a lot more than
a little name-calling to hurt my feelings anymore.

Through the small community of Thunderbolt, I
weaved my way down Bonaventure Road, to the front
gates of the cemetery. Although they'd been open since
eight, the place looked totally deserted—strange for
an August morning. Usually, the tourists were wandering in and out of the keeper's building, meander-
ing through the grounds, and checking out the famous
monuments and infamously interred. I pulled in slowly
past the keeper's redbrick building, following the path
to the far right, and crept along in second gear to the
rear of the property. Bonaventure was the epitome of
the South, with towering, two-hundred-year-old live oak
trees draped in wispy moss, and dozens of narrow dirt
roads leading back into the white marbled statues and
gray headstones of the graveyard. In the spring, pink,
fuchsia, and white azaleas lined the dirt lanes, and vines
of wisteria hung like grape clusters. Quite pretty, actually. A slight salty breeze always seemed to be passing
through, rustling the leaves and anything else that got in

its way. The cemetery itself overlooked the Wilmington River and salt marshes, and I guess if I had to die and be buried somewhere, Bonaventure would be an okay eternal resting place. As long as it was far away from da hell stone, thank you.

I pulled the Jeep over, killed the engine, threw it into first gear, and set the emergency brake, then just sat for a moment as I took in the area. Something felt ... funny. A slight breeze wafted through the leaves of the live oaks, and the faint rustling was the only sound in the cemetery. I scanned the rows of headstones, the white marbled statues and aged crypts, and realized it was way too quiet—even for a graveyard. Not one cricket, bug, or bird made the slightest of sounds. It was totally silent, and it weirded me out. And I don't usually get weirded out. I glanced over at my dog, who had his nose lifted and was sniffing the air. He felt it, too. "Stay, Chaz," I commanded. He whined but firmly planted his backside in the seat. He wouldn't budge until I told him to.

I slid from the Jeep and started walking up the dirt path, my flip-flops slapping my heels, toward the back of the cemetery where da hell stone was located. The closer I got to the crypt, the stranger I felt, and an odd sensation crept over my skin. It tingled for absolutely no reason, and I was acutely aware of it as though hundreds of tiny ants crawled over me. More than once I glanced over my shoulder, and again—*up*—just like the night before. As if my feet had a mind of their own, my pace quickened. Funny thing was, so did my heartbeat, my breathing. It all accelerated.

Once da hell stone was in sight, I stepped off the dirt path and cut across the grass, the weird sensation growing stronger as I drew closer. Probably just my superstitions kicking in, but I was still jumpy, and I hurried even faster.

I got close to the crypt and stared in disbelief. I slowly eased to the jagged opening, only it wasn't jagged at all. The rusted gate was in place, unbroken. It was as though nothing had been disturbed. Squatting down, I lightly ran my fingers over the aged steel; the edges where it fit perfectly against the crypt's opening even looked rusted into place. It was sealed tight. Untouched. Unbroken. *What the hell?* I continued to search the ground, the dirt, the stone, for any signs of what had happened the night before with Seth and his buddies. I didn't even see a Converse footprint. I even inspected some close-by crypts, and they all seemed to be in the same shape. Old, yet intact. No signs of vandalism anywhere. Nothing to indicate a group of teenage boys horsing around and stumbling out of a crypt.

Suddenly, I turned and jumped up at the same time, my hand flying to the back of my neck. It felt as though someone had breathed against my skin. I looked everywhere; no one was around. Far across the cemetery, I saw one of the workers pushing a wheelbarrow, but not a soul was close to me. Certainly not close enough to have blown on my neck. Not to sound like a baby or anything—I've been kickboxing for seven years and did plenty of street fighting before that—but I was done with my inspection of da hell stone. People? They didn't scare me at all. I had handled the very worst of humanity, up close and way too personal. But spirits? Like I said earlier, I wasn't completely convinced they existed, but Preacher was one hundred percent sure about the *wudus*, and that fact alone made me nearly break into a run. I hurried back to the Jeep, where my dog was waiting patiently, jumped in, and drove off like some big damn scaredy-cat. As I pulled through Bonaventure's black pillared gates, I couldn't help but feel like someone watched me, and twice I threw a glance over my shoulder. Very, very weird.

I wondered whether I'd been at the wrong crypt last night. I didn't think so; I grew up here. I knew Bonaventure like the back of my hand, and I damn well knew where da hell stone was. The groundskeeper could have fixed it, but that fast? The gate had been rusted into place. It didn't *look* repaired. It looked ... ancient. And that was why I knew I definitely had to talk to Preacher. Something wasn't right, and I felt in my gut that only he'd be able to figure out what. I'd talk to him tonight, once I finished my last appointment. My thoughts continued to ramble as I made my way back to Factor's Walk, and by the time I walked through the back door of Inksomnia, I still didn't have an answer. It bugged the absolute hell out of me.

Throwing the keys on the counter, I hurried upstairs to shower, Chaz right on my heels. Nyx, my other artist and closest pal, would be here soon, and I was already running a little late. Before I hit the bathroom, I peeked into Seth's room, and the moment I pushed open the door, a wave of heat and brine hit me. The bedroom window was thrown wide-open, stuffy warmth pouring in. Seth was sprawled over his bed, shirtless and still wearing the jeans he'd worn the night before. I walked over, closed the window, and shook his arm. A growl sounded from the doorway, and I turned to see Chaz standing there, the fur at his neck on end. "What's wrong with you, boy?" I asked. "It's just lazy Seth. Go downstairs and wait on Nyx." He growled again, then turned and ran off. Totally strange, but I shook it off and turned back to my brother.

"Hey, butthead, I'm not paying Georgia Power to cool off the riverfront. What's up with the open window?" I asked. Seth's dark brown hair was slick with sweat, his skin all sticky. I smoothed his bangs from his eyes and shook him again. "Hey, Bro—wake up." He continued to sleep, hard, and just when I thought he wouldn't answer, he did.

"A little more," Seth mumbled, and buried his face into his pillow. "Beat."

I stared down at my sweet little brother, who'd never given me a minute's trouble since Mom died, and couldn't resist. "Yeah, whatever, brat," I said, then leaned down and kissed the top of his head. *Teenagers.* I used to sleep like the dead myself. With a sigh, I left his room and jumped in the shower.

By the time I'd pulled on my favorite red-and-black plaid miniskirt (equipped with a really cool steel-ringed belt that was slung low over my hips, and a pair of red lacy boy shorts to wear beneath), clunky ankle-high black boots, and a destroyed black tank that had Inksomnia's logo on the front in red, and tied my long hair in a high ponytail, I heard Nyx moving around downstairs, setting up shop. I fastened a black-corded choker with the cutest little black glass heart charm with a ruby in the center around my neck, hurried from the room, and jogged down the narrow steps. The moment I walked through the breezeway, Nyx turned and flashed me her infamous smile, enthusiastic and bright. Chaz was in his usual spot, on a large braided rug near the corner.

"Hey, Riley," she said, and set down a box of Skin Candy ink that must have arrived while I was in the shower. "Today's going to be a superb day!" She turned, marched over to the storefront window facing River Street, and yanked open the blinds. "Just look at it out there. Sunshine perfectly teeming with lots of happy people who are dying to embark on their first tattoo!" Turning, she glanced back at me expectantly, eyes innocently widened, hands on hips. "Don't you think?"

I grinned. There wasn't another soul in the world like Nyxinnia Foster. "I bet you dinner at Garibaldi's we get at least one man or woman of the cloth in here today, claiming we're doing the devil's work."

Nyx studied me hard, her perfectly arched brows pulled completely together, bunched in the center. Her eyes narrowed. "You're on, Poe."

If there was one thing in my life I could count on now, it was cheerful Nyx Foster always having a cup half full instead of half empty, and I truly loved that about her. We'd gone to SCAD together (that's Savannah College of Art and Design) and had become fast friends the very first day of class. After I'd established Inksomnia, she was the first artist I sought. Like me, she definitely had her own style, her own mentality and outlook on life, and it also leaned toward what people in general would classify as alternative, or Goth—with a few Nyx twists. With straight auburn hair that she wore with bangs and—nine times out of ten—pigtails, porcelain skin that was nearly as white as mine, smoky eye makeup, and red lips, she definitely stood out in a crowd. To us, it was just an artis-

tic expression of ourselves. Knowing today was the first
Saturday of the month, and that River Street would be
jam-packed by noon, she wore one of her favorite out-
fits (I thought she looked fantastic!): black shorts with
suspenders, black-and-white ripped stockings that rose
above her knees, a pair of black platform Mary Janes,
and a red bowling shirt with black piping. On the back of
the shirt was an embroidered spiderweb with a little spi-
der in the center. It matched the one inked onto the back
of her neck perfectly. Nyx was a sweetheart—one of the
most caring, giving people I knew, but the one thing we
didn't have in common was background. While she was
her own unique person and, like me, comfortable in her
own skin, she'd never lived on the street, never been in
trouble, never seen the inside of a police station, and
had a fantastic, supportive family. She'd never even had
a speeding ticket. I'd spent my teenage years as high as
a kite, smoked like a freight train, got into one too many
fights, skipped school, and ran with the badasses. That
crowd happened to be into heavy metal and Goth clubs.
Don't get me wrong; just because someone's Goth or
punk doesn't mean they're dark, gloomy, or dangerous.
I just happened to have hooked up with a bunch of los-
ers who'd fancied their own personal take on the Goth
look. And I'd run fast and hard, right along with them.
Much to my regret, that is. Goth is not what you are.
It's *who* you are. The general public makes that mistake
all the time. And for the record, I'm nothing like I was
back then. Not the crazy, partying, careless teenager. I
am scarred from it. Nothing I can't handle, though.

You see, that's what's funny about Savannah. The
publicized, touristy part—the Savannah you see in travel

magazines? It's idyllic and all historically gorgeous. When people think of Savannah, they think of the Old South, horse-drawn carriages, moss, an original colony with scenic squares, tall church spires, and, strangely enough, Gothic Revival architecture. Maybe even Paula Deen and *Midnight in the Garden of Good and Evil*. The part of Savannah they don't see, and the part society is blind to? It's there, in the recesses of the shadows. Dark. Dangerous. Hidden, unless you're *in*. Hell, there are parts I'm probably not even privy to—especially now. And if you aren't careful, you can be sucked right into the pit of despair. There's always potential to fall into bad shit. I know. I've been there. I fell and *wallowed* in it. And sometimes, when you're in, you stay in. Or you don't leave alive. I escaped, but not without repercussions. Big ones.

We finished setting up the shop and cranked up the music, and by then my appointment had arrived, along with four of his buddies, all military. Rather, *about* to be military, and we get a lot of those guys and gals. Hunter Army Airfield was right here in Savannah, and Fort Stewart was close by in Hinesville. My client this morning was a young guy, nineteen, and he and his buddies were all leaving for Parris Island—the marines' boot camp—in a week. They all sported buzz cuts and were pumped, big-time. God, they looked . . . too damn young. Just four years older than Seth. While the others browsed the art books and chatted with Nyx, my client, whose name was Zac, shyly walked up to me. Tall, a little lanky, but lean, with a pair of clear blue eyes, he flashed a hesitant smile. He was staring at my arms.

"That is some wicked cool artwork," he said. "Can I see the rest of it?"

I lifted one brow and smiled. "You're not as shy as you look."

Zac's face immediately turned as red as a ripe tomato. "Oh—no disrespect, ma'am. I'd heard about it and honestly, I just wanted to—"

I laughed and shook my head. "Take it easy there, Private. No need to get all flustered. I get that same question asked nearly every time my shop doors are opened. I'm always prepared." I grinned. "Swimsuit top underneath, so don't get too excited. Got it?"

Zac laughed. "Yes, ma'am." His buddies were instantly at his side. Nyx stood behind them, a smirk on her face, swinging her hips in a little Nyx dance to the music. I wiggled my brows, and in one easy, practiced move I lifted my Inksomnia shirt over my head and turned around. Everybody always wanted to check out my dragons, and I admit—they were pretty kick-ass. Inked in emerald green, with random ruby scales and lined in ebony, the art started at my lower back and twisted up my spine. The dragons on my arms started at my biceps and wound down to my wrists, the very tip of each tail wrapping around my index fingers.

"Whoa," Zac said with appreciation in his voice. "That is sick. How long did it take?"

"Did it hurt?" one of his buddies asked.

"Who did it?" another inquired.

"That," Zac said, turning even redder, "is freaking hot."

I smiled and shook my head at the questions I'd answered hundreds of times before, and just as I went to turn around, I saw this guy, standing at Inksomnia's large storefront picture window, staring in, and I froze. I felt my breath catch in my throat, and my heart slammed against my ribs. No more than three seconds passed, yet it seemed as though we'd stood there for an hour. Although he wore a pair of dark shades, I felt as though he could see clear through me. I couldn't take my eyes off of him.

When I blinked, he was gone. Yeah, *that fast*. I thought to hurry over to the window, or even better, the door, and look for him, see which direction he went. But I didn't. I have no idea why. Something kept me planted right where I was.

Hastily, I pulled my shirt back over my head and turned to the guys and shrugged. "Eh, hurt a little, but not too bad. It took six sittings, at probably four hours each." I grinned. "And the artist is standing behind you."

They all turned and stared appreciatively at Nyx, who gave a blasé wave. "It was nothin'."

"Awesome," they all said at different times.

I looked at Zac. "You ready?" I asked. "Whatcha got for me?"

"Yes, ma'am," he said again, making me feel totally ancient. But those were the manners of the South, born and bred, and once baked into your brain, they always and forever remained. From his back pocket he pulled a folded piece of white sketch paper and opened it up. He handed it to me, and I inspected it thoroughly. It was a hand-drawn sketch of a Celtic-inspired tribal lizard.

I nodded. "Nice." It was, too. "Fantastic detailing. You draw this?" I asked.

"Yes, ma'am."

"Good work." Inclining my head, I met his gaze. "Let me copy this and run a transfer off the computer, and then we'll be ready to ink."

"I'll fire up the Widow!" said Nyx with excitement, and hurried to my station to start the generator (called a Black Widow). I had Inksomnia set up completely in the spacious front room, almost like a beauty shop—a sitting area with a sofa, two plush chairs, and a few ladderbacks. A square leather-topped coffee table with several albums filled with various art designs took up the corner of the storefront. Two inking stations were in the center, with a clear view from River Street so that passersby could look in and watch. The only thing hidden was the equipment room, situated in the back of the building near the steps that led up to my and Seth's apartment. Upstairs was our kitchen; down a small hall was our living room; then, farther down, were two bathrooms and two spacious bedrooms. It was a great setup, I thought, and had a perfect view over the Savannah River. Preacher had helped me get it a few years before.

About two hours and ten minutes later, I finished Zac's Celtic lizard, and he was totally thrilled with it. I admit— it looked smokin' hot, inked over his right shoulder and shoulder blade, the head just peering over his collarbone. He and his buddies asked to take pictures with me, and of course I agreed. I was always baffled by how I was treated by most patrons as a celebrity; I was an artist who totally dug her job, nothing more. I didn't even have a reality show, yet you'd have thought I did. Nyx said I was a legend in the tattooing industry; I merely loved my artwork. Zac promised to send me a copy of the photo, and they said good-bye. Somehow—and I don't know whether it was because they were so young and full of life, or because I knew they'd eventually be thrown in the center of battle, their innocence gone forever—that good-bye felt sad. Typically, I wasn't the mushy sort, but I was definitely in mush mode today.

It was almost five p.m. before I thought again about my brother.

The shop had been hopping since we opened, time had flown by, and I'd just finished a wicked cat skull on a guy's rib cage, when the fact that Seth hadn't even come into the shop all day suddenly hit me. I hurried upstairs and into Seth's room; he hadn't budged. Fear grabbed me by the throat, and for a second I thought he was dead. Old memories left a lot of scar tissue, and the way I'd found my mom? Emblazoned in my brain forever. I nearly tripped getting to the bed, and I grabbed Seth's hand. It was still warm, and in the back of my head, I'd known it would be. I was just freaking out. "Seth?" I said, and shook him. No response. "Seth!"

I nearly stopped breathing as I waited for my baby brother to respond. I resisted the lack of air in my lungs, drew a huge breath, and followed it with a shout. *"Seth!"*

Part 3

CHANGES

Slowly, Seth's heavy lids lifted, and confusion glazed over his green eyes as he tried to focus on me. "What?"

A breath of relief escaped me, along with the feeling that I was behaving like an overreacting mom. With the back of my hand I felt my brother's cheeks, his forehead, and he just kept right on staring at me as though I'd grown a swirling horn from the center of my head. I searched his face. "Do you feel okay?"

Seth tried to rise but fell back against the sheets. "Yeah. Fine. Just . . . tired."

I brushed the hair from his face. "Thanks to your fun run at Bonaventure, you're probably coming down with something." I wasn't sure that was how you came down with anything, especially in the dog days of summer in the South, but Mom had always said it, and it sounded pretty good now. "Just stay in bed for now and rest. Do you want anything to drink? Eat?"

Seth's eyes were already closing again. "No, thanks."

He turned onto his stomach. "You're not sneakin' smokes, are ya?" he mumbled into his pillow.

At that, I grinned. "No, Mommy. If you keep stressing me out, I just might. Now, get some sleep." Worrying about my baby brother was something foreign to me; he'd never been sick, and as I'd said before, he'd never been in trouble. I suppose that made me a bit complacent. Now? I worried. And I didn't like it. Seth, on the other hand, worried about me constantly. "All right. I'll check on you in a little while." I kissed the top of his head. "Love you."

"Love you, too," Seth mumbled, and was fast asleep before I left the room.

Inksomnia stayed busy the rest of the day. I had appointments until seven p.m., and Nyx usually didn't make appointments on Saturdays at all—she kept that day open for walk-ins, and they kept her Widow running hot all day long. The entire day, I couldn't stop thinking about two things: my overly tired baby brother and that guy at the window. I don't know—something about him struck me *hard*. All I could remember about the guy was a black T-shirt, dark brown hair that was kind of shaggy and swept to the side, and pale skin. He'd been too far away to see detail—except for a pair of perfect full lips. So why had he affected me so much? Secretly, I kept hoping he'd show back up; I was positive he would, and I bet I glanced at the storefront a gazillion times. He didn't show, and it really wasn't a surprise after all; although he'd certainly caught my attention, usually the guys who were attracted to me didn't exactly look like *him*. Let's face it. A guy had to be pretty confident *and* open-minded to be interested in a woman with a dragon tattooed up her back and both arms. Did I mention that I had a black angel wing inked at the corner of my left eye? That one was done in my angsty teen years—my first tat—and to be perfectly honest, I don't even remember getting it. I'd been out partying, woke up the next afternoon, and *bam*—there it was, the delicate skin around it as red as a beet, and in complete contrast to my character, as I was anything but an angel. I must have been pretty wasted not to feel it. Seriously pathetic. But I'm stuck with it now, and I just go with the flow. Besides. If there was one thing I demanded in a guy, it was confidence. Fit that with open-minded, and that right there was probably the main reason I didn't have a boyfriend. Two difficult traits to come already combined. Not that I was actively looking.

"What are you looking for?" Nyx asked. She peered at me over the back of an airman as she inked. She inclined her head toward the front window. "Did I miss something exciting?"

I shook my head. "Hardly."

"Liar."

I grinned, shook my head again, and continued with my work.

Nyx checked on Seth twice, and I ran upstairs just before my last client arrived to check on him myself. He was still hard sleeping. That was a lot of effing sleep, but I chalked it up to . . . whatever. Teenager-itis maybe? I ran across the street, grabbed a couple of funnel cakes, and headed back inside. Nyx and I ate them while they were still hot, the powdered sugar turning to delicious gooey glue. Nothing better.

It was just after seven p.m., and Nyx and I were both

busy inking clients when, finally, Seth wandered into the shop. The moment he came in, Chaz's head lifted from his paws and he growled. "Chaz, stop it!" I commanded. "What is wrong with you?" He'd never growled at Seth, or any of us, before.

"What's up with him?" asked Seth, glaring at the dog. It looked like he'd showered—his hair was wet, and he didn't smell like he had earlier, thank God. But he still didn't seem himself, even after all that rest.

"I don't know," I answered. "Maybe he knows you're not feeling well."

"Maybe," he said, stepping close and inspecting my design. "Looks good, Sis."

I wiped the specks of blood from my client's back with gauze, gave Seth a quick glance, then continued with the needle. "Thanks," I said, and concentrated on my work, the low hum of the Widow pulling me into the zone. "Preacher wants you to help him put up some newsprint, if you're up to it." I finished the section I was working on, wiped, then let off the pedal. "I didn't tell him about last night yet. You know he's gonna freak, so let me do it. I'll be over there once I finish up here. I'm on my last client."

Seth just nodded, then pushed his long bangs out of his face. "Okay. Yeah, I feel all right. I'll see ya." He pulled a pair of shades from his back pocket, slid them on his face, and walked up front. "Hey, Nyx," he said.

"Hey, Little Bro," she replied. "Nice specs."

"Thanks." Without a backward glance, Seth was out the door and headed up the sidewalk to Da Plat Eye. Nyx shot me a questioning look. It wasn't like Seth to blow through so fast. He adored Nyx and never let a day go by without hugging her or picking on her. He was such a lovable guy. Today he did neither.

"He must really feel like crap," Nyx said. "Poor little man."

"Yeah," I agreed, and continued with my work. By nine fifteen, I'd finished my last client, and Nyx was working on a last-minute walk-in. I was cleaning up my station when Gene (named after Gene Simmons, of course) alerted us to another customer. Gene was a big, stuffed, inky black raven, perched right above the entrance, and when someone came in or out, it cawed— loudly. Funniest damn thing I'd ever seen. Nyx had given it to me when I'd first opened Inksomnia. I looked over my shoulder in time to see a middle-aged woman with short hair, pressed khaki slacks, and a blue buttoned-up oxford step through the door. She smiled, laid a pamphlet on the coffee table, and hurried out. Nyx shot me a look, and I grinned as I walked to the front.

"Greetings from Saint James," I read from the pamphlet. I looked at Nyx and lifted a brow. "You owe me dinner, sista."

"That totally wasn't a woman of the cloth," Nyx said with a fake pout.

"*Totally* a nun." I tucked the pamphlet in my drawer. "They don't wear habits anymore, goofball." I made for the front door. "I'm going to check on Seth. I'll be right back, okay?"

"Sure," Nyx said, and I stepped outside for the second time that day. By now, the crowds from earlier were dwindling; a new crowd emerged, a different type of reveler. The night crowd. The ones responsible for the stinky urine and alcohol smell in the back alleys. Lots of interesting things happen after dark on River Street. I've seen them firsthand. I was in quite a lot myself, back in the day.

As I walked to Da Plat Eye, I breathed in the heavy brine from the Savannah River, and a band played down the street. Funny—I could pick Capote's unique sax out of the hundreds of people downtown, and his melody hung on the air as thick as the scent of pralines wafting downwind from River Street Sweets. Damn, those things were addictive. Pure sugar and cream. Just thinking about them made my stomach growl.

I stepped through the front door of Preacher's shop and took in the unique scent of herbs and unknown potions that never failed to intrigue me. The walls were lined with dark-stained oak shelves, and every space was filled with a jar or vial of *something*. Eye of newt? Sure. Graveyard dust? Absolutely. Dead man's nails? Got it. Shredded feathers? Yep. Jars and jars of unknown, wonderful concoctions were everywhere, including tins of tea. The handwoven sweetgrass baskets of all shapes and sizes that hung from pegs on the wall and the wooden rafters were absolutely gorgeous, as were the long strip quilts. The Gullah were renowned for preserving their heritage through language, as well as art, skills, and unique cooking. I had several baskets, quilts, and jars of spices that Estelle and her sisters had made and given me. Everything handmade by the Gullah, and one of a kind.

Estelle emerged from behind the curtain. "Oh, dahlin', your Preacher man had to leave. Your brodder is upstairs, doh, printin' da walls. Dat boy don't look so good. He sick?"

"Yes, ma'am," I answered, and headed to the back. "Or at least he's trying to come down with something. Probably just a cold. Where'd Preacher go?"

"He got called to Da Island for somethin'," she answered. "Wouldn't tell me what. Prob'ly removin' some hex. Won't be back for a few days, dat crazy ole man."

I patted her arm as I passed by. "I'm gonna go upstairs and check on Seth. I'll be right back down."

"Okay, dahlin'," she answered. "I just looked in on him a bit ago. He should be 'bout done."

I eased up the narrow wooden flight of steps, just like mine and Seth's, and for some reason, my stomach felt funny. You know—the kind of funny where you feel something's not right? I hit the five-by-five landing and made my way down the hall. After looking in three rooms, I found him. Stepping inside, I noticed the fresh newsprint plastered to the wall, and Seth, curled up on the floor near the window. My heart jumped again, just like earlier, and I hurried over to him. Once more, I felt his hand, then his cheek, and noticed the slight rise and fall of his chest. Asleep. The little brat was asleep. Again. This time with his shades on.

"Seth," I said, and tugged on his arm. "Come on, Bro, wake up. I'm taking you to the hospital and get you checked out."

"No, I'm good," he mumbled, and shook off my hand. "Sincerely, Ri, I'm good. I feel fine, just . . . tired. I don't need a doctor." He yawned. "I just wanna go home."

I sighed. "Fine. Then, let's get you home. Estelle doesn't want you hanging out in here all night." I tugged again, and this time he allowed me to help him up. I looked at him. "If you don't kick whatever this is, and I mean soon, I'm taking you to the Immediate Med. Got it? You're freaking me out, Bro."

"Sorry," he said, and leaned into me as we made our way to the stairs. "Just so tired."

We eased slowly down the steps and stepped through the curtain. "Have you eaten anything at all today?"

"No," he said groggily. "Not hungry."

"Tough crap," I answered, and slid off his shades. He squinted and looked away. "You've got to have something," I insisted.

"Oh, dat is right, boy," Estelle said, and bustled over. "I got somethin' for him," she said, and hurried to the kitchen, still talking. "I said earlier, dat boy needed to rest. Asked him if he wanted a sandwich, but he said no. He always wantin' food, you know, so dat wasn't good." She emerged from behind the curtain holding a snap-lid container. "You give dat boy some of dis soup, Riley Poe. I jes made it dis mornin'. Chicken." She cocked her head to the side and studied him. "He look awful pasty, girl."

"I know—I'm putting him straight to bed after I force some of this down his throat—not that it needs forcing. I'm sure it's great. Thanks, Estelle," I said, and accepted the soup as my Gullah granny frowned and shook her head. "Call me if you need anything while Preacher's gone, okay?" I gave her a smile. "I'll see ya in the morning."

"Yeah, yeah, I'll have your tea ready, girl," Estelle said. "You take care of dat boy, now."

We went through the back of Inksomnia, just in case Seth decided to barf all over the place. "Nyx, I'm taking Seth upstairs—be right back down," I called out.

"Need some help?"

"Nope—I've got it. Thanks," I answered, and headed upstairs, my brother dragging his feet. Our kitchen is just at the top of the stairs, so we stopped there, and I poured some of Estelle's soup into a coffee cup, draining off the chunks of chicken and vegetables. I pushed the cup into Seth's hand. "Here, lunkhead," I said. "Drink up. At least some of it."

Seth made a face but drained the cup. He wiped his mouth with the back of his hand and set the mug on the counter. "Happy?"

I frowned. "Hardly, but it'll do for now. I knew you were coming down with something. Just get to bed and rest. I'm sure it's just a summertime cold."

Seth turned out of the kitchen and started down the hall, then stopped, walked back, and surprised me with a tight hug. "Thanks for watching out for me, Ri," he said, his long, lean arms wrapped around me like a vise, and he pushed his face into my hair, close to my ear. "Love ya."

Damn, that kid knew how to absolutely melt my heart, and I hugged him fiercely back. "I love you, too, Little Bro. If you need me during the night, come and get me, okay?"

Seth was already walking down the hall, his back to me. "Sure," he answered, then disappeared into his room.

I watched for a minute longer before heading back downstairs to finish up with Nyx. In the back of my mind, though, I worried—about Seth, about why Preacher had to leave in such a rush, especially before I had the chance to talk to him. Preacher was getting a little too old to be hauling ass anywhere, much less hopping a boat to Da

Island. Anything could happen so far out in the sound, but he wouldn't listen.

And of course, no matter how hard I tried, I couldn't get rid of the image of that one guy, staring at me through the storefront, and it irritated me that I dwelled on it. I mean, dozens of guys stare, and dozens come into the shop, and a dozen more hit on me—a lot of them are pretty cute, too. So what was it about *this* guy? Was it because he *didn't* hit on me? The thought nearly made me laugh. Wasn't that a dude's way of thinking?

Surprisingly, the night went by uneventfully, and that was truly a miracle for a Saturday night. We had a pack of punks come in just before we closed, acting loud and obnoxious (and totally reminding me of *me* at that age), and one made a grave mistake. One of the boys walked up behind me and took me by surprise when he put his hand on my arm. Before he could say a word, I had his arm yanked behind him and jacked up high enough that he stood on the toes of his All Stars, yelping, "Hey!," his pubescent voice cracking. He was a big kid, too—at least six feet tall. I jacked his arm higher up his back. "Okay, okay!"

"Oh, yeah," Nyx said apologetically. "You don't want to ever do that." She smiled, her auburn pigtails swinging as she shook her head. "She doesn't like to be touched."

"You guys come back when you find your manners," I said, and gave the kid a little shove. He glared at me, and his friends laughed. I lifted a brow. "And when those IDs are legit, big guy."

"Goddamn, she's hot!" one of them said as they all rushed from the store and headed up the sidewalk. I just shook my head and glanced at Nyx, who grinned. It being so late, I released her from her obligation of dinner at Garibaldi's—for the time being, anyway. I didn't want to leave Seth home alone. Instead, I ordered from Chen's (orange chicken, vegetable lo mein noodles, and two shrimp egg rolls) and stayed in for the night. I worked out (I have a kickboxing bag hanging in my bedroom that I knock the hell out of daily) and took a long bath. Seth was still hard asleep when I took Chaz for a walk around eleven forty-five.

I walked along Factor's Walk toward Emmet Park. No one was close by, although in the distance I saw people crossing Bay Street, and down on the riverfront I could hear laughter and music pouring from the bars. Lamplight burned a dim glow against the cobbles, making the shadows pitch long from the cannon and cross. The slightest of breezes wafted by, and it was at the same moment Chaz jerked to a stop and sniffed the air that the hair on my neck lifted. I turned fast around but found no one. "Come on, boy," I told Chaz, and although he continued to sniff the ground, he'd pause, too, and look cautiously around.

We'd walked all the way to the end of Emmet Park and down the cobbled curve onto River Street, the Waving Girl Statue in view, when the feeling struck again. I jerked a look behind me, scanned the shadows, but noticed nothing unusual. A low growl emanated from Chaz's throat, and I tugged on his leash. "Let's go, boy."

"Nah, don't go yet," a voice said from the recesses of the darkness. "Party's just startin', babe."

Four guys emerged into the lamplight, and I immediately recognized two of them as the punks who'd come into Inksomnia earlier. The one talking was the kid I'd jacked up. Figures. I'd bruised his pubescent pride, and now he wanted to get me back. Chaz growled. "Yeah, I don't think so," I said, and turned to walk away.

"Oh, man, you just got blowed," one said, and they all laughed. The kid I'd jacked moved in front of me, and I stopped. The others, who seemed a little older, crowded around me, but just out of reach of Chaz, whose growling deepened. I tugged his leash. "Down, boy." Great. Here we go. I hated having to kick juvenile ass, but I'd do it if forced. And it looked like I was being forced. "Don't make me give him the command," I said.

I lifted a brow. "Sic balls," I whispered. One of my most favorite movie quotes, from *Stand by Me*. Loved that freaking movie.

"I can change your mind, you know," the jacked kid said, ignoring my humor. Half his face was hooded in shadow, but the other half was all cocky smiles and teenage smugness.

"About what?" I said, barely able to keep from laughing.

"Being touched," he answered, and stepped toward me. He rubbed his hand over his burr-cut hair. "Your friend said you didn't like it, but I think I can change your mind."

I dropped Chaz's leash and glanced at the half circle of guys. "Stay, Chaz," I commanded. "So let me get this straight. You're what? Gonna hold me down while your little friend here puts the moves on me? Really?"

"You're on my turf now," he said, shrugging. "No one around but us, babe."

I laughed, stepped closer, and gave him a seductive

stare. His eyes widened at what looked like anticipation. "Did you really just say *turf*? Please." And just that fast I kneed his crotch. He yelled and bent over at the waist, and I brought my knee up hard and connected with his chin.

"Fuck!" he screamed, and dropped to the ground in agony.

"And don't call me babe," I added, and glanced at the others. They all had blank stares on their faces as they looked at their friend on the ground.

Something moved from the shadows—so fast my eyes couldn't keep up. I stood frozen in place, no time to react. All three guys were lifted off their feet and flung in opposite directions, their muffled curses cracking the night air, followed by heavy thumps as they crumpled to the ground. I twisted and turned, searching in all directions. "Hey!" I hollered. *What the hell?*

Then, from the corner of the building, a figure moved but did not emerge. From the tall, lean shape I could tell it was a guy. I moved closer.

"Don't," he said, and I stopped. His smooth and slightly accented voice crossed the darkness to my ears, firm, commanding. Groans from the fallen punks drifted on the night air. Chaz, who sat still, growled low in his throat.

My insides shook. Not out of fear, but out of adrenaline. What had I just seen? Rather, not seen? And why was he hiding? "You're pretty quick. Thanks—"

"Are you stupid?" he asked, his tone steady, angry, as he interrupted me. "Why would you come out here so late? Alone?" He swore under his breath.

I blinked in surprise. "Uh, my dog had to pee. Thanks for the help." I turned, grabbed Chaz's leash, and started back up the cobbled curve to head home. Who the hell was that guy? A citizen vigilante? He didn't have to know I needed no help at all, but damn. Why was he angry? Not all females were helpless. I shook my head and crossed the park, and I made it all the way to Inksomnia's back door before his voice jolted me. One second I'm pushing the key into the lock and Chaz runs inside, and in the next second, he is standing directly beside me. My reflexes kicked in, and my fist flew up to his jaw, but he easily caught it in one hand. His grip was like steel, and I couldn't budge my arm. I lifted my knee, but before I could cram it into his crotch (in case you haven't noticed, a favorite move of mine), he had me completely pinned against the brick wall of my shop. With the streetlight shining behind him, his face was nothing more than a dark shadow. With one hand he closed the door. My heart thumped fast. This was not a situation I wanted to be in. I stared at his darkened face, waiting.

"You're too careless," he warned. "Those punks outnumbered you. They could've hurt you." He drew his head closer, and I could barely see the outline of a strong jaw, shaggy hair. He looked . . . *familiar*. "I could hurt you," he said, his voice deathly quiet.

I knew he could see every inch of my face—I could feel his gaze searching every feature I had. The streetlamp's light poured directly onto me. I jutted out my jaw and narrowed my eyes. "Well, either hurt me or get the fuck off me," I said, just as quiet. "Now." One scream would have any of my neighbors running outside, but I waited. He seemed to weigh the situation as he stared at me. I felt threatened but not fearful. Weird.

It was several seconds before he released me from the wall. "Don't be so reckless," he said. "You're not as strong as you think."

I wasn't stupid. Even though I felt no fear, I didn't exactly want this guy forcing his way into my apartment, although I guess he could have done that earlier, had he wanted to. I kept my eyes trained on his shadowy face and eased my hand behind me, to the door handle. "I'll keep that in mind." I gently turned the knob. A sound behind my Jeep made me jump—a can rolling, something. I glanced, and when my gaze returned to my almost-attacker, I blinked. He was *gone*. Yeah, just that fast. I took a quick glimpse up and down merchant's drive, but he was nowhere. *No-freaking-where*. I didn't wait for a reappearance. I hurried inside and locked the door. As I got ready for bed and checked on Seth, who—surprise—was still sleeping, I tried to put the whole strange incident out of my head. Who was that guy? And why did he give a rat's ass if I was reckless or not? Finally, I drifted off.

Sometime later, a noise pulled me out of sleep, and I sat straight up in bed. My breath came fast, and I could actually feel my heart pound through my T-shirt. Chaz, on his bed in the corner, kept silent. The streetlamp shone straight into my room, against the aged white brick wall, and for a flash second I thought someone stood in the shadows, watching me. My heart nearly stopped, thinking my personal vigilante had returned. Then I thought better. "Seth?" I said, thinking he'd come in and needed me. "Is that you?" I reached over and turned on the lamp. When I looked again, no one was there. The gauzy white curtains hanging at the balcony's French doors billowed out on a breeze. I didn't remember leaving the doors open. I listened for a few seconds, my groggy head trying to clear. I then realized the TV was on in the living room. Stumbling out of bed, I closed the French doors and followed the sounds to find Seth, sitting on the sofa, watching MTV. With his shades on. I stood in the archway, yawning. "What's up? You feel better?"

"Yeah," Seth answered without turning to face me. "Guess I had enough sleep."

"Good." I glanced around the room. "Did you eat?"

"Nah," he said. "Not hungry."

The room was all shadowy and dark, as you would expect at two in the morning, and the TV threw flickers of light against the wall. "What's up with the shades?"

"Light's hurting my eyes."

I stared at him, all lean muscles, lankiness, and shirtless in his worn, holey jeans, sprawled out on the sofa, and shook my head. "All right. There's more of Estelle's soup in the fridge if you get hungry, and some leftover Chen's. See ya in the morning."

"Yeah," he answered, and I couldn't tell if he had even looked my way once.

Sunday arrived like an ordinary Sunday. I turned on the TV and heard the morning news reporting that a woman's body was found in Daffin Park by a garbage street crew. No details were given regarding the cause of her death, but the reporter described the woman to be in her early forties, and apparently she had been

robbed. I'd assumed murdered. Police were on the case.
For some reason, she remained on my mind for the rest
of the morning. She, along with the mystery guy from
the night before. I heard his voice over and over in my
head, and for some strange reason, I liked it. Don't ask
me why.

Sunday was the only day of the week I closed Inksomnia, and I spent the rest of the morning with Estelle.
Seth seemed to have his days and nights mixed up, and
he spent the majority of the day sleeping. He never had
a fever, so I didn't run him to the ER. But I watched
him, and he just wasn't himself. Not sick, just not himself. Whenever he was awake, he had his shades on, and
he was quiet, aloof, and . . . not Seth Poe at all. Usually
my brother was a sweet, charming kid, with a great sense
of humor. I know things change when puberty hits, but
this was ridiculous. The change had happened overnight.
Now, when he slept, he slept like the dead—literally. I
could barely rouse him. And Chaz's behavior toward
Seth just didn't make sense. He growled every time Seth
entered the same room. Chaz had never been anything
but loving and faithful to all of us, especially Seth, and
the dog usually slept on the foot of Seth's bed. It was
just bizarre, and to be perfectly honest, it was starting
to freak me out. I wished Preacher were here to check
him over, but he wasn't due back from Da Island until
Tuesday. Until then, I'd nurse the peculiar feeling nag-
ging the pit of my gut.

And for the record, I never again saw that guy from
the storefront. Yeah, shamefully, I found myself looking
for him, and yeah, it'd only been one day. But he never
stopped by again, and I admitted only to myself that I

was disappointed. I think it stung a little, too. I had no idea why, but it did.

Sunday afternoon I asked Estelle to keep an eye out for Seth while I picked up a few things at the grocery store. I threw on a pair of button-fly jeans and a white Inksomnia tee. (Okay—I self-promote. Can you blame me? Plus the logo is wicked cool.) I pulled on my black boots and headed out. Food Lion was packed, and I hurried through my list. The moment I left the store, I felt . . . watched. People pushed their grocery carts all around me, the parking lot was full, yet out of all the eyes surrounding me, I sensed only one pair honed in on me. With my shades covering my gaze, I looked around. I saw no one paying any particular attention to me. I couldn't help but wonder if the vigilante watched from his car, or from another store.

When I got home, Seth was still asleep. I made sure he was okay—still no fever, still breathing—and wandered outside with Chaz to the riverfront. Capote was just a few yards up the walk playing, so I found a bench close by; he gave me a nod of acknowledgment, and I listened while I nibbled on a praline from the sweet shop. The walk was still crawling with people, so I ended up sharing the bench with an elderly couple, Chaz at my feet. With my peripheral I noticed them both sneaking peeks at me, and the smirk on Capote's face let me know he noticed, too. I guess my dragons entertained all age-groups.

I decided to walk along the riverfront for a while, just to stretch my legs and give Chaz a little exercise, so I threw a twenty in Capote's sax case. He tipped his hat, and I waved, and Chaz and I wandered off. There was a slight breeze blowing, the sun was starting to drop, and it seemed like a perfect August evening. The *Savannah River Queen* was just pulling in from a river tour, and the passengers lined the railing, waving. The Shrimp Factory's grill spilled the mouthwatering scent of seared spiced meat. Yet the whole time I walked, I felt as though someone watched me, followed me. I had a few quirks when it came to hoodoo beliefs (I do admit to carrying a small container of graveyard dust in my backpack that Preacher gave me, and a special vial of protection herbs), but people did not frighten me. I was strong and very capable, with a six-pack that made most guys jealous. . . . I again wondered whether the shadowy guy from the other night followed me. Once I even turned completely around and stopped, legs braced, hands on hips, and probably looking a whole lot like a freakish version of a Charlie's Angel, yet still—I saw no one. Finally, as the sun sank, the crowds thinned, and I headed back home. I spent an hour ordering supplies online, sent a few e-mails, agreed to do an exhibit at an ink convention in California in November, and called it quits.

Nyx came over later and we hung out, sketching new designs and eating pizza. Seth stayed in his room until around eight thirty, when he wandered into the living room. Yes, with his shades on. Chaz growled, staring at my brother. "Be quiet, Chaz," I commanded. I jumped up from where I was sitting cross-legged on the floor, sketch sheets spread out before me, and hurried over to where Seth plopped down on the sofa. I felt his cheek and forehead. Actually, instead of feeling warm, he felt a little cool.

"Wow," Nyx said, her wide smile seemingly reaching

each ear. "I've never seen this motherly side of you, Poe. It's kinda sweet."

I shot Nyx a glare and turned to my brother. I moved to pull his shades off, and he jerked his head away. The abrupt shift wasn't anything like Seth's usual demeanor.

"Lay off, Riley," he snapped. "Jesus, I'm fine."

This time, Chaz jumped to his feet, head lowered, and moved toward Seth, growling. "Back," I snapped. Chaz froze in his tracks, and I returned my gaze to my brother.

No one, and I repeat, *no one*, had the power to hurt my feelings. Ever. I just didn't have that weakness in me anymore—except with Seth, and maybe Preacher. And that small snub actually wounded me. "Yeah, well," I said, and moved away. "I'm worried about you, Seth."

"Don't be," he said just as sharply. He stood. "And keep that freaking dog away from me." He left the room, and I could do nothing more than stare after him, shocked.

"Hey," Nyx said gently. "Take it easy on the kid, Riley. He's fifteen. Hormones, remember? Just leave him alone for a bit." She patted the floor. "Here, have another slice of spinach and mushroom and finish this design. Looks wicked fab so far." She lifted a wide wedge from the box on the floor and took a big bite. Nyx's appetite was legendary, and hopefully it'd keep her busy for a while, because I just couldn't let my brother walk off.

"I'll be right back," I said, and followed Seth. His door was cracked, so I gently pushed it open and stuck my head in. Seth stood by the window, his back to me as he stared out over River Street. "Can we talk?" I asked. When he didn't answer, I pushed. "What's going on, Seth? Talk to me." Still, he kept his back to me, not answering, and I moved into the room to stand beside him. I could feel the air between us grow cold, and his posture stiffened, as though he couldn't stand me being close. It hurt like hell. "Please?"

"Nothin' to talk about," he said quietly. "Just need space."

I moved closer. "Seth, take your shades off and look at me."

For a moment, he simply stood, rigid, debating whether or not to do as I'd asked, I supposed. Then, with a heavy sigh, he did, but he stared at the floor, at the wall, out the window—anywhere but at *me*. For now, I accepted it.

"Look—I don't know what you're going through right now, but . . . just hear me out, okay?" I asked. "I used to be your age, too, ya know, and not that long ago. Some things I do understand. I'm here for you—no matter what, okay? If there's something bothering you, tell me. Or if Riggs and the guys—"

"There's nothing bothering me, Riley," he said sharply, and this time, he did look at me, and his gaze was cold, angry, the green a shade or two lighter, and he slipped his shades back on and returned his stare to the window. An instant dismissal.

I stared at my brother's profile for several seconds—noticed the tousled brown waves, his straight nose and firm jaw—and suddenly, I couldn't see my baby brother anymore. I saw a young guy. An angry young guy. "Okay," I said, and placed my hand on his shoulder. "But I'm here anyway." I didn't linger or wait for a response, but simply left the room. Inside, my heart hurt—literally ached—from Seth's coldness, but I knew that to stay and try to pry stuff out of this new Seth wouldn't do any good, so I put my brother's behavior behind me for the night. It wasn't easy. I'd gone from street punk to grown-up real fast, and I'd been responsible for Seth since I was nineteen. I loved him more than life, and I now knew what my mom probably went through when I did the same thing to her.

When I walked back into the living room, I instantly saw Nyx's already pale face staring at the TV, a shocked expression pulling her mouth taut. "Oh my God," she muttered, and I glanced at the flat screen to see what it was. The local news was on, and the reporter, standing in front of the Cotton Exchange building, looked grave as he reported the brutal murder of a young marine recruit. A police car blazed blue lights nearby, and the rapid-fire flash recoiled off the black plastic bag covering the body strapped on the gurney. Then a picture of a handsome marine recruit flashed across the screen, along with a name: Zachary Murphy, age nineteen. "Zac," I muttered. My heart seized as I recognized the young guy who'd come in for the Celtic lizard tattoo Saturday, and a wave of sadness swept over me. "Damn, Nyx," I said, and glanced over at her. "That's two murders in one day. I wonder what happened to him." God, his poor parents. I knew exactly what they were going through.

Over the next few days, Seth's condition changed. I'm not positive it worsened, just . . . evolved. What made matters worse was that Preacher had extended his trip to Da Island, so I didn't have his counsel to rely on. Seth's excessive sleeping eased up somewhat, but he wore his shades all the time, indoors and outdoors, sunshine or no sunshine. He barely spoke a word to me, or Nyx, and as soon as it was dusk, he was out, saying he wanted to hang out with his friends before school started. I'd never let him just run the streets—I knew where that could lead, and no way in hell was I about to let my brother screw up like I had. No *freaking* way. So when Riggs and the other boys showed up at Inksomnia at sundown, all wearing shades and looking like a band of thugs, I put my foot down. God, I sounded like an old stick-in-the-mud. But this was Seth, and I wasn't about to let him set even one size-eleven sneaker in the wrong direction if I could help it.

"Hey, babe, where's your brother?" Riggs asked. He leaned a hip against my vacant inking table, arms crossed over his chest, trying way too hard to look cool.

Chaz rose from his rug, the hair along his back bristled, his head down, and the now-familiar low growl emanated from deep in his throat. This time, I let him. I turned to Riggs.

"Babe? Yeah, I don't think so, porcupine. Try again. And take off those stupid glasses," I said, totally irritated.

Riggs' expression turned . . . I don't know, *hateful*, and froze into place like stone. Slowly, he slid his shades off, and if the look on his face had seemed startling, the glare in his eyes was even worse. They seemed like ice, his eyes, without feeling, or anything, really. They even looked lighter than before. How could that be? Inwardly, I flinched, and that shocked me. The boy might be a teenage peckerhead now, but I'd known Riggs Parker since he was a little guy, and until tonight I'd known him to be harmless. Now? He studied me with the intensity of a predator, and that made me want to smack him on the back of the head.

"Where's Seth, Ms. Poe?" His smile was as icy as his eyes. "Better?"

"Hardly."

"Right here," my brother said behind me. "Ready?"

I continued to scrutinize Riggs. "Where are you guys going?"

A small grin tipped the boy's mouth. "Mellow Mushroom. See?" he pulled out a wad of balled-up bills. "My mommy gave me money." He slid his glasses back on and looked up at me. "Don't worry, babe," he said sarcastically. "We'll be home early."

The others laughed—including Seth—and Chaz grew more agitated. He began to bark threateningly. "Chaz, back," I said, and my gaze snapped to Seth as I swallowed the hurt. "By eleven, Bro. Don't make me come looking for you. I'm dead serious."

"Whatever," he mumbled, which again irritated me because we all know what *whatever* really meant. *Eff you*. The boys left the shop. Outside, Riggs glanced back at me through the storefront and smiled, and swear to God, it gave me chills. Chaz noticed and lunged at the window, barking like crazy. I knew the feeling. I wanted right then to go knock the hell out of him, and if he'd been of legal age, I would have.

"What's up with Chaz lately?" Nyx asked, rubbing the fur between his ears, talking soothingly to him. "Don't worry, Riley," she said comfortingly. "He'll be all right." She grinned. "He's just trying to show off in front of his friends. I'll bet you were the exact same way at fifteen."

I continued to stare out of the storefront. "Way, way worse, Nyxinnia. That's what worries me." And that was exactly what I did for the rest of the evening—worried. I beat the hell out of the bag that night, hoping to work out some of the tension, and by the time I'd worn myself out, my knuckles, feet, and shins hurt like hell. I was in the kitchen sucking down a bottle of water when Seth came trudging up the stairs, right at eleven on the nose. He didn't even acknowledge me and instead went straight to his room and shut the door. I almost followed. But Nyx's words rang in my head, so I cut him some slack—especially since he'd made it home on time—and decided to talk to him in the morning. Obviously, something was bothering him, and I hated that he didn't trust me to help him.

I showered and got ready for bed, but sleep evaded me. Instead of tossing restlessly, I wandered out onto the small balcony outside my bedroom. There was just enough room to stand, with a black, wrought-iron railing to keep me from tumbling over. I stood there and stared out into the night, watching the sliver of moon glimmer over the river. The night was still, and I felt vulnerable, not a feeling I particularly liked. My thoughts turned to Zac, a guy I didn't even know, and how he'd been so young and had died so young. What had happened? I couldn't help but wonder who'd done it, and think about how the killer right now walked the very streets my brother and I lived on. I mean, the Cotton Exchange building was two seconds from Inksomnia. I could see it from my back door.

I turned to leave, but before I stepped back inside, that gnawing feeling came over me once more—the one that made me look over my shoulder. I stared out into the night, into the afterlight, searching the darkness. I felt with all certainty that a pair of eyes watched me from the shadows. Swear to God, I couldn't take much more. It was happening all too frequently, and frankly, it was pissing me off. Especially if it was that tough guy from the other night. I closed and locked the balcony door. I did not sleep well after.

Sometime later, I jerked wide-awake with a gasp and sat straight up. At the same time, I heard Chaz's low-throated growl. My blurred vision, groggy from sleep, scanned the dark corners of my room, straining to see. My insides froze. Someone was in my room. I slipped my hand slowly toward the back left bedpost, where I kept a baseball bat. My fingers gripped the handle. I slid my feet slowly to the floor and lifted the bat over my shoulder. A car ambled down the cobbles on the street below, and the headlights cast an illuminated arc across my bedroom wall—*and my brother*. Again, I gasped, taken off guard. "Seth? What are you doing?" I lowered the bat.

Seth didn't speak or move; he stood completely still. I couldn't see his expression now, but I had for a fleeting second as the car had passed. He'd looked . . . vacant, angry. I won't lie—it scared the hell out of me. What scared me even more was that I hadn't loosened my grip on the bat.

"Seth?" I said, not too loud, but definitely assertive. "What's up, Bro? Are you sick?"

Chaz now stood and had taken a few steps toward my bed. His growling grew louder. Seth remained silent.

"Hey," I said, and eased toward him. "Want me to—"

"No," Seth finally said. His voice sounded . . . different. Strained. Deeper.

"Okay, okay," I said, forcing myself to remain calm. "I'm going to turn on the light—"

"No!" Seth yelled, and lunged at me. Chaz lunged at Seth, knocked him down, and latched onto his arm. Seth cried out in pain, struggling to shake Chaz's grip loose. "Get off me!" he cried, and shoved Chaz hard with his free hand. The dog flew across the room and landed against the wall with a shrill yelp. He immediately leapt up and charged Seth.

"Chaz, no!" I yelled, and ran to grab his collar. Seth slammed out of my room, and seconds later the back door downstairs crashed against the wall. Yanking on the shorts I'd worn earlier, I slid into my flip-flops and took off after my brother. What was *wrong* with him? I ran outside, the heavy, early-morning air thick and soupy as a mist rolled in from the river; I closed the back door and searched both sides of merchant's drive but found no signs of Seth anywhere. With my heart in my throat, I edged up the cobbles, ducked into the narrow alley that led to River Street, and hurried to the line of storefronts facing the river. I found myself alone, and I continued up the river walk at a jog. "Seth?" I called out. "Seth!" No answer. I still found myself alone at the west end, past the Hyatt, then made my way up to Factor's Walk and searched Bay Street. The early-hour fog hung like a cloud, and it slipped in and out of the oaks like inching fingers. The air was still; not even the slightest of breezes moved through the moss. I stood still, watched, and listened. Nothing. There was absolutely no sign of my brother.

It was at that point that I realized someone stood close by, and this time it wasn't just a crazy feeling that someone watched me. I *knew* it. I was sure it wasn't Seth. My adrenaline surged as my gaze roamed the area. Shadows fell and stretched from the lampposts, the parking meters hugging the curb, the storefront awnings, and trees; it was impossible to search every nook. I turned and walked up the cobbles, and just as I ducked into the alley next to Inksomnia I was shoved hard against the wall; my breath *whoosh*ed from my lungs. With my front pressed to the bricks and a hard body pressed against my back, I hadn't a clue who held me—until he spoke. There was no mistaking that smooth voice and odd tinge of accent.

"Do you have a death wish?" he said, his voice low and annoyed, his mouth brushing my hair, close to my ear. "Or are you just fucking crazy?"

I tried to push against him, but he held me tight. "You're grating the side of my face into the brick, asshole. Get off me," I said.

"Your face is the last thing you need to worry about." He eased up a fraction, enough for my skin to separate from the mortar. I felt his mouth against my ear, and, swear to God, he sniffed my hair. "It's not safe out here."

"Yeah, I'm starting to get that," I said, trying to look behind me, pushing against his steely weight. "What's your problem? Why are you on me?" Worse was the fact that there was something I found exciting about him. I had no idea what it was—he'd threatened me twice now.

"Get inside and stay there. Understand?"

I did not like being bullied or told what to do. "You don't know me, and you definitely don't scare me," I said angrily. "And I'm not out here for my friggin' health, so why don't you back *off*!" I growled, and shoved hard against him. It was like trying to move a packed freezer. Not a single inch budged.

Suddenly, my body shifted from the wall and pushed up the steps. "What the f—"

"Move," he said, and this *guy's hands* wrapped around my waist to keep me from hauling ass. He all but pushed me along.

"What the hell?!" I said, struggling against him but finding it was no use.

"Shut up and come on," he said. "You need to see something."

I continued to thrash despite the uselessness of it. Now it was on principle. I wasn't going to just meander along at his command.

For the first time in a long, long time, I felt vulnerable, but I'd chew my own arm off before letting him know it.

At the top of the steps he guided me across the walk and up merchant's drive, then down the narrow, dank alley between Inksomnia and the Boho Boutique, where he gave me a shove. I stumbled, caught myself against the tabby wall (made of oyster shell and sand mortar), then sucked in a gasp. The strong scent of urine and metal filled my nostrils, and my quick reflexes jerked me back so fast that I fell against *him*; his steely grip held me upright. The streetlamp behind the Boho poured a hazy amber glow into the alley and onto the sprawled figure on the ground, unnaturally positioned as though all the bones were broken. I stared, unable to look away, my voice trapped inside my throat, at the body of a young male, his chest and throat literally *flayed open*. A dark substance splashed against the tabby wall behind him, splattered around his body. *Blood*. Wide, glassy eyes stared lifeless in the lamplight, and my hand flew to my mouth as I pushed against *him* to get away. "He's freaking dead," I said out loud, and looked into the face still hidden by shadows, at the one who'd forced me to this place. "You," I whispered. I gagged, turned, and fought with fists against him. "Let me go!" I said, choking, and in the next instant my body shifted, and once again I found myself pressed against Inksomnia's back-door entrance.

He shook me. Hard. "It wasn't me," he said. My head snapped back, and again I caught only glimpses of his profile. He was young. My age maybe. "Do you understand now?" he said, his voice dropping to a low pitch, his mouth moving to my ear. "It's not safe anymore. And it's not what you think." He gave me a shove. "Go. I'll find your brother."

For the first time in forever, fear gripped me by the throat. "Leave my brother alone," I warned, my voice quivering. "Swear to God, you'd better leave him the fuck alone."

Just then he moved, ever so slightly, to the side, and I caught a subtle glimpse of his features. Straight nose, cut jaw, and his eyes—they freaking *glowed*. The sight of them made me flinch.

"Get inside. Bolt the door," he ground out as though in pain. He reached behind me, twisted the doorknob, threw open the door, and shoved me inside.

I fell against the stairs leading up to my and Seth's apartment, grasped the handrail, and steadied myself. When my vision focused on the doorway, he was gone. I slammed the door and threw the bolt, my heart slamming against my ribs as I backed away. I quickly climbed the stairs, my mind racing, scrambling to grasp what had happened, what I'd just seen, and none of it made sense. Who *was* that guy? What did he want with me, and how did he know Seth?

An unfamiliar feeling claimed me—panic. I hurried inside the apartment, Chaz whining a greeting as I ran past him and straight to the cordless. The police. I needed to call the police. A guy had been murdered not five hundred feet from my shop. Shit! I grabbed the cordless off the wall, and just as my finger landed on the illuminated "9" button, the phone was knocked from my hand, Chaz barked, and a pair of viselike fingers grasped my neck. My mind didn't have time to react. My vision blurred, and in the next second, darkness swept over me.

When next I woke, bright sunlight streamed in through the window and across my face. I was lying on the sofa, the brushed-wool throw pulled up to my chin. It took a few, but then everything rushed back to me, and I jumped up and ran to Seth's bedroom, threw open the door. A rush of relief crashed over me.

Seth was sprawled across his bed, sound asleep, his window wide-open. I stared, shocked. How had he gotten inside? I hurried to him, pressed the back of my knuckles to his cheek; his skin felt cool against mine. My gaze raked over Seth's body; his face seemed paler, his dark brows and hair stark against his skin. I pushed his bangs from his eyes and sighed. The only explanation was drugs. How could I have allowed my little brother to get messed up in that hell? It was the only reason that could explain his weird behavior. I'd been around users before; I'd been one before. I knew the signs. Closing his window, I pulled the sheet over him. I'd have to talk to Preacher.

Then, the *rest* of last night rushed back to me. The dead guy. The blood. I took off running, down the steps and out the back door. I didn't stop until I reached the alley next to the Boho. When I did, I nearly fell, I halted so harshly. My eyes searched the empty area. There was nothing. Absolutely *nothing*. No body. No blood. My head swam with confusion as I squatted next to the rough-textured tabby wall and ran my palm over its broken-oyster-shell surface. Nothing.

"Lose something, Riley?" a voice said, startling me. I glanced over my shoulder as Bhing, owner of Boho, walked a stack of empty boxes to the Dumpster.

I rose and grinned. "I thought I did," I said, shrugging, "but must have been mistaken. See ya." I walked away, and Bhing waved good-bye. Bhing was Filipino, maybe four feet eleven inches, and her black, shoulder-length, bobbed hair swung with each step she took as she hauled the boxes. Certainly she would have mentioned a murdered guy in her alley, had there been one. I walked away more confused than ever.

After I took Chaz for a walk, I ran over to Estelle's. "Did you hear from Preacher yet?" I asked. Preacher was the action taker, and I needed him. Badly.

"Awe, yeah," said Estelle in her singsong voice, crushing herbs atop a long butcher-block table in the center of her kitchen. "He'll be in sometime today." She frowned.

"Dey got somethin' goin' on over dere, and you know how dem conjurers are. What wrong wit you, girl? Dat brodder of yours any better?"

"I'm not sure, really," I said, not wanting to worry her. "He's just not himself lately. Maybe he's going through some sort of adolescent guy change? I figured Preacher being his male role model, you know, would be able to talk to him?" I didn't dare mention how Seth had reacted last night, or about the supposed dead body in the alley. Definitely not about the mysterious guy in shadows who seemed to be behind it all.

"Oh, now, dem menfolk are funny creatures, you know. Doesn't matter how old dey are." She laughed. "Always younguns. Always goin' through da change."

I smiled, rose, took my cup to the sink, and gave Estelle a hug. She always made me feel better. "You okay here alone? Do you need anything? I can run to the store if you like."

"No, baby," she said, and patted me on the arm. "I'm good jus like dis. You let me know how dat boy is doin', okay?"

I agreed and said good-bye, and headed home to get ready for work. The magnitude of what was really going on with my brother struck later that evening. Struck like a bolt of lightning.

Nyx and I took turns checking on Seth, and this time it was Nyx's turn—she insisted. I was finishing with a client, going over his tattoo-care instructions, so I told Nyx thanks and she disappeared into the back of the shop. It wasn't a solid minute later when I heard her shaky, freaked-out voice holler down the stairs. "*Ri-ley!* Get up here *now*!" she screeched. *"Hurry!"*

"Here," I said to the client, handing him the rest of his paperwork. "Band looks awesome, but I gotta go—sorry!" When he chuckled and said, "No problem," I was already halfway up the steps to my apartment, my heart in my throat. I envisioned every horrible scenario I could imagine, from drug overdose to death—both completely out of character (way out) for Seth, but he hadn't exactly been Seth Poe lately. I beat myself up a hundred times before I reached the top of the stairs, for not getting him to a doctor sooner. But the moment I saw Nyx, standing in the doorway of Seth's room, with a look of disbelief and terror on her face, swear to God, I nearly stopped breathing. I felt like a hole had been knocked through my chest, and I ran hard to the doorway and pushed past Nyx. Once inside, I jolted to a stop. "Whoa!" I shouted, and froze, my eyes glued to what I saw.

The air jammed in my lungs the moment realization hit me. I couldn't breathe, shout, or cry out. I merely stood, mouth slack, staring in complete disbelief as my baby brother's body hovered ten feet above his bed, face-up, body to ceiling, and totally, completely asleep.

"Seth!" Nyx cried. "Wake up! Oh, Riley—what the—"

"Go get Preacher," I said, my eyes remaining fastened on my floating brother, and praying the Gullah had come home.

"But Seth! What's he *doing*?" she said, her voice wailing, and she was literally jumping in place. She was starting to panic, and I was freaking close to it myself. "That's just not real! It's not—"

"Dammit, Nyx, now!" I said sharply. She was already gone and running down the steps before I realized Preacher might not be home yet. Estelle had just called earlier to say he was on his way from Da Island. Deciding not to wait on anybody, I dragged a chair over, climbed on it, reached on booted tiptoes to Seth's ankle, and tugged. His body, weightless, moved with very little pressure, so I eased down off the chair and pulled Seth with me. As effed up and weird as it sounded *and* looked, I positioned his body parallel with his bed, then tugged him down onto the mattress. The moment I turned him loose, he began to float back to the ceiling. "Shit! Seth!" I grasped his ankle again as panic shot through me. What the *hell?*! What was I supposed to do? This was not happening! I scanned the room, hoping my vision would light on something that would give me a clue as to what the *freak* to do with Seth. Was he possessed? On drugs? People didn't *float*. Oh, Jesus, he had to be possessed. I should have paid more attention in my Catholic studies as a kid. I held on to him now, completely out of my mind, and finally, I did the only thing I could think of: I sat on him to keep him down. Seth showed no signs of waking up; he actually looked as peaceful as he ever did when asleep, and I wanted him to damn well stay like that until Preacher arrived.

Within minutes—maybe even seconds, I really lost track of time—a rush of heavy treads hurrying up the steps met my ears, and thankfully, it was more than one set of feet moving. "Hurry up!" I hollered.

Then everything happened at once. Preacher burst into the room; Chaz ran in barking his head off; Seth woke up; Nyx screamed. And in one fluid motion—so fast I didn't even see him move—my brother shoved me off of him with brutal strength, I flew hard across the room and landed against the wall, and Seth disappeared out of the already open window. The moment my body landed, I pushed up and ran toward the window. "Seth!" I called out frantically, and searched the area of cobbles below his window. Vacant. Chaz jumped up, his paws on the sill and still barking like a mad dog, and I searched up and down River Street in the waning light. "Seth!" I called again. It was no use. He was gone. And I was in sickening shock. I didn't think beyond that; I pushed off the sill and ran for the door, screaming my brother's name. "Seth!" No way could he have made that fall and just . . . run off. Unless he was using. Dammit! I made it ten feet before Preacher grabbed me around my waist and pulled me to a halt. "Let me go!" I said, unthinking, and pulled hard against him. He held fast, and I went nowhere. Overcome with distress, I sagged against him. My brain couldn't make sense of anything. "What's going on, Preacher?"

"Girl," Preacher said gently. "Shush now." Somewhere behind me, Nyx wept softly. He touched my chin, and I turned and searched his dark eyes. He asked me nothing, just commanded me with gentle urgency. Obviously, he knew something, since none of this seemed to be freaking him out. "You come wit me now," he said, and headed out of the door. Nothing I looked at was the same as before. Nothing and no one. I don't know why I felt that so fast, but I did; all from just five words spoken from the mouth of a wise Gullah root doctor. Sensations of fear, panic, anxiety, rushed me. That, and the fact that my levitating, drug-using brother had flown out of a two-story building and disappeared.

Knowing what her answer would be, I glanced at Nyx. "Will you close up for me and wait here, in case he comes back?" I asked.

"He ain't comin' back tonight," Preacher said from the hall, and my stomach dropped. "It's time now. Come," he commanded. I drew in a deep breath and numbly followed Preacher out, trailing behind him into the afterlight.

Part 4

INTRODUCTIONS

I had absolutely no idea where we were going, but I followed Preacher with blind faith and silence, out into Savannah's humid dusk. I almost felt like I was out of my body, invisible to everyone around me. All I could think about was my brother; all I really wanted to hear was that Seth would be okay. I doubted seriously I'd hear it right now. Preacher moved wordlessly, and he'd speak when he was damn well ready. Meanwhile, I was dying inside: I fought tears and panic. I felt like screaming at the top of my lungs. I kept my mouth closed, but my silence burned in my throat.

As we hurried along, I knew it wouldn't do me a bit of good to ask the old conjurer where we were headed; he'd either ignore me or tell me to *hush and wait till we git dere*, so I simply kept up. A fair number of people were out and about as we crossed Bay Street; we hurried past a walking ghost tour heading toward the Kehoe House. People were sitting on park benches or strolling through the squares—none of them privy to the fact that something very unnatural had just occurred.

The threat of rain hung heavy in the air, and I could taste it and the ever-present brine on my tongue; no sooner had that thought crossed my mind than distant thunder rolled overhead. Shadows stretched long over the squares as lamplight fell over monuments and benches, making everything seem distorted, aberrant. Even the towering oaks seemed menacing, with long, outstretched arms reaching toward me as I passed beneath, and moss looking more like stringy witch's hair than one of Savannah's icons. The world around me sounded indistinct and displaced, like I was holding a seashell up to my ear. I shook off the weirdness as best as I could, and hurried along with Preacher.

We walked, nonstop and silent, all the way to Taylor Street, where the old Gullah turned right. When we hit Monterey Square, he crossed the street and stopped at the large white-brick historic three-story building on the corner. Black wrought-iron balconies on the second and third stories faced the square; the house was canopied by mammoth, moss-draped oaks—typical of the district. On the front gate hung a brass plate that read HOUSE OF DUPRÉ, 1851. Sure—the Dupré House. I'd seen it a hundred times growing up; I never knew anything about it or its inhabitants, and I couldn't understand why or how they'd be able to help my brother, unless they were some rich, radical interventionists. Preacher, though, he had connections, and I trusted anything—and I mean *anything*—he deemed necessary. Maybe the Duprés were into some of the same dark African magic? I hoped to hell so.

As if Preacher had heard my thoughts, he stopped at the front step and turned to me. It was dark enough out now that I could see only the whites of his eyes, his silver hair against his ebony skin, but I knew he studied me hard. He always did. "You drink your tea dis mornin', right?" he asked.

The odd question stunned me, but I answered. "Yes, sir."

"You didn't skip any mornin's since I been gone, right?"

I knew better than to question right now. When Preacher was dead serious about something, he didn't play around, and right now he was serious—no matter how bizarre the question was. "No, sir, I didn't skip any mornings. I never do." Inside, though, I was screaming *What the freak do you need to know that for?* I wisely kept the comment to myself.

"I know you, girl," Preacher said softly, "and it's killin' you to keep dat purty mouth shut. You wanna know what it is we're doin' here, and how dese folk can help your brodder—I know dat much. You wanna know why your brodder was floatin', and how he jumped and ran off. But I tell you now—don't shoot dat mouth off in dere, even if you want to. You keep dem lips sealed tight shut, and don't make much movement, and for God's sake don't hit nobody if dey put dere hands on you. What you're gonna see and hear in dere? It won't settle in your brain or in your heart right away, and I'm askin' you to just accept it." He placed a hand on my shoulder, and it was strong, warm. "Promise me dat, Riley Poe."

If I wasn't shaken before, I was now. I don't think I'd ever heard my surrogate grandfather say so many words at one time in my entire life. But Preacher man would do anything for me and Seth, and that was what all this was about—Seth. "Yes, sir," I answered quietly. Just the fact that Preacher warned me against someone putting their hands on me put my guard instantly up. He knew I had a thing about people—strangers—touching me. I had reflexes I couldn't help. Besides. Why would anyone in the Dupré House *touch me*? I drew a deep breath and let it out slowly. "I promise," I said, and hoped like hell I could keep it.

Preacher gave a single nod, then turned to the door; he didn't have to knock or ring a bell. The moment I stepped into the porch light beside him, the double-hung slabs of solid oak and brass opened, and an older man in a pristine tailored gray suit stood in the entranceway. Tall and wiry, with close-clipped gray hair, he gave me a double take, then addressed Preacher.

"They're waiting for you in the study, *monsieur*," the man said with a vague French accent. He didn't verbally acknowledge me, but he checked out my dragons, angel wing, and attire: a gauzy flower-print skirt that came just above my knees, a ripped white tee, black leather ankle boots, and a wide black velvet choker. "This way," he said, and inclined his head. He started up the foyer, back ramrod straight, and turned into a room off the main floor, near the back. We followed, my heels clicking sharply against the parquet flooring, breaking a deafening silence. Antique vases, ancient oil portraits, and pristine turn-of-the-century furniture adorned what small portion of the house I could see. The moment I stepped into the room, I stiffened. No fewer than fifteen people were gathered, and all sets of eyes rested on me as we entered. Only six *weren't* Gullah. A young girl, who seemed to be around the same age as Seth, stood beside an elegant, petite older woman and an older man. Immediately, my gaze scanned the room; I noticed two younger guys, around my age I guessed, and then I saw the hot guy who'd stared at me through Inksomnia's storefront window. He stood near the back, the farthest away from me, and four big Gullah guys—I knew them all—stood around him, almost . . . shielding him. Seemingly unbothered by it, he was propped casually against the wall, arms crossed over his chest, brown hair sideswept and falling over eyes that, even from this distance, I could tell studied me with expressionless intensity. Low-slung faded jeans with a ragged hole in the thigh, a leather belt, and a snug white tee covered a lean, well-defined body. Then I noticed his jaw, his profile, and familiarity surged through me. I stared back, slightly unhinged as another profile, in shadows as I was held against a wall, rushed over me. It was *him. What the freak?* But before I could demand what the *hell* was going on, a man's voice pulled my attention away, effortlessly, as if I had zero control. It was smooth, French, and mesmerizing.

"Bonsoir, ma chère," the elderly man said as he slowly rose from a wine-colored upholstered wingback chair near the hearth. His gaze locked directly onto mine as he drew closer, and I found it difficult to think of anyone or anything else except him and his voice. He moved so gracefully, it almost seemed as though he glided across the massive room. Stopping just a few feet from me, he gave a small, sophisticated bow and a warm smile. *"Accueillir à la maison de* Duprè.*"

I stared blankly at the man, and just as I was about to

tell him I had no idea what the hell he was saying, I felt Preacher's hand move to the small of my back. I took that as a sign to keep my mouth shut.

"Oh, Gilles," said the petite woman, also with a French accent, "in English, love." She gave me a glance.

"Ah, *oui—pardon*," the man—apparently Gilles— said to me, switching to English. "My apologies, young lady. 'Tis an old habit difficult to break, I'm afraid." He gave me a curt nod. "Welcome to the House of Dupré." A sharp cerulean blue gaze met mine and held it. "We've been expecting you."

What I wanted to say was, *That's great, really, but how can you help my brother? And what about the guy over there who has been stalking me?* Firm pressure at my back from Preacher kept the question in check. With my eyes, though, I screamed, *What's going on? Why have you been expecting me?*

In the next instant, Preacher began speaking to Gilles Dupré in perfect French. I waited, stunned, and picked up only one word in the fast translation: *Seth*. It was getting more and more difficult to keep my mouth shut, and already I'd had more than I could take of all the silent stares and scrutiny. But just as I was about to lose it, Gilles turned back to me. He grasped both of my hands with his, and I stiffened. Preacher's body went rigid beside me, but I remained calm. Well, calm for me, anyway. At least I didn't flip the old guy onto his back.

Gilles glanced down at our joined hands, and I watched his eyes follow the tail of my dragon tattoo up my arm before finding my gaze. Again, the sensation of complete fascination came over me as he spoke. "Riley Poe. The painted one," he said, almost with admiration.

"You are well loved by your dark brethren here, as is your brother. You are . . . family." He released my hands and gave a grave nod. "I do understand about family, *ma chère*." With a long, elegant sweep of his hand, he glanced to the others. "This is my family, Ms. Poe. There sits my beloved, Elise, my sweet daughter, Josephine, and my boys"—he motioned farther with his hand—"Séraphin, Jean-Luc, and over there in the corner, brooding, is my eldest, Eligius."

I stared wordlessly at the family Dupré. Elise, petite, with perfectly coiffed dark hair pulled back into an elegant ponytail, was at least fifteen years younger than her husband. She smiled warmly at me and gave a short, sophisticated nod. Their daughter, Josephine, stood next to her mother's chair, watching me with inquisitiveness, and looked as though she wanted to say something as badly as I did. Light brown hair hung in naturally wild curls to nearly her waist and parted in the middle, long bangs pinned back hippy style, and wide cerulean blue eyes just like her parents' stared blatantly at me. With a pair of dark skinny jeans, bright pink high-top sneakers, and a black T-shirt with a hot pink peace sign on the front, she looked like every other average teenager. She glanced at my feet, then met my gaze. "I like your boots. And it's Josie." She gave a wicked grin.

Preacher once more pressed firmly against my back, silently telling me to keep quiet. I stared at Josie without saying a word, and her mouth tipped up into a smile—almost as if she knew my thoughts.

Séraphin and Jean-Luc studied me, neither saying a word, and they looked so much alike, they could've easily been twins. Both with athletic physiques and dark blond hair, Séraphin wore his close clipped while Jean-Luc's was longer and crazy. They regarded me in silence, yet their expressions revealed intense curiosity and something else I couldn't define just then. Then Jean-Luc flashed me a peace sign and grinned. All I knew was, no matter how many in the room stared me down, Eligius was the one that affected me most. And that totally irritated me.

I gave only a brief glance at *him*. Eligius Dupré. Clearly, I was familiar with his good looks and harsh stares and was beginning to get really pissed off at him and this whole situation. What the hell was all this about? Why had Eligius been following me, what had happened to the dead body, and—*Shit*! I was confused. Why had Preacher brought me here? How could these people help Seth? And why couldn't I *say* anything? I glanced at Preacher, who also said nothing, but I knew that look. It said, *Do what I said, girl.* Finally, I returned my gaze to Gilles, who warmly smiled. I could do nothing more than wait.

"Now that you have observed *ma famille, chère*, know us well. Just as we know you well; we will all become quite . . . close." He grazed my jaw with a long, elegant finger, and I struggled not to knock it away. He smiled. "Ah, *oui*. Your Preacher has told us of your dislike for human touch." He chuckled and slid a finger across my jaw once more. "I can assure you—'tis not what you think."

The rest of the Duprés chuckled as well—all except Eligius, and despite my previous promise, I just couldn't help myself. I narrowed my eyes. "You've no idea what I think."

Preacher made a hissing sound beside me and muttered an African word whose meaning I didn't know but had a pretty good idea about. I gave him a curious glance. "What?" I asked under my breath, although I knew good and well *what*.

"Come, my fierce painted one," Gilles said. He grasped my elbow and gently tugged me toward the chair he'd vacated earlier, and for some reason, I allowed it. "Sit. We've much to discuss."

I sat down, throwing a curious look at Preacher, who simply stared back expressionless. I didn't have to wait long.

Gilles stood at the hearth, elbow propped against a long, polished antique mantel, and began. "Your Gullah brethren and my family have known one another for many years," he said, his accent light, delicate. "And with regret I confess we've all grown complacent." He sighed, briefly closed his eyes, then looked again at me. "We should never have let our guard down, even for a moment. It was—"

"Gilles," his wife, Elise, said softly. "Please."

"*Oui*, you're so right, love," he said. "Best to just come out and say it." He sighed again. "A contract was made, centuries ago, between Preacher's ancestors and the Dupré *famille*," he said. "They would supply us with . . . necessities, and we in turn would give full protection to the city and outlying islands. A guardianship, if you will."

Gilles watched me, waiting for an understanding that I absolutely couldn't give to him; I had no freaking idea what he was talking about. Although I wanted to question how an old man, a middle-aged woman, a teenage girl, and three young guys could still be carrying on some aged contract to guard an entire city—and from *what*—I kept quiet. A marathon for me, actually, but if Preacher's grave expression meant anything, I knew this was something I needed to chill out with and listen to—for now, anyway. Somehow, this had to link back to what in hell was happening to my little brother. And strangely enough, I sensed a freakish strength radiating from Gilles Dupré. I couldn't explain it, but I think it helped keep my mouth shut and my ass firmly planted in the chair.

Gilles continued. "You see, my painted one, your brother and his young friends disrupted a tomb and inadvertently released two vicious souls—a pair of brothers. Valerian and Victorian Arcos." He stepped close to me and cocked his head. "They, like us, are descendants from a powerful, rare bloodline of the *strigoi* in Romania. They will stop at nothing, *chère*, to take what they want, and trust me"—he gave a wan smile—"they will indeed *want*. They will not be so easy to subdue again."

Strigoi? What the hell? The vacant stare in my eyes had to be blatantly obvious; then, it hit me, and I couldn't believe it. I glanced around at the entire room, despite having Preacher tell me to be still and keep quiet. I just couldn't help it. The Gullah fixed their dark stares on me; the Duprés watched silently, all waiting for my response, I supposed. Slowly, I rose from the chair, shook my head, and gave a short laugh of disbelief. I still couldn't believe it. I turned to Preacher. "Zombies, Preach? Seriously? You think Seth and his friends unleashed zombies from da hell stone? No disrespect—you know I heed your warnings—but zombies? You know I don't believe in stuff like that, and I don't have time for this," I said, and started for the door. I glanced back over my shoulder. "I've got to look for my brother—"

"Stay."

The familiar voice made my head spin around, and I gasped—then swore—in complete shock. Eligius Dupré blocked the doorway and stood so close, I could smell whatever earthy, seductive scent he was wearing. How had he moved so freaking fast? Every Gullah in the room, Preacher included, moved toward me, the room filled with a mixture of frantic African and French languages. All at once, the overwhelming urge to scream, cry, and run like hell overcame me, and I pushed past Eligius Dupré in an effort to try. "Move it, garçon," I said sarcastically as a sob stuck in my throat and my voice cracked—two very unlikely behaviors for me. The foyer was clear, and I ran all the way to the front door, and then out of it. Outside, at the bottom of the steps, Eligius stood, waiting.

"Shit!" I swore under my breath and stopped short. Again—how had he moved so *fast*? Twice! It was . . . impossible, and my brain couldn't—wouldn't—wrap around it. Wouldn't even try. I honest to God could think of nothing better to say and was again in complete shock. "What the hell are you doing?" I asked, breathless with disbelief.

"Trying to keep you from making an ass of yourself," he said quietly, his smooth voice seemingly inside my head. "Now, come back inside if you want to find your brother." He took two steps toward me, his features partially hidden by shadows. "Please."

The look of distrust on my face must have been more

noticeable than I thought, because Eligius gave a slight smile. "Yes, there was a dead guy in the alley last night. I didn't kill him. And we're not zombies." He inclined his head. "Can we go now?"

When someone else said *zombies*, it sounded even more stupid than when I'd said it. What had I been thinking? But where Preacher was concerned, nothing— including zombies—could be ruled out. Preacher and Estelle firmly believed in them, among other things.

"Child, come back in here now," said Preacher from behind me. "Time is gittin' by us, and your brodder is out dere."

Compelled by previous experiences to listen to Preacher, I gave Eligius one final hard stare, climbed the steps, and moved past my surrogate grandfather into the foyer wordlessly, but I didn't miss the look he gave Eligius before following me in. I'd seen it hundreds of times before. It was a *warning look*, with the threat of retribution in his dark eyes. And that just didn't make sense to me, even as I did as he asked. I entered the gathering room, hopefully for the last *effing* time, and was surprised to see everyone pretty much exactly where I'd left them.

Gilles came forward. "My apologies, *chère*. I know this is much to take in. But please"—he gestured to the chair with his hand—"sit. There are things of which you must know."

I glanced at Preacher, who gave a short nod. I crossed the room and eased into the chair. Josie stood close, and she regarded me with an amused look. I sought out the other two Dupré boys, and their expressions were much the same as their sister's.

"As you can see, we're not what you'd call . . . ordinary," Gilles said, pacing slowly now before me. I crossed my legs, folded my arms over my chest, and kept my gaze trained on the older man: his pricey suit, his manicured nails, his aristocratic profile. In my peripheral I noted Eligius by the door, probably blocking any further escapes from me. My mind was a jumbled mess of doubts and panic; I'd do anything to help find Seth. But this was seriously wicked crazy.

"Anything?" asked Gilles. He stopped and looked me in the eye. "Sincerely, *chère*?"

My skin turned to ice; it seemed as if the old man had read my mind, or had I said it out loud? "Yes," I responded in a sure, confident voice, calling off all earlier agreements I'd made with Preacher to keep quiet. And I was a little irritated. "Anything."

Gilles nodded. "*Bon*. Very good to hear." He drew closer, stopped, and inclined his head. "But in order for you to help your brother, you must stay, and listen with an open mind and heart."

"I will," I responded, recalling Preacher's nearly exact same words.

"Children?" he said to his family.

Everything that happened next happened so freaking fast, I could barely keep up. I'd turned my head slightly to glance at Preacher, and when I looked back at Gilles, he wasn't there. Jean-Luc was in his place. I searched out Josie, and while she'd just been standing beside her mother, she was now where Eligius had been, and he was now standing near the hearth. I stood, spun around, confused, only to notice that Gilles and Elise had traded places. No one stood where they once had, and they'd moved right before my eyes. I looked around, unsure, and felt myself beginning to shake nervously. "What's . . . going on?" I asked quietly. What was this, some sort of freakish effing Cirque du Soleil family? French illusionists? Was I losing my mind?

In the amount of time it took me to blink, Gilles stood once again before me. His smile was warm; his eyes gleamed . . . something else entirely different. Then a throat cleared loudly, and I glanced up to see Séraphin perched on the top of a tall bookcase in the corner. He jumped down with complete ease and was at my side in less than—swear to God—a second. I squelched a scream.

"We are creatures of the afterlight," said Gilles quietly. He reached down, grasped my hand, and continued to speak as he drew me across the room. I'm not sure why, but I willingly went as my mind spun wildly, trying to figure out exactly what a creature of the afterlight was. "Nearly two centuries ago I was taken one night by another—an Arcos—and to this very day I know not why." He closed his eyes and shook his head. "I left while my quickening took place, and once I was fully turned, I realized I couldn't bear to be without my beloved family, so I selfishly took them, one by one, as they slept in their beds. I forced them to drink my tainted blood, and they, too, became like me. It was a hellish month of quickening that followed."

"Gilles, *non*," said Elise quietly, and in the blink of an eye she was beside him, her arm linked through his. She laid her head on his shoulder. "Not selfish, *mon bien-aimé*."

Now I shook *my* head, in complete and utter confusion. "Took them—creatures of the afterlight? Quickening? What does all that mean?" I asked. "And what's it got to do with my brother and me?" Afterlight—what the Gullah called dusk—I got that; but the Arcos brothers, vicious killers, *creatures* of the afterlight? None of it made sense.

Eligius was immediately at my side, and his eyes bored hard into mine. "The Arcoses are *vampiric* descendants of the *strigoi*," he said, his voice seemingly inside my head once more. It was weird to finally see a face to match the voice, and I felt as though my gaze was fixed to his. His lips moved, and I couldn't quite take my eyes off *them*, so he must have been speaking out loud. He gripped my arm, and just that fast, my reflexes kicked in. Only, they didn't work. His grip was like a steel vise, and I couldn't budge him. He drew closer, and from the corner of my eye I saw the Gullah men take a step forward. "A bloodline rarely heard of outside of Romanian tales and folklore. We are all considered members of the Kindred, all with a vein of *strigoi* blood, but there are differences. We are immortal and crave human blood, but our hunger has been satisfied in other ways—humane ways—by the Preacher, and his ancestors before him. The Arcoses have been entombed for over a hundred and fifty years, and now they're out, and they're *not* humane. They're hunting." His face was so close to mine, I could see the various flecks of color in his angry eyes. "They have no mercy, no remorse; they cannot be satiated. And they will not stop."

My thoughts jumped to the dead man in the alley, the distorted way his lifeless body lay, the way his flesh had been ripped open, the blood, and Eligius didn't let go of my arm. He held it, steady, his gaze not once leaving mine. My heart slammed into my rib cage, and my skin tingled where he touched. At once, the entire room didn't exist; only us. He'd been the one to give me straight answers, so I asked one more straight question. "What are you?" I said, my voice strong but shaky. I kept my eyes boldly trained on his as I awaited an answer, and I vaguely noticed the flinch in his expression at the word *what*.

"We are vampiric, but not like *them*," he said heatedly, under his breath, and it was the first time I realized the slightest trace of an accent was French. The muscles in his jaws tensed, and again my eyes were drawn to his full lips. "As my father said, we made a contract with your brethren. They have sustained our lives, and we have protected the city against rogue vampires." With his head lowered, his eyes searched mine, and his voice lowered. "But the Arcoses have been freed, and now we have a major fucking problem, *ma chère*."

"Son, that's enough," said Elise, her voice sweet and strong at the same time. A slight shift in the air brushed across my face and made me wince, and when I opened my eyes, Eligius was across the room, leaning against the wall as though he'd never moved.

I looked directly at Gilles. "How does any of this help my brother?" I asked, then sought out Preacher, who stood quietly against the door. "How?" Suddenly, the weight of what couldn't possibly be happening hit me full force in the chest, and I sagged where I stood, unable to breathe. "Seth," I choked my brother's name out, and the lining in my throat burned.

Preacher was immediately at my side, and while he

didn't say anything, his reassuring hands on my shoulders put me at as much ease as I could be.

"Your brother is in the quickening," said Gilles, and I didn't miss the sympathetic note in his voice. "And it takes a moon's full cycle for transformation to complete. We feel that he and his friends, because of their unintentional aid to the Arcoses, are safe for now. Had the brothers wanted to kill them, they indeed would be dead already, I assure you."

It was too much, even for me, to take in. My mind reeled at everything I'd been told, at what I'd seen, and no matter how hard I tried, no matter what I knew of Preacher and his beliefs, I had a hell of a time believing I was standing in one of Savannah's prominent historic buildings with a loving family claiming to be vampires descended from France and Romania; that there were two dangerous, bloodthirsty rogue vampires loose in the city; and that my baby brother was running with them.

That he was going to *become* one of them. My stomach felt sick.

Everything that had happened that night at Bonaventure washed over me in a heavy, suffocating wave: the uneasy feeling I'd gotten, the absence of cicadas, and Seth's slow transformation from sweet, lovable brother to the cold, detached boy I barely recognized. Chaz had noticed it, too, and suddenly all of the symptoms made sense. Seth slept all the time, had hypersensitivity to light and no appetite. At first fevered, he'd grown . . . cooler. Not cold, but notably cooler in temperature. He'd almost attacked me. He'd thrown Chaz across the room. I closed my eyes tightly and tried to breathe. "Oh,

God," I muttered, a pain so fierce lodging deep in the pit of my stomach that it nearly made me double over. I wrapped my arms around my middle. "How can it be true?" I turned to Preacher. "How?"

"There are many things in this world of which most mortals haven't a clue exist," said Gilles, directly by my side now. "Until it's too late, of course."

I turned my gaze on him, unable to do little more than stare. I then took in the room, the Dupré family, my Gullah friends. My brain was in overload and could take not another second more. I turned to Preacher. "I've got to get out of here." He simply kept his gaze trained on me, wordless.

"We thought it may be too much at once," said Gilles, his hands folded behind his back. The weighty expression on his face didn't sit so well with me. "But there's one more thing you should know."

I looked at him. "What's that?"

"You've a rare blood type, Riley Poe. Only the second mortal I've ever encountered with it in my entire existence."

"I'm O positive," I replied. "That's not rare."

He inclined his head. "Have you given any thought as to why so many of your brethren are with us today?"

Glancing quickly around the room, I shrugged. "Not really."

He placed a hand on my shoulder, and every single Gullah took a step forward. Gilles smiled. "They're here to protect you, child. Your blood type is especially rare . . . to *us*."

"Gilles, stop scaring the girl," said Elise, suddenly by his side. She looked at me and spoke freely for the first time. "Your Preacher has masked your blood potency for years," she said softly. "You're in no real danger here, *chère*, and your fellows are here because they love and cherish you. They're just being cautious, and it is that fierce loyalty which has kept our families and the contract bound for centuries. And it shall remain that way."

Preacher put his hand against the small of my back. "Your tea dat you drink every mornin'? It keeps your blood masked."

I looked at him with wide eyes. "You've been drugging me?"

The corner of his mouth lifted, ever so slightly, in a smile only I recognized. "For your own good," he said gently. "We've known of your powerful blood since you was a baby, right. Now, listen to him," he said, inclining his head to Gilles. "Dere's somethin' we have to do for now."

I nodded and gave my full attention to Gilles. "I'm listening." Although I had a difficult time realizing that I was like a filet mignon to these guys.

Gilles clasped his hands in front of him. "The Arcoses will not be stopped easily. They will be difficult to find—as will your brother and his friends. They hide during the daylight and move through shadows in the darkness."

I hadn't thought about that. No wonder Riggs was acting so ridiculous in the shop.

"And I feel they are on more than a hunt. Retaliation in the end, no doubt." He turned to me and studied my face with intensity. "You see, Victorian and Valerian are youths—all of twenty-one and twenty-two years—although extremely cunning and deadly. Their appearances will fool you—never trust them. Their faces are beautiful and innocent; their souls are damned. We will do everything in our power to lure them out of hiding, and we'll need your help."

Again, I nodded, even though everything Gilles was saying felt as though he was saying it to someone else, not me. "What can I do?"

"They're building an army," Gilles said gravely. "From our city's youth—your brother included. It's what they'd intended a hundred and fifty years ago, and it's why they were entombed. They will seek out their troops and victims from the darkest dregs of the city. Now, times are more dangerous, and this time they shall be destroyed." He inclined his head. "You know the underground, *oui*?"

"Underground as in . . . what, exactly?" I asked, although I sort of guessed what he meant. I didn't like it.

"Dark places, drugs," Preacher clarified. "Dem dark dancin' clubs you used to go to, and dos bad folk you hung out wit when you was a youngun."

Inside, I cringed. I'd sworn—*vowed*—that I'd never go back to that life again. I'd put it behind me for good. But this was my brother being dragged into stuff way worse than I ever *dreamed* of doing. I looked Gilles Dupré in the eye. "I said I'll do anything."

Briefly, Gilles closed his eyes, and a slight smile tipped his mouth upward. "*Bon.* For now, we must watch, wait, and try to protect as many as possible. The city has grown—it won't be as easy as it once was. And Eligius will remain by your side at all times."

"Papa?"

"No," I said at the same time Eligius argued. We glanced at each other; then I turned to Gilles. "I appreciate your concern, really, but I don't need anyone to protect me. Preacher lives right next door. I can take care of myself."

With a quick glance at Preacher, who gave one single, short nod, Gilles, in a fraction of a second, grasped my forearms tightly and drew his head close. I blinked in surprise, and just that fast his face grew close and sickly distorted, his jaw unhinged, and every tooth in his mouth grew long, sharp, jagged, his eyes no longer blue but pure white, with only a pinpoint bloodred pupil. I literally shook where I stood, my breath jammed in my throat; I couldn't breathe, move, or scream.

In the next blink, Gilles' face returned to normal— what I perceived as normal, anyway. He was a handsome, distinguished older man. Regret now set firmly in his clear blue eyes. "I'm sorry, *chère*," he said quietly. "But you do now see why you must allow Eligius' aid?"

"Why not Phin or Luc?" Eligius questioned quietly. "I'm not a wise choice."

I couldn't take my eyes off of Gilles. Had what just happened *truly* happened? Was that what would become of Seth? I resisted the urge to reach up and touch his face.

"Oui," Gilles said. "That is what would become of your brother. Worse, I'm afraid. He will have ... no control. A newling, driven by desperate, painful hunger."

I knew then that Gilles could read my thoughts, and I couldn't be sure whether he read them at random, or just when he thought it was pertinent to the situation. That was yet another insane thing for my brain to try and wrangle. I chanced a look at him, and he gave a slight grin.

"And you," Gilles said to Eligius, "are the choice I've

made, *mon fils*. You are the strongest of us and can better protect her. She must carry on her proprietorship as usual, and begin to ease into a life underground. We cannot allow the Arcoses to suspect otherwise, *oui*?" Gilles turned his look to me. "You will be perfectly safe with Eligius. Just . . . make sure you drink your tea." Jean-Luc, Séraphin—rather, Luc and Phin—and Josie chuckled.

After a quick glance at Eligius, I turned my question to Gilles. "Does he do what you just did?"

Gilles gave a nod. *"Oui."*

A cynical laugh escaped me. "And you want him to stay in my house? With me? While I'm helpless and sleeping?"

Gilles didn't answer.

I inclined my head. "Who is Eligius supposed to be protecting me from?"

Gilles' stern, regretful expression made my heart drop to my stomach. "Your brother."

"The Arcoses as well," said Elise. "They're lethal, darling. More than you can imagine. Because of their *strigoi* bloodline they can appear out of body. They can appear in your dreams, if they wished it. And your brother, while still in the quickening phase, has strong mortal tendencies which would lure him to what he's most familiar with—you. Unfortunately, he also has vampiric tendencies, and those would indeed overpower his weak mortal desires, including his love for you." Her look was one of pity. "He'd not be able to help himself."

I felt sickened at the thought that my brother would hurt me, but I knew now that he would. He'd already tried. I had no choice but to trust the Duprés; Preacher did. And I fully trusted Preacher and his family with my and Seth's lives.

Once more, Gilles clasped my hands between his. "Enough for one day, *oui*? I am positive Eligius can give you a Dupré family history and answer any questions you may have." The smile that tipped his mouth was noticeable only by me, I was sure. "You'll be spending a lot of time together, no doubt." Then he cast a severe stare at Eligius. "She goes nowhere without you, *oui*?"

The muscles in Eligius' jaws flinched. "*Oui*, Papa."

"When you begin your searches underground, Séraphin, Jean-Luc, and Josephine will be there, as well."

I shot a glance at Josie, who merely grinned devilishly. "But she's only what? Sixteen?"

"Fifteen in mortal years," Luc answered. Then he grinned wickedly and tossed his sister a glance. "She's more lethal than Phin and me put together. She can handle herself."

I blew out a slow breath. "Yeah, okay," I muttered, then gave Preacher a glance. "So there's nothing we can do to help Seth now? Tonight? I'm seriously supposed to just . . . carry on like none of this is happening?"

"No, girl," Preacher said, and I could see in his dark eyes how much he hated saying those words to me. "For now you do nothing. He's safe for da time being. We get dos *wudus* out da way, and den we git Seth to Da Island." He put his arm around me. "Now, let's go. We'll make it right. I promise." He looked at Gilles; they had a small conversation in French of which I recognized no words, they shook hands, and we left the House of Dupré.

"I really like your inks," said Josie, suddenly right beside me. She studied my dragons, checked out my wing, and nodded approvingly. "Cool." If I didn't know better, I'd think she was any other ordinary, impressionable teenage girl.

I gave her a hesitant smile. "Thanks."

"See ya around," Josie said with a closed-mouth smile.

I gave a nod, and along with Preacher, the other Gullah, and Eligius, who now carried a canvas duffel bag thrown over one shoulder, we left Monterey Square.

The entire way back to Factor's Walk, I was acutely aware of Eligius Dupré's presence, even though he casually hung back about a half block. I would be a liar if I said I wasn't affected by him; I had been since the moment I'd seen him watching me through Inksomnia's window. Even now, when I think back on the incidents in which I saw him only in shadows, I was affected by him. And no matter how much I replayed the entire visit to the Dupré House in my head, I found myself even more stunned at what I'd witnessed than when I'd first seen and heard it. Gilles' chilling, distorted features and deadly strength flashed across my mind, and I involuntarily shivered as a vision of those teeth ripping my throat out became all too vivid. Then I immediately tried to envision Eligius' beautiful face doing the same thing. Don't think for a second that I'm a fool—I knew full well he was just as dangerous, if not more so, than Gilles and the others, despite his boyish, charming looks. It was just . . . freaky to see in my head. And Seth—God, no way could I imagine it. I still couldn't believe this was all real: quickening, *strigoi*, Romanian folklore, the Kindred. Was it actually happening? And despite Eligius being the most lethal, he also somehow possessed the most control. It didn't make sense. None of it did, and the entire walk back I spent trying to rationalize everything that had just happened.

Beneath the lamp separating my shop from Da Plat Eye, Preacher stopped and grasped my hands. He was one of the few people who could do so without my reacting badly. "You did good back dere, girl. Only opened dat mouth a couple of times." He sighed. "I know dis is a lot for you to take into your heart, but you got to do it. You got to do everything dey says to do."

"What about him?" I said, inclining my head to Eligius, who stood a few feet behind us. "What am I supposed to do?" I'd already decided to sleep in my heavy wool scarf. Behind me, Eligius chuckled—at least I thought he did. I shot him a look over my shoulder, and he didn't even appear to be paying us any attention.

"You do what dat boy says to do, Riley Poe. He will do you right. And his brodders will watch out for Nyxinnia."

"What am I supposed to tell her?" I asked, and again, the deathly silence of the night stunned me.

"You tell her dat brodder of yours got into some bad magic, and de Gullah, dey gonna fix him up. Dat's all you gotta say." He glanced toward the darkened skies, then back at me. "It don't feel right out here, Riley Poe. You git inside and stay. And you be nice to dat Dupré boy. I would not let him in your house if I thought he would do something bad. He won't."

Emotions washed over me, and I threw my arms around Preacher's neck and hugged him tightly. "Is all this really happening?" I muttered against the collar of his shirt as I inhaled the odd, sweet mixture of Downy and hoodoo herbs. "Is it real? Is my baby brother going to turn into one of *them*?" I fought a sob that stuck in my already burning throat. I didn't cry often, but when I did, it was torrential—and no one ever knew it happened, because I did it in private. I felt a big one coming on now.

Preacher's big hands patted my back. "Awe, baby, we gonna make things right after all, so dat doesn't happen. You'll see."

I pulled back and *breathed*. "What about you and Estelle?"

Preacher chuckled. "Dat old crazy woman and me, we fine, Riley Poe. Handled things a lot worse dan vampires, dat's right. But dos Duprés ain't like dat, right?" He turned me toward my door and shoved gently. "Now, go git some rest. But come git your tea in de morning; don't forget dat."

"Don't worry—I won't." I stood there beneath my door light and watched Preacher make his way to the back entrance of Da Plat Eye, step through the door, and close it behind him, leaving me alone with Eligius. I looked at him standing there, duffel slung over one shoulder, his dark hair carelessly falling over his eyes as he watched me from the shadows. It thrilled me and freaked me out at the same time. "Come on in," I invited, then turned, stuck the key in the lock, and opened the door. The moment I hit the light switch, he was at my side, and despite being overwrought with sick worry over my brother, my skin heated at his closeness. I was immediately on the defensive. "Back off," I said. I gave him a warning look and moved to the steps. He followed, closed the door, and locked it. And it was at that moment that Chaz came hauling ass into the foyer from the front of the shop, barking his head off, fur at his scruff standing on end.

"Whoa, Chaz, stop it!" I said sharply, and he came to a halt but stood rigid, head down, a low growl rumbling from deep in his throat as he stared hard at Eligius. It reminded me of his reaction to Seth over the past week. "He doesn't like . . . strangers," I said, although I'd meant vampires. I wasn't ready to hear the word come out of my mouth yet; it sounded nearly as stupid as *zombies*, although I was starting to believe in them, too. "Chaz! Down!" I commanded, pointing at the floor.

Eligius turned sideways in the narrow foyer and squeezed by me, our bodies inches apart, keeping his hooded gaze trained on me. "He'll get used to me, too," he said, and drew closer to my bristled dog. Gently, he eased his duffel to the floor and squatted before Chaz, speaking softly in French. Within seconds, Chaz's fur settled, his backside wagged, and he whined as one paw lifted and rested on Eligius' knee. At once I was impressed . . . and betrayed. I grabbed Chaz's leash from the wall and slapped my thigh. "Come on, boy; let's go for a walk." Chaz hurried to me and licked my knee. "That's better, you traitor," I said, and scrubbed the space between his fuzzy ears. I glanced at Eligius, who was still squatted down. "Be right back."

He instantly rose and was at the door beside me. "You go, I go."

"Whatever," I mumbled. I unlocked the door and headed back out into the night. I kept a wary eye on Eligius while Chaz inspected the grass, and finally, I caved.

"So what'd you say to him?" From the river, a tugboat blasted its horn, someone on the walk cheered, and I could vaguely hear music coming from the Boar's Head.

Eligius shrugged and met my gaze. "I promised not to kill you."

"Wow, thanks." I had a hard time swallowing past the lump in my throat, but I didn't let him see that it had bothered me. "As long as I keep drinking Preacher's anti-kill-me potion, right?"

"It'd be a good idea," he said, and the words made me shudder.

Inside, I turned Chaz loose, hung his leash on the wall, and locked the door. As I talked to Nyx on my cell, explaining to her about Seth exactly as Preacher had advised, I watched Eligius move around in my apartment; he seemed to know just where everything was. He walked straight to Seth's room without pause, tossed his duffel on the floor, and stood there, staring at . . . something. It felt weird having him in my home, completely strange and foreign. He looked too . . . normal, in his plain white tee and faded jeans, not what you'd think a vampire looked like at all. No black cape, no coffin. His complexion was flawless, all except for a small mole on his jaw, just below his left ear. Freshly shaved, even, although he had the slightest hint of stubble. Did vampires shave? It was an absurd thought. I almost talked myself out of believing in what I knew he really was. I didn't know him from freaking Adam and had only Preacher's assurance that it'd be okay to have a creature of the afterlight freely wandering my apartment—with me in it. It should be Seth here, and a longing ache for my brother sank deep into my stomach. He was somewhere, roaming the streets with something way worse than anything I'd ever roamed with: *monsters*. Against my will I tried to imagine his young face distorting like Gilles'; I could not. Without my permission, the vision of Seth attacking an innocent human being and sucking all of the person's blood out pushed to the front of my mind. I pushed it quickly away. It didn't seem right. All I could see was his sweet, expressive green eyes divulging every emotion he possessed. Tears stung my throat and eyes, and I hurried into the kitchen, opened the fridge, and grabbed a bottle of Guinness. I had a third of it down when I turned. Eligius was standing no less than a foot away, regarding me closely. I didn't jump—I forced myself not to. With a knuckle, I wiped my mouth, and his eyes followed my movement with intense curiosity.

"What if I didn't have Preacher's herbs?" I asked, his closeness heating my skin. "What if I just stopped taking them?"

Eligius' eyes dropped to the pulse at my neck, and swear to God, his eyes glowed. "You'd be dead before you could lift that bottle to your lips."

Part 5

TEMPTATIONS

Until the day break and the shadows flee away.

—Anonymous epitaph, Bonaventure Cemetery

The night dragged by painfully slowly, and I found myself constantly looking over my shoulder. I knew that if he wanted to, Eligius could kill me; part of me sincerely believed he *did* want to. That skepticism royally pissed me off. I didn't like my life being invaded, especially by a guy so freaking hot and lethal at the same time, he made me burn every time he got close to me. No lie. I'd wanted him from the moment I'd seen him through the storefront. I always was attracted to the bad boy, but this was ridiculous. I supposed he possessed some sort of mind control; it was the only reason I could think of to explain why he made me feel like I was in freaking heat. Again—that pissed me off. I didn't like being out of control, especially when it came to guys. That had happened once in my life—never, ever again.

My apartment is fairly spacious for a historic-district riverfront structure, but when crammed inside with a vampire, I felt like it was a dollhouse. He sat sprawled on the sofa, looking like any other ordinary dude with a remote in hand, flipping through various channels that included all forms of male interest: MTV, motor sports, extreme surfing, *CSI*. Yet he watched me—my every move—and was *blatant* about it. I'd already had a beer and leftover lo mein, and by midnight my insides were crawling with nervous energy. I wanted to go for a run but knew without even mentioning it that if I'd wanted to do *that*, I wouldn't do it without a chaperone. So instead of a run through the historic district, I opted to work out extra hard with the bag. I felt like hitting something, beating the holy hell out of something, and working so hard at it that my lungs caught fire. Maybe then I'd be able to go to sleep and lose the horrible images in my head of Seth.

I grabbed the empty carton of lo mein off the counter, dropped it into the trash, and headed to my bedroom, Eligius' eyes following me the whole way. I ignored him and shut the bedroom door to block his penetrating stare. Kicking my boots off, I yanked my shirt over my head and pulled off my skirt, dropping both into the wicker basket in the corner, along with my socks. A shudder shocked me, and I didn't even have to turn around to know Eligius was behind me, standing in my doorway. I spared him no more than a quick glimpse over my shoulder, and yep—there he was, leaned against the doorframe in a laid-back guy manner, arms crossed over his chest, head cocked, his eyes fastened directly on me, and no shame in evidence. I wore a black lace bra and black boy-short panties. It wasn't like I was naked, not that I'd care about that, either. I turned back around.

"I was strip-searched three times by my thirteenth birthday, so don't think for a second you're intimidating me," I said without looking at him. I pulled on a pair of tight black yoga pants that dropped below my hips, and a white ribbed tank that barely covered my breasts. "You can look, if that's what gets you off." I spread my legs in a wide stretch and dropped my head down to peer at him from between them. "But don't touch." I grabbed my ankles and pulled, extending the muscles in my hamstrings, arms, and back. Rising on my toes, I stretched my calves, then stood straight. I glanced at him. "I'm no part of a contract. Savvy?" In the back of my brain, I knew my cockiness was a bold move; I was teasing a freaking vampire, for God's sake. Somehow, though, I just couldn't help it. Eligius provoked me, and it pissed me off that he was in my house. I moved to my iPod station, chose Breaking Benjamin's *Dear Agony,* selected "I Will Not Bow," and cranked up the volume.

"Eli. Only my parents call me Eligius," he said, and I heard it inside my head.

I pulled on my gloves, watching him with wary eyes, and I didn't respond. His look was anything but wary. I felt the room close in and fill with one hundred percent intense male sexuality, and although it was tough, I turned my back and started punching the bag. After a few minutes, I sank completely into my workout; the music pounded as I kicked hard and struck fast. I didn't forget for a second that Eli was behind me or that my baby brother wasn't coming home. I hit the bag hard, as though it was the very thing responsible for it all, and I felt the shock of it vibrate through the muscles in my arms. Desperation inundated me, and I don't know how long I worked out, but by the time my lungs seized, and my muscles were on freaking fire, tears fell furiously from my eyes. Angered—at myself, Eli, the Arcoses, and everyone else I could think of to blame for Seth's absence—I pulled my gloves off with my teeth and threw them hard across the room. Without a word or a glance, I swore, slung open the double doors to the small balcony, and stepped out into the night. I fought not to literally break down and sob. With my hands I gripped the cool wrought iron until the skin over my knuckles pulled taut, and I squeezed my eyes tightly shut. "Fuck," I said between clenched teeth, astounded by the rage building inside of me. I wanted to scream, shake the iron railing loose, and throw it into the river. I leaned my head down to my shoulder and rubbed the tears off my cheek.

"You'd better pull it together, Riley. You can't be losing it in this game and expect to win," Eli said quietly, so close I could feel him crowd me in the confined area of my balcony. At the same time his body pressed against my back; he placed an arm on either side of me, his hands next to mine on the rail, bracing himself. I reacted, my reflexes leapt, and I grabbed his arm with both hands. Had he not had vampiric strength to stop me, I would have easily flipped him over the edge of the balcony. I let go of him, heart racing wildly. He simply stood, pressed hard against me, keeping me prisoner;

he was aroused, and I felt that, too. It enraged me and turned me on at the same time.

"The monster in me is still there, just below the surface," he continued, as if my reaction hadn't fazed him at all, and his lips barely grazed the skin on the side of my neck. I shuddered, and I know he felt it. "Never forget that. Even with your Gullah magic inside you, I can smell your unique blood," he said, his mouth next to my ear. He inhaled a long, deep breath. "You have no idea how much of a temptation you are to me, Riley Poe," he said, the slight French accent making his voice erotic. "No . . . idea how much control I truly have not to simply taste what rushes through your veins, with barely more than a paper-thin layer of skin to stop me." I shivered as his breath rushed over my neck.

"That and a fucking contract," I muttered, and with what strength I had, I pushed hard against him to escape; he easily turned me around, and now we were face-to-face, body to body, and panic etched into my brain. Exerting the slightest pressure, he bent me backward until I felt the cool iron handrail press against my back. I felt every hard ridge and muscle Eli possessed pressing into me. And I mean *every one.* His eyes searched mine, then dropped to my mouth, where they lingered. "Vampiric cravings aren't the only ones I possess, but they're the only ones I can halfway control," he said. "I've still got the sex drive of a healthy, hot-blooded twenty-five-year-old guy, heightened times a hundred by *what* I am." He dropped his head close, his lips a breath away. "Don't tease me again, Riley, unless you mean it. I can't promise *that* kind of control." He lifted his head and stared, his eyes dark as he searched mine. "I don't think you could handle me."

Desire and fury raged within me, such a lethal combination that I thought I'd come if he pressed his crotch against mine just a little harder, held it there a little longer. I *wanted* him, and I hated myself for it—especially knowing he was just effing with me. "Get off of me," I said quietly. "Now." *Prick.*

The corner of his mouth lifted slightly, and he moved away from me. I pushed past him on shaky legs and waited for him to clear the balcony; then I shut and locked the doors. I started for the bathroom, but his next words stopped me. I didn't look at him.

"We've got three weeks, and despite what your brother's becoming, the desire to return to what's familiar to him is strong. His transformation grows every day as the quickening progresses—get it? Once the cycle is complete, and he makes his first kill—"

I nearly choked at his blatant honesty, and I looked at him over my shoulder and interrupted his chilling words. "Okay—I get it. And I promise you—all abilities I possess to fight and save my brother, I'll use, without hesitation. I might not be a vampire, but I'm as strong as hell, and I don't scare easy. I want him home, here, with me. I want Seth *back*, no matter what it takes." My voice cracked, and I stuck out my chin. "And I'll goddamn get him."

Eli watched me for several seconds, as though trying to determine whether I was bullshitting or for real. He decided. "I believe you," he said, and I could have sworn I heard admiration in his voice.

"Good. Now, can I pee and shower without you watching?" I said.

With his fingers he shoved his long bangs out of his eyes. "Yeah, I guess." He gave a slight grin.

I nodded. "Good. Stay out of my personal belongings. When I'm done, we need to talk. There are things I've got to know, and ground rules that need to be set. Agreed?"

He gave a nod but didn't budge from where he stood. "Agreed."

Rolling my eyes in part frustration because it looked like he was going to stand in my bedroom until I finished, I headed to the bathroom and shut the door. The water was freezing, but I needed it—dammit, I'd never before had a reaction to a guy like the one I'd had with Eli. To think with a clear head, and to be able to look him in the eye during a serious ground-rule-making discussion without screwing his brains out in my mind—*that was* what had to happen. That was what *would* happen. How could I have such a reaction to a guy who didn't even have a freaking pulse? I wasn't even sure I'd make it through the night alive. With my teeth chattering, I hurried through my shower and was seriously grateful I'd spent the cash for laser hair removal on my legs, bikini and pubic area, and underarms; I couldn't afford razor nicks at this point.

Finished, I twisted my wet hair in a towel and wrapped another around me. When I walked out of the bathroom, I saw that Eli had left the room. I was only mildly disappointed. After digging in my dresser, I pulled on a pair of cotton sleep pants and a black tank, and went to find my keeper. I found him flipping channels, once more sprawled on the sofa. I safely kept my distance, parking in the overstuffed chair kitty-corner from him. The TV screen had *Channel 11 News* on, and I stopped in my tracks as another murder report was broadcast. A woman, late twenties, had last been seen leaving the SCAD campus at eleven the night before. Her body had just been found crammed between two parking meters on East Bay. I watched as another black plastic body bag was loaded into the coroner's van. The screen went black, and Eli tossed the remote onto the cushion beside him. He regarded me just as thoroughly as I regarded him. Finally, he rubbed his jaw. "Ground rules?" he said.

I inclined my head to the TV. "Those murders," I began. "They're not . . . normal."

"No."

I tried to get the visions of dead bodies out of my head, pulled up my knees, and locked my arms around them. Time to change the subject, because if I dwelled on it, my mind would never settle down. "Okay. Ground rules," I said, and locked gazes with Eli. "I pee alone and I shower alone. Some things need to remain a mystery, and those are two I firmly believe in."

Eli looked amused, but he gave a nod. "Agreed. Next?"

"Don't interfere with my business at Inksomnia—no matter how crude and rude some of my clients might seem. Trust me—I can handle myself, and I've done it for some time without your help. It's my livelihood, how I plan on putting Seth through college."

This time, he didn't look so amused, if I was reading the hard stare correctly. "I'll do my best," he said.

I gave a nod. "Good." I shifted in my seat, and I ad-mit—I was tired. Drained. But I turned my full attention to Eli. "There are things I need to know," I said.

His eyes never left mine. "And there are things I *want* to know."

"Me first," I claimed, and thought about it. I knew I couldn't find out everything in one night—I had to eventually get to sleep. Eli nodded in agreement, and I thought for several seconds. "About the contract," I started. "Your father said the Gullah provided necessities in exchange for guardianship. What . . . necessities?"

Eli rose and walked to the window facing the water-front. He stood, staring out into the night. "When my family and I first arrived from Paris, we were . . . wild, newlings, completely out of control." He turned to me. "Fresh, young vampires, and we were ravenous. We killed . . . many." He kept his eyes trained on me. "A lot of the yellow fever victims weren't really yellow fever victims, if you know what I mean. Until the contract with the Gullah. Not all Gullah, mind you—just Preacher's kinsmen. Those days were primitive; they supplied will-ing donors, and we took only what we needed to remain alive."

Chills ran through my body at the thought of Eli and his family sucking blood from the necks of *willing do-nors*. I stared back. "So, what—they just lined up, like at a soup kitchen?"

"Sort of."

"And none of the Gullah transformed?" I asked.

Eli pushed the curtains aside and glanced out the win-dow. "No. They have to drink *our* blood to transform."

I froze. "You mean Seth drank the blood of one of those freaks?"

"Yes."

My insides hurt at the thought. "How did they make him do that? And when?"

Something outside must have had Eli's attention; he continued to stare out of the window while he explained. "At the grave, Seth and his friends disturbed a vase containing the Gullah magic that kept the Arcoses entombed, mummified. Like I said, a hundred years ago things were a hell of a lot more primitive and not as effective as our methods today. Back then, once the magic was placed, it stayed *as placed* . . . for as long as it lasts. There's no changing it." He looked at me. "I can only imagine that Valerian and Victorian fed as soon as they gained enough strength, then beckoned their rescuers."

"The woman found dead in the park?" I stated, already knowing the answer.

"Yes."

My insides grew icy cold as I thought of the woman found at Daffin Park, and I slowly rose. "And the guy in the alley?"

Eli nodded. "Yeah."

I drew a deep breath. I also recalled that first morning, when I'd found Seth asleep and his window wide-open. "Why didn't they kill Seth?"

Eli shrugged. "The Arcoses are weak. They need help subduing victims until they're fully restored."

I stared, speechless as that information sunk in. "You mean my little brother is luring innocent people to their deaths?" Yanking the towel from my head, I shook the tangles in my wet hair with my fingers until it hung limp, nearly to my waist. I threw the towel down. "I can't believe that."

"You'd better believe it," Eli said harshly, and drew closer. "A vampire, even in its weakest form, can manipulate a mortal's mind and make him do anything they wish."

We stood now, face-to-face, and yeah—I thought about how easily Eli could manipulate me. But this wasn't about me. "Why aren't we out looking for them now? Why can't we just bring them in, and take them somewhere safe? Why can't we just kill the Arcoses?" Desperate panic began to seize me again, and I didn't know how to control it. "Why do we have to wait?"

Eli's hands grasped my shoulders hard, and I noticed for the first time that his skin was surprisingly warm. "I'm going to say this one last time, and you'd better let it sink into that thick skull. While the Arcoses' physical beings are weak, their minds are as strong as ever. They can't know we're looking for them, or Seth and his friends. They could command them to do things you wouldn't want to imagine—and with just a single, solitary thought. They wouldn't even have to be in the same room with them." His eyes bored into mine. "They would do some messed-up shit and do it just because the Arcoses said to do it. Probably already have."

My mind reeled with every horrible thing a human being could do to another, and I felt sick at the images. "Then what the hell do we do?" I asked, looking into the clearest pair of light blue eyes I'd ever seen. "What?"

"We watch, and we wait. Right now, Valerian and Victorian are too weak to move stealthily through the city. That's why they've got Seth and his friends."

I stiffened, getting more pissed by the second. "We wait and do nothing?"

The look on Eli's face reeked of irritation. "No. We wait; we watch. We try to defuse as many situations as possible. They cannot be destroyed until their physical bodies are fully restored." He looked hard at me. "It's just the way it is."

"Do they know you're here?" I asked, and pulled away as thousands of worries and questions stormed my brain. "Do they know of the contract?"

Eli crossed his arms over his chest and stood, legs braced wide. "The contract was made after they were entombed, and Gullah magic has been in our system for nearly two centuries. They may suspect we're here, but they can't detect it. Our scent is masked—just like yours."

"Can they recognize you? Like, do they know what you physically look like?" I asked.

For the first time in our heated, serious conversation, Eli's expression lightened. "They know what we looked like in 1848. Together, as a family, they'd probably recognize us as the Duprés. Maybe. My mother and father look very much the same. But each of us in a crowd, or walking down the street?" He scrubbed his chin and shook his head. "No. Me, my brothers, and sister—we've evolved with the times."

"Given that you probably used to wear . . . velvet bloomers, lace, high heels, and a ponytail, yeah—I guess you have changed a little," I said, and gave a slight smile in hopes of easing the depressing mood. He must have

been putting the mind-whammy on me; I was even beginning to feel somewhat better.

Eli actually grinned. "That look was hot back then."
He held his arms out. "Velvet coat with tails to match.
Yeah, ruffles, too. I was badass."

I chuckled, although I didn't feel the joy of it go past
my face. "Yeah, whatever. Wicked hot, I'm sure."

"You've no idea."

I studied Eligius Dupré and, again, had the hardest time seeing him as anything other than what faced
me now: a hot guy with a hotter temper. A vision of his
father's frightening features flashed in my mind, and I
tried to put the same horribleness to Eli. It didn't work.
I knew eventually I would have to see it for myself to
believe it. Right now? Hell no. Even I could handle only
so much at one time. Other than going on just his word,
I couldn't imagine him killing. In my gut, though, I knew
just how wrong an assumption that truly was.

I looked at him. "Now?"

He stared back. "Now what?"

"You get your *essentials* in what way?" I had to ask;
no way were the Gullah still forming a soup kitchen for
their blood.

A smile pulled his mouth, showing beautiful, straight
white teeth. "The members of Preacher's community are
still our donors, Riley, but like us, their methods have
moved with the times. They have their own Red Cross, if
you know what I mean. The blood comes packaged, and
premixed with hoodoo magic." His smile widened. "And
only God knows what else. And yeah," he said, meeting
my gaze, "we pour it in a glass and drink it."

I gave myself a quick reminder to think V8 if I ever

watched him drink. Another thousand questions hit my brain at once, and yet my body screamed to get some sleep. I glanced at the clock hanging above the small stone fireplace—almost two in the morning. "I'm in overload," I mumbled, then glanced at Eli. "I've got to get some sleep or I'll be worthless tomorrow." Reaching down, I picked the damp towel up off the floor. "Do you sleep at all?" He looked refreshed and ready to go.

"Yeah," he said. "Just like in the movies, only not all day long." Again, he smiled. "Just a couple of hours, and it's when the sun is at its highest."

I nodded. "Is that the same for the Arcoses? Seth?"

"No. Our genetic makeup is different, and a lot of it's altered because of the hoodoo. The Arcoses will sleep from sunup to sundown, every day. Seth and the others aren't fully transformed; they might wake up, and they might show up here."

"Okay." I moved toward my bedroom. "Do you eat?" I asked, glancing over my shoulder. "Other than your ... Red Cross donations, I mean."

"Yeah, I eat. It's strictly for pleasure, though. We get no nutrients out of it, or feeling of fullness."

Stifling a yawn, I motioned to the kitchen with my hand and continued down the hall to my room. At my door I stopped and looked out at him. "Do I have to bolt my door?"

Eli's stare pinned me to the floor, and I was once again reminded that I didn't see a third of what he really was. "It wouldn't do any good."

I stared at him for a few seconds. "Don't piss me off."

He grinned. "Wouldn't dream of it. Get some sleep. You're gonna need it."

Without another word, I left Eli, brushed my teeth, pulled my hair into a high ponytail, and climbed into bed. In the dark I lay there, my eyes fixed on the beam of light from a streetlamp on River Street streaming in through the French doors of the balcony. Despite how exhausted I was, I knew I'd not find sleep very fast; there were things my brain refused to accept with such little explanation, and vampires were one of them. That one was parked in my living room watching *NCIS* was inconceivable. Yet . . . it was true. I believed it. Without having seen any proof other than, well, Gilles' face totally contorting into something out of a friggin' nightmare, his children and wife moving so fast that my eyes couldn't follow, and Eli's impossible strength.

Okay, I take it back. I guess all that was proof enough. It was weird, and for me to think that was *something*. I'd spent the last seven years under the influence of dark African magic; weird and unusual weren't strangers to me. But when something like this happened—like what happened with Seth—hit so close to home, its in-your-face reality. My brother was—God, I hated to even think about what he might be doing this very minute, what he was going through—and I couldn't help but wonder if he even *knew* he was going through it. Tears welled in my eyes when I thought about the last time we spoke, saw each other—minus the incident in my bedroom. He'd been so cold and disjointed, so . . . *not Seth*. Yeah, Preacher might slap old newsprint all over his walls to keep the *wudus* busy, but he was an herbalist and conjurer, first and foremost. He'd brought me to the Dupré House because it'd been a last resort. He and Estelle had never forced their beliefs on Seth and me; they'd simply offered explanation and left it up to us to do the believing or disbelieving. And you can bet your sweet ass I now believed it *all*. In three weeks, my little brother could turn into a vicious killer.

I wasn't going let that happen.

With an exasperated sigh, I turned onto my side, punched the pillow, and tried to settle down. Somewhere below, in the street, two loudmouths were laughing it up and talking trash—one of the drawbacks of living on River Street, I supposed. Rolling out of bed, I moved to the dresser, grabbed my iPod, and jumped back into bed. I popped in my earbuds and ran through the selections until I found 30 Seconds to Mars. Maybe their music would help drown out not only the drunks on the river walk shouting perverted names at each other, but my constant, nonstop thoughts of what exactly was happening. Although I fought it, I finally drifted off, and a restless sleep claimed me.

Sometime during the night I woke from what would be the first of many dreams. In the dream I was *waking* from a dream. But my room wasn't my room; my apartment wasn't my apartment. *I was somewhere completely different and unfamiliar, and I immediately knew it was a place where I was definitely not welcome, a total stranger. As if I inhabited some weird apocalyptic world, I lived in a derelict warehouse with rats, flaking paint, and broken windows, and when I looked outside, everything was gray, bleak, and lifeless—except for me. Then I saw them—vampires—and at first they were on the street below, maybe eight or ten of them; young, raggedy punks. In the next second, they'd leapt onto my balcony, and I stumbled back, then started to run. All through the ware-*

*house I tried to escape, but they were all around me, leap-
ing from the rafters overhead, toying with me, laughing;
I knew then I'd never outrun them, so I turned to fight. I
was surprised to find a small silver blade strapped to my
thigh; it hadn't been there before. Against a wall I turned,
drew my weapon, and aimed. One flew toward me, face
contorted into monstrous bloodlust and hatred, jaw hy-
perextended. It was Seth. My fingers froze on my weapon.
I couldn't do it. Then the others joined him as they descended upon me, merciless and horrific, and I screamed
my brother's name so hard the lining in my throat was
scorched.*

In the next second, a pair of iron hands shook me
out of my nightmare, and when I came to my senses,
Eli Dupré's face was the first thing I recognized. In the
shadows of my room his eyes were angry, illuminated; at
least I thought they were. He sat on my bed, facing me.
Everything was confusing to me now, and for the second
time in my adult life I felt helpless and out of control. "I
can't stop shaking," I muttered, and was—freakishly so.
I was now sitting up, Eli's hands still grasping my shoulders, and I wrapped my arms tightly around my legs and
pushed my forehead to my knees.

"Breathe, Riley," Eli said, a bit rough, then crooned
in French, and it totally changed his voice. *"Calme-toi."*
I was clueless to the meaning, and swear to God, I didn't
care. The sound soothed me, and within seconds, the
shaking stopped. His hands stayed on me. I wanted them
there.

"I hate this," I said quietly.

With a grip only slightly less ironlike than the one
on my shoulder, Eli grasped my chin and made me look

at him. "It's not going to be easy," he said, "but you're going to have to try."

Through bleary eyes I studied him. "That dream was horrible and . . . so realistic. My brother wanted to kill me; they all did—like I was effing dinner."

"You've no idea how potent your blood is," he said, still grasping my jaw. "Just knowing it's there, masked though it may be, it is a heady temptation."

I blinked, and to be frank it was getting harder and harder to concentrate with his hand on me. "And Gilles sent you to guard me because . . . ?" I let the question hang, anxiously awaiting a decent response.

Eli laughed softly. "Because while I'm probably the most lethal of my siblings, I also have more control. And your Preacher would have no less."

I nodded, he dropped his hand, and I was completely aware of how close his body was to mine. I drew a breath and boldly met his steady gaze. "I learned a long time ago not to depend on anyone's shoulder to cry on, so all this . . . consoling is very weird for me."

Eli's eyes left mine and moved to my shoulder. Without permission, he lifted my left arm, leaned over it, and traced my dragon's lithe body from my collarbone to my index finger, inspecting it closely. My skin warmed immediately. "I think you hide behind your art," he said evenly, then set my arm down and looked at me. "Just because you curse, fight like a dude, and ink your skin"—he lifted a forefinger and traced the wing at my eye—"doesn't mean you don't need a shoulder." He rose. "Everybody needs one of those, Riley. Even . . . us." He gave a slight smile. "I think you're bullshitting. Beneath all that tough-ass exterior you really want someone to rescue you." Crossing my bedroom floor, he stopped at the door while I remained speechless. "Lucky for you I'm not exactly busy at the moment." With a final look of victory that I wanted to smack right off of him, he left the room.

The pillow I threw landed too late; it hit the wall beside the door, and his easy chuckle sounded from the living room. Frustrated, I jumped up, retrieved my pillow, and climbed back into bed. *Arrogant bastard.* "What did that mean, anyway?" I hollered into the living room. "That Frenchy stuff?"

"Quiet down, painted one."

Somehow, those four words affected me. Eli might think it, maybe fully believe it. But I'd never—*never*—admit that he was sort of right. Not completely right, but yeah—sort of. Shoving my earbuds in, I cranked up "Heads Will Roll" by the Yeah Yeah Yeahs and fell hard asleep.

When next I woke, the morning sun was beaming in through the balcony door. My very first thought was *Seth.* And no lie, my second thought was *Oh, shit—I have mouthwatering, one-of-a-kind blood.* Third thought? *I have a hell of a hangover.* Crawling from the bed, I walked into the living room and stopped short. I found Eli on the sofa, Chaz beside him with his big furry head resting in Eli's lap. Chaz saw me and didn't budge; simply wagged his hiniesca (he has no tail).

"Get any sleep?" Eli said, looking like he'd showered and changed—two things I didn't think a vampire would even bother with. He was scrubbing Chaz between the ears.

Crossing my arms over my chest, I frowned. "What did you do to my dog?"

Eli shrugged. "We're friends now."

"Right." I glanced at the clock. "Any bodies turn up this morning?"

Eli regarded me with solemn eyes. "Not yet. But they won't all turn up, Riley."

I nodded. "Gotta get next door and back in forty minutes. My first appointment is at eleven today."

I hurried from the room, hastily brushed my teeth, and pulled on a pair of black board shorts with a small skull and crossbones, a lightweight hoodie, and flip-flops, and walked to the door. I patted my thigh. "Come on, boy. Wanna go out?"

Chaz glanced up at Eli, as if asking permission. Eli inclined his head. "You heard her. Let's go."

My traitorous dog leapt from the sofa, barking. I glared at Eli as we headed downstairs. After a super-quick walk, I put Chaz back inside, fed him, and we hurried over to Preacher's. The moment we walked in, Estelle's greeting shocked me.

"Oh, dere's my boy!" she said, completely ignoring me and rushing to Eli's side. She wrapped her arms around him and hugged tightly. He hugged her back. "Where you been, boy? I been dyin' to see you." She pulled back and looked up at him. "How long's it been? Why you stay gone so long?" She shook her head and swatted him on the backside. "You shoulda come home a long time ago, Eligius Dupré."

I watched their odd, affectionate exchange in fascination for a few moments. Eli had been gone? And all this

time, he'd been close to Preacher and Estelle? Weird
how I'd never noticed. I headed to the kitchen to sit with
Preacher, and he was, as faithful as ever, waiting for me
at the table, tea at the ready. We met each other's gaze as
I sat, he gave a slight nod, and I started in on my first cup
of tea. I poured it from a steaming pot into a mug and
stared at Preacher through the mist. "I look at this tea a
little different than before, Preacher man."

"You're alive because of it," he answered simply, and
I knew it to be the absolute truth.

"Why have I never met him before?" I asked, inclining my head to the first floor, where Estelle's high-
pitched voice could still be heard gushing over Eli. "Or
any of them, for that matter. I mean, it's kinda hard to
miss an entire vampiric family in Savannah, don't you
think?"

"The others you've encountered before; dey jes don't
make a habit of comin' into Da Plat Eye, right?"

The sound of Estelle's and Eli's feet coming up the
steps sounded, and Preacher looked at me. "Dat boy
dere has been gone a few years," he said, taking a bite
of bacon. "Twelve. But you have to ask him why. Dat's a
tale for him to tell."

"Well, no wonder I've never seen him around," I said.
"I was just a punk kid in juvy for the hundredth time when
he was here last." I couldn't imagine what had taken Eli
away from his family for such a long time, unless when
you're immortal, twelve years was just a flash second.
Maybe he wanted to travel the world, see new places. But
then, how'd he get his donated hoodoo-tinged blood?
That thought made an involuntary chill course through
my spine, and I wasn't positive I wanted the answer.

"You don't see dem around 'cause dey know to stay away from you," Preacher said, looking at me over his teacup. "Dat blood inside you is powerful to dem—like drugs, even wit our magic in dem. You don't go wavin' drugs in a junkie's face when dey're tryin' to get clean, dat's right."

The tea still steamed out of the spout as I poured another cup. "Why didn't you ever tell me, Preacher?"

"Didn't need to know till now."

"Does Seth have it? My mom?" I asked.

"No."

"So how'd I get it?" I asked, frustrated. Trying to pry information from Preacher's lips was like trying to crack open a stubborn oyster.

His wise eyes stared at me for several seconds. "Don't know, Riley. Could be passed from your grandmamma or granddaddy, or their grandmammas and grandaddies. No tellin'."

I sighed. "Figures."

"Oh, Preacher man, look at dis boy now, yeah? Ain't he purty?" Estelle said, shuffling Eli into the kitchen and the chair next to me. "Don't worry, girl—he won't bite you. Will you, Eligius Dupré?" she said, then laughed and handed Eli a plate of biscuits and bacon.

"No, ma'am," Eli said politely. He looked at me and lifted a brow, then jammed a piece of bacon in his mouth.

"Good—'cause dat would be bad, right," Estelle said and looked at me. "'Bout time you knew things, Riley Poe. I always kept tellin' your Preacher man, dat girl needs to know things, 'specially wit dat crazy blood inside ya, dat's right." She walked over and hugged me tightly, and I nearly spilled tea in my lap. "Don't you worry, girl. If dere's any one body who can get your brodder back safe, it's dis boy sittin' beside you." She grabbed my face with both hands and squished my cheeks together. "You can trust him, Riley Poe. And, girl, you better eat. Your backside's gettin' bony."

"I can't, Estelle. Just not hungry." My gaze slid to Eli's, then to Preacher's, and back to my surrogate grand-mother, who frowned. "Yes, ma'am," I said, repeating Eli's words. "I'll try."

She let me go. "Good. Now, eat up."

I managed a piece of toast with jam, and just as we finished, Preacher turned to both of us. "Dos boys have gone underground, and Riley here knows dos places better dan anyone. She'll take you, but only after a day or two." He looked at me. "I know you're anxious to do somethin' and you're itchin' to fight. But you gotta wait, girl. Your brodder won't long recognize you as his sister anymore, right? He might know somethin' is familiar, but not your person. If you go too early, he will know you, and dat could mess things up. You watch each odd-er's back, you and dis boy here, and don't go dere for long. Just long enough to get noticed by odders and dey let you back in. Dat's where dos boys will be—dem bad places. Easier to bring victims back to dem bad brodders if messed up wit da drugs. Right?"

I nodded. "Yes, sir, okay," I said, knowing *messed up* really meant *fucked-up*. The thought of going back un-derground, slipping back into a crowd I'd long ago left behind, made me sick. But I'd do it, and no one but me would know how it killed me to go back to the place I'd worked so hard to escape. And not just the clubs; it was rarely the clubs themselves. It was just certain crowds, and I knew Preacher meant *dos people*. And it was in those crowds that I became mixed up with the wrong guy. It'd ended way worse than just a broken heart or an overnight trip in the tank. I pushed the painful memory aside and glanced at the clock. "Oh, gotta run. Shop opens in a few." I kissed Preacher and Estelle good-bye, and we left.

"We'll spend the next day or so going over changes," Eli said as we crossed the cobbles to Inksomnia's back entrance. "There are things you'll need to know and expect. I don't want you sucker punched."

"What about you?" I asked.

"Don't worry about me."

Out of nowhere and all at once, a thought struck me, and it hit so hard I nearly gasped. I turned and looked Eli in the eye. "A young guy was found murdered a few days ago. Nineteen years old, about to leave for Parris Island. I'd inked him the day before." I knew in my heart the answer, but I asked anyway. "Did Seth and his friends do that?"

"No," he said without hesitation. "But they helped Valerian and Victorian find him, or they lured him. There are more victims, Riley. The bodies just haven't been found yet."

My stomach lurched at the thought. All I could think about was Zac, and how sweet and respectful he'd been. And so ready to join the marines. Eli watched me cautiously, and I couldn't take my gaze off him. Blue eyes stared at me beneath long, thick, dark lashes, and I noticed the faint shadowy presence of scruff on his jaw and over his top lip. Skin so blemish free and creamy, any girl would be envious of it. He hardly looked like a killer, but I knew at one time he certainly was. And now my brother was one, too. "I want you to tell me this is all going to be fixed," I said vehemently. I grabbed his forearms and shook hard, urging him to give me the answer I wanted to hear. Needed to hear. "Tell. Me."

"We'll fix it," he answered, and somehow, I believed him. There was still so much I wanted to know about him, and so many questions that plagued me. Hopefully, tonight I'd learn more.

Leaving Eli in the living room with Chaz, I hurried through a shower, dried my hair, pulled my red-streaked bangs into small clips, and let the rest hang down my back. Worn, distressed jeans with a brown leather vest that left my tattooed arms exposed finished my wardrobe for the day, along with a pair of brown, slouched, heeled leather boots. I grabbed a wine red velvet choker from my dresser, tied it around my neck, and left the room, where I pulled up short and froze. Phin, Luc, and Josie Dupré had joined their brother in the living room, and now all four regarded me. "What's up?" I asked, walked to the fridge to grab a Yoo-hoo, and gasped the moment I opened the door. The whole top shelf of my refrigerator was lined with small, plastic, yellow bags, and I knew without asking what they were. I wasn't squeamish or anything, but . . . *damn*—that was just messed up. I grabbed my drink and quickly closed the door.

I can't express how it felt to know that four vampires sat casually in my living room, taking turns petting my dog and watching TV. It was just . . . freaky. And I'm not sure my brain would ever fully wrap around the entirety of it.

"Morning," Luc and Phin said, almost at the same time.

"Your tats are sick," said Josie, staring at my inked arms. She looked at Eli. "Can I get one?"

"Later, Josie," said Eli, and gave me a casual glance. "You intrigue them."

I really wasn't sure what exactly intrigued them. The unique aged claret running through my veins? "Great. Okay, well . . . I've got a client in fifteen, so I have to go. You guys can help yourself to whatever." I really didn't have anything a vampire would want, I suppose—except my blood—but I didn't know what else to offer.

"Thanks," Phin said with a grin. "But we just stopped by to bring Eli his . . . breakfast." He grinned. "We'll take you up on that later, though."

"Can't I stay with you?" Josie asked Eli, and shot me a quick glance. "I want to watch her."

"Not today, squirt," said Eli. They seemed so normal, just like other brothers and sisters, that it seemed weird to think of them as vampires. I supposed no matter what, they were still siblings. "But maybe another day. And you'll have to ask Riley." He inclined his head toward me. "She's the boss."

Josie looked at me with wide blue eyes. "Could I?" she asked. "Please? I won't get in the way, I swear." She nearly squirmed where she stood, dressed in a Go-Go's T-shirt, skinny jeans, and high-tops.

I shrugged. "Yeah, sure." I smiled. "Cool shirt."

Josie beamed. "Cool band."

"Damn straight," I agreed. "Okay, I seriously have to go now."

Luc looked at me and smiled. *"La paix hors."*

In the next breath, they were gone, and I literally heard Josie giggle just as the downstairs door closed. I would *never* get used to that. Eli stood, watching me, amused. "He said, 'Peace out.'"

"Oh," I responded. "Okay, come on." Running against the clock, I hurried downstairs, Eli and Chaz on my heels. At the bottom of the steps I turned, and Eli stood on the step above me, not quite a foot away.

"Look," I said, grasping the wooden handrail and looking up at him. "You're about to meet one of my favorite people in the entire world. She's very buoyant, optimistic, and sweet—and she's my best friend. She's already freaked about Seth, so don't make it worse by staring at her all day, okay?"

Eli's smile was subtle but effective. "Why do you think I'd stare?" he asked.

"Because you stare at me constantly," I answered.

He drew closer. "Are you freaked-out?"

I fought the ever-growing urge to touch him and instead glared at him. "No."

Again, he smiled. "Good. So what are we going to tell her?"

I cocked my head and stared, keeping my voice down. "A big fat freaking lie, that's what." I poked his chest. "I can't tell her about . . . your heritage. *I* believe because your father proved it to me—in my mind it's indisputable. Hard to grasp, but I can handle it. I'm not sure if Nyx would be able to. For now you're just an apprentice hanging out for a little experience. That's it. No connection to what she witnessed with my brother. He's gone to rehab on Da Island. Got it?"

"Understood," Eli said, then, with his forefinger,

grazed my angel wing. "You look"—his gaze raked over me with appreciation—"amazing."

Why that compliment affected me, I haven't a clue. But it left me a little breathless, a little shaky, and, strangely enough, wanting a lot more. "Thanks," I answered, and tried to seem like it was no big thing, but Eli's smile proved he knew otherwise. I rolled my eyes, turned around, then stopped again. I regarded him. "You're not going to be tempted by Nyx, are you? Because if you hurt one little hair on her head—"

"She's safe," Eli interrupted. "I've got Gullah blood in me, too, don't forget."

"One more thing," I added. "Nyx is a hugger. She hugs me every time she sees me. She will hug you. It's what she does. So just . . . deal with it."

Eli's blue eyes gleamed. "Yes, ma'am."

The moment I opened the door, Nyx, just flipping the OPEN sign in the storefront, turned. In total Nyx fashion, her huge blue eyes lined with heavy black liner widened. "Riley! Oh my gosh, I've been so worried! How's Seth?" she asked, hurrying across the room and launching herself at me. I hugged her back as tightly as she hugged me; then she pulled back and studied me, seeking answers. "Is he going to be okay? Have you heard from him today?"

Just her concerned questions made my heart sink; knowing the truth of what was happening to my brother, and keeping it from Nyx, *hurt*. It hurt like freaking hell.

"No, I won't be talking to him for a while," I said, not exactly lying. I *hated* lying, especially to my best friend. But in this circumstance I had no choice. She didn't need to know how much danger my brother was in, and she'd never understand the truth. "Not while he's in detox."

Tears came to Nyx's eyes. "Oh, Riley," she said, and gave me another hug. Nyx was a big hugger, and I was so not—except with her and Preacher and Estelle. And Seth. "Everything's going to be fine; I just know it. Don't—oh, hello," she said, and pulled back.

I glanced at Eli, who'd been standing in the foyer, waiting for an introduction. "Oh, Nyx, this is Eli. He's apprenticing and is going to be with us for a while." I shrugged. "Sort of a last-minute thing."

Nyx's bright red lips widened into a welcoming smile only Nyxinnia could give. She immediately hugged Eli. "Hi, Eli! Welcome to Inksomnia! You're going to love it here. Riley is the best artist you'll ever work with."

Eli chuckled and hugged Nyx back. "So I've heard," he said, and gave me a quick, amused glance over her shoulder, then pulled back and looked at her. "Nice to meet you. Riley says great things about you."

Nyx grinned and looked at me. "Oh, she has? She's so sweet!" Then she mouthed the word *hot*, and although I didn't hear Eli make a sound, I could just tell he'd seen it. "Well, come take a look around." She turned and headed toward the front of the shop. As always, she wore her hair in two high ponytails, and today she wore her favorite spiked collar. She grinned at him. "I'll show you how we set up. First, we rock the house. I can't work without music. How 'bout a little Metric?"

With a grin, Eli followed, and I gave him over to Nyx while I prepared for my first client and printed out the transfer I'd created for her. She showed right at eleven, and after a brief chat about the design—a pair of barbed dark wings, one on each shoulder blade—I set to work. The design itself included intricate scrolled detailing and color on the wingtips, so I knew it'd take me a handful of hours to complete. Which was fine. I needed something to take my mind off my brother, and off the vampire who was learning how to set up the Widow with my best friend. Metric's "Sick Muse" thumped overhead, and it pulled me right into the zone.

The early afternoon went by without a hitch, and around one thirty I sent Eli on some errands for a couple of hours. I didn't tell Nyx that his errand included going upstairs, sucking blood from a bag in my fridge like it was a Capri Sun, and sacking out on my bed, but I knew he needed it. He'd watched me work on the dark wings for nearly two hours, completely intrigued—or so it seemed. Nyx had enthusiastically talked Eli through every step of the dragonfly she'd inked on a girl's lower back, and more than once I looked over at his dark head bent close to Nyx's work. Finally, he went upstairs. I never checked on him; I figured he'd been doing his thing for nearly two centuries and didn't need my help. True to his word, after a couple of hours he returned to the shop, looking refreshed and ready to go. Good thing the Arcoses were out cold until the sun dropped.

The rest of the afternoon flew by; I'd done two wicked armbands, one of which was a bike chain, which I thought was pretty cool, and was finishing up a screaming phoenix on a marine's rib cage when the shop phone rang. Nyx answered.

"Hey, Riley, it's for you," she said.

"Okay, could you tell them to hold just a sec?" I asked. Inking the side of a marine's solid six-pack was challenging—lots of hard ridges to work over—and I leaned close, wiped, and inspected my work. The marine, lying on his side with his arm above his head, glanced at me and grinned. "How does it look?"

I gave a nod. "Freaking awesome. I'll be right back." I peeled off my gloves and went to the front desk to answer the phone. "Inksomnia. This is Riley."

"I'm . . . sorry to bother you, Ms. Poe," said a distraught female voice. "This is Karen Parker—Riggs Parker's mom." She paused. "Have you seen him? He was supposed to be staying with Todd Sawyer, and, well . . . I just can't find him. It's been a few days." She paused. "He usually checks in."

"Mrs. Parker, hi," I said. My insides froze over, and I stilled. My eyes immediately sought out Eli's, and I found he was already watching me. He moved instantly toward me, and I covered the mouthpiece and spoke softly. "It's Mrs. Parker—Seth's friend's mother. He was with Seth that night."

"Give me the phone," he said quietly, and I did. In a voice so faint I could barely detect it, Eli spoke to Mrs. Parker in French. I have no idea what he said. Then he hung up. As he moved away, he leaned close to my ear. "I eased her mind. She'll be okay for now."

I looked at him and fully understood, although I had no idea how Eli did it. I didn't care at this point, as long as he *did*. I knew Riggs was with Seth, and as much of a peckerhead as he'd been before, I wanted him safely returned back to normal, back to his mother and deserving a good ass kicking. God, I knew without hearing the angst in her voice that she was going through hell. "Thanks," I told Eli, and went back to the marine who was waiting for me. In less than twenty minutes I was finished, screaming phoenix complete and looking pretty sick, if I did say so myself. He proudly examined his new ink, the skin around the design flaming red. I gave him a sample tube of medicated ointment and tat instructions, and he left.

Nyx finished early, and she finally confessed to having a blind date. Eli helped her clean up, and as I watched my alternatively dressed best friend pick up her station with a vampire, I knew my world was unlike anyone else's. Nyx gathered her big black shoulder bag with pink skull and crossbones, gave me a hug, gave Eli a hug, and said good-bye. The only reason I wasn't apprehensive about Nyx walking the streets alone after dark now was because I knew one of the Duprés had her back. I felt somewhat guilty for keeping it all from her, but it had to be the best choice. It wouldn't do any good to have Nyx worried about things out of our control, and she loved Seth like a brother. I watched her through the storefront window until she disappeared down the cobbled street and into the dusky light, auburn ponytails swinging with each step.

"She's a good person," Eli said, suddenly at my side. "She has a good soul."

I nodded. "She does." Out of the corner of my eye, I looked at him, and memories of the night before, when he'd crowded me on the balcony, his hard body pressed against mine, flashed to the front of my mind. I tried to decide just how unsafe Eligius Dupré actually was, and I couldn't. Part of me was terrified of him. The other part of me wanted to fuck him until he passed out. Or I passed out.

Eli chuckled.

And then, nearly twenty-four hours later, it hit me.

I frowned and turned to fully face him. "Can all of you read minds?" I asked, and watched his reaction warily.

A smug, nonchalant expression crossed his perfect features, and he shrugged. "Yeah, sure. And we can co-erce, too." He rubbed his chin. "I'm not sure yet which is more to my advantage." He lifted a dark brow and stared. "Right now I'm thinking mind reading."

"Ground rule number three: Stay out of my head," I said, and felt only vaguely mortified at my pornographic thoughts of him.

Eli simply smirked. "Whatever." He shoved a hand through his bangs and swept them to the side, then shoved his hands into the pockets of his jeans. "Tomorrow night we begin." He regarded me. "Are you ready?"

Turning toward him, I boldly inspected him, from booted feet to the top of his head. I shook my own head and walked off to tidy up my station and start a list of needed supplies.

"What?" he asked, dismayed.

"I'm not going anywhere with you"—I turned and pointed at him—"looking like that."

Eli glanced down at himself. "What do you mean? What's wrong with the way I look?"

With a critical eye, I studied him. "Do you know where we're going to search for my brother? They're the types of places where a pretty boy who looks like he just stepped off the pages of *GQ* or . . . *Men's Health* or something sticks out like a sore thumb. You'd look wicked ridiculous and draw unwanted attention. You've got to blend, dude."

A slow grin played across his face. "So you think I'm hot? *GQ* hot?"

I ignored his arrogant, blunt question, locked the front door, and set the alarm system. "Come on," I said, moving past him.

He was at the back door ahead of me, and I stopped short. All I could do was try not to look as surprised as I was.

"Where are we going?" he asked, leaning against the frame and blocking the door.

"Walgreens. A friend's house. Liquor Warehouse. Mellow Mushroom. In that order," I answered.

Eli laughed a totally guy laugh and regarded me. "Okay, I won't ask. Let's go."

After quickly letting Chaz out, we locked up, jumped in the Jeep, and headed first up Bay Street, then hit Abercorn. The usual after-dark traffic crept along until we passed the intersection at Victory Drive; then the pace quickened as we moved along the oak-lined streets. The heavy brine and warm, sultry air rushed over us as we drove, and I knew he watched me—could feel his gaze on every inch of my body as we passed beneath each streetlamp. At the next red light I hit the clutch, downshifted into second, then first gear, and came to a stop. I looked over at him, and shadows played over his sharp jaw, cheekbones, Adam's apple. I noticed he had absolutely perfect lips, and the way his eyes studied me with such intensity made a thrill shoot through my insides. He was the kind of guy who would have never given me the time of day in high school, but I didn't care. We sat, staring wordlessly at each other beneath the streetlights and with cars all around us, and I knew then, at that very moment, that we'd have mind-blowing sex in the near— very near—future. It was inevitable, and I felt it clear to my bones. The tension between us was palpable, and I couldn't help but wonder just how much vampiric control he'd be able to maintain. Would he lose it and kill me? At the time would I even care? The light must have turned green, because the driver of the truck behind us blew its horn, and I jumped. Eli grinned; I frowned, although it really wasn't a sincere frown, and I shifted into first and eased off the clutch. Soon we were crossing DeRenne, and Eli glanced to his right as we passed the big globe.

"You know," he said, "my brothers and I had a pissing contest off the globe once. It was new back then, too, and Papa was furious at us." He laughed again. "We liked to think we took a leak from the top of the world."

I glanced in my rearview mirror and changed lanes, then gave him a quick, bewildered look. "Vampires *pee*?"

"Only if we drink a lot of beer," he said with a grin, the wind blowing his hair all about and making him look more like a carefree young guy than an aged vampire. Why I constantly questioned myself about that, I don't know, but I did.

As I made the long drive down Abercorn, I pushed my hair from my face and glanced at Eli. "Preacher said you've been gone for twelve years. Why?"

The muscle in Eli's jaw flinched, and he stared straight ahead. "That's none of your business."

Anger pushed me. "You're supposed to be guarding me, right? A vampire capable of killing me, staying in my house while I sleep. I have a right to know."

"No, you don't."

I looked at him, but before I could say a word, his face grew alarmingly still. "Drop it, Riley."

I did, for the time being. After several stoplights, we pulled into Walgreens and parked. Releasing my seat belt, I hopped out, and Eli did the same. I didn't say a word as I entered the store and turned down the aisle lined with hair color, grabbed a box of L'Oréal black, and checked out. Eli looked only vaguely puzzled; I'd asked him to stay out of my head, but I couldn't decide whether that was something he could voluntarily do, so he may have known my plan. If I had the power to scope people's thoughts, I'm not positive I could turn it off. So much temptation. So little time.

On to our next destination. I pulled into the drive of a single-story Savannah brick home just off Largo—quite deceiving on the outside, since the interior was decorated in a unique decay look. I yanked the emergency brake, put the Jeep into first, and looked at my passenger's questioning gaze. I was still pissed so was short on formalities. "Mullet Morrison's house. I went to high school with him. He's cool," I said. "And one badass tailor. He designs and sells one-of-a-kind Goth and urban wear online and makes a freaking killing at it. Calls it Gnaw Bone Brand. Come on."

At the door, Mullet welcomed me as he always did: enthusiastically. Despite his name, he wore a totally shaved head, a goatee, baggy shorts, a ripped camouflage shirt, and combat boots—his usual attire. He was a prince.

"Whoa, man—my favorite hot inked chick," Mullet said, and glanced at Eli briefly. "Wassup, cuz?" he asked me, and bumped my fist. "Welcome to the kingdom of Gnaw Bone." He regarded Eli. "What can I do you for?"

"We're looking for some decent stuff," I said, and inclined my head at Eli. "For him."

"Excellent, excellent," Mullet said. "No offense, dude, but you could use a little darkness. Black? Ripped? Junkie?"

"Yeah, on all three accounts," I answered. I gave Eli a short glance; then we followed Mullet inside. "Oh my God, Mullet—how many more times can you watch *Jackass*?" I said, glancing at his monstrous flat screen on the wall.

Mullet laughed. "Never enough *Jackass*, I always say." He glanced at Eli. "This way, dude." He looked at me. "Been to the Panic Room lately?"

"Nah, not in a while. Busy at work. Thinkin' about going, though," I replied, and he gave me a nod.

"Sweet," he said. "Maybe I'll see you there."

We didn't spend much time at Mullet's—didn't have to. Mullet had an entire showroom full of clothes on racks, and boots that he bought wholesale. There was so much to choose from that we had no problem picking out appropriate gear for Eli. He was silent through most of it, and I'm positive he thought I'd lost my mind. Two pairs of postapocalyptic urban pants, a black pair of junkie-fit jeans with side laces, two long-sleeved decayed shirts, a gray ripped shirt, and a pair of buckled black combat boots later, we left. I'd also picked out a two-inch leather finger band with a sterling-silver skull in the center. Wicked cool.

I called Mellow Mushroom on the way and ordered a sausage, pepperoni, and mushroom with extra cheese, stopped off at Liquor Warehouse and grabbed a six-pack of Yuengling Lager, then picked up the pizza. Finally, we made it back to Inksomnia. Upstairs, we dumped every-thing onto the kitchen table, and I turned to Eli. "Ready for a makeover?"

He shrugged. "You're the boss."

As I gathered a few things from the bathroom—comb, scissors, towels—I noticed more than ever how cramped I felt in the same apartment with Eligius Dupré. I tried to ignore it, tried to ignore him as he watched me with such scrutiny. Quickly, I changed into a pair of low-rise cutoffs and an old black cotton cami, scrolled through the iPod home unit and chose Chevelle, pulled a stool from the bar into the kitchen, and inclined my head to it.

"Sit," I said.

He did so wordlessly.

"Lose the shirt," I commanded, "unless you want it stained."

Without a sound he grasped the collar behind his neck and yanked the white tee over his head, leaving a perfectly cut chest and sculpted abs bare and flawless. Quick reflexes always served me well, and I dropped the towel in his lap. "Over the shoulders," I said, and with an arrogant chuckle he did as I'd asked. I began his dark transformation.

With Chevelle's "Don't Fake This" thumping through the apartment, I settled into my task. Coloring Eli's hair proved to be an erotic experience. His breath brushed the bare skin of my exposed stomach as I lifted my arms to apply the dye, and gooseflesh followed. I was sure he'd noticed, and positive he knew it had affected me. His hair was slick and wet and fell through my fingers as I applied the color, and as I moved around him I noticed how his hand rested casually on his crotch, and how my thigh brushed against his, or how I leaned into him to reach a certain spot. Yeah, I did it on purpose. Swear to God, I couldn't help it. He was a total turn-on; my mind and body hummed with sensations, and I knew I played with fire. *Knew it*, and still did it.

While we waited for the color to set, I grabbed us each a Yuengling, handed Eli one, grabbed us each a slice of pizza, then hopped onto the counter in front of him. With black dye all over his head, I regarded him as I sipped the beer. Silently, he watched me as he swallowed, his eyes moving over my body. Neither of us said anything for several moments, and that may have been even more erotic than the coloring.

"Why don't you have a man?" he asked, blue eyes gauging my response as he bit the pizza in half. I watched his teeth flash and wondered what else they'd sunk into in times past.

Mood killer. I immediately had my guard up now. "If I need one, I find one," I said, taking a bite, chewing, and chasing it with another sip.

"A permanent one," he restated. I'd already known what he meant. I just wanted to provoke him.

I sat the bottle and pizza on the counter beside me and wiped my mouth with a knuckle. I lifted the hem of my cami to expose my ribs, and touched a jagged, three-inch-long scar midway up my side. "Reason number one," I said, and Eli's eyes followed my finger. Before I knew it, his hand shot out and, grasping my side, he used his thumb to trace the old wound. "What happened?" he asked, his voice odd, almost . . . strained. He dropped his hand.

I shrugged. "Thought I was in love with a psychopath," I answered. "That was my first warning never to leave him." I met Eli's hard stare. "I should've listened then."

"Why?"

Although it was an old memory, it was still as painful as hell, and my throat burned at the thought of it. I trained my eyes on his. "Because the second warning came when I found my mother strangled and drowned in her own bathtub," I said, and shook my head, painful visions filling my mind. "My mom warned me about him and tried her best to get me to break up with him. I never dreamed he'd do . . . what he did to her." I looked at Eli, who remained stonily silent. "I was seventeen and was one messed-up kid. Seth was only seven." I drew in a long breath. "My mother worked for Preacher and Estelle, and they'd been left by her as guardians for Seth and me. I'd always wondered if she knew her life was in danger; she'd made sure we'd never be separated or put in foster care." I drained the rest of the bottle and tossed it in the recycle bin. "I'd given her hell—a total fuckup and into just about everything a teenager could get into. Smoked like a freight train, toked a little Mary Jane, drank, drugs, runaway, sex—you name it." I studied Eli hard. "I was changed after that night, though. Seeing my mother like that?" I shook my head. "Something in me snapped. Preacher saved my life, put me through detox on Da Island, the Gullah way. Then I went to college and started raising Seth here. I owe Preacher and his family everything." When I swung back around, his gaze still remained dead on me. "You know?"

"Yeah," he answered quietly. "I do know."

I gave an understanding nod. I supposed he did know.

The Gullah had helped Eli and his family, too—in a huge way. Had molded them into something completely different from what their destiny had tried to determine. I ate the rest of my pizza and had another slice, Eli had three, and by then the timer on the oven buzzed. "Well," I said, not really knowing what else to say. "Time to rinse." I beckoned Eli to the sink and turned the water on warm.

With his hair on end and now totally black, he moved to the sink and bent over, resting his forearms on the counter. Moving over him, I rinsed his hair with the spray gun, moving my fingers through its wet silkiness, my breasts brushing his shoulders, until finally, the water ran clear. I applied the conditioner and rinsed again. My skin flushed hot just standing close to him. Part of me hated my easy reaction to his raw sexuality; part of me wondered whether the underlying threat of arcane danger was what turned me on. If so, I was indeed a freak to the nth degree. One thing was indisputable: I was incredibly, undeniably drawn to him. And he knew it.

I struggled to sound calm and collected. "Okay," I said, running my hands through his hair and squeezing out the excess water. Grabbing the towel that was half draped over his shoulders, I pulled it onto his head and scrubbed. "Done. Let's have a look."

Eli straightened, grabbed onto the towel, and dried his hair, and I couldn't help watching the muscles move and flex with the motion; creamy smooth skin stretched taut over the hard ridges of his stomach and chest; his biceps bunched into rocks, shoulders broad. Long veins snaked up his arms, and wide hands moved over his head in a careless, guy manner. When he dropped the towel and looked at me, we were standing too close; I knew it and did nothing about it. Eli's new black hair hung in wet, shaggy strands over blue eyes that grew dark and dangerous as he looked down at me, and I couldn't move. He leaned a hip on the counter, braced his weight with an arm behind me, and leaned close. My heart began to race erratically, and I moved a bit closer. I felt like I'd been placed under a spell, knowing in the back of my head that what I did was a bad move but unable to help myself at the same time.

"You play a dangerous game, Riley Poe," he said with steely restraint, and his gaze dropped to my exposed cleavage, then rose to my mouth, where it froze. A muscle flinched in his jaw. "I suppose I'm part to blame." He looked at me and moved closer, his mouth at my ear, his voice even, low. "Ever since I heard you say you wanted to fuck me, I haven't been able to shake you." Eli moved his entire body in front of mine, all bare chest and ripped abs trapping me against the counter, his arms now locked on either side of me. With ease, he grasped my hair behind me and pulled with just enough pressure to force my face upward to meet his gaze, then held it there. He inhaled deeply, his face inches from mine. "I sensed it the first day I saw you through the window, and it's grown stronger with each encounter." He searched my eyes, his voice lethally quiet. "Do you want to know why I've been gone for twelve years, Riley?"

I could barely breathe, much less talk. Never had I been held under such a tight restraint as Eli's penetrating gaze. "Yes," I finally said, forcing my voice to be strong and wondering why the hell he was torturing me. He was so close that his warm breath brushed my neck, my chest, making me thrilled and shivery at the same time.

"Because I lost control," he warned, emphasizing each word as a low, painful growl, his breathing becoming more ragged. I could feel the air snap between us with a mixture of sexual tension and tightly reigned rage as he struggled. "So stop twitching your tight little ass in front of me," he said, and let his gaze drop to my breasts once more. His stare lifted and bored into me. "You're a greater temptation to me than your mortal mind could possibly grasp." He let my hair go. "And I don't know if I'd be able to stop with you." He pushed off the counter but kept his eyes trained on mine. "There's too much at stake here to risk that."

My heart was beating so hard and fast, it hurt; my breathing burned my lungs. Inside, I shook, and all I could make myself do was stare at him like some fucking mute and move past him. Rejection in any form sucked; rejection tinged with fear sucked even more, and I wanted to escape the living room, escape Eli's scrutiny. So twisted inside that I could hear my own heartbeat, feel it beneath the thin cotton of my cami, I hurried to my bedroom. I'd escape the mortification of the moment now; in the morning I'd be cool; his transformation could continue. I still needed to do something to his hair, and I didn't exactly trust myself with a pair of scissors right now.

I felt his eyes on me as I disappeared up the hall, but even though rooms separated us, I could feel him still on me, his voice inside me, his breath brushing my skin, and I wanted to scream until it vanished. I wanted it all to go away—the Arcoses, the Duprés, everything.

The moment I stepped into my bedroom, I knew

nothing would *ever* be the same again. I stumbled to an abrupt halt as I laid eyes on my brother, standing at the now-open double doors of my balcony. Reaction to action took over, and I moved toward him. "Seth!" I said, my voice cracked and jagged with holes, emotion.

The look in my brother's eyes froze mc; they were feral, frigid, vacant, and terrifying at once. He looked like himself, yet didn't; he looked . . . *starved*. Before I could move or say another word, a gust of air blew past me, and Seth lunged viciously toward me, out of control and as fast as lightning. I hadn't even seen Eli move, but he now had Seth by the throat in a tight grasp, hanging him over the balcony's edge.

My scream reverberated off the centuries-old bricks of my bedroom.

Part 6

UNDERGROUND

Seeing my brother's body writhing in a frenzy to escape Eli's grip—in an attempt to get at me—ripped my heart out and terrified me at the same time. It also kicked in my adrenaline, and I reacted. As scared as I was, I hurled myself at Eli and grabbed his arm. "Don't hurt him!" I yelled, and pulled hard. "Eli, *stop it*!"

As if in slow motion, Eli turned toward me, and his beautiful face had grossly distorted into the same elongated, unhinged-jaw, fanged creature Gilles had turned into—only more frightening. I physically flinched, my insides turned frigid, and I froze at the shock of seeing Eli transform, but something snapped inside of me, and I didn't release his arm. All-white eyes with tiny pupils bored into me, almost challenging me, maybe even a little ashamed. And it was in that very instant that everything became crystal clear. If Seth and I survived, our lives would never, *ever* be the same.

Over Eli's shoulder, I glimpsed my brother. Seth

didn't seem to care that a vampire had him by the throat; all he wanted was to get at me, and my unique blood, which now tempted him. Seth's eyes were wild and hungry, and while his face wasn't contorted, he clawed and kicked the air as he struggled against Eli's hold. Deep in his throat, Seth made a noise that . . . didn't even sound human. Definitely not Seth. I can only explain it as desperate. If I hadn't known better, I would have thought he was on drugs, and trust me—I knew the look all too well; his long, choppy bangs were sweaty, his skin pasty, his eyes rabid. If only it *were* drugs.

"Are you sure you want me to let him go?" Eli asked, and his voice, too, was somehow different. Darker. Edgier. Seth growled and struggled harder.

"No," I answered angrily, and I hated saying that word more than anything. I knew it wasn't Eli's fault that Seth was in transition, but I blamed him all the same, and he obviously read my mind, because he narrowed his eyes. "Leave us."

I stared first at Eli, then at Seth, and my heart ached to hold him, smack the hell out of him, and shake his lanky adolescent body until he snapped out of it. But I knew that wouldn't happen, and no amount of shaking would change anything. It killed me to obey Eli, but I did. "Don't hurt him," I stated, and stared hard at Eli. He didn't agree or even acknowledge my request, but I knew by the way he looked at me that he'd not hurt my brother. I turned and headed for the door, and just that fast, a gust of briny air brushed the side of my face. When I looked over my shoulder, they were both gone. Uncertainty and an agonizing pain I couldn't define washed over me and sucked every ounce of energy from my body, and my knees collapsed. I sat down right there on the floor. I wanted to run to the window, to see where Eli and Seth had gone, *how* they'd gone; I couldn't. My insides were locked, and an inescapable feeling of helplessness overcame me. Then, the tears. The goddamn tears. I hated them, hated the weakness they represented, and hadn't allowed myself the luxury of them since the day I found my mother dead in a bathtub. By the time we'd had her funeral, I was angry and the tears had dried, and I hadn't shed one more tear until last night. *Fuck it.* Pulling my knees up to my chest, I locked my arms tightly around them, put my head down, and cried.

How much time lapsed, I couldn't say; I must have seriously been in a haze, because when next I was conscious of my surroundings, I was in my bed. I could come up with no conclusion other than that Eli had put me there, because I didn't remember crossing the floor and climbing beneath the covers myself. The lights were out, the room shadowy, and my mind was fuzzy with cobwebs. Pushing up on my elbows, I looked around, noted the familiar stream of light coming through the French doors, and remembered everything I wished to hell wasn't really happening. I sat up and rubbed my swollen eyes.

"Go back to sleep, Riley." Eli's steady voice came from a dark corner of the room. "It's early."

"I think you've confused me with someone you can boss around," I answered, just as steady. "Seth?"

There was a long pause, and my heart leapt. But then Eli answered. "Safe for now."

My body eased at his words, and I shoved my fingers

through my hair and searched the darkness. "Why are you hiding?" I asked.

In the time it took me to blink, he was standing over me. The light from the French doors morphed his figure into a silhouette, his face nothing more than a black cutout. "It's called sentry, smart-ass. I'm watching over you."

Carefully, I regarded his dark profile. "Thanks for not hurting my brother," I said, and managed to say it with some sense of strength.

Again, another pause, this one longer than the last. "Had he hurt you, he wouldn't have been so lucky."

My insides shook at Eli's words. I knew he was dead serious, and while it pissed me off, it intrigued me as well, and I couldn't help asking, "Why?"

"It doesn't matter," he said flatly, and I knew then he'd never tell me his reasons. "Now, go to sleep." Still, he stood above me, next to the bed.

I sat there for a while, rebellious and determined that Eli Dupré's self-prescribed supremacy over me would not get the better of me. Why the hell did he want me to go to sleep so badly? Apparently, I sat there too long. With my next breath he'd pushed me flat back onto my pillow, his arms braced on either side of my head. Although he wasn't as hot-blooded as I was, the electricity remained, and my whole body tightened at his closeness and the tension it caused. You could feel it in what little air there was between us.

"Aren't you afraid of me?" he asked with a steely, almost angry voice.

"No," I said just as steely. "I'm not."

He moved his mouth close to my ear, and the sensation of his breath brushing my neck made me shiver. "You really should be," he said, and although he meant it as a warning, it turned me on instead. Releasing one of his hands, he moved it to my chest, and with a forefinger grazed the exposed flesh above my heart. "I can hear your heart beating a mile away," he said, his voice raspy, thick. He laid his palm flat against my chest, his fingers brushing the swell of my breast. "When it pounds harder, or faster, I can feel it inside me. It's like you're fucking everywhere—inside my head, my body"—his hand remained against me, heavy, erotic—"and it's really starting to piss me off." With a sudden jerk he pushed off of me, the impact causing the air in my lungs to *whoosh* out as if the breath had been knocked out of me. I gasped, staring after him until his silhouette had retreated into the shadowy recesses he'd emerged from. We were both silent for several moments; I couldn't even tell how much time had lapsed. I was shocked and still reeling from his intimate touch, alluring admission, and harsh action.

"The body you saw, behind the alley? His throat and chest were ripped open because a *strigoi* vampire desires blood directly from the heart. So be afraid of me, Riley," he said quietly from the darkness. "It will keep us both alive."

I sat up, breathless, and became so conscious of my heavy breathing and thumping heartbeat that I tried to force both to slow. I'd never been known for my shyness, or the ability to keep quiet, so I drew a few more calming breaths, then spoke. "I don't scare easy," I said, and I heard Eli snort—or something. "But why both of us?"

Eli groaned, frustration thick in his voice. "Because if I lose control and something happens to you by my hand, the contract will be broken, and Preacher and his kinsmen will destroy me." He gave a soft laugh. "And my father will let them."

"Pretty sick contract," I said, and when Eli didn't respond, I decided to keep my mouth shut for the time being. It was already difficult enough to try to fall asleep with him in the room; the current in the air between us snapped like it was alive, and swear to God, despite his *strigoi* threats, I couldn't help the perverted thoughts that stormed my brain at the memory of Eli's hand on my body, his mouth so close to my skin. When he was near me like that? A relentless, seductive, feral desire surged through me, one I couldn't control, and visions of his hands touching me everywhere invaded my mind. I wanted his mouth and tongue on me; his hardness inside me; the two of us naked and slick with sweat; Eli standing and holding me as my legs wrapped around his waist while he pounded into me against the brick wall of my bedroom; and for a half second I thought I'd die where I sat if I didn't get it *right then*. There was something else, too—something deeper, something more intimate than mind-blowing, nasty sex, and it was *that one thing* that made my brain shift into reverse and seize. I couldn't even name it, but it scared the holy hell out of me.

In the shadows, I heard Eli's muffled groan—at least I thought it was a groan. Then another sound broke the darkness, barely there, quiet, but I heard it just the same. It was skin against skin, and the only conclusion I could come to was that Eli had read my dirty thoughts and had decided to take care of business himself instead of putting us both at risk by taking me. I could have been mistaken, but I probably wasn't, and it totally turned me on. All I could do was lie there in the darkness and think about Eli. My mind filled with vivid images of his hands moving painfully slowly over my bare flesh, his tongue and lips tasting my throat, my breasts, down my abdomen, and settling between my legs in a long, erotic kiss that had me writhing with need. My hand moved without command, and the moment I touched myself, I came. I wasn't as shocked at myself as I thought I'd be, having done that in the same room with the very subject behind the act. In the shadows, I felt him; I didn't hear him, but he was everywhere.

It irritated me that sexual thoughts of Eli could push their way to the forefront of my mind even in the midst of the chaos that had become my life. Eventually, I drifted back to sleep, but it was a restless, agitated slumber that I fell rebelliously into.

The breaking dawn fell across me the next morning, and I cracked open my eyes and immediately sought out the corner where Eli had last been. He was no longer there, and I really wasn't that surprised. Sitting up, I scrubbed my eyes with my knuckles and tried to ignore the feeling of the morning after, especially frustrating since we hadn't actually had sex. Somehow, though, it had felt real enough. I pushed it from my mind, got up, and began the first day of my new life—life as a rogue vampire bounty hunter. That was what I thought of myself as now. Amid the tossing and turning and turbulent sex thoughts of Eli, I'd come to a shocking conclusion: I could no longer whine and cry about what was happening to my brother and me. This was no time to be a wimp. I'd been a tough-ass since age nine and had grown only tougher as I'd aged. I was a fighter, and now was definitely the time to fight. I wanted my brother back, and I'd get him, swear to God. No matter the sacrifice. It'd be worth it. The only thing I'd have to learn to control was my growing desire for Eli. Anyone with a rational mind who actually believed there were vampires among mortals would probably repel the idea of sex with one. They weren't natural. They weren't living. They had no souls, and they were damned to hell. Supposedly. To be frank, I thought that nothing more than a load of horseshit. But that's just me.

With those empowering thoughts in mind, I jumped up, pulled on some ratty jeans and a T-shirt, slid into my flip-flops, brushed my teeth, and headed downstairs. Eli was standing in the storefront window looking out over River Street, Chaz at his side, and both turned when I entered the room. Chaz barked and wagged his whole back end but stayed directly by Eli. I ignored the cold shirk from my dog and reflected on my revelations. I'd shed all my anxieties from the night before; I was ready to kick vampire ass, and not Eli's but the Arcoses'— the little pricks. It seemed Eli hadn't released quite as easily as I did. His penetrating stare shook me, and I knew—*knew*—he was still thinking of what he'd seen in my mind the night before. He may be a vampire, but at the root of that monstrosity was a dude. A young, hot-blooded, horny dude.

I gave Eli a smile. "First, gotta let Chaz out, then run

next door to Preacher's, then back here to finish your makeover." I headed for the door. "Coming?" I glanced back, but he wasn't there.

When I turned around, Eli was at the door, waiting, his hands shoved into the pockets of a pair of faded 501s. "I took Chaz out earlier."

I lifted a brow, frowned at my dog, then nodded. "Well, good for you. Let's go, then." I reached for the door, but he blocked it. "What?" I said, trying to keep the irritation from my voice.

Silently, he moved aside, and we stepped out into the muggy air. The first thing I noticed was a custom chopper, parked next to my Jeep. I knew it had to be Eli's, and I inspected it. A Martin Brothers Silverback, it was titanium platinum with some pretty sick black scroll-work on the tank and fenders, a wide, fat back tire, and a narrower front one. "Wicked bike," I offered, and I meant it. I'd always wanted one.

"Ride's sweet," he said. "We'll take it tonight."

I admitted only to myself that the thought of it thrilled me. At Preacher's, Estelle bustled about making break-fast, but my surrogate grandfather kept his eyes trained on Eli and me. I could tell he knew something was up. Not that anything had happened, but that there was something in the air between us, something dangerous and palpable. He ignored it, though, and we finished our breakfast and left. I couldn't help thinking the whole time, *What the freak are they putting in my tea?* Drinking it just wasn't the same anymore, which was a little depressing. I'd loved the tea, back when I'd thought it was just tea. Maybe one day, I'd get used to the idea that it was now for the sake of my life, not just for the hell of it.

I made quick work of finishing Eli's makeover; I snipped his bangs to make them jagged and swept across his forehead, partially hanging over his eyes, and had him change into a pair of black junkie-fit jeans, a gray ripped shirt, and buckled combat boots. I helped him strap on the leather finger cuff and noticed that he already wore a leather band around his neck with a silver medallion. Then I walked around him, examining him thoroughly, and was pretty satisfied with the results. *Almost*.

I looked hard at him. "You need a piercing."

Eli raised a brow. "Where?"

Studying his face and following that raised brow, I pointed to it. "Right there. Small silver hoop."

Surprisingly, Eli shrugged. "Whatever you say." He glanced toward the door and inclined his head. "My brothers and sister are downstairs."

"I guess I might as well get them a key made," I muttered as I jogged down the stairs. I opened the door, and Phin, Luc, and Josie stood, waiting. "Come on in," I said, and led the way upstairs. "Check out your bro."

"Whoa," Phin said, walking around Eli and ruffling his hair. "Goin' dark, huh, Eligius?" he said, and Luc joined in, patting Eli on the ass. "Nice threads," he added.

"If you're going to go where we're going to go, I suggest you get some of the same," I said.

"I'll try the skins, but no one's touching my hair," Luc said, threading his fingers through his careless dark blond locks. "Hell and no."

"Puss," laughed Phin, then turned to me. "My hair's too short, but we'll go along with the clothes."

"Piercings, too," I added, then opened a drawer in the kitchen and grabbed a notepad. "Here's the name of another ink shop that does piercings," I said, scribbling the address, tearing it off the pad, and handing it to Eli. "It's on the west side, not too far from Mullet's. You remember how to get to his house?"

Eli gave me a wicked smile, and it made his blue eyes dance beneath the pitch-black jagged bangs. "Yeah, Riley. I got it." He glanced at Josie. "You stay here with her, squirt," he said. "Watch her back."

"Yes!" Josie said excitedly. "I brought some drawings to show you," she said to me, patting the backpack she carried. "I've got them on my laptop."

I hid my skepticism at having a fifteen-year-old vampiress watch my back, and nodded. "Cool. I've got about an hour before the shop opens." I inclined my head. "Let's have a look." Josie busied herself setting up her laptop, and I found Eli's gaze; he gave an approving nod.

"We'll be back in a few," he said. In less than a blink, the Dupré brothers had disappeared down the stairs. An accompanying roar of three motorcycle engines echoed in the alley behind Inksomnia at once, and I glanced at Josie.

"Boys and their toys," she said very maturely, and I had no option but to agree and laugh.

"Ain't that the truth," I said. For a split second I paused and thought about the Duprés. Even though I'd seen the horror Eli could transform into, I had the hardest time picturing Phin, Luc, and Josie doing the same thing. Especially Josie. It all seemed so surreal, fantastic, and mind-boggling at once, and I wasn't positive my brain would ever fully comprehend and embrace it.

I turned my head, gasped a muffled scream, and stumbled back. Josie stood no more than two feet away, her sweet, youthful face contorted into the same unhinged-jaw, jagged-teeth terror that I'd seen on Eli and Gilles. Her white eyes stared curiously at my reaction, and once she'd seen it, her face immediately re-formed back to the sweet teen Josie I knew.

"There," she said matter-of-factly, a bit arrogant, and with a wicked little smile. "Now you don't have to wonder anymore." She inclined her head to the open laptop on the counter. "Wanna see my pics?" she said, as if she'd not just completely transformed in front of me.

"Whoa," I muttered, and tried to force my racing heart to slow its pace. "Okay. Let's see." I scrolled through the file and inspected Josie's art—amazing, highly detailed sketches of everything from Pictish symbols to lizards and spiders to faces reflected in the infamous stain-glassed window of Notre Dame. They literally blew my mind.

"Wow—this is your brother?" Josie said from the living room.

I glanced up and noticed that she was looking at the picture I'd taken of Seth from the top of Tybee Light-house in June. "Yep, that's Seth," I answered, and just hearing his name out loud made my heart heavy.

"God, he's *so cute*," Josie muttered, and continued to stare at it.

I couldn't help but grin. "These are seriously fantastic," I told her, scrolling through more drawings. "Despite the fact that you're over a hundred and fifty years old, you're too young for me to hire," I said, "but I'd love to commission some of your art. They'd make kick-ass tats."

"Seriously?" Josie said excitedly. "That'd be freaking awesome!"

"Good. Okay it with your mom and dad, first," I said, then thought how funny it was that her mom and dad were nineteenth-century vampires. "Listen—I've got to get ready. Help yourself to . . . whatever," I told her, and headed to my bedroom. "I'll be right back.

"Okay," Josie answered.

After a quick shower, I changed into a pair of black side-laced skinny jeans, a gray T-back Inksomnia tank, and black chunky Mary Janes, and added a black lace choker. Pulling my hair back, but leaving my red-streaked bangs free, I added makeup and was ready to go.

Nyx took right to Josie, and vice versa—just as I'd figured. There wasn't a soul around who could refuse Nyx—even if that soul was damned. I'd simply told Nyx that Josie was Eli's younger sister, and after I'd shown her Josie's incredible artwork, they hit it off.

It was just after noon when Eli, Phin, and Luc walked into Inksomnia, and so stunned was I by their changes that I paused in midink to stare in appreciation. Don't get me wrong—they were totally fan-freaking-fine before. All three had the bad-boy look, reckless, faded jeans, T-shirt, boots. But now? Now they'd stroll straight into the Panic Room and no one would be the wiser; they'd think the Duprés were truly into the Goth/urban scene. I grinned. "Looks like Mullet did you guys right," I said, and inspected all three. "Poster boys of Gnaw Bone Brand Urban Wear."

"Sweet," Nyx said with approval, and I introduced around the room. Nyx hugged everyone.

Phin's already close-cut hair fit perfectly with the

dark gray urban decayed pants, black ripped T-shirt, and
thick-buckled boots. He walked up to me, grinned, and
stuck out his tongue. "Ouch," I said as I checked out the
new silver tongue ball. "How'd that feel?"

"I'll tell ya later," he said, smirking.

Luc, who, true to his word, hadn't changed a single
strand of hair on his head, stood with his arms folded
over his chest, his postapocalyptic jeans and ripped
gray shirt making him look like a Panic Room regular.
I peered closer and noted the small silver hoop pierced
through his bottom lip and the silver balls adorning his
ear lobes. I smiled and gave a nod of approval. "Nice."

Eli stood back, watching me with intensity as I inspected his brothers, until I turned my full attention to
him. "Come here," I said, and he walked closer. A small
silver hoop pierced his left brow, and I admit—it was
dead sexy. I nodded. "Good job." I ducked my head back
to the tribal serpent I was inking on the shoulder of an
army guy, and vaguely listened as Nyx carried on, showing the other Duprés the ins and outs of Inksomnia. She
uploaded one of Josie's art filcs to our computer, then
printed it out as a tattoo transfer. Josie squealed and de-
clared that it was totally cool.

After a while, all four Duprés left and went upstairs
for their two-hour vampire siesta. Nyx finished up early
and headed out, while I inked a few more clients. Eli
strolled in while I was wrapping up a barbed armband
on a young woman who taught English to seventh grad-
ers. For some reason, I found that freaking hilarious. As
I gave her samples of ointment and paperwork, I saw
Eli watching me closely. When Gene the Raven cawed

as the woman exited Inksomnia, I locked the door and flipped the sign to CLOSED. I stood staring out into the waning afternoon as tourists wearing Bermuda shorts, T-shirts, and capris bustled by, and noticed the dark clouds swirling overhead and moving in over the riverfront. Even indoors I could feel the change as something dark, ominous, settled over the city. Maybe it was because I was privy to it; maybe it was because I anticipated it. Either way, my adrenaline rushed through my body at the thought of facing unimaginable foes—ones who held my brother prisoner—and I couldn't help but wonder what Seth was doing at that very moment. Or even whether he knew he was Seth anymore. Eli was suddenly standing beside me, his presence heating my skin.

"Tonight will be the beginning," he said with an assured voice. "If you have any hesitations at all, you'd better speak up." I glanced up, and at the same time, he looked down. "Once we start, there's no turning back, and things will only get harder. If they sense you, they'll hunt you. And trust me—they won't stop until they have you."

"Hesitations aren't in my genetic makeup," I answered tightly, fearless, even though I was sure by *they* Eli meant *Seth and his friends*. "As long as those effers have my brother, I'm in."

Eli turned me around and pushed me against the wall, his hands braced on either side of my head. He appeared more . . . menacing with his black hair, pale skin, pierced brow, and darker looks. "If they ever caught a whiff of that blood running through your veins, you would not be able to stop them." He cocked his head and studied me. "They would descend upon you like a pack of hyenas. Your brother's strength and agility grows every day. Only, their stomachs aren't prepared for human blood yet—and that's what saved you the other night. They have the craving, the desire—but don't know how to act on it." He frowned. "Yet."

"So teach me how to protect myself," I said, sensations rippling through me as Eli crowded me against the brick wall of the shop. I knew then that my desires had become his. *Knew* it. They'd become powerful and all consuming, forcing the edges of the spacious tattoo parlor to slam in around me. "If I can't beat them, or outrun them, teach me how to kill them."

A look of disbelief crossed Eli's features. "Would you be able to ram a dagger through your brother's heart if he came after you?" he asked.

Sickening nausea crept up my throat at the thought of it, and I knew I'd die before ever turning on Seth. "No," I said. I lifted my chin and met his gaze. "But the Arcoses I'd kill. No problem."

Eli studied me for several seconds, and I waited as patiently as I could. Patience wasn't exactly a trait I'd ever claimed, and the lack of it was now kicked into overdrive as Eli's body hovered so close to mine, silent, powerful, exotic. Slowly, he pushed away from me.

"I'll speak to my father," he said. "And he'll speak with Preacher." Although he'd pushed away from me, he was still close, and I swallowed the desire to grab him by the collar of his already ripped shirt and yank his mouth down to mine. "There are ways for a mortal to kill a vampire, but they're old ways—primitive, and not for the squeamish." He dragged a knuckle over my jaw, and I regarded him as his gaze raked over me. "You squeamish, Poe?"

My body reacted without my brain's permission; I jammed my knee sharply in Eli's crotch. Although I didn't get the same reaction I'd gotten dozens of times before with mortals, I was fascinated to watch as Eli's eyes dilated just a hair, and he stifled the shallowest of gasps. Balls were balls, I guessed. Still, he stood over me, and a small, wicked smile lifted the corner of his mouth. I grinned back. "Not squeamish at all."

He nodded. "Dirty street fighting will buy you minimal time with a vampire," he said matter-of-factly. "More than anything, they'll be intrigued. But it won't stop them."

I shrugged and crossed my arms over my chest. "So when you say primitive, you mean wooden-stake-through-the-heart primitive?"

His eyes never left mine. "No. That only works in Hollywood. In real life it's silver, and it can't just pierce the heart. It has to go all the way through it. Ultimately it's best if ripped from the chest wall, driven with silver, and burned."

I considered that. "Sounds wicked disgusting, but I could do it."

Eli glanced away and gave an arrogant laugh—a totally mortal guy's move, and it looked even sexier on a vampire. He glanced back at me, then out into the afterlight, and inclined his head. "Go get ready. We leave in an hour."

"An hour? Why so early?" I asked. "We don't just show up at the Panic Room at seven o'clock. We have time to kill." I looked around. "Ever think about get-

ting some ink?" I asked, and inspected him. I admit it.
I'd wanted to ink him from the moment I'd laid eyes
on him.

Blue eyes fastened to me, studied me intently for several moments. "Really? And why's that?"

I scowled. "Stay. Out. Of. My. Head."

With a slight grin, Eli looked away and shrugged.
"Yeah, I've thought about it." He picked up a design
book and thumbed through the pages. "If I decide to do
it, you'll be the first to know. Now, come on."

With narrowed eyes, I frowned. "Again—you've confused me with someone who takes orders." I turned to
go. "Besides. That's way too early to hit the Panic Room.
Learn some manners, Dupré." Eli's silence followed me
to my bedroom, where I hastily kicked my clothes off
and jumped into the shower. With steaming water pelting my back, I measured exactly what I was doing, and
what was about to happen, and I'd be lying if I said it
didn't make me a little apprehensive. Before, when I
was heavy into partying and getting effed up, things just
didn't matter to me. I thought I was invincible, that nothing and no one could ever hurt me. I could kick ass and
was proud of it. But I'd left that life. Now? I was about to
dive headfirst right back into it. And the thought of seeing Seth involved in the dark stuff that happened in the
back rooms of the clubs I used to hang out in? It made
my stomach hurt.

The entire time I showered, I felt a presence, as
though someone watched me, and thoughts of Eli
crowded my mind. I peered through the clear glass doors
of my shower, to the bathroom door I'd left cracked
open, but didn't see him. I didn't like how drawn I was

to Eli; he was deadly, like holding a gun to my temple with the trigger half cocked, hoping the odds would keep it from firing. He of course knew it, too. Although I'd asked him not to read my mind, he did it all the time. Actions I could mostly control; private thoughts I totally could not. So I was pretty sure he knew right now that I wanted him in the shower with me, slick, wet, and totally out of control. My better judgment kicked in, though, and I turned the shower off, wrapped a towel around my body, and climbed out. I couldn't help one last thought: *How long can we resist each other?* Maybe Eli could take it longer than me; he was, after all, immortal. I wasn't, and hadn't nearly the amount of resistance or control he did.

I dried my hair and left it loose, pulling various strands into tiny black clips. I left my bangs down, and they hung just to my jaw. It was the underground we faced, so the makeup I applied was a little heavier than usual, with dark liner and purple shadow that sparkled when the lights hit. Ruby lipstick and rouge made my skin look paler than it actually was, but beneath the club's black walls and strobe lights, it'd prove the perfect effect. I added a pair of black webbed earrings; a black lace choker with a silver cross hanging from its center; a metallic hot pink push-up swimsuit top barely covered by a skimpy leather vest that sat about two inches above my navel; my favorite pair of second-skin leather pants, which laced up the sides; and black six-inch spike-heel ankle boots completed my Panic Room attire. I added a few black leather finger cuffs studded with silver, and a spiked wrist cuff, and was ready to go. With a quick final inspection in the full-length mirror in the corner of my bedroom, I grabbed my small black leather backpack and left the room.

"Okay, ready," I said as I stepped into the living room. Eli stood at the window facing River Street, and he turned to look at me.

Alluring blue eyes slowly took in my appearance, lingering at the swell of my pushed-up breasts and skintight-leather-clad legs. Slowly, he moved toward me, and I noticed then that with six-inch heels I looked him square in the eye. I held my ground as he perused every inch of my body. I won't lie; I enjoyed it. It *empowered* me, because I knew I affected him, too. Good. I didn't want to be the only one on freaking fire.

Finally, after a prolonged, silent inspection of me, Eli met my gaze, and I immediately saw raw male desire laced in those blue depths. "You," he said slowly, evocatively, "are hot."

I gave a little smile and a shrug. "Thanks." I gave Eli a quick assessment, and he looked just as mouthwatering as he had before. "Not so bad yourself. Ready?"

Shaking his head, Eli moved toward the kitchen table and grabbed a box. He handed it to me. "For you."

With brow raised, I gave him a skeptical look and took the box. "What is it?" I said as I opened it.

"Protection," he answered.

I nodded. "This size box could hold a lot of condoms," I said, grinning, and Eli chuckled. Once I got the flap opened, I peered inside and was surprised to see a flat black half helmet with a metallic purple tattooed butterfly painted on the side. I lifted it out and looked at Eli. "Cool. Thanks." I grinned and gave an approving nod. "Biker chic."

He shrugged indifferently. "No problem. I already took Chaz out. Let's go."

I stopped long enough to scrub the fur between Chaz's ears, and we stepped outside into the fading daylight. "Where exactly am I going to fit on that bike?" I asked, knowing that Eli's Silverback had a single scooped seat. I didn't have a wide ass, but that was definitely a seat made just for one. Then I looked beneath the streetlight at his bike and noticed a single seat had been mounted on the back, and a set of foot pegs had been placed directly behind Eli's.

"I had it done while we were getting pierced," he said. "No room for you on the scoop."

"Yeah, I got that," I said, and walked to the bike and inspected the seat. I gave it a tug.

Eli pulled on a solid black half helmet, I did the same, and once he'd started the bike I climbed on behind him. The rumble of the engine hummed through my entire body as I settled my heeled boots onto the foot pegs; I wrapped my arms around Eli's waist, and he took off. As he pulled out of Factor's Walk, he turned left. I leaned close to him. "You're going the wrong way," I said, knowing the Panic Room was off Martin Luther King Boulevard on Williamson.

"You said we had some time to kill, right?" Eli answered, and continued on his way. "There's something I want to check out first."

As we rode along President Street, then Highway 80 toward Tybee, I nearly forgot that I sat clutching a nineteenth-century vampire and we were looking for others. Eli's muscles flinched beneath my hands, and I could feel the ripped abs under his T-shirt. He seemed like an

average hot guy riding a chopper; I knew he was anything but, and I found myself wishing hard that things
were different, and that Eli wasn't a vampire, and that
Seth wasn't becoming one. It was useless wishing and
an utter waste of time, and yet I found myself constantly
doing it. Pissed me off, really.

Highway 80 had its usual backed-up traffic, so it was
slow going toward the island. The air was thick with
pending rain; it carried that indisputable scent, and it
even permeated, or enhanced, the heavy brine of the
marsh. It was low tide—I could tell without even seeing the water. The rotting sea life was always thicker at
low tide. Cattails and oyster shoals sat visible in the river
muck as we crept along.

After we crossed over the main bridge to Tybee, Eli
turned into the first subdivision and down several streets
before stopping at a stilted house at the end of a cul-de-
sac. An old white caddy sat parked in the driveway. I
climbed down, and Eli turned the engine off, threw his leg
over the tank, sat, took off his shades, and looked at me.

"What?" I asked, and looked around. "What're we
doing here?"

"There's something you need to know," he said, and
beneath the streetlight I saw his eyes studying me.

I had no idea what to expect. "Okay," I said, and
waited.

"Remember when you asked if any of Preacher's
people had changed, way back when?" he asked. "And I
told you a mortal quickening couldn't occur unless they
drank the blood of a vampire?"

"Yeah," I said slowly, not liking at all where this was
going. "So?"

"Well," he said just as slowly. "That's not completely true."

I could do nothing more than stare and wait for the rest of the explanation.

"More than just the Gullah were used, at first. If a mortal is fed upon, and too much blood is taken, they die. Plain and simple. But if they're bitten and live, they gain . . . tendencies." He gauged my reaction. "Vampiric tendencies."

I shifted my weight and cocked my head. "And they include . . . ?"

Eli shrugged. "It all depends on who did the biting, their genetic makeup. Excessive speed. Ability to jump high, maybe defy gravity for a while. Read thoughts. Crave raw meat." He shrugged again. "They live longer, with a slow rate of aging. They also have the ability to rapidly heal."

"Okay," I said, not fully understanding. "And are there a lot of these people still around?"

"Yes."

I nodded and considered that enlightening news. "All right. Weird, but okay. So why are we *here*?" I inclined my head to the stilt house.

"Ned Gillespie. Bitten in 1912, when he was fourteen years old."

I stared in disbelief. "You bit a kid?"

Eli shook his head. "Josie did." He looked at me. "But back then, yeah—I would have. We were just learning to be humane, Riley. We couldn't help it."

"So why are we here to see Ned Gillespie?" I asked, glancing at the two-story house perched above the marsh.

"He and Josie were . . . close, I guess, until they outgrew one another," he answered. "Ned knows about the Arcoses—can sniff a vampire thirty miles away." He climbed off the bike. "I thought maybe he'd heard something or . . . smelled something." He nodded toward the house. "Come on."

As we walked up the inclined drive, I glanced at Eli. "Is Ned going to freak me out?" I could only imagine what *tendencies* he might have.

"Yep," Eli answered, and I took a deep breath and followed him to the door. Just as we walked under the porch light, the front door opened; there stood a young guy, mid- to late twenties, with crazy brown hair and frosted tips, a yellow and black Led Zeppelin T-shirt, and destroyed jeans. His eyes crinkled in the corners as he grinned and bumped fists with Eli.

"Dude, what's up? Haven't seen you in a while," he said to Eli, then looked at me. "Whoa. Who's the babe?" He leaned closer to Eli. "Is she a bloodsucker? That's sick, man." Then his eyes landed on my dragons. "Damn—sweet tats." He walked around me, looking. "Sweet."

Eli shook his head and laughed. "No, Ned. She's"—he looked at me—"a friend. A mortal friend." He inclined his head. "Ned Gillespie, Riley Poe."

Ned stuck out his hand to shake mine, and I allowed it, although I was in shock to see Ned as a young guy instead of a hundred-and-twelve-year-old. *Weird.* "Well, Riley Poe, this is the dawning of the age of Aquarius, don't ya think? Vamps, Tendies, and mortals, chillin' together. Pretty awesome, huh?"

I shot a quick glance at Eli. "Yeah, sure." I thought I'd

fallen through a time warp and straight into one of Bill and Ted's excellent adventures.

"Well, come on in to my humble abode," he said. "Come in."

Eli gave me a glance and a nod, and I went inside first. It was an open floor plan, with cathedral ceilings and a walkway at the top that encircled the entire room. No sooner did Ned close the door behind us than a cell phone rang, and he patted his pockets, then cursed.

"Be right back," he said, and swear to God, had I not seen it with my own two eyes, I'd never have believed it—even knowing what I now know about vampires, I wouldn't have believed it. In one leap Ned cleared the wooden railing of the walkway—an easy twenty feet if not more. He disappeared into a room, and in the next second he was leaping down again. He looked at me as he landed.

"Missed call," he said, as if what he'd done was absolutely normal.

I could do nothing more than lift my brows in astonishment.

"Listen, Ned," Eli said. "Have you sensed any other vampires lately?"

Ned dramatically lifted his nose to the air and sniffed. "Yeah, dude, I have. It's not strong, though—so weak actually I thought it was farther up the coast. Why, what's up?"

"The Arcoses," Eli said. "You haven't seen or heard anything?"

Ned looked at Eli, and seriousness replaced the carefree attitude he'd just had.

"There's a pack of them. Young, not fully transformed, but a load of trouble, if you know what I mean," Eli said, inclining his head toward me. "One of them is her brother."

Ned regarded me. "That sucks."

"Have you sensed them around here?" Eli asked. "On the island?"

Ned shook his head. "Been in Atlanta at a gaming convention." He glanced at me and grinned. "I created Urban Bloodsuckers," he said, waiting for me to comprehend. "The computer game? You know, software? Badass."

"Congratulations," I said, and he shrugged.

Eli and Ned exchanged few more words, and then we said good-bye, with Ned's promise that he'd contact us if Seth or the others showed up on the island. I felt skeptical—Ned seemed to be in his own little software world despite the superpowers having been bitten by a vampire had awarded him. "Live long and prosper," Ned hollered from his front door as we climbed on the bike and left. Eli explained over his shoulder, "He's a big Trekky." I fully could see that—especially since he'd been around since before Captain James Kirk was even a spark in his daddy's eye.

A spitting rain had begun just as we turned off of President Street and onto Bay, and we made it to the Panic Room just before the bottom fell out. A nondescript brick building, the club was completely void of neon lights or signs; the entrance was a plain set of haint blue double doors, and if you didn't know of the Panic Room, you'd never have found it on your own. It was sort of a word-of-mouth type of place, and only a select few could waltz right in. A lot of shit happened in the

Panic Room—drugs, sex, prostitution—but the owner's attorney was a pit bull. They'd already sued the city for a bust without probable cause and a warrant, and not only did the attorney rake in the dough because of it, but the incident had made the SPD extremely cautious about raiding the Panic Room again. We parked the bike along the sidewalk and hurried to the entrance.

"Who's the big guy with the braid?" Eli leaned toward my ear and whispered.

I turned into his neck and was surprised by the thrill that shot through me at the intimate closeness. "Zetty's in his midthirties, from Tibet. He serves as the Panic Room's resident doorman." Zetty, with a black braid that reached his waist, always dressed in traditional Tibetan clothing, with a long red yak-wool wrap and black baggy pants tucked into a worn pair of shin-high leather boots. "He was once a Shiva follower," I said. "See the symbol of a god inked into his forehead?"

Eli looked down at me. "Yeah."

Tattooed into Zetty's forehead were brightly colored squares of yellow and red adorned with dots that extended just down the bridge of his nose. He wore round, brightly colored stone earrings and carried a traditional Tibetan knife in a multicolored, handwoven sheath secured across his chest. "I've seen him use that knife, too, so don't be stupid." No one fucked with Zetty.

"Don't worry," Eli said, and placed his hand to my lower back and urged me forward.

Zetty smiled at me as we drew close, and recognition made his eyes shine. It was the kind of look that made his already intimidating features even scarier. "Riley

Poe. What are you doing here?" he said in his heavy Tibetan accent, and grasped my shoulder.

Eli immediately stiffened and moved slightly in front of me, causing Zetty's gaze to move from me to Eli. Zetty frowned.

"It's okay," I said quietly to Eli, and placed my hand on his back. "Zetty's an old friend." I looked at the bouncer. "Just here to hang out. So how ya been, Zetty?" I asked.

"Cannot complain," he answered, but his attention was now on Eli.

"Good. Nice seeing ya," I said, and tugged on Eli's arm.

Zetty turned his eyes on me. "Stay out of the back rooms, Riley," he said with a deadpan tone. "Nothing there for you anymore."

We walked away, and I averted my gaze from Zetty.

"What's up with him?" Eli asked as we passed through the small foyer where the music reverberated through another set of double doors that led into the club. "He seems too protective over you."

"He probably thought the same thing about you." I smiled. "Zetty does his job and only his job," I said, glancing at him. "He always hated that I'd gotten messed up, and while he knows what goes on in the back panic rooms, he doesn't get involved." I shrugged. "Except for once. He pulled me out of a bad situation and almost killed a guy doing it. Otherwise, he merely stays up front and keeps the peace."

"He knows what I am," Eli said matter-of-factly.

"I wouldn't doubt it," I answered, knowing he'd read

Zetty's mind, and to be honest, I wasn't all that surprised. Zetty had been sort of a mystical man in Tibet, mysterious and deadly. I was always grateful he liked me, for whatever reason.

As we pushed into the crowd, the black walls and strobe lights swallowed us, and "The Raven and the Rose" by My Dying Bride slammed through the sound system and hummed through me; Eli's body crowded mine, his palm and fingers pressed possessively to the bare skin of my lower back as he guided me through a sea of smoke, black leather, silver spikes, and exotic makeup. This part of the Panic Room was tame—the club part, the dancing, the music, the drinks, and most of the people. What I knew lay in the back rooms—the dark *panic rooms*—was something else altogether. I'd experienced them, and I'd be a liar if I said it didn't bother me to be back. And yet with Eli's hand against my skin, and the music bounding through my body, it sort of thrilled me, too.

"I'd ask what's wrong, but I already know," Eli said, his mouth grazing the shell of my ear as he leaned close. I turned and looked at him, our faces close, intoxicating, erotic. His eyes were mesmerizing, and I was drawn to them. Him. I was drawn to *him*.

"This is the easy part," I said, and I knew he understood that I meant where we were now. "Kelter Phillips owns this place. I know how to get in, know how to act. And I know *exactly* what to do to be accepted back." Now I pushed my lips to Eli's ear. "You say the Arcoses are into the dark stuff, right? It's where they'll gather their freaky vampiric army?" I purposely pressed my mouth to Eli's jaw. "Then it's this place they'll come, and

I swear to God, I'm not leaving here tonight without finding something out about my brother or those assholes that have him under their control." I pulled back and held Eli's gaze with my very determined one. "You're going to have to back off, Eli, and trust me. These aren't vampires. They're people." I lifted my chin. "I can damn well handle people." He stared hard, contemplating probably, then gave a begrudging single nod, and his eyes flared as they bored into mine. I couldn't tell whether he was impressed or turned on. With his hand resting on my hip, Eli guided me to the bar; I ordered a shot of whiskey, and to my surprise Eli did the same. As I lifted the glass and swallowed the fiery liquid, Eli watched, his gaze following the path of the whiskey as it slipped down my throat. Raw male power and deliberate sexual hunger lit his eyes, and to say that the sensation it stirred within me was erotic was a freaking understatement. He was driving me crazy, and I had to literally make a conscious effort not to put my hands on him. It was so easy to submerge into the seductive darkness of our surroundings; the music, the forced intimacy, the whiskey—they were all drugs in their own right. And I was an ex-junkie to it all.

"Someone's coming, and I don't like him," Eli said close to me, and he turned to the bar. I waited, although I knew who it'd be. I was right.

"Riley Poe. Damn, it is you," a throaty voice said behind me. "All grown-up."

I turned and amid the strobe lights stared into a face from my past—one I hadn't ever planned on encountering again but knew I'd run into tonight. Average-sized, Kelter Phillips wore his usual attire: a collection of black

leather, chains, spiked cuffs, and collars, and his signature
bald head and black goatee looked exactly as they had
when I used to hang with him. Ten years my senior and
filthy rich, he now sported a large tat that started at his
brow and stretched over his head in a six-inch-wide strip,
Mohawk style. The tat was a list of the seven deadly sins,
written in Old English and inked in black, with black
vines and bloodred roses along the side. The words above
his brow read *Fuck Virtue,* followed by *lust, gluttony,
greed, sloth, wrath, envy,* and *pride* in intricate calligra-
phy. Damn, he always thought he was a badass. He could
smell fresh meat a mile away, and to him I'd always been
meat—only back then, I hadn't known or cared. I pushed
past my revulsion and gave Kelter a seductive smile. Eli
tensed beside me. "What's up, Kelter?"

Kelter gave Eli a curious glance and a nod. "Friend of
yours?" he asked.

"Yeah, a friend," I assured him. I'd get nowhere fast
if Kelter thought I had the scrutiny of a boyfriend, and
I nearly snorted out loud when I thought of what he'd
think if he knew Eli was a creature of the afterlight. Beside me, Eli smothered a chuckle. *Get out of my head,
jackass,* I thought. I knew Eli had heard.

"Come with me," Kelter offered, completely ignoring Eli, and I tried not to shiver with revulsion when he
placed his hand on my bare lower back.

"Sure," I said, looking directly into Kelter's black-
lined eyes. I slid from the barstool and allowed him to
guide me into the throng of people dancing. Before I
got too far, I glanced over my shoulder; Eli sat watching
me with a deadly glare in his eyes. *I'll be okay,* I told him
in my mind, and allowed the crowd to swallow me up. I

wasn't kidding myself; I knew Eli could see me, hear my heart, and would hear if called for him.

And God help anyone in his path.

Megadeth's "Bite the Hand" roared through the Panic Room, and I moved seductively to the music; strange bodies moved with me. With my peripheral, I noticed someone standing close to us, and when I turned, the person had slipped back into the crowd. I stared hard through the smoky darkness. It was Eli, and he was everywhere, moving so fast the human eye couldn't track him. I knew to look for him, and although I couldn't see him actually change locations, I glimpsed him hovering closer, like a hawk. I got one glimpse of his face; he looked like he wanted to rip Kelter apart. *Take it easy, Dupré,* I said in my mind, and turned my attention back to the scumbag I was forced to deal with.

Kelter watched me intently as his hands slid down my hips and pulled me closer, and I knew he was already half lit and turned on, the smell of whiskey, marijuana, and cigarettes clinging to him. Suddenly, his hands were on my ass, his crotch grinding against me, and his mouth pressed to my ear. "You look good enough to fuck right here," he said, obviously thinking his controlling dirty talk would do it for me, and it made me sick to think that at one time, it *had* done it for me. Now it made me profusely sick, and I tried not to let it show. "That ink is goddamn hot," he said, and traced my dragons up both arms, then back down again. "All professional now, huh? Got your own business," he said, moving behind me and groping my hips, pulling me hard against him. His dick was already hard—it probably stayed that way.

With all the crap Kelter took, it wouldn't surprise me to know he'd added Viagra to his repertoire of drugs and walked around with a twenty-four-hour woody. "Wanna go to the back?" he said in my ear, and turned me back around to face him. "Old times, huh, Riley?"

"Depends," I said loudly over the pounding music. "On what you got back there."

Without warning, Kelter grabbed my hand and pushed it against his crotch, and he throbbed beneath the leather pants at my touch. I tried to control my reaction; seriously, I did. But a lot had happened since my wild, reckless days at the Panic Room, and I *reacted*. I grabbed his balls hard, yanked upward and in, and twisted; Kelter's eyes widened, and he smothered a painful gasp. I could tell he was getting no air at all if the squeaking from his throat and stretched eyeballs meant anything. I pressed my lips together to keep from laughing.

"Nobody forces me anymore," I said, staring deadpan at Kelter's agonized face. I squeezed harder. "Like you said—I'm all grown-up, and I didn't come here for a lay. I don't trade shit for it anymore. I'll pay. Cash." I glared at him. "Understand?"

Kelter nodded because he couldn't breathe, and I released him. He coughed and drew a few deep breaths, and finally gave me a skeptical look. "Always did like it rough, didn't you, Poe?"

I shrugged and turned to leave. I knew he'd stop me. He did.

"Okay," he said, nearly grabbing my arm but thinking better of it. "Come on." He inclined his head but didn't touch me. "You remember the way?"

"Yeah," I said, and followed him. Weaving through

the sweating bodies and haze of cigarette smoke, I made my way to the panic rooms. Behind the main floor of the club was a horseshoe-shaped, dimly lit corridor that held the bathrooms. It swung in a half circle back to the main hall, and I knew that in the back was a set of double doors that led to six small rooms—rooms where crazy-weird stuff went on: sex, prostitution, drugs, fantasy role-playing—just about anything. As we squeezed past the people in the corridor, I winced as memories of my old self resurfaced. Near the back, a couple made out against the wall, her short leather skirt riding up her hips as his hand disappeared between her legs. She looked over his shoulder as I passed by and gave me the slightest of smiles, just before her eyes rolled back. Turning my head, I ignored her and continued on. Another small group of people hovered close by, and one guy in particular who stood off alone didn't really surprise me: Eli. His head was bent, but as I passed he lifted it, and a hot, penetrating gaze met mine, followed by a look of pure hatred at Kelter. *I got it,* I mouthed to him, but it didn't change his glare. All I wanted to do was get back into the scene, or at least make Kelter think I wanted back in. Lowlifes of various ages abounded in the panic rooms—but they were mostly buck-wild teens whose parents had no effing clue what they were up to, and Kelter, the sicko that he was, supplied whatever, whenever. Perfect recruits for the Arcoses. *Not if I can help it . . .*

Kelter stopped at the double doors, withdrew a key from his pocket, and opened the lock. He inclined his head for me to enter, and I did, and the moment I stepped through, the heavy scent of marijuana billowed out. My eyes burned as we walked down another short hall to Kelter's office. He opened the door, and in a rush, a body flew by me, slamming into me so hard that I stumbled and fell against the wall.

"Goddamn it!" Kelter yelled. At the door, the figure stopped and turned. The figure wore dark ratty jeans and a black hoodie, and a pasty white face peered back at him. My insides froze to ice. It was Riggs Parker. And he turned directly to me and stared.

Part 7

————◆————

OBSESSIONS

Riggs stared at me for several seconds, and I knew right away that he didn't recognize me. The feral gaze in his eyes reminded me of a junkie, or worse— a starved animal, one who'd been chained in a grass- less, dirt-covered backyard with no food, no water. It sent shivers down my spine, and just when I thought I couldn't take it anymore, he looked away and focused on Kelter. It took everything in my power not to scream, *Riggs! You peckerhead! Snap out of it!* I knew it would do no good.

"Val says the next time you lock me out, you're dead," Riggs said, smirking, dangling a gallon-sized ziplock filled with small, plastic-wrapped packages the size of sausage links in the air, his voice heavy, dark, menac- ing. A maniacal smile tainted his youthful features. He barely even looked like the Riggs I knew. "Well, look at that," he said, cocking his head and scrutinizing Kelter. "Looks like you're already dead, man." Without another glance my way, he turned and disappeared out the door; I pushed off the wall and ran after him.

In the corridor, I pulled up short and caught a glimpse of Riggs as he pushed out a single steel door. I took off after him. My mind was void of everything; I thought of nothing but finding Seth. The metal bar of the steel door stung my palms as I slammed into it and ran outside and into the dark, dank alley behind the Panic Room. The putrid scent of urine mixed with rain and trash from the Dumpster made me gasp for air, and at the end of the alley, beneath a streetlamp, I saw Riggs. He and several others—I counted seven in all—wore dark hoodies, and they paused and glanced back at me. I knew Seth was one of them, and I drew in a deep breath and yelled. "Se—!"

My eyes widened, and I fought against the steely grip around my waist and mouth. I knew it was Eli without even looking. I watched, stunned, as Riggs and the others did something that literally blew my mind. With a series of shrill yells, extreme leaps, and acrobatic moves, running up the trunk of a tree and swinging off limbs, railings, window ledges, they dispersed to the building across the street like a freaking circus troupe. One of them picked something up from the ground and smashed it into the window of a parked car, and the night air filled with the shrill sound of an alarm, followed by adolescent laughter. Within seconds—no lie, under a minute—they were all on the rooftop. I held my breath because I knew one of them was my brother and they teetered dangerously close to the roof's edge. Finally, the blackness of the night swallowed them up as they leapt out of sight. If I hadn't known any better, I would have sworn they'd flown.

"Free running." Eli's voice spoke quietly against my ear. He released my mouth but not my waist. "They're learning fast."

"We've been watching them all night," said Josie as she emerged from the darkness. Phin and Luc flanked her.

"Wicked urban freestyle," Luc said, nodding. He crossed his arms over his chest. "They're getting pretty damn good."

"And their quickening grows fast," Phin said, and glanced at Eli. "As does the brothers' rejuvenation. Faster than we thought."

I moved out of Eli's grip and stared in the direction Seth had gone. "My brother can barely walk and chew gum at the same time," I said, mostly to myself, and then looked at Eli. His beautiful features were cast in half shadows, seemingly haunted, as he met my gaze. "I don't understand why we have to be here. Why can't we just go after them? Take them away from the Arcoses, and let Preacher get Seth and the others to Da Island."

"You know why," Eli said quietly. "We've already been over this. I know it's tempting to just grab them, but it'd do a hell of a lot more harm than good. There are three weeks left in the moon's cycle." He put his hand on my shoulder. "No way will the Arcoses rejuvenate faster than a cycle. We'll be ready."

"Yeah, and we can't get too close, Riley," Phin said, leaning against the wall. "Victorian and Valerian are smart little bastards. They may be weak, but they're still deadly. We wait."

I considered that. "Back in Kelter's office, Riggs mentioned Val being angry that Riggs had been locked

out of the office. Then he took a plastic bag and ran."
I looked at the Duprés. "The way it was packaged, it
looked like pills. OxyContin probably." I rubbed my
arms. "You crush it, melt it, and smoke it—gives you a
high like heroin." They all looked at me like I'd lost my
mind, but I knew what I spoke of. I'd gotten the same
bag from Kelter before. "Val is Valerian, isn't he?"

Eli nodded. "Yeah, he's sort of the . . . leader, I guess
you could say. He's the eldest of the two. Apparently
he's already zeroed in on Phillips."

"How has he already established a drug trade?" I
asked. "The Arcoses have only been free for—"

"Mind control," Eli said. "From the moment the tomb
was broken both Arcos brothers had complete mind
control. They can make Phillips do whatever they wish.
They won't stop until their army is complete."

"Valerian is as mean as hell," Luc added, his face
grave. "No mercy. He gets off on torture—"

"Luc, enough," said Eli.

Pacing seemed to help, so I did it, but soon the stench
of the alley made my stomach roll. "What am I supposed
to do with loverboy in there?" I said, inclining my head
to the back door of the Panic Room.

"Go back in," Eli said. "Let him think you're interested in buying, but not tonight—not after what just
happened. Let him think you're rattled."

"What will buying drugs do to help us against the
Arcoses?" I asked. "And I think after having his balls
yanked into a twist, he knows I don't rattle easily."

Luc and Phin chuckled, and Eli glared at me. "It
keeps us from getting kicked out. Better to watch who

your brother and his friends pick up. Just do it, Riley. And we'll leave by the front entrance. You don't want that big Tibetan on your ass."

"You want access to their supplier," Phin added. "And to the rooms. It's apparent that Valerian has your brother and his friends using this place. Not just to gather more kids for his army, but probably to lure victims." My stomach sank at that last part.

"Did Seth's friend recognize you?" asked Josie, who'd been quietly watching.

"I don't think so," I answered. "He stared at me for a few seconds like I was a pork chop, but that's it."

Luc and Phin chuckled; Eli did not. He just stared at me, angry, and I couldn't understand why he was so pissed off at me.

"Okay, guys, let's go," said Josie, and headed up the alley toward the street. She glanced over her shoulder, then stopped and looked directly at me. "Bye, Riley. Don't worry—we'll keep an eye on Seth."

"Peace out," Luc said, following her, and Phin grinned and hurried up the alleyway. I watched in awe as the Dupré siblings mimicked Seth's and Riggs' free-running moves, using every ledge and flat surface to spring effortlessly off of—and at a much faster pace than Seth and the others had. At the rooftop of the building across the street, Josie stopped, turned, and waved, and then the three disappeared into the darkness.

"Come on," Eli said, his voice angry, edgy. "Let's get this over with and get out of here. Place makes me sick." He opened the door and held it for me, and I held his gaze as I walked through. I didn't look back as I walked to Kelter's office, and when I got there and turned, Eli had gone. Inside, I found Kelter at his desk, smoking a joint, which smelled just as bad as the corridor.

"That little prick owes me money," I said, making up something on the spur of the moment to explain why I'd run after Riggs. I leaned a hip against Kelter's desk. He was pasty white and didn't seem to really hear what I was saying. Of course he was half lit with liquor and pot, but his tolerance was usually a little higher. "So, what do you got for me?" I said.

He regarded me through a vapor of Mary Jane, but the cockiness from before was gone. He looked genuinely scared, and I felt no pity for him at all. "What do you want, Riley?" he asked. His eyes squinted as he pulled another drag.

"Tonight, nothing. Not after the stunt that kid just pulled. Later? A couple dozen Oxys," I said, the familiar words feeling dirty against my tongue. "Enough for a party. As long as you're still in good with your cousin?" Kelter's cousin was on the SPD, and yeah—a dirty cop.

"Tonight's a freebie." Kelter reached into his desk drawer and retrieved a ziplock similar to the one Riggs had taken, only smaller, quart sized, and rolled like a cigarette. He stood and eased around the desk, leaning close to me, and handed me the dope. When I reached for it, he grabbed my arm and held it tightly. I resisted the urge to shove my knuckles into his carotid.

"Room four, babe," he said, and moved his other hand to my thigh. "That's our old room, remember? When you're ready for the seven deadly sins, let me know. You remember the rules, right?" he asked, and slid his fingers along the inside seam of my leather pants. "Or do you need a little reminder?"

Inside I screamed; I wanted to knee his nuts so bad it hurt. But instead I put on a pouty face and nodded. "Yeah. I remember. There are none."

He laughed. "Good," he said, and drew another toke from his joint. The scent was making me nauseous, and I wanted out of there. "And here I thought all this time you'd cleaned your ass up and made something of yourself." He chuckled, and I swear his pale face made him look like a ghost. "Guess I was wrong, huh?" He dropped the bag in my hand. "Once a junkie, always a junkie. See ya round, Riley."

I didn't answer him; instead, I shoved the dope in my pocket, pushed away from him, and left his office, slamming the door behind me. It didn't drown out his laughter. What a nasty freak. I was halfway to the double doors when Eli stepped out of the shadows. Immediately, a protective hand went to my lower back. Within the horseshoe, it was like some seedy club in a movie; two guys were standing close, sharing a joint; another couple was hot and heavy against the wall not two feet away, her laced leather shirt completely undone and his hands all over her breasts. Two girls had staked out a dark alcove near the bathroom, one sprawled across the other's lap; they faced each other, making out and feeling each other up. The one on top had on a short plaid schoolgirl skirt with her knees pulled up, and her thonged ass was hanging out. Swear to God, people these days had no freaking humility. I wasn't a prude or anything, but damn. "Get a room," I muttered, but no way did they hear me, and even if they did, they didn't care. The pressure of Eli's hand guided me past all the club lovers and into the main room, where we entered a mob of people dancing. Not once did his palm leave my skin. People bumped and knocked into me as they moved to the music, and each time they did, Eli's grasp tightened against my flesh. I could feel his entire body pressed against me as we weaved through the crowd, and my body hummed with awareness. I liked it.

Close to the door we ran into Mullet and a tall, leggy girl with a pitch-black bob, straight-across bangs, black pants, and a red tank top with suspenders. Her Goth boots made her an easy two inches taller than Mullet. He made quick introductions; then we left. Mullet had never gotten into the bad stuff, like what went on in the back rooms. He was strictly a partier of music and drink. A really good guy. I sometimes wondered how he remained my friend when I'd been into so much awful stuff.

At the door, Zetty gave me the stink eye; he knew something was up, and although I hadn't been around him in some time, it didn't set right with me that he thought I was into Kelter's shit again. But I couldn't tell him otherwise. I waved good-bye and felt his all-knowing mystical Tibetan eyes on me until the door closed.

Outside, the heavy, wet air from the recent rain hung thick around us, the salt marsh from the Savannah River throwing off a weighty scent, and I breathed deeply, relieved to be outside. I glanced back at the Panic Room and again wondered how such a nondescript building could contain so much . . . sin. And how easily I had become a part of it, way back when.

"Get on," Eli said, the anger back in his voice. I looked at him like he'd lost his mind, wondering why he was so mad—especially at me. He said nothing more, so I climbed on and we headed up Martin Luther until we reached Bay.

"Head to Congress Street," I said over his shoulder. "Molly McPherson's."

At the traffic light he stopped and half turned to look at me. He said nothing.

"Because I don't feel like going home yet," I said, and I didn't. Home was where Seth wasn't, and it was where Eligius Dupré would be, and the walls of my apartment would close in on me. "Please?" I asked, and really didn't like having to plead. Eli didn't answer, but he made the right turn, and we parked across the street from Congress and walked to Molly's.

Inside the atmospheric Scottish pub, I weaved through the small crowd gathered at the long, polished mahogany bar to Martin, the bartender, then grabbed the corner booth by the front window and ordered another whiskey. Eli slid into the booth across from me, his mouth drawn tight, brows pulled together in a pissed-off expression. He didn't order anything. His light eyes regarded me with such depth, and although he usually observed me in such a manner, tonight was different. There was something different gleaming there, and I wanted to know what it was. I waited, thinking he'd tell me on his own. Too much to expect from a guy, I suppose—even a vampiric one.

The whiskey arrived, the waitress left, and I leaned forward. "What the hell is wrong with you?" I asked, now feeling angry myself. "It's *my* brother out there. Not yours." I literally boiled inside, all of a sudden, and since no one else was around who could take the blame, I put it all on Eli. I let it all out. "My whole life is screwed up. One day I'm doing well; my brother is smart, safe, and doing super in school; my business is going great and we're happy—despite our mother being murdered by a freaking psycho and our loser father a lifer in some penitentiary. Now? I wake up and discover . . . unexplainable *things* exist, my little brother is fast becoming one of them, I have to drink drugged tea to keep an entire family from making me their main course, and I'm trying hard to understand it all, and do what I can to get things back the way they were. So lose your sucky attitude." I sat back, glaring, my heart beating fast. "I didn't ask for any of this."

Eli regarded me for several seconds, then leaned forward. "I am not a *thing*," he said, his voice deadly low. "And I didn't ask to be your fucking babysitter." He raked furious eyes over me and muttered something in French. *"Deal."*

I kept my eyes locked on his as I lifted my whiskey, downed it in one gulp, pulled two bucks from my pocket, and dropped them on the table. "Duties relieved," I snarled, and headed for the door. I was the last person who needed a freaking babysitter; I'd gone through too much in my young life and handled a lot of problems most never encounter in their entire existence. Screw that. I threw a hand up at Martin when he said, "Take it easy, Riley," and I pushed out into the City Market nightlife crowd. It was nearly midnight; the tourists had somewhat thinned, but the locals, the SCAD students, still hung around, and would for a few more hours. It wasn't like I blended into the crowd; I stood out because of more than my choice of clothing. I was tall on top of it, and I knew that if Eli wanted to come after me, he'd have no trouble. Still, leaving returned to me some sort of control; I'd lost it, and dammit, I wanted it back. I didn't like my every move being tracked. It was . . . suffocating.

As I walked up Congress, moving farther away from Molly's, the air grew somewhat quieter, and Capote's familiar music tinged the air; I headed straight for Johnson Square and found him among the mossy oaks. When he saw me, he lowered his sax.

"Now, dere's a sight," he said, grinning. "How you walk in dem things?" he pointed to my boots.

I walked up and hugged the older Gullah, and he patted my back. "Dere now, baby. You don't worry about nothin', you hear? You listen to da Preacher man and do what dem Duprés say." He chuckled the laugh of a man who'd seen it all. "I known you long enough, Riley Poe, to know you ain't takin' fast to havin' someone tell you what to do, right? But you keep dat temper down." He looked at me. "You mind dem."

I gave Capote a smile and a nod. "I'll do my best." I inclined my head to his sax. "Don't stop playing."

"Ha-ha," Capote laughed, and gave a nod. "I never do, baby." He started again, his music soothing and enlightening all at once. So, even old Capote knew about the vampires of Savannah. Somehow, I wasn't shocked. A slow, light drizzle began again, but I didn't care. I stood there surrounded by towering live oaks draped in moss, and I watched the long gray clumps sway in the breeze. The streetlamps cast a tawny glow against the slick brick and cobbles, making them seem glassy, and I inhaled a long, deep lungful of sultry August air. It almost calmed me, until I remembered the cicadas. Rather, their absence.

A couple walked up, wrapped in each other's arms, and stood close by to listen to Capote play. I stood there for a moment longer; then with a wave, I left and started walking up Whitaker toward Bay. I let my thoughts ramble. I was somewhat shocked that Eli had allowed me this much freedom; perhaps he sincerely was sick of babysitting and had gone back to his parents with a refusal to do it any longer. I couldn't blame him. I'd been a bitch. I'd allowed the situation to overwhelm me, and I'd called him a . . . *thing*. I of course hadn't meant the Duprés were *things*, but at the time, it had sounded that way; maybe I'd allowed it to sound that way, too. Some small, sick part of me wanted to make Eli sting, and I didn't know why. I thought of Eli as *anything* but a thing. I found him intriguing, mysterious, and disturbingly unique. The attraction I felt for him seemed real, not just heightened because he was a vampire. Hell—I sometimes had to remind myself he really *was* a vampire. Other than his exceptional capabilities, and his transformation in my bedroom when Seth had lunged toward me, I'd not witnessed anything overt. He and his siblings and his mother and father certainly weren't like Hollywood vampires. They seemed like an ordinary, loving family. Yet . . . I *felt* it. I felt that they were anything but ordinary—that, and much, much more. Precarious circumstances were keeping things settled. I knew that. Just like I knew that one day very soon, I'd see them. *Really see them.*

Just as I crossed Bryan Street, I heard them. I don't know how I knew it was Riggs, Seth, and the others, but I did—maybe it was their distinctive, squeaky, adolescent laughter. I searched the darkness, down Bryan Street, and there they were: seven altogether, wearing dark hoodies like some weird fight-club, free-running hoodie cult, surrounding some skinny dude on the sidewalk. He was alone, and the boys were harassing him, crowding the guy against a car parked on the curb. I couldn't tell which one was Seth; they all looked alike from my vantage point. They weren't full-fledged vampires yet, still just a bunch of stupid kids experiencing quickening, so I changed directions, ducked into the shadows, and moved toward them. I knew I could take at least three of their skinny little asses out; maybe then they'd run off and leave the guy alone. Junkie or not, I wasn't going to stand by and watch while they killed him, or lured him. Whichever.

By the time I'd gotten close, the boys had surrounded the guy and were pushing him, laughing, calling him foul names. I could tell right then that the guy was as high as a kite; he just flailed between the boys, and they laughed, and he even laughed with them. It enraged me. He didn't deserve what they had for him—either transformation by the Arcoses, or ending up as their freaking dinner. Both were unacceptable.

No sooner did I step out of the shadows than I was pushed back into them, and Eli's body pinned me against the brick wall of an empty historic residence that had a FOR SALE sign in the yard. Damn, he was fast. *Freaking* fast, silent and strong. I pushed with all my strength and couldn't budge him a fraction of an inch. I hadn't even heard him coming. We were front to front, our bodies pressed intimately together. He looked down at me as the brick scored into the bared flesh of my back, and he put his finger to his lips. *Shushing me.*

He glanced over his shoulder and then lowered his mouth to my ear. "No matter what you see, stay here," he warned, and when he lifted his head and looked at me, I saw just how much he meant it. I nodded, and just that fast he moved off of me. I barely felt the air shift as he stirred.

In the next breath, Eli stood among the boys and in one lightning-fast move pushed the junkie clear; he landed on the other side of the car with a thud and a moan. Now the boys surrounded Eli, and they became a pack of wild dogs, darting at him, growling; in the middle of two streetlamps, a long shadow fell over Eli, and as I watched, my gut in knots, I saw his transformation. It took all of two seconds, and as I caught glimpses of his horrible face, opaque eyes, unhinged jaw, and jagged fangs, my insides clinched with fear. It was still a hard thing to comprehend. *Don't hurt them!* I yelled inside my head. I wanted their asses kicked, not killed. They were just boys, and one of them was Seth. Eli had two by the throat; I couldn't tell who they were, but their faces were so pale I could see their seemingly luminescent skin almost glowing from where I stood pressed against the brick. Eli dangled them high, their sneakers completely off the ground; then he threw them— threw *both* of them. They landed in the street, and like strung-out users, they jumped right up, unfazed, and lunged at him again. The others followed. Next, adolescent bodies flew everywhere as Eli tossed them like rag dolls; the boys got right back up and surged toward him. Snarls and curses filled the air as they fought; I don't know how much control Eli issued to keep them alive, but he somehow managed. I couldn't take it anymore. Maybe with two, they wouldn't make such bold moves.

The moment I stepped out of the shadows and into the street, one of the rabid boys noticed me and lunged. I mean freaking *lunged*. He was on me in seconds, and I found myself flat on my back in the middle of the street. Beneath the hoodie I stared into a pair of opaque eyes and a pale face; relief washed over me when I saw it wasn't Seth. It was his other friend, Todd, and I grabbed the boy by his skinny throat and held his gnashing mouth away from me. The sensation of his Adam's apple bobbing up and down against my palm made me want to shake him off. But the kid was as strong as a friggin' ox, and it took all of my strength to push him back and shove him off of me. I rolled and crouched, and just as Todd lunged again, I kicked with the flat of my shin and knocked him back. It was almost as if he hadn't felt it; he rushed me again, and this time I gripped both of my hands together to make one big fist and swung upward as he neared me, then elbowed his solar plexus. Still he came at me and in seconds had me on my back again. As much as I hated it, I fished the dope out of my pocket and dangled the baggie in front of Todd with my free hand; his eyes averted from mine, and he grabbed it. Then a smile pulled at his mouth, and it made my insides ice over. His fist came down on my mouth with blinding speed; I didn't even have time to deflect it. Warm liquid spilled onto my lip, and the pinpoint pupils in

Todd's white eyes widened as he stared hard at me, at my mouth. At my blood. *Damn.*

Out of the darkness, the other Duprés emerged and descended upon the boys; it took all of three seconds for the boys to realize they were outweighed. Todd leapt off me, and he and the others took off down the street, laughing, leaping off ledges, and doing crazy, mindless jumps that landed them into handstands; they kept on running, kept moving. I could hardly believe one of them was Seth. Seth wouldn't believe he was Seth. Phin, Luc, and Josie took off after them in the same manner, until darkness swallowed them all. Only their echoes bounced off the buildings of the historic district.

By the time Eli emerged by my side, he'd transformed into the beautiful guy I'd grown painfully used to; all traces of his previous horror vanished. Now he looked more pissed than he had before. His gaze lit on my bleeding lip, and his frown deepened, nostrils flared.

"What in the hell are you doing, Riley?" Eli asked, and yanked me up hard, nearly flinging me across the street. "Can't you listen to anyone? Something wrong with your goddamn ears?" he asked. He looked down, shook his head, and then clasped his hands behind his neck and stared up and off into the shadows. "Wipe the blood off your mouth. Now," he said with almost a growl.

Pulling my minipack off my back, I opened it and searched for something to get the blood off my lip. An old Krispy Kreme napkin wrapped around a wad of gum sat in the bottom; I quickly used it.

"Throw it down," Eli commanded.

Without question, I did as he asked. I knew that having fresh blood on my face was stupid. I wasn't about to push Eli. Not now.

"One of them could have easily killed you," he said without looking at me. Then he turned on me. "All of them would have left nothing for the coroner to piece together."

"I—," I started.

"If you say you can take care of yourself one more damn time, I'm gonna explode," he ground out between clinched teeth. In a blink he was at me, grasping my shoulders and all but shaking me. "You can't, Riley. Not with this. This is way out of your capabilities, no matter how much of a badass you think you are." He did shake me then. "Do you hear me?" He drew so close, our noses nearly touched, and his eyes bored hard into mine. "When I tell you stay put, *stay the fuck put.*"

I could do nothing more than scowl at Eli. I didn't like being chastised, even if he was right.

He shook me harder, his expression lethal. "I don't care that you don't like being chastised. Next time"—his face hardened—"listen."

"Let. Go. Of. Me," I said, emphasizing each word with as much venom as I could muster. He did, and I turned on my heels and began walking, back toward Whitaker, Eli a few steps behind. I played with my cut lip with my tongue and didn't say a word until we stopped at the cross light on Bay. "If your brothers and sister follow Seth and Riggs, why is it that we still don't know where the Arcoses are . . . restoring, rejuvenating, or whatever it is they're doing?" I asked, frustrated. "Won't the boys lead them?"

"No," he said flatly, the light from the streetlamp behind him throwing his whole face into darkness. "They will play all night until dawn, jumping the rooftops and gathering forces, reveling in their freedom and new-found powers; they'll eventually disperse and run in different directions, and the Arcoses will continue to move. Even if we did follow the boys, they'd never be able to lead us to the brothers. The Arcoses are too smart for that. Weak as they are, they'll move, too." He ducked his head and caught my gaze. "Patience."

I glanced back down the street, where the junkie was just stumbling up the sidewalk. "They were going to kill that guy," I said, sickened by the thought.

"No," Eli said. "They were going to either lure him to the Arcoses or force him. Either way, yes—he would have died. They prey on people like him—homeless, junkies, prostitutes—because they're easily overlooked in the public eye."

"What if your parents helped? And Ned? If we all gathered and followed Seth and the others, couldn't we just take them?" I said angrily. "I just don't get it."

Eli grasped me by the chin and held my head in place as he looked at me. "You're forgetting about the Gullah magic, Riley," he said harshly. "They're untouchable until fully regenerated. It might get your brother and his friends killed if we overstepped the boundaries of the magic. Understand?"

I had a hard time breathing; Eli's face in shadows, the glassy reflection in his eyes—even his angry voice all but lulled me into another zone. "Not really," I said, equally angered. "But I guess I have no choice but to go along with it, huh?"

Eli dropped his hand and stepped away. "Yeah. It'd make things a hell of a lot easier if you did."

Thunder rumbled directly overhead, and just that fast, heavy drops of rain began to fall. "Let's go," he said, and we started home. The cars on Bay rolled by on the wet pavement with a hiss, and the warmth of coastal Savannah mixed with that unique smell only rain has. I inhaled deeply. It seemed the last of normalcy for me, and I greedily sucked it in. The rain fell faster and harder, and before we'd even made it to merchant's drive, we were both soaked. I stomped up the cobbles in my spiked boots, my hair like a pile of wet moss hanging in thick, sopping hanks, my skin slick from the rain and the lotion I'd used earlier.

Everything hit me at once: Seth, the Duprés, Eli, the Arcoses, *strigoi*, the Kindred, Kelter and his dirty hands—it all overwhelmed me, and I began to shake. Goddamn, I hated being weak! I yanked my pack off my back and frantically dug for my house key.

Eli's body pushed close to mine. "What are you doing?" he said.

My gaze flew to his, emotions taking over me. I remembered his words in Molly's, and it pissed me off all over again. "Why do you care?" I said vehemently. "You're just a *fucking babysitter*, right?" I found the key and tried to jam it into the lock, but my unsteady, frustrated hands prevented it, and I cursed under my breath. "What happens to me, to Seth—it doesn't matter to you." I looked at him again through a sheet of rain highlighted by the glow of lamplight. "We're nothing to you. Just part of a contract, right, Eli?"

In a move so fast I didn't know it'd happened until it had, Eli grabbed my bag and threw it on the cobbles, then shoved me hard against Inksomnia's back door. He pushed in and crowded me, and I had nowhere to go. I felt his presence all around me, and as the rain fell against my face, it dripped from his hair, too, and onto my face, my chest; I could do little more than stare at him incredulously. "Get off of me," I said angrily, my voice cracking, deep as I struggled not to lose it.

Eli shook his head and studied my face. "No," he said, his voice softer, not as angered as before. His hands moved to my hips and yanked me against him. He drew his face even closer. "You have no idea how much restraint I've used to keep my hands off of you," he said, his hands slipping under my leather vest and along my bare rib cage. I shivered beneath his touch. "I've wanted you from the second I saw you through your storefront, and every dirty desire and thought you've had became mine." He leaned heavier against me, his gaze dangerous, fierce. "I nearly lost my mind the night you thought of me and touched yourself," he whispered against my ear. "I almost took you then," he said, his gaze fixed on mine. "I've wanted you every second since. I can't control myself anymore." His hands skimmed my rain-slicked lower back, grasped my ass, and pulled me against his hardness; his gaze grew dark, and he lowered his mouth to my ear and whispered erotically, "It's been a pleasure being your *fucking* babysitter, Riley Poe. But now I want more."

Never had any form of the word *fuck* sounded so sensual, but falling in a whisper from Eli's sexy mouth, in the context he'd used, his voice heavy with need and with his breath brushing my wet neck? A total turn-on, and my skin flushed with heat despite the rain. I wanted his hands all over me; I wanted out of the leather. I wanted him inside me, and whatever consequence came along with it. As long as it was Eli, I didn't care. Danger and fear of what could happen was easily forgotten as sensations took control. My mind was of myriad sexual pleasures I couldn't help but think of, and Eli cued in on every one of them by invading my thoughts. I invited him, welcomed him, and let him take control.

Perfect, sexy, curved lips hovered close to mine, and his eyes watched my reaction as he grasped the zipper of my leather vest and slowly lowered it, exposing my abdomen and the hot pink swimsuit top that pushed my breasts up; I know he heard my breath catch at his touch—I could see it in his eyes. My leather pants were low-riders and sat a good two inches below my navel, and with one hand Eli explored the rain-slicked skin and muscles of my stomach; then the other pulled me free of the vest. I leaned into him, reached up and threaded my fingers through his wet hair and grasped the back of his neck, and for a split second, we stood motionless, staring. He could kill me in under two seconds, my blood a fiery temptation, and I didn't even care. As long as he kept his hands on me, fear escaped me. He ran his palm up my side and over my breast, and stilled it over my heart. It pounded wildly against his hand. I had no idea what ran through his mind, and I wasn't too sure I wanted to know. But desperation and awe filled mine; I couldn't remember ever needing someone so badly—my insides actually ached with want, desire, and I wasn't even sure why. But it had to be now. And it had to be Eli.

With the rain falling against my face, Eli lowered his head and pressed his mouth to mine; it felt like a match had been struck, and I gasped at the contact. A current soared between us, palpable and hot, and Eli shoved me hard against the wall as he kissed me, both hands leaving my body to push into my hair and hold my head in place. His tongue against mine made me struggle for breath, struggle for more, and I slid my hands up his shirt to feel the hard ridges of his abdomen. He groaned against my mouth, then tore his lips away to press against my ear. "Inside," he said, his voice dark, dangerous, on edge. "Now."

Without waiting on me, Eli turned me around to face the door; I struggled to jam the key in the lock. Behind me, Eli's body pressed against mine, his front to my back, and as his fingers pushed my hair aside, his lips sought my neck and his hands slipped around my waist, down over my hips, where he pulled me against him. Urgency and raw need ripped through me at his touch, so much that it didn't even strike me to think that a vampire's mouth was on my throat—skin that barely sheeted a vessel carrying a unique, druglike blood type. Honest to God, I didn't care at that point. I did *not care*.

Finally, the key worked. I grabbed my pack off the ground and opened the door, and we stumbled inside. Eli's hands never left my body, and as the door shut, the pack dropped from my hand, and we fell back against the door, his body pressed into mine, our tongues entwined, tasting, not getting enough. I felt him everywhere at once; every nerve ending throughout me hummed with heat, and the unique way he tasted made me crave, beg with my hands as I slipped my impatient fingers over the buttons of his fly. There was nothing gentle about either of us. I wanted him *yesterday*.

"Upstairs," he muttered against my ear, and before I could hit the first step he'd pulled me against him again, both hands on my face as he lowered his mouth to mine; he kissed me long, then pulled back, and only the stream of light shining in from the storefront caught his eyes, making them appear dark, almost black. Never had I seen desire so heavy in a pair of eyes. "Hold on," he said, his voice husky, raspy, and as I slid my hands around his neck, he lifted me, and I wrapped my legs around his waist. It was sixteen steps up to my apartment, and he kissed me the whole way.

Upstairs, I slid from his arms, and we stumbled together in the shadows, down the hall and into my room, our lips fastened, hungry, and I found myself once again hard against a brick wall, my fingers desperately grasping at Eli's button fly and unfastening a few. I pushed his shirt up, and he took over, yanking it over his head; my palms skimmed the ripped muscles of his stomach, his chest, and I eased my hand inside his fly and over the hard ridge of his cock; his painful groan escaped his throat at my touch, and I slid my other hand around his ass and pulled him harder against me. When his gaze met mine, his eyes were dark, glassy, dangerous, and lost in desire. It turned me on even more.

Without words, Eli slid his hands up my stomach and over my breasts, where he nimbly released the single clasp keeping my top together. He slid it off my shoulders and dropped it on the floor. At the same time his mouth claimed mine once more, his hands claimed my breasts, and I pushed my body against him with blinding need. I couldn't get close enough, fast enough—as though I wanted to just sink into his skin. I wanted him all over me, everywhere.

With deft fingers Eli trailed his hands down my abdomen to the buttons of my pants, and as he released each one I shivered with anticipation. I kicked out of my boots, he kicked out of his, and finally, we were both free of clothes and restrictions. The only thing that remained was a pair of slender black G-string panties; even those felt more like armor than the weightless, seductive cloth they were meant to be. I wanted to rip them off; Eli read my mind, lowered his hand, and did it for me, then tossed the shredded material to the floor.

We were nothing more than silhouettes and shadows as we stared at each other, with only the tapered band of light streaming in through the French doors. Eli's hands slid to my hips, over my ass, his eyes watching me intently. "Turn around," he said, his voice neither a whisper nor a growl but something in between. It sounded more inside my head than in my ears, and I did what he asked, my front now facing the wall.

Eli's hands pushed my heavy hair aside; his fingers drifted to my lower back, then slowly up my spine; he was tracing my dragons, and continued up my shoulders and down each arm, where he slipped his fingers between mine, his lips and tongue tasting my neck, my shoulder. I shuddered with anticipation. It was the only thing gentle that occurred between us after that. In a blinding move, he spun me around and pinned me against the aged bricks of my bedroom wall and kissed me frantically, desperation in every suck, every lick, every taste, and I met his fury with the same enthusiasm, gasping in between. His hips were muscular and narrow, and I glided my hands around them to his ass and pulled him against me. Eli's hands were everywhere, touching every curve, every valley, and when his hardness throbbed heavy against my thigh, a groan escaped my throat, and I reached down, found it, and palmed its sleek ridges. In one effortless move he lifted me, the grainy bricks scraping my back, and as I wound my legs around his waist, he pushed into me. The deep groan that came from Eli's throat made me shiver, and he muttered something in French. God, I was so wet, out of my mind with need, and Eli satisfied it in three hard thrusts; lights exploded behind my eyes as the fiercest orgasm I'd ever experienced wracked my body, and Eli continued to pound into me, his mouth buried in the crevice of my neck and shoulder, his groans muffled, his orgasm violent as his body spasmed against me. Strong hands grasped mine, spread them out against the wall, and laced his fingers through mine. The kiss that followed nearly undid me all over again; different from the frantic kiss from before, it was slow, erotic, and Eli took his time tasting every inch of my mouth and neck. Without words and with me still clinging to him, he walked backward, turned, and laid me on the bed. There wasn't anything either of us could have said; everything was still fresh, tantalizing, and my whole body hummed with pleasure. For a moment, my eyes drifted shut, but when they opened, Eli stood over me, and I froze. His eyes had turned opaque—literally luminescent as he stared down hungrily at me.

"Eli?" I said warily, and when he didn't move, I repeated myself, except stronger this time. "Eli!" No other words would come out of my mouth. I was scared. And I could tell he struggled for control.

He quickly turned, grabbed his clothes off the floor, and left so fast my eyes couldn't follow. I wasn't in total shock. Now that my mind and body had started to recover from the mind-blowing sex I'd just shared with Eli, I recalled how many times he'd said how he wasn't sure his control could last. It had *barely* lasted. What did shock me, though, was that he didn't just leave my room. He left my apartment. Leaving me totally alone—as in wide-open prey for the Arcos brothers and their growing hoodie cult.

As I slipped beneath the sheets, I reached over, switched the ceiling fan on low, and closed my eyes, letting my mind wander. I was a big girl, and I'd been through a hell of a lot in twenty-five years. I'd been used in the very worst of ways; rejection and abandonment weren't unfamiliar to me. I'd be a liar if I said it hadn't stung to watch Eli walk out, but I understood. I guess I wasn't like other girls in that sense. Being a crybaby just wasn't in my repertoire. I'd learned over the years not to be greedy; take what little bits of life's pleasures you could, while you could—you might not get another offer.

I turned onto my side and stretched, pulling one of the spare down pillows to my middle and cradling it against my bare body. Before slumber dragged me under, I replayed the past hour of my life with Eli, and I knew then that another man would never be able to satisfy me like he had. The way I'd responded to his body, his mouth, his touch . . . no one could ever live up to that. *Never.* I knew what I spoke of, if you know what I mean.

I wasn't sure whether I should be pissed, or grateful for the experience. Part of me knew—felt it in my gut—that something much deeper than wild, nasty sex had occurred with Eli Dupré, but it'd do no good to dwell on it now, and it may very well have been solely on my part. He'd almost transformed, almost lost control. I mean, seriously—he'd lived for nearly two hundred years. He'd had plenty of experiences, and I'm positive I wouldn't be the last orgasm he'd ever experience. For a hot minute, it was a nice thought. But like I said—I wasn't stupid. Rough around the edges maybe, definitely a little perverted at times, but never stupid. I was a survivor. I'd damn well survive this.

Finally, I drifted off to sleep. I knew, even though Eli had left my apartment, that he was still close by. I knew one night of hot, rampant sex certainly wasn't a marriage proposal. Not that I wanted one. But if I knew Eli at all, I did know he wouldn't leave me unprotected. He was out there, somewhere. I knew it. Watching. Just like he had been when I was oblivious to the fact that vampires existed.

Sometime during the early-morning hours, before dawn, I awoke with fear choking me—literally. I was coughing as though I'd been strangled; my heart slammed hard against my ribs, and adrenaline surged through my veins. I sat up and tried to catch my breath, and the bare threads of a nightmare rushed back. Sweat plastered my bangs to my face, and I pushed them behind my ears and rubbed my eyes, trying to remember.

In the dream, *I couldn't tell where I was; long shadows blocked street names and building signs, but it was desolate—almost postapocalyptic. Everything was gray,*

colorless—except me. My black hair with red-and-fuchsia
highlights, and white skin stuck out like a sore thumb, and
dressed in nothing but a short leather skirt, tall leather
boots, and a vest, I ran, fast, down a cracked, broken side-
walk. What few cars sat parked along the sidewalk were
as abandoned and derelict as the buildings. Where I hur-
ried to, I didn't know, but I knew something chased me.
Maybe more than one. They slinked through the shadows
overhead, on the rooftops. I glanced behind me, only for a
second; when I turned back around, he was there. Young,
virile, flawlessly beautiful, and very, very powerful; his
very nearness caused me to burn for him. Seductively, he
licked his lips, and just that fast I envisioned his mouth
and tongue between my legs, erotically caressing until I
fell to my knees as spasms of orgasm wracked my body. I
didn't want it—I couldn't help but take it. It infuriated me,
his seduction, and I knew then that he would haunt me
always, and never cease his pursuit of me. He had power
over me. He wasn't Eli. . . .

I sat up with a start. Somehow, I'd fallen asleep again,
even after remembering that most vivid of dreams. It
left me feeling dirty; it left me with heavy desire. Early
dawn was just beginning to break, and as I slipped from
the bed, I noticed the French doors were wide-open.
They were closed before. . . .

Crossing the room, I closed the doors and latched
them, then jumped in the shower. As the hot water ran
down my body, I felt drained; my energy had dissipated.
Once I finished, I quickly dressed in board shorts and a
tank top and dried my hair, and just as I walked into the
living room, I pulled up short. Sprawled across the sofa
watching TV was Phin Dupré, Chaz's head resting in his

lap. Both glanced up as I walked into the room, and Phin regarded me with eyes so much like Eli's.

"I guess you're the new babysitter, huh?" I asked, although I already knew the answer. I met Phin's gaze as I pulled my hair up into a ponytail, then glanced at the TV. I looked at Phin and lifted a brow. "*The Lost Boys*?" I asked, noting the eighties cult vampire movie as it played across my flat screen.

Phin gave a cocky smile. "Freaking awesome movie," he said. "Classic."

I shook my head and grinned, and it struck me as funny that a vampire would dig a cult vampire movie. "Yeah, it is." I wanted to ask where Eli was, but I didn't. I kept it to myself and figured that whatever was going to happen would happen. Like I said before—I wasn't the crying-over-spilled-milk type of girl.

"So yeah, I'm the new babysitter," he said, then scrubbed Chaz between the ears and stood. I glared at my dog, whose only response to me was a little hiniesca-thumping against the sofa cushion.

"What'd you do, brainwash my dog?" I asked, scowling at Chaz.

"What? Come on, dogs love me," Phin said, and moved toward me. He cocked his head and crossed his arms over his chest. "What'd you do to piss off Eli?" Before I could answer, realization crossed his features. "Ah—never mind." He shook his head and mumbled something in French that sounded something like *sack ray blue*, rubbed his jaw, and regarded me even more closely. He shook his head again. "Damn."

"Look," I said, and turned directly to Eli's brother. "I don't know what's going on here, but I have to have a game plan to get my brother back. If it's changed from before, just tell me—"

"It hasn't," Phin said. "Not exactly."

I slid my flip-flops on. "What does that mean?"

"My father and Preacher agreed to your training," he said, "at Eli's urging. Mainly for safety purposes."

As I let that congeal in my brain, I realized that was what I'd wanted all along, and Eli had known it. "Great. Vampires training me to kill vampires. When do we start?"

He chuckled. "Today. Tonight we'll run the streets a little, and tomorrow night we'll hit the Panic Room along with a few others, if you're up to it. This time, you're hangin' with Luc and me."

"Sounds good to me," I answered, although the void Eli had left suddenly seemed larger. I stood there, contemplating, then walked to the door. "Come on, Chaz—"

"I already walked him."

I stopped and did not look back. "My control over my life has fizzled into nothingness," I said. "I can't even walk my freaking dog anymore." I walked to the door and let myself out, Phin directly on my heels.

"Sorry," he said as we made our way to Preacher's.

"Not your fault," I said, although I wanted it to be someone's fault.

As we crossed the cobbles to Da Plat Eye, Phin leaned close. "So, Riley," he began casually. "What's the story on your friend Nyx?" He chuckled. "She's pretty hot."

I snapped a glare at him. "Don't even think it, porcupine."

Phin rubbed his close-cut hair and grinned. "I'm just sayin'."

After breakfast—I had to sit through forty-five minutes of a wicked stink eye from Preacher man—we left. I needed some air, so I took Chaz for a walk down the riverfront and contemplated my next moves. *Without Eli* was what I thought, and was glad as hell he wasn't around to listen in.

The day was overcast, with a residue of last night's rain clinging to the air, as I walked by the river, Chaz at my side. The bricks were wet and dark from rain, and not even the slightest breeze shifted the thick, muggy air. The familiar cooked-sugar-praline scent from River Street Sweets wafted by, but I discovered that even that simple pleasure didn't sit well with me. A few people were out and about, tourists taking pictures of the *Savannah River Queen*—an old-time riverboat—and the storefronts. Most businesses were closed on Sundays; the others opened up later in the day, so only a few people were out and about, which was fine with me. I was in a foul mood, and I didn't feel like dealing with anyone—not even a total stranger.

My thoughts returned to earlier, at Preacher's, where Phin had gone over very little of what I'd be learning while in training. I already knew how to fight; that was a plus. He said I'd learn the rest from his papa at the House of Dupré. Preacher had looked hard at me, then stated that two of his boys would remain at the house with me at all times. Seemed kind of silly; if a house of vampires decided to take me—one little ol' mortal—down, I'm pretty sure they could do it, and no one would be able to stop them. It was about trust. Like I'd trusted Eli last night, I'd trust the Duprés now. Really—we had no choice. I had no choice. My life for Seth's? Hell yes, in a second.

Returning home, I gave Nyx a quick call; then, changing into a pair of black Lycra yoga pants, a white ribbed tank, and a pair of black Adidas workout shoes, I tightened my ponytail, left my apartment with Phin, and headed to the House of Dupré. A mortal with an extremely rare blood type strolling directly into a house of vampires. Yeah. I'd lost my freaking mind. Again.

Part 8

MARTYR

The moment I stepped foot through the back entrance of the House of Dupré, I knew Eli wasn't there. Somehow, in all of the four-thousand-plus square feet of the historic landmark, I could sense he was gone. I tried not to let his absence bother me, but it did.

Gilles, Elise, Luc, and Josie were in the main sitting room when Phin and I walked in. I immediately noticed Jack and Tuba—two of Preacher's great-nephews—standing near the back. Both were big guys, and they both carried several familiar pouches attached to their belts. I would bet at least one of them contained graveyard dust. I gave them a nod and greeted the Duprés.

"Welcome again, *chère*," Gilles said. He looked just as aristocratic as he had the previous time, and it was weird. He seemed so genuine. A smile touched his lips, and I wished like hell I could command my thoughts instead of rambling on. He was just as bad as Eli about reading my mind.

"I would speak with you alone, if I might?" Gilles asked.

"Sure," I said, and when he directed me to the hallway, I followed—and so did Jack and Tuba. I turned to them both and held up a hand. "Guys, seriously."

Neither looked happy, but they stopped at the door.

"You are quite a brave young lady, Riley Poe," Gilles said in the foyer. "My eldest son was right about you after all."

That got my attention, but I tamped my reaction down. Way down. "Oh? And why is that?"

Gilles gave a soft, all-knowing laugh. "My dear, you do not have to hide anything from me." He rubbed his chin and regarded me. "Not that you could. Still," he said smiling. "I applaud your attempt." He paced before me, his footfall tapping the parquet flooring of the foyer. "He confessed to me his actions last night."

It takes a lot to mortify me these days. Like I've said—I'd experienced a million indecencies and humilities in my youth, and I thought all modesty had flown out the window. But when Gilles Dupré told me his son had confessed his actions with me? *Eesh!* "I hope he didn't tell you everything," I said.

Gilles' blue eyes sparkled. "His mind is just as easy for me to read as yours, *chère*." He inclined his head. "He's at the isle with your dark fellows. He felt he needed a . . . rejuvenation, I suppose you would say."

I stared incredulously. "You mean, he needed some extra hoodoo herbs in his blood?"

"*Oui*. And if I may be frank with you?" Gilles asked politely.

I gave a short laugh. "Of course," I replied, as if he could be any more frank.

"Eligius nearly took your life last night, Riley Poe. He exerted more control than you could possibly comprehend by mating with you and . . . leaving you alive. That's why he left, and why Phin is in his stead." He cocked his head and seemed to study me, beyond my eyes and deep into my soul. "Eligius cares for you. And I know you care for him." He moved closer and stroked my cheek with a long finger. "But when a vampire cares for another, it is . . . different. Deeper. And 'twill end badly, *chère*," he said quietly, with remorse in his eyes. "Between our kind and mortals, it always does." With that, he turned and left me alone in the foyer.

I forced myself to swallow past the hard lump in my throat, and I really didn't know what to do next. I supposed Gilles was right. How could anything have ever worked out between Eli and me? It was the age-old reason found in every vampire romance novel, every vampire movie: The vampire would never age, and the mortal woman would grow old and die. Same old, same old. It was so cliché, but so freaking *true*.

"Are you ready for your first lessons?" Phin said, startling me out of my dreary thoughts.

"Absolutely," I replied, and when he inclined his head to follow, I drew a deep breath and followed, as did Jack and Tuba.

On the top floor of the Dupré House was an enormous room, complete with a martial arts mat, kickboxing bag, boxing bag, and other apparatuses that I couldn't identify. Luc and Josie were setting up three full-sized dummies on the mat at one end of the room. Silver throwing blades of various sizes and shapes lay on a long table at the other end.

I gave Phin a curious glance. "So my training is going to really be about becoming an expert knife thrower?" I asked.

He chuckled. "Sort of." He glanced at me. "You're going to have to learn how to aim, throw, and score while running, jumping, rolling, and flipping." He grinned. "How's that sound?"

I shrugged. "Almost as crazy as a family of vampires teaching a mortal how to kill vampires."

His grin widened. "We're not vampires. We're creatures of the afterlight. We're . . . special."

So for the next several hours, I did a lot of watching and a lot of throwing of practice blades made of stainless steel. The pure silver blades, handcrafted in France and shipped to the House of Dupré, were to be used for the sole purpose of killing other vampires, and they were locked up.

"Okay. Your goal for the day is to simply try to hit the marks—the heart, of course—of the dummies, i.e., the Arcoses." Luc sidled up beside me, placed a steel blade in my hand, closed his fingers over mine so that I'd grasp the short hilt, and then lifted my arm so that my hand rested directly behind my ear. "Like this," he said. "Don't let the blade loose until your arm is fully extended and pointing at your mark."

"Got it," I said, and did as he'd instructed. The blade flew across the room and landed square in the dummy's forehead.

"Heart, Riley," Phin said. "Aim for the heart."

"I was," I said, and everyone chuckled. An hour later, I finally hit the mark. I thought my arm would fall out of its socket, it was so sore.

Then Phin and Luc put me through a series of tests to gauge my existing fighting skills. That was one category where I efficiently proved myself. Of course, Phin and Luc were way stronger and faster than I'd ever be.

"You're not even out of freaking breath," I said, breathing hard, keeping my eyes fastened on Luc as he circled me, and waiting for the pounce.

"Cool, huh?" he said, grinning, his handsome face determinedly fixed on mine. "Vamp perk."

I lifted a brow and inclined my head. "Where'd you get that headband?" I asked, noting the one keeping his long bangs from falling in his face. "The eighties?"

Luc's expression darkened, and he lifted a hand to his band. "Hey, I—"

With a wide roundhouse kick, I knocked Luc's feet out from under him and put him right onto his ass. I followed him down and straddled his middle. While his siblings laughed, Luc graciously accepted the fact that I'd gotten the best of him, and he laid there, sprawled out, arms spread wide in submission. "Nice move, mortal," he said, then in one breathless move leapt up, flipped me, and had me flat on my back while he straddled *me*. He grinned. "Don't hate the headband."

He jumped up, bent over, and offered a hand up. I took it, then swept his legs with one solid kick and again had Luc on the mat.

"Dude, you might as well give up," Phin said.

Luc glanced over at me and grinned. "You know I'm just fucking with you, right?" he said. "Building your esteem."

I laughed. "Yeah, whatever."

He rolled and got up, and this time I did let him help me stand. I wiped the sweat from my brow.

"You're a pretty sick fighter," Luc said, crossing his arms over his cut, bared chest. "But let's add a few obstacles."

I shrugged. "Okay, whatever you want."

Luc grinned, and it made me shudder. *That* made him and Phin laugh.

When it came time to add in jumps and rolls and throwing blades while running? God, I needed practice. At least it would keep me busy, and part of my brain thought that was what the whole thing was about anyway: keeping my mind off of Seth. *And Eli.*

The real shocker came later that afternoon. "Hey, Luc, why don't you and Phin be moving targets?" Josie said, smiling. "I think that would be wicked cool."

I'm not sure why it took me by surprise, but it did, and I suppose the alarm was evident on my face.

"No, seriously—it's fine," Luc said, and flung a practice blade directly at Phin. I watched it sink into his flesh, all the way to the hilt.

"Whoa!" I hollered when Phin pulled it from his chest, flipped it, and flung it back at Luc. Luc caught it in midair. No blood anywhere, but then vampires don't bleed their own blood, do they?

"Totally not real silver, don't forget," said Josie, who sat perched on the windowsill, swinging her skinny-jean-clad legs and All Stars. "The practice blades are sharp, but fake—steel. That's why they're *practice blades*."

I glanced at her, then at Eli's brothers. "That makes me feel lots better."

They all laughed.

Over the next couple of hours I worked on moving targets, and I was glad not to have a squeamish stomach. It took a little getting used to at first—flinging a sharp blade at a live being, although technically, Luc and Phin weren't alive. I missed—a lot.

When Phin laughed at a blade that pinged off the wall, I turned to him. "It's a hell of a lot easier hitting still dummies than moving ones." He merely laughed again.

Practice was grueling. I had good aim, though, and a steady hand—so said Gilles as he and Elise came to watch, and eventually I hit my mark—Luc and Phin— a few times. Jack and Tuba stood near the door like a couple of bouncers and kept their gazes trained on me. Big and silent, they were in fact intimidating. I'm not convinced they'd be a match for the Duprés, though I'd never confess that to Preacher. Maybe there was a lot more to Gullah magic than I originally thought. Rather, Preacher's sort of magic. He and his family were definitely unconventional Gullah.

The last of my first practice day consisted of Luc and Phin tag teaming me while I threw. One would be the moving target; the other would come after me.

I started running from the back of the room, Luc and Phin flanking me. I aimed my practice blade at Luc and threw, then kept my eyes trained on Phin as he lunged toward me. I ducked, rolled, and hit my feet running,

but he was too fast. His body full-impact hit me, and I
landed on the mat with a heavy thud. His eyes twinkled
down at me with victory. "This is the most fun I've had
in a hundred years," he said with a smirk.

"Get off me," I said, struggling to breathe.

"Again," Luc said.

I groaned.

I hit the mat so many times, I lost count. It was a
hard workout for me, effortless for the Duprés. They'd
crammed all the lessons into one day. Apparently I'd
be doing the same every day from here on out. I could
barely wait.

I jogged home from Monterey Square, Phin beside
me, and dusk was just approaching. A slight breeze now
shifted the moss hanging from the oaks, and I dodged
tourists as they window-shopped the myriad antique and
specialty stores lining the historic district. We jogged past
a walking ghost tour, the tour guide dressed in Colonial
wear and swinging a lantern, flashes from the tourists'
digital cameras lighting the darkness as they aimed at
various structures. As I ran by, I noticed a horse-drawn
carriage with a couple snuggled together, and the woman
in the carriage glanced down and smiled at me. The first
thought that crossed my mind was, *You have no freaking clue what's really out there, do you?* How cynical I'd
become. Phin chuckled.

After a quick shower, I quickly ate a can of Spaghet-
tiOs and changed into something Phin suggested: comfortable, movable clothes. I wasn't exactly sure what that
meant, but I took no chances: a pair of baggy jeans that
sat below my hips, a black ribbed tank, and a pair of well-
worn Vans. I pulled my hair into a high ponytail, slipped

on a belt to keep my baggy pants from falling around my knees, and was ready to go. At least, I thought I was. I was learning real fast to always expect the unexpected. I popped four ibuprofen tabs to keep away the soreness I knew my body would be experiencing— was already starting to feel— from the Dupré workout. It was well after dark when we left, and Luc as well as Josie joined us.

For the first hour, we simply mingled in the streets with the tourists. Sunday nights were typically slower than the rest of the week, but there were still a good handful who stepped out into the historic district to wallow in Savannah's atmosphere. I found myself obsessively searching for a crowd of delinquents wearing dark hoodies but never caught the first sight of them. We hit all the main squares, walked Broughton Street east and west, and even strolled through Starbucks. Mullet was in there with his übertall girlfriend, and I spoke to them for just a few seconds before leaving.

It was nearly midnight when we found ourselves in a small alley two blocks over from the Panic Room, and that was when I caught sight of them. Huddled together, they knelt on the sidewalk next to a streetlamp, completely engrossed in . . . something on the ground. Phin grabbed my arm as I moved forward.

"No way, Riley," Phin said, and we all fell into the shadows. "Watch, not approach, or don't you remember the other night?"

I glanced at him. "Yeah, I remember." Todd could have killed me.

"They grow stronger every day," Josie said beside me. "And Seth doesn't know you anymore."

I'd already known it—Eli had said as much. But somehow it hit harder now, and it hurt. An ache spread through my chest at the thought of my brother not knowing me. I studied each of the boys and couldn't determine which one was Seth.

Just then, one of the boys shifted, and I saw all too clearly what they were so intrigued by: a *body*. By the size of the chunky black boots I estimated a male; I couldn't tell whether he was dead. My stomach lurched at the thought, and I wanted to react. No way in hell was I going to sit by and watch as my brother sucked the blood of some dude lying on a dirty sidewalk. I moved, and a hand abruptly stopped me.

"We can't drink the blood of the dead," Phin said, grasping me with a steely grip. "It's lethal for us. That's why they use dope."

"To sedate and subdue," Josie said flatly.

I felt my face lose what little color it had. "Will they kill him?" I asked, afraid of the answer.

"No," Luc said. "They can't make their first kill until the quickening is complete."

"They'll take him back to the Arcoses, and they'll kill him," Josie offered.

In the next instant, I shifted—barely a movement, from one foot to the other—and one of the boys heard. Several hoodies glanced my way, but one in particular had enough light from the streetlamp illuminating his face for me to get a good look. Seth's extraordinarily pale face and lightened eyes stared hard at me; blood was running from the side of his mouth. I reacted—I *lunged*. And Seth lunged back, both of us at the same instant. He was close enough now that I could see the depth of his eyes: crazed, unfamiliar, incoherent—nothing at all remained of the loving, sweet brother he once was. The others stood, glaring; the energy around us snapped, and I knew they were ready to pounce.

"Shit—get her out of here!" Phin yelled, and Josie grabbed me and yanked so hard I thought my arm had popped the socket. She all but dragged me away, and behind us I could hear the fight that had started. We ran—hard—I had no choice, really. It was run or be dragged. I followed Eli's sister and rolled beneath a red-tip shrub and into a neighboring yard. The grass was damp and cool with dew, prickly and stiff. We both jumped up, crossed the lane, and started running.

"You have to go back and help them," I said breathlessly. "I'll go straight home—promise. But seven against two are bad odds—even for a vampire."

Josie stopped and stared hard at me. "Promise?" she asked, then frowned. "Swear it."

I nodded. "Swear it. Now, go," I said.

She watched me for a split second longer, gauging her trust of me, no doubt, then took off. I ran in the other direction, toward home. While my gut told me to stay and fight, my brain told me to get the hell out—I was nowhere near capable of handling myself against a newling—much less a group of newlings. It ate at me to run away—it just wasn't in my nature. But all three Duprés together could fight off Riggs and the others, and my being there would be a total and possibly lethal distraction—to both parties. As I ran hard and fast beneath the streetlamps, my Vans pounding the paved sidewalk, I prayed the Duprés wouldn't accidentally hurt my brother.

I turned at the intersection at Martin Luther King and ran up River Street, the lights and activity at the west end not nearly as heavy as at the east end, but I'd get there soon enough. I hurried up the cobbles, the old Atlantic Paper Company on my left, then past the Hyatt. I crossed over to the river walk, slowing now to a jog. I glanced over my shoulder and didn't see any hoodies, so I began to walk, out of breath. I couldn't help but wonder who the victim on the ground was; I'm glad I hadn't seen his face. I knew I'd never rid my mind of Seth's pale skin, with blood dripping off his chin; it was too horrific. I felt like screaming at the top of my lungs; I felt like hitting something—I felt sick to my stomach. I started to run again—ran *hard*. Very few people were out on a Sunday night at midnight—even on River Street, and I had free rein on the walk. I jumped over the short wall barrier and headed to the river. At the section across from Inksomnia, I stopped, leaned over the rail, and threw up. Never, ever would I forget what my brother had looked like, what he'd unknowingly done. I hated this. I hated *all* of this.

I stood there grasping the metal railing, breathing hard. The night air was stagnant, the low tide making the scent of the marsh pungent, and the shoals of oysters bubbled and popped across the river from Dafuski Island. The mosquitoes were out in armies, and I slapped my neck as they bit. Damn, I hated mosquitoes. I pushed off the rail and turned to go inside—but gasped and jerked to a halt as I stared straight into the vacant, opaque eyes of my brother.

I stood frozen in place; my eyes widened and my insides quivered as I stared at Seth. I hated being afraid of my brother, but I was. He almost looked dead, with his skin so pale and translucent, his eyes a completely different shade of green—nearly white now—and his lips a darkish blue. Dried blood streaked his chin. His nostrils flared as his gaze settled on the side of my throat, at my carotid, and I took a step back. With a sound emanating from his throat that no longer sounded human, he moved slowly toward me. Again, I froze, and he stopped. I know he didn't recognize me, and was pretty sure he'd followed only because he'd caught sight of me. Josie and the others had said more than once Seth wouldn't remember me or his previous life. Had she been wrong?

The air tensed around us; Seth and I were both on edge and about to lunge—I could feel it. I slowly eased back a few more steps, until my flesh grazed the rail, and my hands followed, encircling the metal in a tight grip. "Seth," I said quietly, steadily, my eyes directly on his; hopefully he would concentrate on my face and not my hand movement. I was going to freaking jump in the river if I had to, despite the bull sharks that patrolled the waterways—another thing not mentioned in the tourist mags and brochures. I inhaled slowly, and even that slight movement was noticed by my brother. He flinched and jumped at me. "Seth!" I said, louder, and he jerked as though he'd been struck. His chest rose and fell rapidly, faster than human, and his Adam's apple bobbed unnaturally—like he was swallowing something rapid-fire, over and over.

Then his face drew taut and his eyes widened, and in the next second, he lunged for me. In the same breath I threw my legs over the handrail, and before I could drop, Seth's body just . . . stopped coming at me.

I tightened my grasp and held on to the railing, suspended, until my hands started to sweat and my fingers grew cold and numb. Nothing happened. I had no idea whether he stood there, waiting, or . . . what? No more than thirty seconds passed, and I'd decided a swim with the bull sharks was going to be my finale for the night. Then Phin's face appeared over the rail, and he reached down with one hand, grasped one of mine, and effortlessly hauled me back over. "Riley—what the hell are you doing?" he asked.

I looked at him, then looked around. "What'd you do with my brother?" I asked, ignoring his question, still scared but trying to shake it off.

In the lamplight, Phin's flawless pale face, chiseled features accented by the light dusting of scruff on his jaw, all but glowed. Even though he had different colored hair he looked a lot like Eli. He cocked his head. "What are you talking about?"

I glanced up the river walk, toward the west end. I saw nothing. "I left Josie and ran here, stopped, and barfed over the railing." I looked at Phin. "When I turned around, Seth was right behind me." I met his gaze. "He knew me, Phin. I could see it."

Phin's face turned hard. "In his opaque eyes, you mean? He didn't recognize you, Riley. Not this far into his quickening." He shook his head. "No way."

I crossed my arms over my chest, glanced upward at the more than half-circle moon that slipped in and out of misty clouds, and sighed. "He did. He lunged at me, and when I called his name"—I looked at him—"he flinched. He stopped when he didn't have to."

Phin rubbed his neck. "Then, where'd he go?"

Glancing at the place where Seth had just stood, I shrugged. "He lunged for me, I threw my legs over the railing, and he just . . . disappeared." I stared up both ends of River Street. "What about the guy? Back in the alley?"

Shaking his head, Phin grasped my elbow. "Don't dwell on it, Riley. They took him, probably to the Arcoses. Come on, let's go," he said, then mumbled something French beneath his breath. "Eli would kick my ass if he knew I let you off alone," he said to himself, but I'd clearly heard.

We crossed the cobbles and old trolley rails, gained the sidewalk, and walked to the narrow alley next to my building. "Why's that?" I asked. I knew it was fake coy, but I didn't care. I wanted to hear it. We climbed the steep concrete steps to Factor's Walk, and Phin gave me a sly look.

"He just would," he answered, and continued to look at me with curiosity. "Why'd you barf?" I looked at him, and he held up a hand. "Ah—never mind."

"Right," I said, and fished the key out of my pocket as we mounted the top of the steps and turned down the merchant's drive. The moment we reached my back door, images of Eli kissing me hard against that very door raged through my mind, and so did everything that followed: his hands, his mouth, his body inside of mine it overwhelmed me. I found it beyond weird to think I'd known Eli for such a short time. It seemed like years. I wasn't a virgin; I'd had sex before. That night with Eli wasn't sex. It was something else that to me had no name, no origin, and obviously something I'd never experienced before—probably never would again. I accepted it as that and pushed everything else out of my brain.

Chaz barked as soon as he heard me push the key in the lock; he had to go out. Grabbing his leash, we walked him for a few, then headed inside for the rest of the night. I made a peanut-butter-and-jelly sandwich, and Phin sat on the counter while I ate.

"My father says you'll need to close your business for the last week of the quickening," he announced. "I was supposed to tell you earlier, but I forgot."

I stared, midbite. "No way." I bit, then continued to chew. "I'll take off, but Nyx can run the shop. This is high season for me, and unlike you, I didn't come from money."

Phin smiled. "I confess—that is a pretty sweet deal. But Papa made us each invest—even Josie. We all have our own money." He smiled. "Microsoft."

"Do you have a social security card? Driver's license?" I asked, and took another bite. I chased it with a long gulp of milk from the carton and regarded him. "Insurance on your bike?"

He grinned. "Of course," he said. "We pay taxes, too."

I shook my head and rinsed my plate in the sink. "I don't even want to know how you manage that."

Phin just chuckled, hopped off the counter, and flopped onto the sofa. To look at him, or Luc, you'd think they were just a couple of hot young guys without a care in the world. But I'd seen them in action. They were tough-asses to the max.

"Pretty impressive fighting today," he said as I walked from the room. "Sincerely."

I turned and grinned. "Yeah? You too, Dupré. Night."

Phin laughed a total guy laugh, said good night, and flipped on the TV.

I had to constantly remind myself that he used to suck the blood out of innocent humans.

After a shower, I left my hair wet, wadded it up high on my head, and wrapped a band around it to keep it in place. I pulled on a cami and a pair of black boy shorts, and sighed. I was sore and exhausted; my mind whirled around seeing my baby brother in his quickening state, and wanting—*needing*—Eli. It'd shocked me to learn he'd gone to Da Island to get rejuvenated—whatever that exactly meant. It had taken a lot of control for him to walk away from me, and Gilles' words, or warning, felt heavy in my head. '*Twill end badly, chère. Between our kind and mortals, it always does.* I crawled into bed, glanced at my closed French doors, and drifted off to sleep with Gilles' words still ringing in my ears.

In my slumber, another dream claimed my conscious-ness, and *I found myself in a dark, hazy underground club—I didn't recognize it, nor did I recognize the pa-trons. Was it a masquerade party? Halloween? Themed? Everyone was dressed in modified Victorian garb; wom-en's gowns dipped exceedingly low, revealing heaving breasts and nipples, and slits up the front and back of their flowing skirts exposed their nakedness when they moved. The young men wore dress velvet coats with tails and ruf-fles, their pants laced in the front but with laces loose and mostly undone; some openly groped themselves as they sucked an exposed breast. A themed orgy? An odd mix-ture of music played, one of Gregorian monks chanting*

*and the ancient strings of a harpsichord. I glanced down
at myself and noticed that I wore the same as the others;
my breasts and nipples were also exposed, and I had no
panties beneath my skirts. No one seemed to notice me,
and I eased away from the corner I was standing in and
moved along the edges of the crowd, seeking an exit, covering myself with my arms folded over my chest. I had no
idea why I was there, only that I wanted to escape.*

*Then he was suddenly blocking my path; I knew I'd
seen him before but didn't know his name. He was not
Eli. A black-haired woman was at his side, her face hidden in his shoulder, her fingers entwined in the laces of
his breeches, fondling. The man was flawless and beautiful; his gaze raked over my body, and wherever it lingered, my skin burned, tingled with desire. His hand
lifted to the woman beside him, and he grazed a thumb
over her hardened nipple; I felt it and gasped with pleasure. A smile tipped his sensual mouth, and he leaned to
the woman and whispered; I heard it. He said, "Stroke
me." The woman's hand slipped inside his breeches and
palmed him, moving slightly up, then down; I felt it, too,
hard and sleek in my hand. His gaze never left mine, and
I hated how excited he made me. I wanted to escape; I was
powerless to move. He whispered to the woman, "Taste
me." With her back to me she knelt before him, freed him,
pulled it into her mouth; I felt it in mine, and I grew wet
between my legs as I watched her head bob against him.
He stared at me with a gaze so intense and powerful, I
hadn't the ability to move, and he smiled seductively at
me, and whispered, "You look good enough to fuck," and
then licked his lips, sending me into a breathless orgasm;
then his eyes rolled back as he found his. I hated him; I*

wanted to be closer to him. It was then that the woman shifted, exposing a piece of bared back. At the same time I recognized my dragon tattoo, she turned and looked at me, smiling as she delicately wiped her mouth with the tip of her finger. The woman was me. All of the other patrons stopped their orgy at once to look at me. I blinked, and their faces contorted into those of monsters, their teeth jagged and gnashing from unhinged, exaggerated jaws, and they lunged at me. Terror gripped me, and I began to run, faster, and everything became barren and bleak. And suddenly I was no longer at a Victorian orgy but in a heavily wooded forest filled with long shadows and darkness. I was being hunted. . . .

"Riley!"

As my name being said out loud made it through the webby edges of the dream, I gasped and lunged forward, and steely hands were there to catch me. My heart pounded mercilessly, and I was breathless, grasping onto . . . someone. At first, I thought it was Eli. It was still dark, but I soon realized it was Phin.

"Whoa," Phin said, trying to comfort me by patting my back. "Slow down, girl. What's wrong with you? You're gonna have a freaking heart attack." He pulled the sheet that I'd kicked out of to cover up my lower half.

"Bad dream," I said, and suddenly felt a wash of weakness overcome me. I fell back onto my pillow. It was just like before—I had no energy.

"Tell me about it," he said. "It always helps."

"Thanks," I said, my heart slowing, and I closed my eyes. "But you don't wanna know." I didn't even want to know, but unfortunately I did. I remembered it all. And it was freaky-weird. *Who* was that *guy*? I wasn't into orgies, and I'd never been to one. Why in hell would I not only dream of one, but get off from it? Nasty, Poe. Just freaking nasty.

"You need to sleep with this shut and locked," Phin said, and when I looked he'd moved and was closing the French doors.

"I closed and locked those before I went to sleep," I told him, and he looked skeptically at me. "Swear to God."

Phin latched the doors and sat at the foot of my bed, rubbing his neck. "That," he said, "is not good." He cocked his head. "What was the dream about, Riley?"

I cracked my eyes and looked at him in the shadowy light.

"Don't make me go in there and get the info myself," he said, pointing to my head.

I sighed. "Fine. But don't say I didn't warn you. It's freaky. And it's not the first one I've had." When he lifted a brow, I continued. "They're just . . . weird sexual dreams. Ones where an amazingly hot guy can make me . . . you know?" Phin lifted the other brow up. "Yeah, that. Well, he can do that without touching me." I put my hands over my eyes. "God, Phin—do I really have to give any more detail?" I wasn't shy, but some things were personal. "I don't think a porn dream is something you need to know about."

He stroked his chin. "Uh, yeah. I think you should tell me every sordid detail of both dreams. Don't leave anything out. Sincerely." He leaned forward like a freaking psychiatrist, imaginary notepad and pen in hand. He gave a slight nod. "You may begin."

I threw a pillow at him. "Get out of my room, pervert. I need more sleep."

He regarded me, then rose and left the room. "I'll be in here if you *need* me." I heard him chuckling at himself in the living room. A vampire with a sense of humor. Sweet.

The rest of the night went by without incident; no more funky erotic dreams, no further opening of locked doors, and so on, and I carried on my usual Monday-morning routine. Nyx was hopping around like a little prairie dog when Phin and I walked in to Inksomnia, and she wanted an update on Seth.

Nyx pulled me into a tight, squeezing hug, then looked at me. "Riley, how much longer does Seth have to be out there?" she asked, and guilt gnawed at me for telling my best friend a lie. She adored Seth, and I knew she was going through a tough time with his supposed drug rehabilitation. If she knew what was really happening—no, she'd never be able to handle it. Not Nyx. I met her gaze with what I hoped was a reassuring one. "He'll be home soon, Nyx. We don't want him flying through rehab and getting out too early, do we?" I hugged her back. "Trust me—I want this to be his last terrible experience. And that's why I'm going out to Da Island to be with him."

Nyx's eyes widened. "When?"

"In a couple of days. I need to call and reschedule several appointments today." I looked at her and cocked my head. "Can you handle the shop alone? Oh—and would you take Chaz? If it's a problem, then Estelle and Preacher—"

Nyx gave me her signature thumbs-up. "Of course

I will, on all accounts! No prob." She smiled, talking with her hands as she did when excited. "I'm glad to see you're going to be with your little man. He needs you now more than ever."

I sighed. It wouldn't be the first time, unfortunately. "I really miss him."

"I know," she said, then smiled through her worry. "So do I. And you're doing the right thing." She began to set up. "So where's Eli?"

I shrugged, but inside my gut wrenched at the sound of his name. "He's around. Maybe he'll drop in soon. Until then," I said, distracting her from Eli, "how 'bout showing his brother the ropes? They've all sort of taken an interest."

"Sure!" she said, and waved Phin toward her. "Come on. There's a lot to learn about . . . ink!"

The day progressed more slowly than any I'd experienced over the past couple of weeks. I made tons of calls to clients to reschedule inking appointments for the following two weeks, and only one out of twenty-two decided to use another artist. I spent the rest of the day ordering Nyx enough stock so she wouldn't have to handle it and the ink jobs. Plus I did a few inks myself, and I tried to put my personal hell aside long enough to do good-quality artwork. It wasn't easy, but I managed it. Inksomnia had been my passion, my savior after I'd managed to get a decent life going once Preacher and his family scoured the drugs and idiocy from my system. Now? My heart just wasn't into it. Knowing Seth was experiencing some freakish ancient vampiric quickening and fast turning into a vicious killer sort of put a hold on the rest of my life. I loved that kid more than anything, and I would die to make things right again.

At six o'clock, Nyx flipped on the flat screen in the sitting area; she always wanted to find out what was happening in the low country. Me? Too depressing, so I avoided it. Until today, when the desperate plea of a woman's voice blasted across the shop. I crossed the room and watched with Nyx, and my heart dropped.

"Please," the woman sobbed, and sagged against a man—I assumed her husband. "If anyone has seen Jared, please—I . . . just want my son back." The camera flashed to the reporter, who described Jared Porter as sixteen years old, five feet seven inches, approximately one hundred and forty pounds, with short blond hair and brown eyes. A picture of him flashed across the Crime Stoppers screen, and my insides went icy. Jared had been missing now for almost a week and was last seen around eleven p.m. leaving River Street with his friends.

"That poor mother," Nyx said, shaking her head. "It must be so awful."

I had no doubt that Jared Porter had joined Seth and the others. It made me angry and more determined than ever to bring those bastards down.

Nyx helped me close shop, then headed out to Wilmington Island to have dinner with her parents. Luc and Josie had come in just as Phin and I headed upstairs. I quickly showered and dressed—this time with Josie digging through my closet. She reminded me of a little sister, and I had to give it to the kid—she had rockin' taste. She pulled out a pair of ripped skinny jeans and a black tank with a spiderweb tattoo design on the back.

"Sweet," she said, and handed them both to me. "I

wish I could go," she said, pouting. She pulled my hair into a funky half-up, half-down sort of do, with my bangs long and free. "But Papa said I should just let the boys go with you for now." She looked at me, her brows pulled together. She glanced at my chest, then back to me. "I wish I'd been a little older when Papa changed me." She looked down at herself. "I'll never have boobs like you. I'm flat chested forever. It sucks."

I smiled. "I know it seems like it sucks," I said, and then flushed when I remembered Eli's words. I inclined my head. "But boobs are more trouble than they're worth sometimes anyway. I have a hard time fitting into clothes sometimes. Pain in the ass." I grinned. "Tell ya what. Why don't you pick out a choker? I've got a hundred of them."

"Cool, thanks!" she said, and dove back into the plundering. "Any of them?"

"Sure," I said, then grabbed my navy All Stars and headed into the living room. "Ready?" I said to Luc and Phin, both standing near the window looking out. They turned, and I gotta say—it's one thing when you get a reaction from a regular dude that they think you look hot. It's another experience altogether when it's a pair of century-plus-old vampires ogling. I shamelessly confess to liking the ego being boosted a little.

"Damn, Riley," Luc said, looking more like a wolf than a vamp.

"Double damn," said Phin, and he grinned at me. He was remembering my dreams, although I never did go into detail. I didn't have to. I'm sure he slipped into my thoughts. I could so tell.

I shook my head. "Pervs. It's just jeans and a tank.

Let's go. And I'm driving." I glanced at them both appreciatively. Luc had on a pair of frayed jeans and a black formfitting tee with black boots. Phin wore a pair of black slim-fit jeans with a chain hanging from the pocket, a pair of black All Stars, and a gray long-sleeved mesh shirt. "Pretty hot yourselves, by the way," I said, and headed to the door. I scrubbed Chaz on the head—Josie had taken him out earlier—and the Duprés followed me out.

We dropped Josie off in front of the Dupré House and made our way over to Martin Luther King. The plan was to hit the Panic Room, followed by a trip to the Morgue—another dark alternative club. If there was time, we'd hit one more: the Asylum. God, I hadn't gone to any of those in quite a while. But Seth and the others would be hanging around the darker clubs for—I hated to say it—victims. So I had to put my fears aside despite my reservations. It hadn't been easy giving them up, but once I had, I was done. I'd figured that if I was going to get clean and straighten my life out, and give Seth a good life, then I needed to cut clean of all things that would be a temptation to me. Now, some people, like Mullet? They went for the sheer fun of loud, head-bangin' music, dance, and drink. I'd started out that way, but I became something else—a big-time clubber, long before reaching legal age, who couldn't assert self-control. I didn't even have the desire to go anymore. Weird.

The night air whisked through my opened Jeep as we cruised up Martin Luther King and turned down Williamson. I parked a street over, closer to the River Street side, and we got out. Much to the surprise of both Duprés, I tucked some bills into my bra, and my Jeep key in my pocket. I then gave Luc and Phin a heads-up on Zetty.

Just before we got to the entrance, Phin stopped me. His look was grave. "Preacher told us about, you know— when you were young. If it gets too much in here for you, just say the word."

I gave Phin a smile. He really was one considerate vampire. "No prob. That habit left my body once the Gullah washed it out of me. But thanks for some good lookin' out."

Zetty greeted me the same as the other night, and greeted Luc and Phin with his hand resting on his trusty traditional Tibetan blade. His eyes followed us all the way inside.

Luc and Phin simply looked at each other and shrugged.

The moment we pushed through the doors, "Bad Company" by Five Finger Death Punch was pounding through the surround sound, and the familiar, sickening scent of smoke and liquor tinged with body sweat and pot hit us in the face. I knew Kelter would find me. It was like he could smell me, which really freaked me out. Luc went to the bar to order me a drink, while Phin and I melded into the throng of people dancing—or doing whatever it was they were doing.

I moved to the music, and Phin stayed close. I leaned in. "Pretty good moves for an old guy," I said in his ear, and he laughed. While he seemed to be a free-willed young dude dancing with a crazy chick, I knew how serious he was taking this issue with the Arcoses. While he laughed, his gaze raked the crowds, searching for any of the boys with Riggs and Seth. Every once in a while I caught a glimpse of something dark in his eyes that was . . . beyond frightening. I'd seen it in Eli's eyes, too. They were not to be underestimated. That much I knew.

We danced for a few more minutes, then made our way to the bar. "We're going to leave you alone, but we'll be close," Phin said. "All you have to do is think me to you, and I'll come." I nodded, and he and Luc moved away. The black walls and strobe lights made the inside of the Panic Room surreal and dreamlike, and to me it was no surprise how so many people lost themselves. It wasn't the club's fault—the music rocked, and people drank in clubs every day and didn't get screwed up. It was the fault of scumbags like Kelter, who added that little extra something that made innocent lives go to straight to hell, becoming completely submerged in the darkest dregs.

After almost forty minutes, there were no signs of Riggs, Seth, or any of the other boys, and Kelter hadn't shown up. I decided to take a walk to the back of the club to see whether I noticed anything unusual. I eased away from the bar and moved into the crowd.

If I'd had a buck for every stray hand that felt my ass in the four minutes it took me to get to the horseshoe, I'd be filthy rich. But to find the body those hands belonged to would have taken a CSI team. Everyone looked as guilty as hell. Freaky-guilty, male and female alike. So I squelched my desire to knock the hell out of every potential ass grabber and hurried through the crowd. Once in the horseshoe, I made a beeline for the office doors, weaving through a line at the women's restroom and the usual couples pawing each other against the wall. I tried the doors, found them locked, and turned to leave but stopped abruptly. A girl stood directly behind me. Almost as tall as me, with platinum blond hair streaked with black and purple that hung to her waist, and dressed head to toe in black leather, she glared at me with kohl-rimmed eyes. She was maybe all of eighteen.

"If you're looking for Kelter, he's not here," she said sharply, and inspected me critically from the tips of my boots to the top of my head. Disgust crossed her face. "I saw you here the other night with him," she said, and lifted a cigarette to her lips and pulled. She blew smoke in my face and leaned close. "Back off, whore," she whispered, and her breath smelled like stale beer and cigarettes. "Kelter's mine."

I nearly choked. Not on the smoke but because I couldn't believe that anyone would purposely want Kelter Phillips. It was freaking hilarious. I gave her a slight grin, although I really felt sorry for her. "Don't worry—I don't want him anyway." I pushed past her and left, and I found I couldn't get out of the Panic Room fast enough. Her eyes shot daggers at me the whole way out—I could feel them ricocheting off my back.

Phin and Luc met me in the middle and guided me to the exit. Zetty stared at me as we left and gave me a single nod. He held the door as we passed through, and closed it firmly behind us.

"Cheerful dude," Luc said. "No gains there tonight. On to our next destination."

Outside, the air had grown heavy, muggier than earlier, and very, very still. We climbed into the Jeep and pulled out onto MLK. "The Morgue," I supplied, and within fifteen minutes we were pulling into the parking garage on Drayton and walking down the narrow alleyway to the entrance. Again—this wasn't the sort of place listed under "Nightlife" in the travel brochures for Savannah. Inside, the Morgue was home to a rougher class of partiers; gangs that liked to call themselves Vamp-Goths dominated the club, male and female alike, and only the nonsqueamish, extremely confident—or crazy—dared make an entrance. I knew some of them, and they were pretty freaking cool—I had probably inked most of them. Others were just wannabes, dressing the part and making a lot of noise to get attention. I couldn't help but wonder whether any of them *really* believed vampires truly existed. Or was it just the idea? The portrayal? If they did, I'd bet my ink shop none of them thought they were anything like the Duprés.

Unlike the Panic Room, the Morgue was under new ownership; it prevented me from having an in—and part of me felt thankful. One Kelter was all I could handle. I suppose I didn't need an in anyway. The club was dark and thumping. I stepped through a veil of smoke and moved through the crowd to a vacant spot near the wall. Phin rounded on me and lowered his head to my ear.

"We'll spread out and see if we spot any of the hoodies," he said. "Let's give it forty minutes, tops. Then we're out." The look he gave me was grave. "If you need me, just think it."

"Right," I said, and watched the Dupré brothers split up and disappear into the crowd. For a Monday night, it was a heavy mix. People were jammed into the Morgue like sardines, and as I edged the perimeter I scanned the clubbers and began to weave into the center. The dark interior and flashing lights made it pretty difficult to see any sort of distance, so I moved in and out of the dancers and fought off several groping hands, my sights set on the opposite side of the club. A hand to my crotch—yes, my *crotch*—stopped me abruptly, and I reacted. I grabbed the wrist taking privileges and yanked upward, and I separated the offender from the tightly knit group of people around me. A young guy, maybe nineteen or twenty, with burred black-dyed hair and a silver mesh sleeveless shirt stared at me with cold, almost black eyes. The side of his neck was inked with a massive wad of barbed wire; in the center was a naked woman, clinging to the wire, a look of terror—or ecstasy, I couldn't tell which—on her face. It was a shoddy art job, in my opinion.

The guy pushed toward me, his face close. "I know what you want," he said in what he probably thought was a seductive, turn-me-on, throaty voice.

I dropped his arm. "I doubt it," I said, and turned away. "Freaking perv."

From behind, he pressed into me and grabbed my hips to hold me in place.

"I mean, I know *who* you're looking for," he said against my ear, and then a hot wetness crept over my lobe as he licked it.

I stopped and looked at him over my shoulder. "Is that right?" I said, repulsed but hiding it. "And what exactly do you know?" Maybe he'd seen Seth or one of the boys. It was worth checking out.

"This way, babe," he said, and nudged me forward through the crowd; the whole time, his hands stayed gripping my hips. "Hands off," I growled, and he laughed but removed his hands. As we moved, I continued to

search faces, but no one seemed familiar—not even
Phin or Luc appeared. Finally, we broke free, and when
we did the guy totally took me off guard and shoved me
against the exit door. In the next second he was pressed
against me and we were falling through the door, into
the alley. With a heavily booted foot he kicked the door
closed behind us and was on me, my front slammed into
the bumpy painted concrete of the building, and *this
guy* was grinding his hard crotch against me, mouth buried against my neck, one hand feeling my breasts, the
other one groping my crotch. "It's me you're lookin' for,
right?" he said, grunting in my ear.

Oh, Poe. You dumbass.

"Wrong," I ground out, and he merely laughed. He
had me pinned pretty good, but I was a tall girl, strong
and athletic; I pulled my legs up while he sucked on
my neck, wedged the balls of my feet against the wall,
and pushed hard. We both fell back, and I leapt up. Before he could get off his ass, I'd kicked him in the jaw,
and his head jerked back; he spit blood from his mouth.
"Bitch," he growled, and spit again. "Stupid bitch."

Adrenaline must have kicked in, because he jumped
up like a cat and lunged for me. He never made it. A
figure moved so fast from the shadows and grabbed him
by the throat that my brain hardly had time to process it.
I watched the perv's body fly against the Dumpster and
hit with a heavy thud. In the next second, Eli emerged
from the darkness, his face a mask of fury, his eyes lightened but not yet opaque. He moved closer but did not
touch me.

"What the hell are you doing, Riley?" he said, his
voice dark, angered, shaking with rage. "What?" Those

light eyes regarded me, held me captive. I couldn't have looked away if I'd tried. Thankfully, he did. He grasped his neck with both hands and looked skyward. *"Tu me fais mourir,"* he muttered in French, and of course I had no idea what it meant. "You're killing me," he clarified, and then drew a deep breath and looked at me. "You. Are. Freaking. Killing. Me."

I glanced toward the Dumpster. The perv hadn't budged. "You didn't kill *him*, did you?" I asked.

Eli's face became even more infuriated. "No. But I should."

I would be lying if I said my heart wasn't soaring at seeing Eli. It'd only been two days, but it'd felt like forever. Pretty mushy coming from me, and I can promise you—it took some getting used to. I didn't want to care about him. It made zero sense and made everything much more complicated—especially since Gilles had pretty much given me fair warning to back off.

"He did *what*?" Eli asked, moving closer.

I turned my back and headed for the door. "Oh my God, Eli—stay out of my head." No sooner did my hand grasp the metal than Eli was behind me, stopping me, and the memory of our night together, with him crowding my body like he was now, made my head swim, my senses heightened. My heart raced at the thought of him touching me, and my breath quickened at how he *had* touched me. I didn't dare move.

"I'm sorry I left, Riley," he said, close to my ear. "I had no choice."

I made myself breathe, and steady my voice. "Yeah. I know."

Just then, Phin entered the alley from the street side;

he cast a quick glance at the guy lying against the yellow Dumpster and stared at me. "Why didn't you call me?"

I shrugged. "I had it. Besides—he led me to believe he knew who I was looking for. I thought it was worth a shot to check out."

Phin rolled his eyes and threw his hands up. Yes. A vampire *rolled* his *eyes*. "Never do that again. Besides— we just spotted three of the kids." Phin glanced at Eli. "They were with a new kid—a little older, but not more than eighteen. A total badass. They're headed down to the river. Lots of warehouses down there. Luc's on them." His gaze returned to Eli. "Lots of gangs hang out down there, too. Glad you're back." He slapped his arm.

"Well, let's go, then," I said, and turned up the alley. A steely grip stopped me, and I turned to stare at Eli. "What?" I asked, hiding the thrill that shot through my arm at his touch. He couldn't possibly read *every* thought I had.

"You stay with me," he said flatly.

I could tell there'd be no arguing, despite the fact that being close to him made me want him all the more. I'd have to get over it and deal. "Fine," I answered. "Then, move your ass. I want to see where my brother's been hanging out."

Eli stood there, his face unreadable, and stared. It certainly would be nice to have that mind-reading ability, because he was like a stonewalling poker player. I had no idea what he was thinking. Might be a good thing, now that I thought about it.

"Oh-kay," Phin said sarcastically. "Let's go."

We moved through the shady treelined streets of the

historic district, past tourists and locals, then slipped through a chain-link fence into the dregs of the industrial riverfront. Two older guys sat near the river, the embers of their cigarettes dotting the blackness with an occasional orange glow. As we edged closer, they turned their heads and stared but kept to themselves. Probably homeless and harmless. Phin slowed and reached into his pocket, grabbed his vibrating cell, and read the text. "Luc says it's three warehouses down from here. Nine kids in all including the three that just left the Morgue."

"If all nine complete the quickening, we'll have a large vampire problem on our hands," I whispered. "Damn."

"They're not all in the same phase," Eli said. "But it's still a problem. Big problem. Their tendencies grow each day, and the last time I faced your brother's friend, he was damn strong. And fast."

We crossed a patch of soggy, stinky sod that smelled more like rotting sea creatures than the marsh, and edged close to the building. Yeah, an empty warehouse. Just like in the movies. Nothing good ever came from an empty warehouse.

"There's Luc," Phin said, and we made our way to where he was standing. A row of dirty windows stretched from one end of the metal building to the other, and a flicker of light came from an old metal barrel. When I neared the window to get a better look, Eli pulled me back and pinned me behind him. I frowned at his back and knew it'd do no good to try to force my way around him. It'd just cause unneeded noise.

"They're here," Eli said under his voice. "Arcoses. I can sense them."

"They weren't before," Luc said. "I didn't sense them, and my sense of . . . sense is better than yours."

"Doesn't matter," Phin said. "Eli's right—they're here now. They're weak, but their vigor has improved. Greatly."

"Fourteen now, not nine," Luc said, peering into the window. "Shit."

Eli glanced at me. "How many were at the cemetery that night?"

"Four, including my brother," I supplied. "And there's fourteen now?"

"Twelve. Two in there are the Arcoses," Eli said. He craned his neck around, then looked at his brothers. "Not good."

A man's scream broke the silence.

I leapt at the window to see what had happened; that scream was the kind that speared your soul; I could *feel* it inside me. He was terrified. Eli pulled me back.

"Riley, don't," he said quietly. "It's too late."

Part of me—obviously the sick part—wanted to see. I wanted to know what kind of hell I was dealing with. I tried to pull out of Eli's arms, but he held fast. He moved his face close to mine, his eyes pinning me with a dark glare. "I said *no*."

I again struggled. "We've got to do *something*!" I hissed.

Eli's fingers tightened around my arms. "I said, it's too late." When I jerked again, his face grew angry. "Do you really want to see, Riley?" He shook me. "Do you?"

"Yes!" I said furiously under my breath. "I do."

In a move that nearly made my head rush, Eli spun

me around. Through the hazy glass and firelight from the barrel I could vaguely make out three guys—bigger than the rest. Two held the struggling a man, and one had his mouth planted at the guy's throat. The man's legs twitched and kicked as he tried to break free; the others—the kids—watched. Then, even from the distance I stood away, I watched as the attacker's face contorted, long fangs dropped from his mouth and he snatched the struggling man away from the other one who held him and tore into him like a rabid dog. First his throat. Then his chest. The man's screams died in a drowning gurgle, and I almost gagged. My mouth went dry; I hadn't even realized I'd started to shake until Eli forced me away from the window. *So much blood . . .*

"Let's get out of here," Phin said.

All the strength had drained from my body; I'd never felt so weak and helpless in my entire life—except once, and that was the day I'd found my mother murdered. I remember holding her in my arms, shaking her hard, yelling at her to wake up. I didn't like the memories. I hated *this*. But Christ Almighty, there'd been blood everywhere. That guy never had a chance. *And Seth was in the midst of it.*

I was silent as Eli and I walked back to the parking garage. Without asking, Eli took the wheel and drove. Luc and Phin stayed behind to watch the boys, and that comforted me very little. My mind rushed around in myriad directions; I wanted to be furious, pissed off and ready to kill. But I was scared. Scared shitless. What they'd done to that man . . .

I leaned my head against the seat as we drove through town, and the city I once loved didn't look the same anymore. Everything looked darker, menacing, uninviting. Rather, inviting death. The Spanish moss that I'd always loved hung limp and lifeless; every shadowy alcove and alley, every intricately carved piece of black wrought iron beckoned evil, and behind my closed lids I could envision it happening all over again. Seth's face flashed before me, and just that fast he transformed, and sunk his mouth into the throat of a stranger. I pushed the pads of my fingers into my eye sockets hard, trying to rid myself of the sight. It wouldn't go away.

"Riley," Eli said, and in the next breath his hand was on my thigh. I wanted it there; I didn't want it there. I wanted more; I'd get nothing. I was a loser in this, no matter how I looked at it. My brother would have . . . tendencies, and only if the Arcoses could be destroyed and the boys taken to Da Island for rehab. My mind, though, would never forget what I saw. *Never.*

I barely noticed when Eli passed Bay Street, and thought nothing when he turned onto Victory. I had no idea where he was headed, and frankly, I didn't care. The balmy wind swept over me as we drove, and I closed my eyes to try to block the visions invading my brain. It didn't help.

Then Eli reached over, laced his fingers through mine, and held my hand, and the simple gesture comforted me. I opened my eyes and turned my head to find him already looking at me, and that comforted me, too. When he moved his gaze back to the road, I continued to watch him. His profile was so perfect, his hair blowing sexily against his jaw, his forehead, catching on sensually arched lips that worked magic against my body. Somehow, it made me calm. "Where are we going?" I asked.

He didn't look at me, but he smiled. "Ever been to the lighthouse?"

I laughed and shook my head. "I grew up here. Of course I've been. Why?"

He laughed a total guy laugh and glanced at me. "Were you born a smart-ass, or did that fine quality just develop over the years?"

I smiled. "Shut up."

Eli chuckled and continued driving. When we reached Tybee he pulled into the vacant parking lot next to the lighthouse. At this time of night, the shore was empty, and I preferred it that way. He cut the engine and we sat for a moment, the surf pounding the sand, the wind ringing through the night. Stars studded the black sky, and the moon hung, a half circle, above the water. Sea oats rustled in the breeze.

Almost a perfect night, the exception being the vicious bloodsuckers taking over the city.

"They're not going to take over the city," Eli said, taking liberties with my thoughts. He turned in his seat to look at me. "And I won't let anything happen to you, Riley."

I laughed softly, cynically. "It's not me I'm worried about, Eli, and you know it."

In the amount of time it took me to blink, he was out of the Jeep and standing at my door. Silently he opened it, clicked my seat belt, and pulled me out. With little force he urged me back against the fender and placed a hand on either side of my body, trapping me. For several seconds he regarded me, searched my face.

"Yeah, I know it," he said quietly. "You make sure everyone knows how tough you are, all the time." With one hand he grasped my jaw and dropped his head closer to me. "You're a fragile human, Riley," he said, his hand sliding to my throat. "So fragile, so delicate, so easy to kill." His grip tightened. "When are you going to get that through your thick skull?"

I stared at him, my gaze unwavering. Instead, the unavoidable happened—something I hated; something that seemed to happen more and more since I'd met Eli Dupré. Tears formed in my eyes and rolled down my cheeks. I lifted my chin. "Never," I said, my voice cracking, determined.

Something flared in Eli's eyes, and then they softened. His hand loosened and slid from my throat upward, his fingers threading into my hair, and he leaned his forehead against mine. I breathed in his scent, unique, sweet, and earthy, and slipped my arms around his waist.

"I can't let anything happen to you," he whispered against my ear. "You've become too important to me, Riley." He pulled back and looked at me, his eyes dark pools in the shadows. "Understand?"

"Not really," I whispered, and I didn't. "But if you think I'm going to cower in some corner while my brother experiences the quickening, you're crazy. I promise to be careful."

Eli's features tightened, his jaw flinched, and he sighed, as though he was holding something back and it was not something he wished to discuss. He stared at me for several seconds, then inclined his head toward the lighthouse. "Come on."

I didn't ask how Eli had a key to the lighthouse; I just followed him inside. He grabbed my hand and led me across the shadowy interior. "I was just a ways up the shore when they installed the first Fresnel lens," he said. "Pretty cool. Always did like lighthouses. They fascinate me."

I laughed. "I keep forgetting you're so old."

"Yeah, right," he said.

We made it to the steps. "I'd race you, but I'm sure you'd cheat and use your vamp powers to beat me," I said, then craned my neck and peered above me at the steps as they spiraled upward. "Seth and I used to race them all the time. One hundred and seventy-eight steps to the top." I laughed, but it was with sadness. "He always got such a kick out of it." I felt the beginning of panic seize me once more, and again, Eli was there to rescue me.

"Wrap your legs around my waist," he said, moving close. "And hold on."

I did, and slipped my arms around his neck. We were face-to-face, body to body, and sensations soared within me. Eli read my mind and lowered his mouth to mine and kissed me, a long, gentle, sensual kiss that had my head spinning. He tasted sweet, just like his scent, and I knew it wasn't anything like a mortal scent. It was a scent only a creature of the afterlight could possess. And Eli possessed it fully.

With a sensual pull of my lips into his mouth, and a sweep of his tongue, Eli ended the kiss and took the one hundred and seventy-eight steps to the top in seven. Yeah, seven. Traveling that fast while hanging on to someone, in a spiral staircase? It was better than any amusement park ride I'd ever been on. My head spun, adrenaline pumped, and somehow, my sexual desire for Eli tripled. *Quadrupled.*

At the top, Eli lowered me onto the platform and eased open the door that led to the outer balcony. The wind was wicked strong, salty, and . . . perfect. Without a word, he shut the door behind us and urged me to the rail, where he crowded behind me and placed his arms on either side of me. I admit—I liked the feeling of being trapped by Eli's body.

"Good," he whispered against my ear. "Get used to it."

A shiver shot through my body, and I looked out over the darkened Atlantic. Several lights blinked from the fishing boats off the sound, and the glow from the moon rippled steadily over the water. Somewhere close, an oyster shoal bubbled, and the wind carried the ever-present brine to my nostrils.

"It's strange to think we've shared this place," Eli said, sliding his hands over my waist. His mouth sought the tender area of skin beneath my ear—something that should have had me on guard since he was a vampire, but it didn't. He had the ability to make me forget all of it. "The two of us, in the same city but totally different worlds," he whispered. He turned me around, my back to the rail, and looked down at me. Moonlight flashed off his eyes. "Same world now."

I didn't have to wait for his mouth to descend upon mine; it happened instantly, and the burning desire his touch created felt just as new as the first time he'd ever sensually laid a hand, or his tongue, on me. My skin heated under his touch, and sensations rocked me as his tongue tasted, his teeth nipped, and he suckled my bottom lip as his hands swept over my back, cupped my ass, and pulled me against him. I kissed him back, lost in the atmosphere and in *Eli*, and as I slipped my hands beneath his shirt and caressed the ridges of his abs, he gasped against my mouth. With his fingers buried in my hair, he held my head still and looked at me.

"I thought I could bring you out here, talk to you, comfort you," he said, his voice strained. He leaned closer. "But all I can think of is being inside of you." He kissed me, dragged his lips across my jaw, then back. "And staying inside of you," he whispered against my lips.

"I'm comforted, so let's go," I said hurriedly, because I wanted the same thing.

With a laugh, Eli gave me a quick kiss, grabbed my hand, and led me back down the steps of Tybee's lighthouse.

I'd never look at it the same again.

The drive back to my apartment was excruciatingly long and sensually painful at the same time. We didn't speak—not with words, anyway. Eli read every sexual thought I had, and I knew it, so I let my mind wander freely. It was so easy, and almost amusing. I'd think about how I wanted to run my hand along his thigh, to his crotch, and before the thought actually was completed, Eli had my hand in his and had moved it to his leg. I edged as close to him as my seat belt would allow, and nuzzled his neck, drew his earlobe into my mouth and sucked while my hand roamed over his thigh, cupped his crotch. Slowly, I unfastened the buttons of his jeans and eased my hand inside, and the sound of his pained groan and my name on his lips made a flash of heat spread between my thighs. I was so turned on that I didn't think either of us would make it back to Inksomnia. We did—barely.

We parked, and Eli reached over, clicked my seat belt, and dragged me onto his lap, our mouths melding together as we tasted, kissed, panted. Stumbling out of the Jeep, we somehow made it to the door; somebody—I can't remember whether it was Eli or me—opened the door, and once inside we fell against the wall. His kiss was fierce, desperate, and we didn't linger there. He carried me up the stairs and straight into my bedroom. With a loud slam he kicked the door shut. He crossed the room, and we fell onto the bed together, writhing and pawing at each other until every stitch of clothing lay on the floor. Our kisses were no longer gentle; they were frantic, and we each struggled for control. Eli touched me everywhere, dug his fingers into the flesh of my hips as he pulled me on top of him, and I straddled him and took his hard length deep inside of me. My head dropped backward, and I gasped with pleasure as the sensation of Eli filling me rushed through me. His hands left my hips and covered my breasts, trailed the dragons on my arms, and grazed my thighs.

In the next second, he flipped me, and Eli was on top of me, his weight resting on his forearms, and as he began to move inside of me, he lowered his head and pressed his mouth to mine. I wrapped my legs around him and moved with him; his mouth left mine as he buried his face in my neck. I shoved my hands through his hair, and as the orgasm gained strength I cried out Eli's name, then went breathless as shots of light fired behind my eyes. Eli found his release at the same time, intensifying mine, and it went on and on as our bodies writhed in pleasure. The residue of orgasm began to retract, slowly, and as it did, Eli's mouth moved to my lips. He kissed me, his hands buried in my hair and cradling my head gently; then he pulled back just enough that our gazes locked.

"Mine," he whispered against my mouth. He kissed me again. "You are *mine*."

In the shadows I stared into the eyes of a vampire, grazed his mouth with my finger. "No, you're *mine*."

Over the next few days I felt rejuvenated. Where I'd felt catatonic before, now I felt ready to *kick some ass*. It wasn't so much because of what I'd seen at the warehouse. It'd been gruesome, absolutely. Horrific. And, strangely enough, it wasn't my amazing relationship with Eli, although I have to admit, it was seriously empowering. But even that wasn't it. It was the deep responsibility I felt for that man's life, for all the kids' lives in that freaking warehouse, Zac the almost marine, the woman in the park—everyone who had been slaughtered just so a couple of satanic undead creatures could revitalize their powers. It *pissed me off*. Even deeper was a responsibility to *end it*. To destroy the monsters. I wanted to do something, not sit around on my ass and wait.

Every day that passed, I missed my brother even more. We were so close; it was like a part of me was missing, like I'd lost a body part. It hurt. My chest actually, physically *hurt*—especially knowing where he was, what he was doing, and what he was fast becoming. Every time I'd look in his room, my body went numb. Seth was the only blood family I had left. I wanted my baby brother back, dammit.

Despite Eli's run to Da Island to get protection against killing me, and the threat that was always present, I wanted him. Desperately. I mean, I hated sounding like some weakling who can't make it in life without a man, but damn. We'd clicked. I'd felt it. And I *wanted* it. I wanted *him*. And

he wanted me—he made no effort to hide it. I didn't care
that he was undead, and I didn't care that he'd outlive me.
Yet Gilles' words rang in my head continuously—almost
as though he kept doing it on purpose to keep me from
caving in to my desires. Actually, he did put a thought into
my head. He literally told me that Eli would have his head
better in the game if he wasn't preoccupied by me. Say
what? It was hard—don't get me wrong. I've never experienced so much difficulty keeping my hands off a man in
the whole of my life. Worse than that, I had to pretend that
it didn't bother me so much, that I didn't care. God*damn*, I
did care. Too much for my own good. And he affected me.
Whoa. Did he ever. And who am I kidding? He knew it.
The guy freely dug into my thoughts.

I did pretty well, keeping my distance those few days,
and Eli actually allowed it. I'd made it perfectly clear
that we needed to focus on this mission and not get
caught up in a lust affair. Eli had made quite an effort,
too, at the urging of his papa; he'd stayed away, and Phin
continued to be my babysitter.

The dreams continued.

I had two more nights at the apartment. I'd agreed
to spend the rest of Seth's quickening at the House of
Dupré, mainly to train. If anything, I was a workaholic,
and hell yeah, I'd train my ass off if it helped take down
the Arcoses. I'd dreamed the two nights before; I'd kept
them to myself because of the nature of the dreams. They
were highly intense, erotic, at times freakishly kinky, and
part of me thought they came over me because of what
I went to bed each night thinking of: Eli. The first night,
after the warehouse, I found myself back at the Panic
Room, in one of the back rooms, completely naked,

my limbs spread and roped to the bed—something I'd
never been into. I liked control too much, I guess. *He* was
there—always the same beautiful, flawless, freaky guy—
and he did nothing more than stare at me. He whispered
nasty-bad things in my head, things he wanted to do to
me with his tongue, how many different positions he
wanted to take me in, and it was like a drug. I wanted to
break free and escape the panic rooms, and put as much
distance between us as possible; I wanted him inside me
first. It was insane. Not once had this dream guy ever
physically touched me. Afterward, I felt wicked guilty.

The following night I found myself alone at an amusement park on the waterfront—sort of like Coney Island,
I guess. *He* pursued me through the park, slowly, never
relenting. I ducked into the house of mirrors, only to find
him there, watching me. When I looked in all the mirrors, I saw us, naked and entwined. I ran to escape, and
ran so hard I woke up with chest pain. Weird. Both very
weird. I'd never seen this guy in my life, and all I knew of
him was that he was one horny little toad who had some
major control over my brain.

I climbed out of bed and got ready as usual. I had only
one client, and then I'd be heading over to the Duprés'—
along with my entourage of Gullah bodyguards. I don't
know why, but I felt safe with them. I know it sounds
crazy, but I firmly believed the Duprés were a much different breed of undead than . . . any other undead out
there. Besides, Estelle had given me a canister filled with
my special brew.

No sooner did I pull on my jeans, black fishnet long
sleeve, and white ripped Inksomnia tank than a harsh
banging at the back entrance made me jump. When

I stepped into the living room, Phin watched me; I shrugged, and jogged downstairs to see who it was. When I opened the door I was surprised—and repulsed—to see someone I'd hoped never to lay eyes on again.

"Well, Ms. Poe," Detective Claude Murray said. His eyes regarded me a little too closely for comfort. As they always had. "All grown-up, I see."

I inspected him. "And I see you're still packed into that suit like a sardine."

He grinned—looked like he still chewed tobacco—and shook his head. "Grown-up but still a smart-ass, eh? Figures." He glanced at his watch. "You need to take a little trip down to the station for some questions, little miss tight pants."

"Why?" Phin said from over my shoulder. I could feel his tension rolling off him in waves. Phin might look innocent, but he was anything but. I knew he could rip Claude's arms off in less than five seconds.

Claude ignored Phin and stared hard at me. "You'll find out. Let's go."

I gave a short laugh. "If you think I'm riding anywhere with you, you've grown senile in your old age, Murray." I grabbed my keys off the hook. "Why am I needed for questioning?" I asked, hooking my pack onto my back.

Claude Murray, a graying man in his midfifties and getting more portly by the second, gave me a hard stare. "Looks like your past is coming back to bite you in that little ass of yours, Poe," he said quietly. "Your old boyfriend Kelter Phillips just turned up at the city morgue." His gaze raked over my body, and I literally felt like I needed a bath. "And according to his girlfriend, you were the last to see him alive."

Part 9

QUICKENING

I was pretty sure that perv Murray noticed the shock on my face about Kelter, and was even surer he took pleasure in delivering the information. Not that there was any love lost—not by any means. It's always a shock when someone dies unexpectedly—even a scumbag like Kelter. I was actually surprised he'd lived as long as he had.

On the way to the police station I gave Phin the skinny on my background with Detective Claude Murray. I stared at a traffic light through my shades and began. "Ol' Claude had a thing for me back then—yeah, gross, I know. Even though I was just a kid, I could tell he was a freak. I'm sure I wasn't the only juvy he had a thing for."

"What do you mean?" Phin asked, his voice growing dark, like Eli's did.

I shrugged. "You know—his touch lingered way too long when cuffing or uncuffing me, and whenever we were alone he'd touch my hair, brush against me—sick stuff like that." I laughed cynically. "I guess because I was a little junkie at the time, he thought he could get away with it. And he had. I'd been privately scared of him back then. Now? I'll kick his ass, even if it means a night or two in jail."

Phin sat quietly in the passenger seat and listened, his face growing angrier by the second, and I knew then that Detective Claude Murray was now on the Duprés' lifelong shit list.

"Hey," I said, and punched him in the arm. "I got it. No worries. I'm a big girl now, not some crazy little drug-gie teenager. Okay?"

He glanced at me, and although I couldn't see his eyes through his shades, I knew he was scowling. "Right."

I parked the Jeep and popped some quarters in the meter, and Phin walked into the station with me. He stood against the wall and waited, arms folded over his chest, and I was led into the back. When I glanced back, he had his cell phone out, and I knew he was calling Eli. Oh, boy. Phin shrugged, and I continued down the hall.

I knew the way, of course, and saw that things really hadn't changed in ten years. Claude was waiting farther up the hall—the inside of the station reminded me a lot of junior high, with dingy white concrete walls and tile floors, wooden doors with little brown nameplates screwed onto them. And . . . it smelled funny. Weird-funny, and it brought back old, unwanted memories. Claude smiled at me as the police officer escorted me to the interrogation room, and I went quietly in and sat down.

"So you're hanging out with old friends, Ms. Poe?" Claude asked.

"No. Just went by for a few drinks."

Claude leaned over my shoulder. "I have a witness that says she watched you enter the back rooms with Kelter Phillips after making nicey with him at the bar. And you know *we* know what goes on back there."

I gave him a glare. "Get to the point, Detective. Yes, I saw him that night, but so did hundreds of others. When I left, he was very much alive."

"Alibi?" he asked.

"Sure. Why don't you ask the doorman, Zetty? He watched me leave."

"Were you with anyone?" He walked around to face me. "Oh—let me clarify that. Were you with someone whose last name you knew?"

Prick. "Yes."

Claude blinked and waited. "Well, are you going to give me a name?"

I looked him in the eye, although I hated bringing Eli into this. "Eligius Dupré, and I was with him all night."

"We'll need to speak with him."

I didn't even blink. "No problem. Can I go now? I have an appointment."

Claude's slow, thin-lipped grin stretched over tobacco-stained teeth. "I bet you do." He inclined his head. "You're free to go. But we may need to drop by and have a look around."

I stood and shrugged. "Be my guest. I have nothing to hide." I gave him a look that I hope mirrored my revulsion. "Later, Claude. Much, much later."

I walked out and let the door slam behind me. When I reached the waiting area, Eli stood next to Phin and Luc, an infuriated look on his face. I walked up to him. "I'm sorry—but he wanted to know if I'd been with anyone at the time we left the Panic Room." I felt awful. "He wants to talk to you." I lowered my voice. "Did you kill him? Kelter?"

Eli said nothing, and I guessed that meant no. He walked to the counter and spoke to the clerk, and within seconds another officer escorted him down to interrogation.

I glanced at Phin. "Did you tell him?"

"Yep."

"Everything?" I asked.

"Yep," he confirmed.

I let out a sigh. I'd known he would, but no way would Eli be able to hide his anger at Murray. Surprisingly, within minutes, Eli strode from the back, his eyes glued to mine. Still furious. "Let's get out of here," he said.

The afternoon went by relatively quickly, and I heard nothing else from Murray; Eli and the guys disappeared while Nyx and I wrapped up appointments. I always dressed the part on workdays—clients had come to expect it of me. It was as much a part of my reputation as my artwork. So I wore a kick-ass outfit: a burgundy leather minidress, sleeveless and laced from the waist up, and a pair of over-the-knee black leather boots. A plain black velvet choker and matching velvet wrist cuffs completed my attire. The clients were more than satisfied. Nyx had decided to take the next day off and take care of some family business with her parents on Wilmington Island; she finished up just before I did; it was almost seven. As she grabbed her skull-and-crossbones shoulder bag, she came over and gave me a tight hug. "I'm going to miss you," she said, and looked at me with those big, round, always-wide-open blue eyes. "Don't worry about a thing. If the police come by to check the place out, I'll make sure I'm here."

"Thanks," I said, and rubbed her arms. "I'll be around until late tomorrow afternoon anyway. And I really appreciate your help, Nyx. Call me on my cell if anything comes up."

We said good-bye, Gene cawing sharply as Nyx left out the front door. I locked up—earlier than usual, but I'd canceled all my appointments and still needed to handle a few loose ends for the business. I flipped the sign to CLOSED, pulled the blinds, and cranked up some Linkin Park. I was at the computer, printing out some of my latest designs on transfer paper for Nyx, when I felt Eli's presence and glanced up. He stood leaning against the doorjamb with his arms crossed over his chest, watching me.

"Hey," I said, casual, as I'd tried to keep it since his return. I continued my work. Eli pushed off the frame and walked up front, plopping down on the sofa. He picked up a design album and started thumbing through the pages.

"I wanted to kill that detective today."

I glanced up. "Yeah, I've had that same thought myself before," I said, trying to lighten the mood. I gathered the transfers and hung them on the backlights—similar to what doctors use when viewing X-rays. I stood there, inspecting for imperfections, and suddenly felt Eli directly behind me.

"No," he said quietly. "You don't understand. I wanted to *kill* him."

I turned around and met his enraged gaze. "Why?"

And it was then I saw that anger had been brewing in Eli all day.

"Because of how he treated you as a kid," he said. "And for his thoughts today." His eyes bored into mine. "It would have been so easy."

I placed a hand on Eli's chest. "I appreciate your chivalry. Really. But he's just a stupid mortal. I can handle him." I smiled. "Trust me."

The air around us stilled; Eli's gaze grew dark. "What do you feel when you touch me?" he asked, and slid my hand over his heart. "Anything?"

It was something I'd been avoiding; it hadn't been easy. The thing between us was palpable, dangerous, and I'd known it went deeper than sex the moment we'd met. He'd told me quite seriously that I was his. I'd told him the same, yet the subject hadn't been approached again. What did *mine* actually mean? I lowered my hand and moved away. "I don't know, Eli."

Silence gripped the interior of Inksomnia for several moments before Eli surprised me with a request. "I want you to ink me."

I looked at him, gauged him. "Tats are for life—and with yours that's a long damn time." I cocked my head. "Do you know what you want?"

Eli kept his gaze on mine. "Yes." He lifted the medallion from his neck. "This. It's our family crest."

Bending my head over the medallion, I inspected the design and detailing. I'd not noticed it before, and I now found it fascinating. A griffin clutching a pair of daggers sat in the center of a fleur-de-lis, encased by a thorny vine. At the bottom, the name Dupré. I looked at him. "That's pretty wicked."

"Can you do it?" he asked.

I grinned, grasped him by the hand, and shoved him in the chair. "Sit." I grabbed a pencil and sketch pad and within minutes had the entire design on paper—it was roughly the size of an orange. I showed it to Eli, and he nodded.

"Perfect," he said.

I scanned the design, then printed out a transfer and walked back to Eli, whose gaze remained locked onto mine. "Where?" I asked.

"Between my shoulder blades," he returned. "Black ink."

My heart beat faster, and I nodded. "Off with the shirt, and let's get going."

Eli pulled his shirt over his head and turned onto his stomach on the inking table. I slowly wiped his skin with antiseptic and let it air dry, then laid the transfer print-side down, directly between his shoulder blades. I started the Widow, pulled on my gloves, loaded the ink, and bent over to Eli's ear. "This might sting a little." I settled into my chair.

He chuckled. "Yeah, okay."

"No laughing," I warned. I peeled the transfer off and began. Eli didn't even flinch. "Nice," I said, and concentrated on my design. I admit, it was a pretty cool design and would make a sick tat. With a steady hand I inked the Dupré crest over the muscular back of the eldest son. Tattooing Eli under such intimate conditions was beyond erotic—my breathing increased; my heart quickened. My breasts brushed his side as I bent over him, and even through gloves the contact of my skin against his aroused me. His scent radiated off of him in waves, and I drew it into my lungs, and that aroused me, too. It took about an hour and forty minutes to complete, and swear to God, I didn't want it to end. Finally, it was finished, and it looked badass.

I handed Eli the hand mirror, and he turned and checked out my work. "Nice," he said appreciatively, then turned to me. "You're a superb artist."

I shrugged. "Thanks," I said, then took a deep breath and tried to push away the intense sexual feelings just being in the same room with Eli stirred within me. I busied myself cleaning up, then turned off the Widow. I crossed the room, and the whole time I felt Eli's eyes on me.

"Why are you blowing me off?" he said, following me. *Shirtless.* "It's not like you."

I flipped the lights and walked to the stairs in the back. "You're right, Eli. It's not like me. But it's what I feel is best for both of us."

He grabbed me just as I reached the staircase. "You feel it's best, or are you afraid of me? Disgusted by what I am?" He pulled me against him, and his hot glare struck me. "The truth, Riley."

I glared back. "Let. Me. Go. I'm not arguing in the staircase."

His hand dropped my arm like it'd been burned. "Let's go, then."

I knew I ventured in very dangerous territory by walking those stairs and trapping myself between my apartment walls with Eli Dupré again—especially since Gilles had warned me to keep away. But in the heat of the moment, and argument, it seemed the only thing to do. The tension between us over the past several days since Tybee had been nearly unbearable, and to settle things before I actually had to stay under the same roof with him *and* his entire family was my intention. I stomped ahead of him, knowing full well his eyes were on my ass; I didn't care. Inside the apartment, the long, hazy shadows crossed the room and rafters as the dog days of August waned through the picture window. It suddenly struck me that neither my brother nor my dog was present; everything I loved was gone, and nothing would ever be the same again. I rounded on Eli. "What exactly do you expect from me? I can't lie—you regularly read my mind, so I'm sure you already know how badly I want you *all* of the time. It's like some freaking sickness, or a hex. You know I'm not scared of you because of what you are. You *know* it."

His eyes and voice gentled. "You should be."

"Shoulda, coulda, woulda," I said, sounding like a child. "I guess rule following and good-choice making aren't in my nature, either."

Eli moved closer, his eyes locked onto mine. "I can't stop thinking about you. I can't stop thinking about that night. Both nights."

"Oh, I get it," I said, and sank into the plush cushion of the seat in the picture window. Whether mortal or vampire, both male species are led around by their peckers, it seemed. "So it's the sex you're obsessed with?"

"It's *sex* with *you*," Eli clarified, and stepped closer to me. "With *just* you." His body closed in on me as he leaned against the wall next to me. Still, he didn't touch me, but I felt my will busting up. "It's the way you move, the sound of your voice," he said, his voice dark, seductive. "The way you thought about me that night, about what you wanted me to do to you, and how you touched yourself. The way you smell—not your perfume, or the shampoo you use," he said, lifting a long strand of my hair to his nose and inhaling. "*You*." He shoved his hands into his hair with frustration. "I've watched you, Riley—even before we met. You . . . intrigued me, and I found myself at your window, inside your room." His eyes searched mine. "It's about *you*."

"You watched me from inside my room?" I asked, my voice shaky, quiet. The thought thrilled me. "Why?"

"You intrigued me," he said, his body brushing mine. "Because I had to."

Already, my heart was beating faster, and I struggled to breathe normally. I couldn't stop staring at the muscles in his chest, the way his abs were cut, and his face; the shadows had grown long, and the room was nearly cast in darkness, yet there was just enough surreal light to make out his features. His pitch-black hair hung across his forehead and luminescent blue eyes, and when he spoke, his lips fascinated me; they were full, perfectly shaped, and the memory of them against my skin made me burn for him all over again. His jaw, dusted with just a shade of growth, made his pale skin flawless and sensual. My fingers itched to touch him. My heart yearned for him. My brain had turned to gravy.

Without taking his eyes off me, Eli drew closer, grasped my hand and placed it over his heart. "Again, I ask. What do you feel when you touch me?"

My eyes closed as his hand covered mine and pressed it against his chest. "I feel . . . a sensual energy that I can't get enough of, that lingers on my skin, inside of me, and drives me crazy," I said quietly, my chest rising and falling faster with my ragged breathing. I looked at him. "An obsession. I feel *you*."

Eli slid even closer and pressed his palm over mine. "But no heartbeat."

I rose, slipped my hands over Eli's hips, and guided him onto the cushion I'd just vacated. Grasping his neck, I climbed onto his lap, my leather dress riding up as I slid my legs on either side of him and locked them behind his back. He sat silent, completely still, and I knew that if he did have a heart that beat, it'd be pounding like crazy right now. His hands slid to my hips as his eyes searched mine.

I palmed his chest and brought my lips closer to his. "My heart beats enough for the both of us," I whispered against his mouth. "Just don't . . . kill me, okay?" I shoved my hands into his silky hair and kissed him softly, and he sat still while I explored his mouth. I sucked his bottom lip, slowly, then traced his teeth with my tongue, and the unshaven scruff on his jaw against my palm turned me on and made me slide closer. I slid my hand down his throat, and he ran his hands over my bared thighs, pulled me hard against him, and deepened the kiss. My mind went completely blank as his tongue grazed mine, and his mouth moved erotically over my lips, and everywhere his hands touched made me burn for him.

"Did you mean it when you said I was yours?" he asked quietly.

I looked into his eyes. "You know I did."

Eli stood, and although he held on to me, I slid from his embrace and turned around, threaded my fingers through his, and tugged, urging him to my room. He wordlessly followed, but he pulled me close while we

walked, my back to his front, and he dropped my hand
and slid his fingers over my hips and held me tightly
against him; the feel of his hardness pressed into the
small of my back made me hot and wet, and I wiggled
against him, stretched my arms up, and clasped them
around his neck. His hands slipped upward, skimmed
slowly over the buttery smooth softness of my dress, and
cupped my breasts, and even through the thin leather
it caused sensations to ripple through me, turned me
on even more. His mouth teased the skin at my throat,
and my heart pounded with anticipation. I completely
trusted him. I wholly wanted him.

In my bedroom, Eli stopped and kept me tight against
him; we simply melded together. I'd forgotten to power
down the iPod station in the shop, and music from below
rose up and drifted through the ventilation, and darkness had now claimed the shadows. Only shades and
planes of half-light played against our features, obscur-
ing full detail, leaving everything else up to other senses:
touch, taste, scent. I lost myself in Eli; to me, he wasn't
an immortal; he wasn't a vampire. He was . . . *necessary*.

"Eli," I said, unaware I'd even spoken his name out
loud. I relaxed against him while his hands explored
me; with tortured slowness he pulled the laces loose at
the bust of my dress, my breasts spilling out and Eli's
palms covering them. My flesh turned warm, then hot,
and his hands trailed down my sides to my hips, where
he tugged my dress up higher, caressing my thighs and
pulling my ass against his swollen crotch. He groaned in
my ear; I nearly came at the sound of it. When his hand
moved to my inner thigh, and over a little more, I shifted
my hips; his fingers slipped first into the small triangle

of silk, then eased slowly into my wetness. My head fell back against his chest and my body began to seize, but he moved his hand and stopped the orgasm. I almost touched myself, I was so frantic with desire and need. He stilled my hands, held them tightly.

"Don't," he said against my ear. "Not yet."

I willed myself to stop throbbing, and it almost didn't work. But Eli lifted me up in one swift move and laid me across the bed. He grabbed three pillows and stacked them behind me, pushed my dress up over my hips, and pulled my panties off slowly. Every nerve ending in my body hummed with pleasure; his strong hands slid up my thighs and pushed them apart, and as his head lowered and he tasted me with his tongue, I exploded, sparks went off behind my eyes, and I pushed my hands through his hair and held on. His fingers gripped my hips and tasted deeper, and my body seized with ecstasy. Before my orgasm was completed, he moved away, and I needed no cue. I was dying to have him inside me, and I followed him off the bed.

This time, my need was too powerful to rein in—he'd done it; he'd caused it. I couldn't help it. We traded places. I pushed him backward onto the bed; I peeled out of my dress and boots and knelt between his legs as I deftly unfastened each button on his fly. I felt savage, feral, and nothing and no one could satisfy me except Eli. With a fierceness that surprised even him, I pulled off his jeans, only to find him bare beneath. I looked at him then, and his eyes were nothing but glassy black orbs in the darkness. I kept my gaze on his as I slid my hand over his hardness, rock hard and smooth at once; I drew him into my mouth; he jerked, groaned, and it made me wet all over again. I couldn't take much more. I moved back, eased first one thigh over his, then the other; I straddled him and took him in completely. The sensation of Eli filling me took my breath, and I gasped first, and then he grasped me and turned me onto my back, and followed me down. He stared at me, threaded his fingers through mine, and lifted my arms over my head.

"Do you trust me?" he asked, his voice thick, raspy.

"Yes," I answered in a hoarse whisper. "I do."

In the most sensual move I'd ever experienced in my life, Eli wrapped his arms completely around my back and held me as he began to move. Every inch of our bodies melded together, and he moved faster, we moved together, and the orgasm I'd been denied twice exploded fully and my body jerked with uncontrolled spasms as I clutched desperately to Eli. His body moved with mine, and I felt his shudders as if they were my own. He slowed; he stopped; he didn't move off of me, his arms wound tightly around my body. He lay very, very still.

Too still.

Oh, hell.

I grew as still as Eli; I barely breathed. After nearly two minutes—that's a long, long time—I drew a slight breath. "Eli?" I asked, barely a whisper.

He didn't answer.

Oh, shit.

Then, slowly, he lifted his head. I breathed a sigh of relief as a pair of nonopaque eyes stared down at me. A slight grin tilted the corner of his very sexy mouth. "You are amazing." He kissed me. *"Mine."*

I punched him, and he laughed and buried his head

in my shoulder. Then, while we were still completely wrapped around each other, Eli Dupré lowered his head and kissed me, gently, softly, taking a very long time to explore every inch of my mouth that may have been overlooked during our passion. Then he lifted a finger to my angel wing and touched it softly, following the etching as it fanned out to my temple. "You're such a variance, Riley Poe," he said. "A sign of dark purity inked onto your face"—he stroked it again—"and disturbingly caring inside." He placed his hand over my heart. *Incredible* vaguely described lovemaking with Eli Dupré. I knew then I was spoiled for eternity.

"For the record," he said, catching my bottom lip between his teeth. "My pecker doesn't lead me around."

I laughed, and he quickly hushed me with his lips, his tongue, and then he eased to the side of me, pulled me close, and wrapped an arm over my stomach. He rested his chin on top of my head. "Go to sleep," he said. "I'll be here when you wake up."

Content, for a while, anyway, I closed my eyes and drifted off.

For the first time I felt cherished, and worthy of a morning after.

How a dream could plague me after sex with Eli, I have no idea, but *I found myself in a horse-drawn carriage, my eyes turned to the window, where I peered outside into a dense forest of massive trees, gray foliage, and rock. Everything looked gray, bleak. The horses' hooves pounded the terrain at a gallop, and the carriage veered precariously close to the edge of a cliff before changing direction and plunging into the shadows, deeper into the wood. The horses slowed to a trot, and I eased back against the cushions and closed my eyes. I don't know how long I kept them shut, but when I opened them again, he sat across from me. Dressed in black breeches, tall black boots, and a blood burgundy velvet coat, with white ruffles at the neck and cuffs, he watched me, studied me with intensity as though trying to figure me out. The auburn-haired woman sat beside him, her face hidden, pressed against his chest, her hand possessively resting on his thigh; sleeping, I supposed. It was difficult to determine, as she was very, very still. His gaze wundered seductively over me, shameless and bold, and then with his eyes still fastened to mine—as I was powerless to look away—he leaned his head down and whispered to the woman, yet I heard it clearly in my own head. "Unlace my breeches." Only her hand moved, and she skillfully loosened the laces as though she'd done it many times before. I didn't want to watch; I couldn't pull my gaze away. "Touch me," he whispered again, and once more I heard the words in my head as though he'd spoken them to me. The woman slid her hand slowly into his breeches and stroked him; I could feel his hardness in my own palm, and I sat, entranced. He was enjoying me watching, and I wanted to look away so badly, but I hadn't the will. "Ride me." The woman kept her back turned as she lifted her skirts and straddled him. He watched me over her shoulder as she rode him, and I jerked at the heavy sensation of him between my legs. I didn't want to come; I couldn't help but seize with orgasm. His beautiful face tensed with pleasure at my weakness, and then he pulled the woman's blouse down, baring her back. As I stared in horror once again at the familiar tattoo winding up her spine and over her arm, she glanced over her shoulder and stared. Her face was pale—too pale—and her lips were bloodred, her eyes opaque. She was me. It was then that I noticed the movement outside of the carriage; winged creatures with unhinged jaws and jagged teeth flew by, their faces distorted into those of horrific creatures. They looked in at me. They were hungry, and they wanted my special blood—I knew it. Yet when I turned back to him, he smiled, two long fangs dropped from his top jaw, and with a gentle touch he pushed the woman's head to the side, sank his teeth into her, and drank. I felt the pain in my own neck, felt the life draining fast out of me. The winged creatures began beating on the side of the carriage, screeching, clawing to get at me. I screamed. . . .*

"Riley!"

I bolted up, my heart out of control, gasping for air. My body ached, as though I'd run a triathlon, and I fell back to the pillows just as quickly. I tried to catch my breath, but I was hyperventilating. Then I saw Eli, bent over me, concern etched into his perfect features.

"What's wrong?" he asked, and placed a hand over my heart. "Take it easy, Riley. Breathe." He kept his hand on me, and for some reason, it helped.

"The dreams," I said, my breathing slowing. "They're so freaky. I don't like them."

"What dreams?" he asked, and part of his face was illuminated by the light coming through the French doors. I glanced at them—they were closed.

I shook my head and put a palm over my eyes. "I've had, like, four of them," I said, thinking I'd lost count. "They're hideous, and nasty erotic."

Eli's voice grew steely. "Tell me."

"They're humiliating," I said, and was surprised by

my own reaction. "Don't take offense—I don't have any control over dreams, and in the dream I am *not* a willing participant," I started. "I try my best to escape. But they're weird—always the same guy, very hot, and he ... talks dirty to other women, gets them to touch him." I glanced at him. "You know? And ... he watches me get turned on by it."

Eli stared incredulously at me. "What else?"

I sighed. "Something horrific always happens at the end. Death. Vampiric death. And the woman he talks dirty to? When she turns around and looks at me, it's *me*. She has my tattoos and everything."

Shoving his hands through his hair, Eli sat up and propped his elbows against his knees. "Describe him." His voice was edgy.

"I ... don't know," I said, and realized suddenly I didn't know much about him at all. "He's just ... gorgeous. Beautiful, actually. Long dark hair. Dark eyes." I looked at Eli. "That's all I can remember."

Eli slowly rose from the bed and walked; the light from outside cast sharp shadows across his naked, perfect body, throwing dark planes against the ridged muscles of his abdomen, and I didn't think I'd ever seen a more beautiful man in my life. Way more beautiful than the guy in my funky porn dreams.

"Thank you," Eli said, casting me a slight grin. He continued to pace. "This is not good, Riley." He sat on the side of the bed and tucked my hair behind my ear. "We need to tell my father."

I slapped my own forehead. "Oh my *God*, Eli. Are you kidding me? First Gilles learns we have nasty sex— did you know he dug in your brain to find that juicy morsel? And now you're going to tell him I have porn dreams?"

"Yes."

I sat up and stared at him. "Why?"

Eli's gaze darkened with concern. "Because. It sounds like one of the Arcoses."

My stomach twisted at the thought. "How is he invading my dreams?" I rubbed my eyes. "They're so . . . realistic."

Eli turned his head and looked at me for a long time. "He's been here. Because he's a direct bloodline of the *strigoi*. They have the power to invade the dreams of mortals." He shook his head. "He must be very taken with you."

"Why?" I asked, and already my insides ran cold.

Eli dragged a knuckle over a loose strand of hair and brushed it out of my face. "He could have just as easily killed you, or taken you. Although in his weakened state he more than likely can do nothing more than cast dreams." He closed his eyes and sighed. "It must be Victorian. His brother is much too vicious to waste time with dreams. He would have taken pleasure with you, or not; then he would have killed you."

"But his strength has grown, right?" I asked, and Eli laced his fingers through mine. "Why is he still making me dream? And how can he do it with you sitting right beside me? How does he even know who I am?"

Eli's gaze searched my face. "I don't know. But he's taken with you. And the *strigoi* are powerful beings, Riley." He pulled me to his chest and settled against the pillows. "Do you dream more than once at night?"

"Not so far," I replied, draping my arm over his

stomach. "And *taken* isn't quite the term. More like obsessed."

"You're right. Now, go back to sleep. I'll be right here."

I was quiet for a while, my thoughts rambling, and finally, slumber took me again, and Victorian blessedly left me alone.

When next I woke, bright morning sunlight streamed through the French doors. I was on my stomach, and the gentle, erotic touch of Eli's fingers dragging across my spine, tracing every intricate detail of the inked dragon, aroused me. We explored each other, touching, kissing; while we began against the softness of the down topper on my bed, we ended up on the hardwood floor, and we finished in the shower. Eli washed my long hair, and I washed his crazy-sexy black hair. I gave him a soapy Mohawk, and we laughed. I can't remember ever having a man wash me with such ... enthusiasm before. And I'm pretty positive I haven't had a man stick around long enough to have a laugh with me the next morning. Eli was an anomaly, one I feared my heart was laid wide-open for.

I finished first, and Eli wanted to enjoy the hot water a little longer. So I pulled on a pair of hipster shorts, a cami, and flip-flops, and ran down to the shop to turn off the iPod home system and gather a few things I'd be taking to the Dupré House. I was flipping through the supply books when a knock at the back door made me jump. Not so much to my surprise, Detective Claude Murray in all his too-tight-suit glory stood there, a smirk on his face.

"Mind if I take a look around?" he asked. "You've nothing to hide, right?"

I threw the door open and cast a hand out. "Be my guest. Shop's this way." I started for the front, and I felt Claude's eyes on my ass the whole time. I heard the door shut with a click, and Claude's stressed-out loafers crossed the floor behind me. I continued with what I'd been doing, and the detective slowly perused Inksomnia.

"I always knew you were a little freak, Ms. Poe," he said, glancing through the art books. He looked up and smiled. "Now that you're all grown-up, I bet you're even freakier, huh?" He moved to the desk and computer. "No appointment book?"

"Welcome to the twenty-first century, gramps," I said. "Everything's on the computer." I didn't like him in my shop, and I didn't like him touching my belongings. I wanted him gone.

"Do you mind?" he said, inclining his balding head toward the screen. "Just pull up the files for last Friday."

This forced me to move closer to him, and I swallowed my rage and did so. I logged on, pulled up the client appointment file—although I had no idea what he thought he could find there—and turned the screen toward him. "Enjoy."

In the next second, Claude moved behind me and brushed against my ass. I jumped, and he laughed. "You remember back when your punk ass was in my jail on a weekly basis? All strung out and high as a kite?" I froze, and he leaned closer. "You'd fuck anything for a fix back then." He dropped a small, cellophane-wrapped object the size of a roll of dimes on my desk, and his hand moved to my ass. "How 'bout now?" he said, his voice thick, his breath thicker. "For old times' sake?"

I reacted; I knew it'd get my ass landed in jail, but I didn't care. Elbowed him in the gut; when he fell back, I laced my fingers together into a tight fist and swung up, catching Claude right smack in the nose. He stumbled back, wiped the blood trickling down his face. He wasn't shocked or surprised; it seemed to have turned him on even more. "Rough little bitch, aren't ya?" he said, grinning. "That'll cost ya."

But he surprised me; in a move I didn't expect, he popped me right in the mouth. I felt my lip split again, and in the next breath I kneed him in the balls. Claude didn't have time to react after that; he didn't even have time to fall to his knees.

Eli emerged—was suddenly there, enraged, and I watched in horror as he grabbed the detective by the throat and lifted him off the ground. Eli's face contorted—his jaw unhinged and jagged fangs dropped long; his eyes grew opaque—and urine ran down Claude Murray's leg and onto the floor. Eli pulled his face close to the detective's. "Leave. Her. Alone," Eli growled, his voice not his own, dark, menacing. Claude gasped, choked, and right before my eyes I watched the color drain completely from his face. His body jerked, twitched, and then grew still. Very, very still. Lifeless eyes stared at me, and my insides froze. Eli dropped him onto the floor. The detective had just died of fright.

I stood there, shaking, as did Eli. His face returned to normal; his fangs slipped back inside. His eyes remained opaque as his fury slowly subsided. I said nothing, simply stared at the body of an SPD detective lying dead on my floor.

"Call my brothers," he said, his voice edgy, and turned

his back to me. "Call Preacher." He grabbed the dope and shoved it into his pocket.

I did as he asked, although my mind was buzzing. I called Preacher first, then Phin. Preacher showed up first.

My surrogate grandfather walked in through the back and came straight to me. "You tell me what happened, girl," he said, and reached out with a thumb and wiped the blood off my lip. I told him about the Panic Room, about Kelter, and about me being questioned yesterday.

"The detective showed up while Eli was showering. He . . . wanted to check the place out." I rubbed the back of my neck. "Then, I don't know—he started talking dirty to me, then put his hands on me." I looked at Preacher, and it was only then that I noticed that the other three Dupré men, Gilles included, had walked in. I glanced at them and continued. "I reacted—I elbowed him, and then I punched him." I looked at Eli, whose eyes were almost back to normal, but he was still silent, furious. "Eli didn't kill him," I said fervently. "He didn't. I think . . . he had a heart attack after seeing Eli change."

Preacher began speaking in French to Gilles; I of course didn't know what they spoke of.

"Preacher's telling my father what Murray did to you as a child," Phin offered, and I gave him a nod of thanks.

I glanced at Gilles, and he looked at me. "Worry not, *chère*; all will be well. You will soon learn that a creature of the afterlight cherishes beyond mortal imagination what is his, and will protect fiercely if challenged." He glanced at Eli, down at the detective, and back to me. "We no longer routinely kill; in this case, it could not be helped." Gilles and Preacher stepped off together and continued to speak in French. Eli grasped me by the elbow.

"Go upstairs, Riley," he said. "Josie and my mother are on their way." He glanced behind him, at the detective. "We have to take care of things now." He brushed a knuckle against my cheek. "I couldn't help it."

I covered his hand with mine. "Yeah, I know." Our gazes lingered for a moment, and I'd never felt the full weight of a man's stare before like I did with Eli. "Tell me this is going to be okay," I asked. I wanted him to say it badly.

"It will," he said. "I promise."

I left then, without a backward glance. I didn't want to see any more than I already had. I didn't want to think of how they'd get rid of the detective's body, his car, or any trace of him being and dying in Inksomnia. I had to trust Eli, and I found myself surprised once again— I truly did trust him. It wasn't until I was upstairs, and Josie, Elise, and Estelle were sitting in my kitchen, that I felt how my energy had drained. I sat at the table, Estelle made me a pot of tea, and two vampires, a Gullah root doctor's wife, and I kept one another company. It was so weird I almost laughed out loud. And if I thought that was weird, later on, when we all drove to Wal-Mart to pick up a few necessities for my stay at the Duprés'? Now, *that* was funky. As we stepped inside the double automatic doors, a woman in her midthirties or early forties standing at the bulletin boards caught my eye. Her despondent expression as she thumbtacked a picture to the corkboard made me ache inside. I watched her for several moments as she stared at the photo, and my eyes followed hers to the picture—a young guy Seth's age, wearing an Atlanta Braves baseball cap and smiling like there was nothing better in life. She stroked his face and walked away, and I continued to stare at that wall. In three of the pictures I recognized Seth's friends. There were many more hanging there.

"It'll be over soon, *chère*," Elise said, placing a hand on my shoulder. "We'll get the boys to safety and fix this. My husband, Eli and his brothers, your dark fellows, they never fail."

"Dat's right, baby," Estelle said, and she linked her dark arm through my snowy white one. "Dem boys are tough as nails. Dey won't give up. Neither will your Preacher man, dat's right."

Josie watched me curiously; she amazed me by how much of her environment she soaked in by merely listening to others. Even she gave me a smile. "No worries."

Later that day, as I was packing up in the apartment, the news came on announcing the death of one of Savannah's finest, Detective Claude Murray; he'd succumbed to a long-standing cardiac problem. His funeral would be in two days. I didn't ask how, or why. I simply felt relief—and a little guilt. I'd hated that freaky guy, and inside, I wasn't sad he'd croaked pissing his pants over the sight of Eli's transformation. Not one bit sad.

Over the next several days, the Duprés put me under the most strenuous workouts I've ever experienced. During the day, I remained in the donjon on the top floor, and everyone got a poke at me; every family member had something unique to offer. Josie taught me the latest in acrobatics; I could now run toward a wall, run up it a ways, and flip completely over. My body felt strong, vibrant, alive. I felt like those guys in *The Matrix Reloaded*. Call me Neo. I am the *One*. Rather, I *was*, until Luc laid me flat on my ass. You know, there are those fight-club guys who kick and punch and just go nuts when they fight; then there are those like Luc who can almost remain perfectly still and catch you completely off guard while knocking you senseless. He showed me a few moves, and I began practicing. He let me win a couple of times.

Phin was a fantastic dodger and roller. Of course, moving like lightning helped, but seriously—he was a fine, fine free runner in his own right. When we weren't in the donjon, we were outside, working every plane and flat surface of the Dupré House, its outbuildings, its wall. I already had natural abilities and athleticism, but perfecting the moves of a free runner was going to take a little time. Still—when I made it to the roof for the first time, I squealed like a cheerleader.

Elise was an expert markswoman when it came to throwing a blade; she'd been taught by the best: her husband. Thank God they didn't participate in the practices where I used a moving target. No way could I have thrown a blade at that sweet little woman—no matter that she could rip a throat out in the blink of an eye.

Of course, in my opinion, Eli was the master of all. Yes, *all*. On and off the donjon mat, I might add. He was wicked fast, could free run like a mofo, and rivaled his mother with blade accuracy. I supposed when you live for as long as they have, you tend to just get good at stuff. I didn't have a century's worth of training, but I had a heart full of determination. I knew this was the only way for me to be able to help my brother. No way would Eli let me get near the boys, so close to the completion of their quickening, without a little more training. I worked hard, all day, every day. It wasn't until the fourth day of training that I began to feel weary. Extraordinarily weary, like I was coming down with the flu or something. My body ached—and it was more than just soreness from the workouts, or the sex marathons with Eli. I didn't want to seem like a wiener, so I kept it to myself. I hated a complainer anyway.

The interior of the Dupré House was enormous; you could literally go days inside without running into anyone, if that was what you wanted. As vampires, they pinched about two hours of sleep during the middle of the day; the rest of the time they were awake, out and about, mingling with Savannah's society. Elise loved antique shops. Gilles loved to go to the shooting range and had a massive gun collection. It was all very eye-opening.

I stayed with Eli; there was no question about that from the get-go. The moment I'd arrived, he'd carried my bags and led me straight to the west wing of the third floor, to a massive chamber. Inside were a large fireplace, a king-sized bed with intricately carved posts and headboards, and a gauzy white bed curtain. It was . . . perfect. Gilles and Elise were on the first floor; the others had rooms on the second floor. Philippe the butler had a room in the back of the first floor, and stayed with the Duprés twenty-four seven. He was a cool enough guy, and I always caught him checking out my inks. Pretty damn funny if you asked me. I bet he wanted one himself.

So while my days were filled with boot-camp, Parris

Island–type, bad-vampire-slaying training, my nights were filled with edging the darkest, seediest places in the historic district, and tracking the boys. The Arcoses moved to a different place each night, making it more difficult to keep an eye on them. They were chronic, though—dark places where kids looking for trouble would certainly find some. They offered drugs, alcohol, even women. Horrified, I'd witnessed two prostitutes being killed; we'd prevented several others from becoming prey. I knew where the darkest of souls hung out after dark; I used to be one of them. After Kelter Phillips' death, the Panic Room had closed its doors. Now the Morgue and the Asylum both were filled to the gills. Rarely did Eli let me out of his reach when inside, either. He knew I could fight; he'd watched me kick Luc's ass plenty of times, although Luc had toned his skills down to match my mortal ones. Still, Eli was severely protective over me and my body. One groping hand to the ass and he'd scatter the crowd just to find out which one did it. Honestly. I'd dealt with scumbags so often in my past that they didn't offend me. These guys were pathetic, and it didn't take much for me to jerk an arm behind some pig's back, or twist a set of nuts until the jerk squealed like a girl. Eli didn't like others touching me; he secretly loved how much of a badass I was. I knew it.

It was my third night in the Dupré House, and Eli had left me soaking in a bath to go speak to his father. "I won't be long," he said, his eyes caressing me, making me shudder. "Wait for me."

I grinned. "I'm not going anywhere." I wasn't usually a bubble-bath type girl, but damn. This wasn't an ordinary tub. It was a copper tub, and it was freaking huge.

Who could pass that up? So I closed my eyes and rested my head against the air pillow, and honestly, I didn't mean to fall asleep, but I did.

I'd hoped being in another vampire's lair would keep the dreams away; I was so totally wrong. What was worse was that, after the incident with the detective, we'd sort of forgotten about telling Gilles. Rather, Eli forgot—which surprised me. I didn't forget. I just wanted to be spared the humiliation. I supposed Eli let it go once we settled in together, and the dreams seemingly stopped. They were now back.

I was running through a dark, dense wood. Everything around me was gray, desolate, colorless, yet the forest was alive. I ran, frightened, barefoot, my long black hair hanging free down my back, and a thin, gauzy white slip with thin satin straps clung to my pale body. A light rain began to fall, and soon the slip was completely drenched and see-through, and still I ran, though I didn't know whether I was running to something or from something. I was afraid. As I passed trees, I noticed him. He wore black breeches tucked into tall black boots, and a white gauzy shirt with billowy sleeves and laces at the neck. His pale, flawless skin was in stark contrast to the darkness of his hair, and dark brown eyes followed me as I ran. When I thought I'd left him behind, he emerged from another tree, then another, without seeming to move at all. This time, he was alone. No other woman. Just him, me, and the forest.

No, I sensed another—another man. I couldn't see him, but I knew he was there, lurking. I continued to run until I tripped over a root hidden by fallen dead leaves. He was suddenly there, pulling me up, and I gasped at his beauty. That was when I heard the shrieks overhead, above the canopy of the forest. I knew the winged, fanged creatures were back, and they wanted me. I also knew him now: Victorian. I didn't want him to know I knew. "If you want your brother freed, you must come to me," he said, and his eyes turned opaque. "I want you for my own. All those things I've showed you are my dreams. Come to me, Riley Poe, but don't tell the others. Come alone, and I will set your brother free of his curse. Your life for his." He stroked my breast through the sheer wet material, and I shivered. "You will not regret it." Upon my chest he laid the bud of an unopened, bloodred rose. . . .

My eyes fluttered open, and I found myself still alone in the massive bathroom. The water had turned tepid; the bubbles had dissipated. A breeze drifted in through the open floor-length window, and when I glanced at the water, my heart seized. Floating beside me was the unopened bud of a bloodred rose. Victorian's words rang in my ears. *Your life for his.* I shivered, grabbed the bud, and stepped out of the tub. How had he been here without the others detecting him? Creepy. Sincerely creepy. Why was he so obsessed with me?

It would be a last resort. I'd try the Duprés' way first. I wanted to actually be around after my brother recovered. But in the end, if it came down to it? Yeah, hell yeah, I'd trade my life for Seth's. I tried with all my might to envision the Arcoses from the warehouse. It'd been far enough away for me not to have seen their faces in detail—not until they'd transformed, anyway. But I had a difficult time believing that the beautiful guy in my dream—Victorian—was one of the guys at the warehouse. They were—what had Gilles said? Twenty-one and twenty-two? I was having porn dreams about a twenty-one-year-old? *Oh, Father.*

Like I was saying: Every day was spent training. Though I certainly wished that I'd never have to actually use any of my new skills, I worked hard and hoped that if it came down to a fight, my training would pay off. At night we'd run the streets, stalk the clubs and the alleys outside of clubs, and search abandoned buildings. We'd not been able to find the Arcoses since that night at the warehouse, and time was running out. Soon they'd be fully restored, and Seth's quickening would be over. He'd kill. He'd become a killer.

Once we'd finished running the streets, we'd go to the Duprés', and Eli and I would head to our little slice of heaven on earth. He was the only thing that could relieve my mind of the problems at hand, the only soul who could comfort me. There wasn't a word to describe sex with Eli; I'd tried several out, and all fell short. The man literally made me lose my mind. His look alone turned me on. His hands and mouth made me beg for release. It wasn't merely sex. It was . . . something I couldn't define. Something I never wanted to see end. Something I sadly felt would.

When the dreams stopped being dreams and started happening while I was wide-awake—that was when I knew the shit was about to hit the fan. I don't know how he did it, but somehow Victorian placed thoughts into my head—images, visions, requests. At first, I'd turn around to see who'd spoken to me. I'd find myself completely alone. The words were always seductive: *Come with me. I want you. I need you. Let me touch you. Feel me inside of you. Kiss me. Take me. Love me forever.*

The words rattled me; I didn't know what to expect, or whether he could hear me if I responded. I never did; I just kept them to myself.

The day Preacher showed up at the House of Dupré with a dozen Gullah, I knew our time was running short. I made a solemn vow to learn French once this was over. Whenever Preacher and Gilles got together, it was all they spoke.

"The quickening is almost here," Josie said beside me, listening to them. We were just getting ready to head out for the night when they'd shown up. "Preacher says the Arcoses are nearly fully rejuvenated." She looked at me. "He's making sure we protect you."

I had on my leather pants and boots and a snug black Lycra tank, and beneath the black leather jacket I'd stashed multiple silver blades in the various pockets and holsters. Yes, all that leather in the dead of August. I was as hot as hell, but it was good protection. Eli had loaded me up, and when the hole didn't quite fit the blade, he made it fit. I had two stuffed into each boot. I just prayed I didn't impale myself. It was just past sundown when we left.

We made our way on the bikes up Whitaker, stopping by several places with no luck. Not one sign of Riggs, Seth, or the Arcoses. We checked the docks; nothing. We even checked the warehouses at the west end of River Street. Nothing. We ran nearly all night—even once Eli checked in with Ned Gillespie, who claimed zero vampiric activity from the Tybee area. It was almost dawn when we got back to the house, and not once had we spotted a single hoodie. My stomach burned at the thought of the quickening coming to fruition. I wasn't going to let it happen. And *that was* why I came up with a plan.

I'd lost my mind. Again. But for my brother I'd do anything.

We walked into the small kitchen area—Gilles and Elise each had a large glass of "V8," and I sat down and looked both of them in the eye. "I want to stop using the herbs so that my blood will lure Victorian and Valerian out of hiding."

"No," Eli said immediately, and not to me. "No way, Papa."

I ignored Eli's pleas and searched Gilles' light blue gaze. "Please. You know it would work. And we have no more time." I grasped his hands with mine and begged. "I want my brother back. Please."

"I forbid it," Eli said angrily. "Riley, hell no."

Gilles' stare didn't waver; he looked nowhere else for approval. "You are a reckless warrior, *ma chère*," he said, and his gaze bored deeply into mine. "Do you fully understand what it would mean for you to cease drinking your special herbs?"

"Yes," I said.

Eli grabbed me and yanked me out of the chair. "No, Riley, you don't understand!" he said, infuriated. "Have you ever witnessed a pack of dogs penned up without food or water for two weeks? Do you know what they do to anything remotely edible?" He pulled his face close to mine. "That's what the Arcoses would do to you, as well as Seth and the other newlings." He shook me. "Get it?"

"Son, let her go," Gilles said. "He is right, though, my dear. It is risky. We"—he motioned with his hands to his family—"would certainly have to be extra-dosed by Preacher."

"Papa, you're not seriously considering it?" Eli said.

"It's her decision, not yours."

I didn't even have to think about it. "Yes. It's what I want to do." I looked at Eli. "I'll be okay. I want this over with, Eli. I want my brother back safely."

Eli stared at me in disbelief, then gave a cynical laugh. "Oh my God, Riley." He walked off, hands around the back of his neck. *"Fuck."*

"Don't let his temper worry you, *chère*," Elise said. "He's very protective over you, as you can see."

"Besides," said Gilles. "With the herbs out of your system for just one day, your blood won't reveal full potency. Maybe, though, just enough."

"That's a relief," I said, and gave him a sincere look. "Thank you."

My internal clock had returned to my teenage schedule: out all night, sleep all day. Only, Eli was pissed, and he wasn't about to let me sleep all day. By noon he woke me up, angry, desperate to change my mind. He tried everything—including sex. No, as potent as that was, my mind wouldn't be changed. He stormed off even more pissed than he had been before. We worked out in the donjon. He kicked my ass.

Preacher came by with a supply for the Duprés—the third one that day. Talk about getting tanked. Phin held his washboard stomach as he downed another glass. "I'm too full."

I found that weird and hilarious at the same time. "Wow. Getting sloshed with unknown herbs just to keep from sucking my blood out. Nice."

He grinned. Luc grinned. Josie grinned.

Eli remained unapproachable.

By nightfall, we were ready.

"Only one thing to do, *ma chère*," Gilles said. "You must wait to do it. Too early and you'll cause a frenzy that even my children, I and Elise, and your dark brethren may not be able to control."

"Okay," I said. "What's that?"

He pulled a blade from my belt. "You must cut yourself and expose your blood. In its watered-down state it may not have the potency it usually does."

"Great," I said, and nodded. "Okay."

"Wait for Eli's word," he warned. "Understand?"

I nodded. "Don't worry." Loaded with silver and a body full of tempting O positive, I headed out with Eli. He was tense; anger boiled just below the surface, and it showed.

"You do exactly as I say to do, Riley," he said, turning and glaring at me on the bike. "Swear to God, you'd better."

"Don't worry," I reassured him. "I promise I'll wait for you."

We hit the Morgue and Asylum and came up empty before finding a place called Decay 11—a punk joint in an abandoned garage off of East Broad. It was new to me—not around in my teen years—and I had to make a few calls to get directions. We found it in a plain metal building that had once housed an automotive oil and repair shop; the smell of stale motor oil still filled the air. Once inside, we noticed nothing unusual—not at first. I'd sidled up to the bar and overheard a guy on a cell phone talking about a party at Bonaventure—a party not for chickenshits, according to him.

"Sounds like a bitchin' party," he said, glancing at me and grinning. "Yeah, they've already headed out there. I'm right behind you, dude. This place blows tonight." He closed his cell, pocketed it, and eased closer to me. "Hey, babe. Wanna go to a party with?"

Not a bad-looking guy, with short-clipped brown hair and his eyes a nice shade of blue. I shook my head. "Thanks for the offer, but I'm with someone."

He grazed a thumb over my jaw. "Too bad. Bonaventure if you change your mind." He grinned and left. I watched him move through the crowd until he drew close to the door. I figured it was worth checking out, especially since we were running out of time. There was only one way into Bonaventure Cemetery after hours, and that was to sneak in. Over the black wrought-iron fence. I was glad this time I had on pants. No moonshine tonight.

Just as I was about to call Eli, he appeared. He moved his hand to my back and leaned close. "I heard. Let's go." He looked at me. "For the record, that guy almost lost a finger."

I didn't doubt it a bit. Outside, Phin and Luc met up with us—Gilles, Elise, and Josie would meet us at Bonaventure—and we headed down the sidewalk, climbed on the bikes, and headed toward the Wilmington River. We parked the bikes along Thirty-sixth Street, just before it turned into Bonaventure Road, and walked the rest of the way to the cemetery. The full moon, a large white lunar sphere, cast a hazy glow over the cemetery.

At least it wouldn't be dead pitch-dark. Before we even reached the front gates, laughter rose from the river. "They're in the back near the river," I whispered, leaning against Eli. "Da hell stone is back there." I looked up at him. "Why would they do that?"

"No reason," Eli said, grasping my arm. "Maybe it's victory to them. Some weird little coup. Who knows?" He glanced at me, his face stern. "I don't like how this feels, and I damn sure don't want you here."

"There's over a dozen of them," I reminded him, "and only six of you, plus me."

"We only need to kill two—the Arcoses," Phin said. "Besides, Preacher's boys are pulling in right now."

I looked, and sure enough, Preacher's van parked directly behind the bikes. Eight big guys ducked out of the vehicle and started moving our way. "Well. Great," I said. "My Gullah grandfather is bringing a bag of dust to a vampire war. I feel better."

"He's stronger than you think," Eli said. "Trust me. He can handle himself better than you think."

"I hope you're right," I answered. It still worried me. Preacher was too old to be here.

Eli grabbed me and turned me to him. "This could get . . . ugly, Riley. Really bad," Eli said. "Don't forget your promise to me."

"I know," I answered. "I won't forget. I'm ready."

Eli's stare bored into mine. "I can smell your nervousness."

"But can you smell my special blood?" I asked, and hell yeah, I was nervous. I was like a cartoon steak with legs running around a pack of mouthwateringly hungry dogs.

"No," he said quietly. "I can't."

The Duprés' Mercedes parked, and Gilles, Elise, and Josie got out and walked to meet us. "'Tis time," Gilles said, as though he'd heard the entire conversation. He and Elise slipped away into the darkness. I'd almost have to see it to believe it—Gilles and Elise in a vamp brawl. Josie must have read my thoughts because she gave me a wicked grin.

I guess the partiers had jumped the fence to Bonaventure, just as I had that night not too long ago. But I was in the company of young, free-running vampires, and they leapt and scaled the gates so fast it made my head spin. I followed—just a bit slower, with Eli right behind me. I was actually proud of my new skills—even though they were much slower than the Duprés'. Once inside, we crept along the iron fence toward the back, following the laughter coming from the river.

"It's going to be a bloodbath," Luc said, glancing around. "I can feel it."

"We're experienced, not like those newlings," Josie said. "We're ready for them."

As we walked among the graves, a half-moon filtered through the canopy of live oaks and dogwoods and caused long shadows to fall from the ancient headstones and marble statues of Bonaventure. A slight breeze grazed my cheek, and I noticed the moss swaying, could hear the sawgrass rustling at the river's edge, the water lapping the shore. Still no cicadas, or crickets, not even frogs. My skin felt icy, my insides cold. Like Luc, I had a bad, bad feeling. Eli must have read my thoughts, as his fingers found the small of my back.

We moved silently, and as I passed a white marble

statue of a young girl, her arms outstretched, and the saddest expression on her face, I shivered. The way the shadows fell across her and added a menacing expression to her sadness? It seemed dark, terrifying, and . . . just not right. I'd never been afraid of the cemetery, but tonight, I was leery. On edge. Cautious. Adrenaline ripped through me, penned up, anxious to be released.

You belong with me.

I twisted my head left and right, looking for the speaker of the words until I realized it had come from inside my head. It was him. *Victorian.* I'd now recognize his voice anywhere.

Yes, it's me. A bloodbath can be prevented if you come to me.

I looked at Eli; he had no clue what was happening. Neither did Luc, Phin, or Josie.

Only you can hear my voice. Not the Duprés, nor your Gullah magic men. Just you, love. Your brother will die tonight unless you end it now. Come with me. I crave you, Riley. I crave your body. I know by your reactions you crave me as well. I have to have you. I vow you will never regret it.

I searched all around me; I saw nothing but the faint flicker of firelight near the river, menacing headstones, shadowy trees. My heart pounded fiercely, and Eli turned to stare at me.

"I can hear your heart racing," he said, grazing my cheek. "You don't have to do this."

"I'm fine," I insisted, and after he stared at me for several seconds, we continued. The sultry, thick air tinged with brine hung like a mist over the gravestones; sticks crackled as they were tossed into the fire near the river;

beer tabs popped, brew fizzed, laughter rose. We had to hurry.

You were meant to be mine, Riley Poe. You cannot resist me. I've watched you in the dreams and felt your tremors of ecstasy. I made you come more than once. Do you remember?

I didn't answer him. I wanted to, but I didn't.

It doesn't matter. I can still hear your every thought. And while you make love to the one in front of you, you'll forget him soon enough. You'll know nothing but my touch, my tongue. Forever. I know you burn for me. I've watched you.

Just then, chaos erupted around us. From the trees and crypts at the river, the hoodie boys leapt and swung and descended upon the group partying by the fire. The smell of pot wafted on a breeze. My insides froze as no fewer than fifteen kids moved like lightning, and I knew that Seth was one of them. The guys at the fire swore; one threw a can of beer. The kids—*newlings*—advanced, slowly now. Toyed with them. And then it began.

A hooded kid swung from a low-lying oak branch and dropped into the circle of partiers. With strength that caught me off guard, he grabbed a guy and yanked him up, and in the flickering firelight, I watched fangs drop from his jaws; his young face contorted, and he sank them into the throat of the screaming partier.

Then the screams began.

"We've got to move now," Eli said. He looked at me. "Wait for me."

A melee broke out at the fire; as the group of partiers tried to flee, newlings leapt and chased, and behind them the Duprés closed in. Luc threw two newlings to the

river, another far across the fire to a crypt. Josie fought
a younger hoodie—I somehow imagined it to be my
brother, although I couldn't see his face. Phin rushed three
hoodies at once, and behind him, I saw Eli. He moved
fast, so fast my eyes couldn't keep up. He fought like a
madman and threw three hoodies like rapid-fire rockets.
I saw some of Preacher's kin step in; Gilles and Elise, as
well. It was all so surreal, unbelievable; my legs turned
rubbery. I couldn't move. The screams heightened.

*Come to me, Riley. You can end all of this right now.
I'm here, to your right, across the stones. You can end the
killing if you come to me. . . .*

As if I had no control, I eased toward the right. I
hoped and prayed that Eli would forgive me, but no way
was I going to allow these young innocent kids to be
slaughtered because of what they became against their
will. No *freaking* way.

All at once, Eli, Luc, Phin, and Josie ran forward, into
the mix of hoodies and pot smokers; Gilles and Elise
joined them, and it was like watching a medieval battle
scene. I wasn't going to wait another second. Not for
the Gullah, or for Eli. He didn't realize that I no longer
needed to cut myself to lure the Arcoses; I had one of
them waiting for me. It didn't seem like the Duprés were
stopping the bloodbath. It was up to me. In one fluid
motion, I eased a silver blade from my belt, grasped it. I
continued to move toward Victorian's voice.

That's right. Come to me. I am here, waiting for you.

I ran then, where I didn't know, but screams from
the campfire rose into the night air and hung there, tor-
menting me. I glanced behind me and watched in horror
as the newlings continued their rabid attack. Screams

filled the night air, the sickening metallic scent of blood tainted the briny air, and bones snapped. God, I'd been too late. We'd all been too late. I stumbled through the darkness, up a long dirt path that led . . . somewhere. I didn't know anymore. I just wanted to lure the newlings away from the mortals, and Victorian would be the one to help me. Victorian, and my blood I knew Eli and his family would follow.

Just then, a figure moved from behind a large oak. I stopped in my tracks; my breath shortened; my heart slammed hard against my ribs. I met his gaze as I grasped the blade and yanked hard. I hissed as pain shot through me. I had the most potent of blood sliding from my palm and landing on the dirt and gravestone I stood by. But my gaze became utterly transfixed on *him. Victorian.* I prayed the newlings would get a whiff of my blood and come after me.

"I knew you would come," he said, and stepped into the moonlight. Like in the dreams, he was beautiful; he wore nineteenth-century clothing: dark breeches laced up the front, a billowy white shirt, and tall black boots, and his dark hair was pulled back in a loose queue. Moonlight spilled a hazed glow across the cemetery and cast shadows across his stunning face—flawless, pale, just like in the dream. I felt catatonic, awed. He smiled, and his face became even more exquisite. He seemed a lot older than twenty-one.

"Let us leave," he said, and held out his hand.

"No," I said, managing to find my voice. "You said you could stop this. My brother—the others?"

"Your Duprés have it under control. All will be well; I vow it. Now, let us move. If my brother—"

"If your brother what?" a dark, menacing voice said from behind me. He was so close, his voice racked my insides.

I turned quickly and faced another almost equally beautiful young man. Modern clothes, though. Dark hair, dark eyes, pale skin, but different all the same. Harsher. Merciless. That I could tell immediately. Silently, I screamed for Eli. Thankfully, he heard.

"Riley!" Eli's voice shouted from the river. I knew, even as fast as he was, he'd never make it to me in time.

Valerian's gaze suddenly shifted, his eyes rolled back, and he inhaled the air. Immediately, he spied my bleeding hand. "Thinking to keep this pet for your own, Tory?" he asked his brother. Two sharp fangs dropped from Valerian's jaw, and he moved toward me, his eyes turning opaque, boring into me. "He never did like to share."

"No!" Victorian shouted, and lunged at his brother.

Too late, Valerian had my hand to his mouth, sucking with all his might. Victorian pushed him off, and Valerian flew against a headstone. Before I could blink, he was up and advancing toward me, eyes pure white, no pupils. I reached for the blade jammed into my belt, and by the time I had it palmed, Valerian had grabbed my wrist so hard I felt—heard—my bones snap, and I gasped. The blade dropped, and pain gripped me, causing stars to flicker behind my lids. I had no time to move or shift; he had complete power over me. With one arm, he held me, and his mouth dropped against my throat. The moment his fangs pierced my skin, I screamed. They sank deep into me; I felt every inch, and my body convulsed. He sucked hard for all of three seconds.

Suddenly, Valerian was off of me. Eli stood there, facing him, his transformation complete, terrifying. "Leave her," he commanded, and moved forward.

Valerian laughed and transformed, but he was different. Very different. Winged and silver skinned, he looked . . . hideous, not even humanlike, and he lunged at Eli; Eli lunged at him, and they met, midair, and fought. Valerian threw Eli against a crypt; he was up and had Valerian by the throat in under a second.

"Come with me," Victorian said at my side, his voice darker than before. His eyes had also turned and were now staring at the holes in my throat left by his brother. "Forgive me. I . . . cannot resist," he said, and in the next second, sharp, long fangs dropped. Like his brother's, they pierced my skin and sank deep into an artery; I was completely powerless and in so much agony, I was paralyzed. He held my body against his tightly, almost like a lover's embrace, while he drank. One hand cupped my breast; the other held me intimately around the waist. His drinking of my blood was . . . different. His arms touched me lovingly, not brutally. I was dying just the same. I could feel it. I could feel Victorian's urgency in the way he suckled me. My breathing became more shallow, my heart slowed even more, and I fought to keep my eyes open.

Just as fast, Victorian dropped me, and I was shoved— I knew it was hard, but I had no idea how hard until later. I just knew that I crashed against something solid. I didn't even know who did it. I lay there, my face pressed against the moist moss and damp pine straw of the cemetery grounds, my heart slowing, and my inhalations far apart. My vision became blurred, and the last thing I recalled was my body being lifted. Someone carried me, and I didn't know who. Through the haze of my vision I saw chaos: bodies on the ground, blood, tall dark men, opaque eyes, others in the shadows. I felt light, weightless, and my breathing became faint. I wanted my brother. I wanted Eli. Then, complete and total blackness engulfed me. Blackness, and excruciating, mind-numbing pain.

Part 10

✦=✦=✦=✦

TENDENCIES

Sad I am without you.

—Anonymous epitaph, Bonaventure Cemetery

My eyes cracked open slowly, my lids so heavy they felt like steel weights sat upon them. I blinked several times to rid my vision and mind of the cobwebs. Everything was hazy, surreal, and my entire body burned. Like, my joints, my skin burned. Suddenly, I became fully aware of deep pain, and I cringed.

"You're awake," a desperate, deep, gentle voice said close to my ear. "Riley?"

"Don't bother her, boy," a familiar voice said. "Dat girl dere has been through it now, right? Shoo. I'll let you know if she wakens all de way."

"I'm not budging, Estelle," the voice said.

"Oh," the familiar voice replied. "Ornery today, dat's right. I'll be over dere seein' to my odder patients, den."

I forced my eyes to open despite the pain raging through my body. My vision cleared just enough for me to see the silhouette of a man. The longer I stared, the clearer my vision became. Finally, I saw pitch-black hair, pale skin. *Beautiful.* "Eli."

"I'm here," he said against my ear. "How do you feel?"

Memories rushed back so fast, I felt dizzy. "Seth?"

"He's here," Eli said. "He'll be fine."

Relief washed over me in a heavy wave, and I exhaled. "Thank you."

"Now," he continued, and I felt his fingers stroking my arm. "How do you feel?"

I didn't want to sound like a baby, although it felt as though fire ripped through my veins. "I feel fine."

"You are a terrible liar, *chère*," Eli whispered. "I'll tell Estelle. She can get you something for the pain." His soft lips pressed against my forehead. "I'll be right back."

I couldn't move; my body felt stiff and weighted. But my other senses worked fine, and I smelled . . . the salt water. Not old, briny air, but fresh, salty air. A breeze drifted over my face, and I felt the warmth of the sun beaming in through . . . something.

"You're at Da Island, baby," said another familiar voice.

I smiled. "Preacher man." I tried to find his hand, but I couldn't move.

He found mine, and I felt his large calluses as he cradled my palm. "You know how to make an old man skip a heartbeat, dat's right," he said. "I almost lost you, baby. If it wasn't for dat Eli and his brodders and sister, and his modder and fadder . . ." He let the words drift off. "I'd take a stick to your backside if you was well enough."

I smiled again. "You can make good on that as soon as I can lift my own arms."

Finally, my fuzzy sight became clearer; I looked into Preacher's dark, handsome face. "What happened?" I was on a cot in an open-air cabin on Da Island. Seagulls screamed overhead; the smell of the ocean engulfed me. It was like . . . heaven.

Preacher looked down at me and tapped my nose. "Dat's a story for your Eli to tell. He was right dere after you passed out."

"Who threw me?" I asked.

"That was me," Luc said, walking up. "No one's ever accused you of being a lightweight, huh, Riley?"

I squinted through the filtered sunlight and smiled. "Since I can't lift my arms, I'm flipping you the bird in my mind," I said. "Thanks, Luc."

"No prob, cuz," he answered.

Estelle arrived with . . . whatever it was she concocted, Eli by her side. She gave me a sip of it, handed the cup to Eli, and left. He sat beside me. "What do you remember?"

I thought a few seconds. "Everything up until your brother tossed me," I said. "Valerian?"

Eli's gaze hardened. "Dead."

Relief gripped me. "Victorian?"

Eli glanced away, then returned his gaze to mine. "Not dead, but he's gone. Ned can't pick him up."

"Oh," I answered. "I remember seeing . . . bodies. Blood."

Eli's face grew grave. "Some of Valerian's newlings made their first kill on the guys down at the river. Six in all, and they escaped with Victorian. Phin and Luc cleaned up while we gathered you and the others to bring here."

"How did you manage that?" I asked, trying not to think about the innocent boys whose lives are now those of monsters.

"It wasn't easy. Newlings desiring their first kill are ... tenacious. But we managed. They're all here."

"Riggs? Todd?" I asked, then remembered a desperate mom on TV pleading for information about her missing son. "Jared Porter?"

"Yeah, they're here, too. They're all fine, Riley."

Tears came to my eyes; I couldn't help it. They leaked out the sides and down my cheeks and into my hair, and I couldn't even lift a hand to wipe them. "Can I see Seth?" I asked, my voice trembling.

"Not yet," Eli said, wiping my tears with a finger. "His rehab is going to take a bit longer than yours."

My eyes sought his. "Why can't I move my body?"

Eli knelt on the ground beside my cot and leaned close to me. God, I'd never seen a more beautiful man in my life. I couldn't believe he was really mine.

A smile cracked his pale features. "So you consider me yours, huh?"

I smiled back. "You jackass. I'd smack you, but ... why can't I lift my arms?"

The smile faded. "It's been over a week, Riley, since that night at the cemetery. You were bitten. Both Arcos brothers—they both drank. You collected some of their venom."

"There's *venom*?" I asked, horrified. "You never told me there was venom."

The slightest of smiles returned. "Yeah, there's venom.

That's what causes the tendencies. You didn't get much, but you did get some—from two very powerful *strigoi* vampires."

I frowned. "So . . . what does that mean? Am I paralyzed for life?"

Eli shook his head. "No, not by far. It means you are going to have tendencies, Riley. You and Seth both will, but yours will be . . . different."

I thought of Ned Gillespie.

"Yeah, like Ned. Only . . . way different."

My mind whirled. "Could you please let me finish my own thoughts and say them before you answer me?" I asked with a smile. "Now. How different?"

Eli pulled his knee up and propped his arm against it. With his fingers, he played with my hair. "Only time will tell. It's too early to know."

I tried to let that congeal in my brain. It really was too much to take in at one time. So much had happened, and in such a short amount of time. "As long as my baby brother is safe, and okay," I said, "I'm totally content."

"Totally?" Eli asked, and leaned closer. He dragged a finger across my bottom lip.

"Can you kiss me, or is it too dangerous?" I asked.

"Dangerous for whom?"

I smiled and gave him a somber look. "Thank you, Eligius Dupré. You saved me. You saved my brother, and I will be grateful forever."

He leaned over me then, brushed my hair back, and cradled my face. "I had no other choice," he said quietly, and lowered his lips to mine. He kissed me gently, as though afraid of hurting me. It was soft but possessive; it was a brand, and I relished it. Eli's unique taste and scent lured me, and had I not been paralyzed, I would have pulled him to me and never let him go. He raised his head and sought my eyes with his. "Is that a fact?" he asked, grinning.

"Yeah," I answered. "That's right."

His gaze grew serious and bored straight through me. "Mine," he said, matter-of-factly. "You're *mine*, Riley Poe."

My insides seized, and I didn't think a man could ever say another thing to me so incredibly possessive or romantic at the same time. I smiled.

Eli knew exactly what I was thinking.

Estelle's hoodoo medicine kicked in, and my eyelids grew heavy. I fell asleep with Eli's fingers entwined with mine, but even after my body slumbered, my brain continued furiously. At least, I thought it was my brain. At first. Until a familiar voice crowded my thoughts.

I will come for you, Riley Poe. That potency which rushes through your veins has lain against my tongue. It's inside of me. You're now a part of me, like my venom runs through you. We are meant to be together, forever. I will come for you. . . .

Read on for an excerpt from
the next book in the Dark Ink Chronicles,

EVERDARK

Coming in June 2011 from Signet Eclipse.

"**Y**ou've been dreaming of him again," Eli said, his eyes hard, his voice low, accusing. "Haven't you?"

I ignored him, extended my leg fully, and, with a quick snap, kicked the bag. I followed it with three sharp jabs. Anger and a little hurt built inside me, and after a few more kicks, I broke a sweat.

My body whipped around, and Eli's strong hands grasped my shoulders. "Don't ignore me, Riley." He drew his face close to mine. *"Don't."*

I frowned, totally pissed. "Then don't accuse me, Eli." I shook his hands off. "You know I can't help those dreams. You *know* it."

Eli stared at me several long seconds, then shoved his fingers through his hair, muttered some French expletive, and walked to the window. He looked at some distant point across the river. "You desire him."

Anger flashed inside me, and I crossed my arms

over my chest. "How freaking old are you, Eli?" I asked. "Sixteen? Oh, no, that's right. You're over two *hundred*." I walked up behind him, grabbed him by the arm, and turned him around to face me. Brilliant blue eyes searched mine, and I knew he was reading my thoughts—digging through them like a madman was more like it. "You're acting like a jealous high school boyfriend," I said, a little gentler. I grazed his jaw with my index finger. "Seriously, Eli."

Another handful of seconds dragged by before his face went emotionless, his eyes dulled, those beautiful full lips that worked magic against my body thinned. "You don't deny it, do you, Riley?" His voice was low, even, tinged with a heavier-than-usual bit of French. I'd learned fast that the heavier the accent, the more pissed off Eli Dupré was.

"Victorian forces the dreams on me," I said harshly. "Just like he forces the emotions within them." I stepped closer. "I. Can't. Help. It."

Anger pulled his features tight. "Do you think this is some game? He is deadly, Riley. He will drain every ounce of your blood. Regrets will come after it's too late." His eyes grew somber. "I think you enjoy the dreams a little too much," he said, moving past me. At the door, he stopped, staring straight ahead. "You could have come to me."

"What would you have done, Eli?" I said. "You can't go into my subconscious and change anything. You can't make him stop."

"You don't know what I can do," he said angrily. "You didn't give me a fucking chance."

He moved so fast, I didn't see him actually turn and

leave. Only the sound of the back door closing alerted me to his absence.

I walked to the window overlooking River Street, propped a hip against the ledge, and stared out into the growing darkness. Leaning forward, I pressed my forehead against the cool pane. He wasn't right, not by far. I did not enjoy the dreams, nor did I desire Victorian. In the dreams, I want him to stop, to leave me the hell alone, but he never does. He returns to me, time after time, with the most erotic, out-of-control dreams that make me respond to him in ways that mortify me.

Worse, Victorian had begun speaking to me during my waking hours. Somehow, he'd gotten inside my head *outside* of the dreams. I thought I could handle it. I wanted the bastard dead; I was the only one who could get close enough to do it. *Dammit.*

"What was that all about?"

I turned and met Seth's gaze. I was a balled-up bundle of hot electrical wires, and I needed to burn off a little energy. It was either that or bang my head against a brick wall. "Nothing, Bro. You wanna go for a run?"

My brother gave me a crooked grin. "I'll pass. I'm meeting Josie for a little roof jumping." He wiggled his brows at me.

Seth Poe was definitely enjoying his vampiric tendencies. The kid had serious free-running talent. I grinned. "Gotcha. I'll catch ya later." I yanked on my sneakers and headed out into the early-September air, crossed the merchant's drive, climbed the metal steps to Bay Street, and took off.

Savannah in September was still warm and humid, and the brine from the river clung heavily to the air. I drew it in fully as I ran, the muscles in my legs stretching with each stride. I could go faster—much faster—but that would draw serious attention. Instead, I kept it to a mortal's pace, crossed Bay behind a group of late-night ghost walkers, and headed up Bryan Street. Finally, I found myself alone, and I increased my speed, stretched my legs. Long shadows fell from lampposts, parking meters, and the massive oaks that lined nearly every side street in the historic district. Everything looked distorted. I turned the corner and glanced over my shoulder.

An arm shot out of the shadows, clotheslined me, and knocked me onto my back. I'd barely felt the sidewalk beneath me before I leapt up, adrenaline rushing, body rigid, poised and ready to fight, and stared into the shadows.

I knew who awaited me before he emerged.

"My apologies for using force to stop you," Victorian Arcos said in a low, seductive voice. "But you're amazingly fast."

"Thanks to you and your brother," I answered. "What are you doing here? They'll kill you if they find you."

Victorian stepped fully into the lamplight, and again, I was stunned by his beauty. Gone was the eighteenth-century clothing from before. Although he still kept his sleek black hair long and pulled in a queue, he was now dressed in a loose white button-down shirt hanging untucked from a pair of worn jeans and scuffed boots. It was difficult to believe he was only twenty-one years old. Well, that plus several hundred years.

"I can barely smell your blood," he said, ignoring my threat, stepping closer, inhaling deeply. "Your dark brothers must have changed the drugs they use to mask your scent." Light reflected in his deep brown eyes, and they studied me closely. "I had to see you."

A car turned up the street, and the headlights flashed toward us. In the blink of an eye, Victorian stepped in front of me, pushing me backward through the thick grass and into the shadows of an aged-brick historic house that dominated nearly an entire block. The car passed. The headlight beams swept above our heads, and then left us in total darkness. Victorian, who stood six feet tall, moved slowly, crowding me, forcing me to back up. I stopped when brick touched my back. I felt completely powerless, as though I possessed zero control of my actions, my thoughts, and the younger Arcos brother took full advantage.

He stared down at me, desire radiating off his body in waves. "You torture me, Riley," he said, his Romanian accent making his words seductive, erotic. "I think of nothing else but you"—he leaned close, his mouth brushing my jaw—"of what I want to do to you." His soft lips grazed the skin at my neck and made me shiver. "It causes me physical pain to stay away." His mouth moved to my jaw, dragging his lips to my chin, close to my own mouth. "I want you now," he whispered. "I want to keep you forever."

I was shaking, my mind numb, sensations tingling across the skin where his lips moved so erotically. I gathered my strength—God only knows where it came from—lifted my hands to his chest and pushed. Victorian flew backward and landed on his back several feet away. He lay there, staring at me. Smiling.

When I blinked, he'd risen, crowding me once more, his hands grasping my wrists and pinning them to the brick wall at my back. He lowered his head, his lips whispering against mine.

"Your tendencies do nothing but excite me even more," he said. "What other tricks do you possess that I can enjoy?" His alluring scent surrounded me as his mouth covered mine . . .

"Riley? Wake up."

My eyes fluttered open, and I stared into Eli's questioning gaze. He frowned. "You were dreaming."

Inside my head, Victorian's seductive laugh echoed . . .